The Water of the Hills

....

Jean de Florette
& Manon des Sources

....

TWO NOVELS BY

Marcel Pagnol

Translated by W.E. van Heyningen

First published in Great Britain in 1988 by André Deutsch Ltd
Reprinted 1988 (twice), 1990, 1992
First paperback edition published in 1991, reprinted 1992
This revised paperback edition published 2004 by

Prion
an imprint of the
Carlton Publishing Group
20 Mortimer Street
London W1T 3JW

Published in the United States of America by North Point Press
a division of Farrar, Straus and Giroux, LLC

ISBN 1-85375-529-X

A catalogue record for this book is available from the British Library

Printed in Great Britain
by Mackays

TRANSLATOR'S NOTE

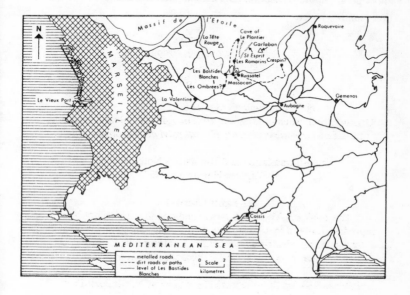

The Water of the Hills is set between the wars in the foothills of the Massif de l'Etoile, less than a dozen miles from the outskirts of Marseille. The description of the fictional village of Les Bastides Blanches is a topographically faithful picture of the real village of La Treille, scene of the long summer holidays so lovingly described in Pagnol's childhood memoirs, *My Father's Glory and My Mother's Castle*. Born five kilometers away in Aubagne, Marcel Pagnol lies buried in the cemetery a little way down the hill from La Treille, together with Pique-Bouffigue, Giuseppe the Piedmontese, Jean de Florette, Ugolin, and the Papet.

The map shows the area as it was at the time the events of the novels take place. Internal evidence suggests that Les Ombrées might be where the present village of Camoins les Bains is. The fictional village of Ruissatel occupies the site of the real hamlet of Gratiane, near the foot of the actual Ruissatel hill. Crespin must be east of Les Bastides Blanches and west of Roquevaire, and so has been placed where the real village of Les Boyers now stands. The single contour line is largely guesswork, to show the level of Les Bastides Blanches and Ugolin's house, Massacan. Everything north of the line is higher; everything south is lower.

W. E. van H.
Oxford, 1986

Jean de Florette

CHAPTER *I*

Les Bastides Blanches was a village of a hundred and fifty inhabitants, perched on the prow of one of the last foothills of the Massif de l'Etoile, about ten kilometers from Aubagne. A dirt road led there on a slope so abrupt that from afar it appeared to be vertical; on the hillside beyond, nothing but a mule track left the village, with a number of footpaths leading off it to the sky.

About fifty rows of houses, whose whiteness remained only in the village's name, lined five or six streets that were neither paved nor tarred—streets that were narrow because of the sun and tortuous because of the mistral.

There was however a fairly long esplanade that dominated the valley on the west; it was supported by a rampart of trimmed stone a good ten meters high, finished off with a parapet under a row of ancient plane trees. This place was called the Boulevard, and the old people came there to sit and talk in the shade.

In the middle of the Boulevard a very wide flight of a dozen steps rose to the town square bordered by facades around a fountain with a stone shell attached to the middle. This was the origin of the village. Fifty years earlier, a summer resident from Marseille (two or three would come during the hunting season) had left a small bag of gold coins to the community, and this had made it possible to conduct sparkling water from the only important spring in this part of the country to the square. It was then that the small farms scattered about the valleys and hillsides had been abandoned one by one, and the families had grouped themselves around the fountain, and the hamlet had become a village.

All day long one saw pitchers or jars under the jet of water and gossips listening to their rising music while they exchanged the news of the day.

Around the square there were a number of shops: the *bar-tabac*, the grocer, the baker, the butcher, and then the wide open workshop of the carpenter next door to the blacksmith, and at the end, the church; it was old, but not ancient, and its bell tower was hardly higher than the houses.

A small street left the square on the left to lead to another shaded esplanade that stretched out before the biggest building in the village.

This building was the town hall, as well as the meeting place of the Republican Club, the chief political activity of which was to organize the game of lotto and the *boules* contests. The *boules* tournaments took place on Sunday under the plane trees in both esplanades.

The Bastidians were rather big, lean and muscular. Born twenty kilometers from the Old Port of Marseille, they resembled neither the Marseillais, nor even the Provençals of the big suburbs.

Lastly, a peculiarity of the Bastides was that there were only five or six surnames: Anglade, Chabert, Olivier, Cascavel, Soubeyran. To avoid possible confusion, the first name of the mother, rather than the surname, was often added to the first name: Pamphile de Fortunette, Louis d'Etienette, Clarius de Reine.

They were probably the descendants of some Ligurian tribe, driven long ago toward the hills by the Roman invasion; that is to say they were perhaps the oldest inhabitants of the Provençal country.

Because the road that led to them stopped at the Boulevard, they saw "foreigners" only rarely; and because they were content with their lot, they went down to Aubagne only to take their vegetables to the market. Before the 1914 war it was still possible to find old people on the farms who spoke nothing but the Provençal of the hills; they would make the young people who came from the barracks "describe Marseille," and they were amazed that it was possible to live with so much noise, and to brush with people in the streets whose names one did not know, and especially to meet policemen everywhere!

All the same, they chatted willingly and had no objection to cock-and-bull stories. But always, whether talking about everything or nothing, they rigorously respected the first law of Bastidian morals—"Stay out of other people's business."

The second law was that Les Bastides was the most beautiful village in Provence, infinitely more important than the market towns of Les Ombrées or Ruissatel that had more than five hundred inhabitants.

Like all the villages, it had its jealousies, its rivalries, and even its stubborn hatreds, founded on histories of burnt wills and testaments or badly divided lands. But faced with attack from outside, like the intrusion of a poacher from Les Ombrées or a mushroom gatherer from Crespin, the Bastidians all banded together, ready for a general squabble or collective false witness; and this solidarity was so strong that the Médéric family, while not on speaking terms with the baker's family, always bought their bread from him, but using signs, never addressing a word to him. Even though they lived on the hill, and the baker of Les Ombrées was nearer to their farm, nothing in the world would make them eat the bread of a "foreigner" in their community.

Their great fault was that they were morbidly avaricious, because they had little money. They paid for bread with wheat or vegetables, and in exchange for three or four cutlets they would give the butcher a hen, a rabbit, or a few bottles of wine; as to the sous they sometimes brought from the market at Aubagne, these vanished like magic, and five-franc coins were not to be seen except when the peddlers came by, to pay for espadrilles, or a cap, or pruning shears.

The garigue of the Bastidians was nothing more than a series of immense plateaux of bluish limestone, separated by deep ravines, which they called vallons. Here and there in these vallons were level patches of shallow earth, deposited over the centuries by the wind and runoff from the rain, and that was where they established their fields, bordered by olive trees, almond trees, and fig trees. There they cultivated chick-peas, lentils, and buckwheat, that is, plants that were able to grow without water; and the little Jacquez vines that had defied the phylloxera. But around the village, thanks to connections made to the pipeline to the fountain, there were rich vegetable gardens greening, and orchards of peaches and apricots, whose fruits were taken to the market.

They lived on their vegetables, the milk of their goats, the lean pig they killed every year, a few hens, and most of all on the game they poached in the immensity of the hills.

Nevertheless, there were some rich families, whose fortunes represented the savings and privations of a long line. These were the gold coins hidden in the beams, or in crocks buried at the bottom of the cistern, or bricked up in the thickness of the wall. These were never touched except for a marriage, or to buy a joint property. Then all the family would redouble its efforts to replace the diminished treasure as quickly as possible.

The mayor was Philoxène de Clarisse. Forty-seven years old, large and round with fine black eyes, and a Roman profile without beard or moustache. His

hairy hands were rather fat because they never touched a pickax. He was proprietor of the *bar-tabac*, obtained thanks to a war wound that brought him a
pension. He was respected for the wound (otherwise invisible), but above all
for the pension.

He called himself a lay anticlerical socialist, he openly read *Le Petit Provençal* on his terrace, and freely vituperated against the Jesuits, who were leading France to its ruin. Thus he was the leader of the unbelievers, who numbered
no more than five or six, and whose anticlerical activity was not displayed except on Sunday mornings when they drank aperitifs on the café terrace instead
of going to mass. Nevertheless, at municipal elections he always got a majority,
fairly small, but enough, because it was said that he had "a head," as if the others
did not.

People went to him for advice on all difficult questions because he knew a
little of the law; he was able to keep up his end of the conversation with towns-
men, and he talked with unparalleled ease on the telephone in his bar. He was
not married, but lived with his sister, an active and discreet old maid—and (a
question of solace) he descended on Tuesdays to Les Ombrées to get tobacco
and in passing to greet a fresh and plump young widow who wished him well
without at the same time spurning the postman—a pleasant blond young fellow—nor the pharmacist, nor a gentleman who came from time to time from
Marseille in a varnished tilbury with luxurious rubber tires.

The joiner-carpenter-wheelwright was Pamphile de Fortunette. He was
thirty-five years old, with a jolly chestnut moustache, and the only pair of blue
eyes that had ever been seen in the village. Since he was less stingy and less
secretive than the others, the elders considered him a daredevil, sure to end
up impoverished—a prognosis aggravated by the fact that he had married fat
Amélie d'Angèle. She was a nice girl, but enormous, always having crises of
mad laughter or shattering temper. She never stopped eating bread and sausage, or figs and cold black sausage, even walking down the street. Philoxène
said it cost less to fill her that way than to feed her properly. But Pamphile
worked hard, and was really capable. He replaced rotten beams, repaired carts,
made mangers, stable racks, and heavy peasant tables; and when he had no
orders he made coffins—to measure for the country people, or in a series of
three sizes for an enterprise in Marseille, where the people died quite easily. In
addition, he set up a chair in front of his workroom on Sundays and did hair-
cuts.

The baker was a big lad of thirty years; he had beautiful teeth and straight black hair, always powdered with flour. He laughed freely and interested himself in all the women in the village, even in his own, a pretty girl of twenty who adored him. His name was Martial Chabert, but since everybody called him Boulanger people forgot his name.

Ange de Nathalie was dark, lean and tall, his cap on his ears. He was rather nervous, and his voluminous Adam's apple constantly rose and fell, as if he was trying in vain to swallow. He was a peasant, and the fountaineer—that is to say he supervised the two-kilometer pipeline that brought the water to the fountain; in addition he regulated the flow of the connections that supplied the small ponds of the vegetable gardens on the way.

He was well liked, especially by the men, because his pretty wife never refused more than once if she was asked politely. But nobody ever spoke about this.

Then there was Fernand Cabridan who was called "Big head small bum" at school—a summary description of his person as a child, and still valid after thirty years. It is quite true that his small ass had a sad look in his corduroy trousers that hung like a curtain; but in his big head there were two great brown eyes, attentive eyes, with a pure and luminous look.

He already had two children, and he was poor. He possessed only a small house in the village, and a little field lower down with a very small pond; but he produced chick-peas as big as hazelnuts and so tender they melted in the mouth. They were at a premium at the market of Aubagne, where everybody (even the people of Les Ombrées) called him the King of the Chick-Pea— modest enough royalty, but it sufficed him amply.

Casimir the blacksmith was proud of his powerfully muscled arms, so completely covered with hair one could not see his skin. He did not have a vegetable garden, but he did wield a pickax once or twice a year, because he occasionally filled the function of a grave digger to the general satisfaction. There was also the old Anglade, with his thin neck, his hooked nose, and his falling moustaches. He was the sage of the village. His piety was celebrated, and it was he who came every morning to ring the first Angelus before leaving for the fields with his two sons, Josias and Jonas, who were twins and stuttered equally. Finally, the most important person of Les Bastides—this was César Soubeyran, of whom more later.

On Sundays one also saw, besides these notables, a number of peasants from the vallons, where they lived on their little farms, sometimes grouped in threes or fours, sometimes entirely isolated, such as those of La Pondrane or La Tête Rouge. They arrived for mass at ten o'clock, perfectly clean under their black felt hats, but practically all their chins were marked with little cuts made by trembling Sunday razors. The women, under their flowery scarfs, had fine features, but their brows were prematurely wrinkled, and their hands withered by washing soda. The girls, under hats stuck with flowers, and sometimes with fruits, were as pretty as the girls from Arles.

Comparing the two generations, the effect of the open air could be seen, so quickly extinguishing the youthful sparkle of cheeks and tarnishing the purest brows.

César Soubeyran was approaching sixty. His thick coarse hair was yellowish white, streaked with red; black spiders' legs emerged from his nostrils to attach themselves to a thick grey moustache, and his words whistled through greenish incisors lengthened by arthritis.

He was still robust, but often martyred by "the aches," that is, by rheumatism that cruelly inflamed his right leg; so he supported himself on a stick with a bent handle when he walked, and worked in the fields on all fours or seated on a little stool.

Like Philoxène, but longer ago, he had had his share of military glory. After a violent quarrel—and perhaps also, some say, on account of a disappointment in love—he had enlisted with the Zouaves and had taken part in the last African campaign, in the extreme south. Twice wounded, he had returned, around 1882, with a pension and the military medal whose glorious ribbon ornamented his Sunday suit.

In days gone by he had been handsome, and his eyes—still deep and black— had turned the head of many a village girl, and even others . . . Now he was called the Papet.

The Papet usually is the grandfather. But César Soubeyran had never married and owed the title to the fact that he was the oldest surviving member of the family, in sum a paterfamilias, bearer of the name, and the sovereign authority.

He lived in the large old house of the Soubeyrans, at the highest part of Les Bastides, near the windswept area that overlooked the village.

It was a farmhouse with a long facade, separated from the hill track by a strip of ground supported by a stone wall, and called "the garden" because there was a border of lavender along the path to the door. The shutters, according to family tradition, were repainted light blue every year. Moreover, the bourgeois reputation of the Soubeyrans was firmly established on the fact that instead of lunching in the kitchen like everybody else, they had always taken their meal in a special room, the "dining room," where one could admire a little citified fireplace that did not draw well, but was of real marble.

The Papet lived there alone, with an old deaf-and-dumb servant, more stubborn than a red donkey; she pretended not to understand orders that did not please her and did nothing about them and went her own way. He put up with her because of her talent as a cook and her hard work. Above all, he had no fear that she would listen at the door, or gossip.

The Soubeyrans had large holdings around the village and in the hills, but they were nearly all uncultivated because the family had been devastated by misfortune. Of the Papet's four brothers, two died in the war of '14 and the other two committed suicide in turn, one because he thought he was consumptive, because of a bleeding tooth, the other after the death of his wife, aggravated by a drought that had scorched his artichokes.

It was this last who had left him Ugolin, supreme hope of the race of Soubeyran.

This nephew lived in the shadow of his uncle, who was also his godfather. He had just turned twenty-four . . . He was not big and was as lean as a goat, but he had big shoulders and was strongly muscled. Under a mop of red frizzled hair, he had one continuous eyebrow in two waves above a nose that was slightly twisted to the right and rather thick, but fortunately shortened by a blunted moustache that hid his lip; finally, his yellow eyes, fringed with red eyelashes, never rested for a moment, constantly looking in all directions like those of an animal fearing surprise. From time to time a tic caused his cheekbones to jump and his eyes would blink three times; it was said in the village that he "twinkled" like the stars.

He had done his military service at Antibes with the Chasseurs Alpins. On his return from the barracks the Papet, who continued to live alone in his house, had bought him a little farm called Massacan, after a former owner.

The farmhouse was a fairly tall building, in front of a dense pine wood near the top of a hillside, just opposite Les Bastides, and separated from it by a narrow deep vallon. Below the house stepped fields descended right to the bottom of the hillside; they were strips of earth supported by little dry stone walls. Here and there were olive trees pruned in crowns, almond trees, apricot trees, and crops of tomatoes, corn, and a little wheat.

A rocky dirt road zigzagged up to the house, and then petered off toward the vallon of Les Romarins, up in the hills. As it approached the house the road broadened out into an esplanade—a small level area—at the far end of which rose the house, near a covered well under a large fig tree. In front of the door there was a very old mulberry tree whose enormous trunk was no more than a cylinder of bark, spread all around with richly leaved shady branches.

On giving him this little farm in advance of his inheritance, the Papet had told him:

"When I die you will live in the Maison Soubeyran; but until then put Massacan in order, that way you will be able to let it to some peasant, or give it to one of your children . . ."

But Ugolin thought that he would never marry, that he would let the house in the village to some gentleman from town, and he himself would finish his days in his little farmhouse on the hill where he could talk to himself as much as he liked and count his gold pieces with all the doors locked.

His father had left him thirty-two such coins, in a little cast-iron crock that he had buried under the foot of his bed in the big kitchen. Every four or five months he added a louis to this treasure, which he would then scatter on the table and count again by the yellow light of a candle, with his loaded gun at his side. Then he would caress the gleaming medallions and let them slide against his cheek. Finally, before putting them back in the crock, he would kiss them, one after the other . . .

From time to time the Papet, who wanted to resuscitate the family, would suggest to him some village girl who would not be displeased to espouse the Soubeyran territories and add some parcels of her own land to them. But Ugolin always replied:

"I haven't got a mule, since you lend me yours. I have no chickens or goats, because they destroy everything. I don't wear socks, because they tickle. So what use would a wife be to me?"

"There are other things in life," said the Papet.

"Oh, as to that," replied the sensible Ugolin, "nearly every week when I go to Aubagne I stop for half an hour at Le Figuier, to refresh my ideas . . . I've calculated it costs me about fifteen francs a month, and I can choose . . . While

I would have to feed a wife and clothe her, and she would talk to me all the time, and she would take up all the room in my bed. So, we'll see."

The Papet did not insist. But one day when he came to lunch at Massacan, he looked at the vast kitchen and shook his head and said:

"Galinette, you can't go on like this. This house is a dunghill. Your bedclothes are nearly rotten, your shirt is in rags, and your trousers—one can see your bottom. Don't get married yet, since that doesn't suit you, but you should have a woman here from time to time. I'll find one for you."

And thus he returned that same evening with Adélie. She carried a brand-new straw broom and a scraper with a long handle on her shoulder. She was a widow of forty, with unkempt flaxen hair and a bosom floating in a blue camisole. She had great cow eyes and a wide mouth, and in the middle of her cheek there was a mole ornamented with a comma of blond hairs.

"Here is Adélie," said the Papet. "She's a good girl and she's a tremendous worker."

"She's going to come every day?" asked Ugolin uneasily.

"Three days a week! Thirty sous a day. That's not dear, and worth it. There, look at her!" Délie, armed with the broom, was already pushing piles of fluff from under the armoire toward the door.

"Don't hurry, Délie," said Ugolin. "Come and sit here a little and drink a glass of wine, so we can talk."

Délie came forward and took a chair without relinquishing her broom.

"It's all settled," said the Papet. "She'll come here on Monday, Wednesday, and Saturday. At seven in the morning. She'll bring your bread, she'll clean your house, and she'll prepare your midday meal for two days. In the evening there's no problem because you always have your supper with me. Besides, she'll take your linen to wash it, and she'll do the mending. And in the evening she'll leave at six."

"On Saturday," said Ugolin, "it would be better if she slept here."

"To do what?" said Délie.

"To keep me company. You haven't got a husband anymore and I haven't got a wife. It won't harm anybody!"

"Why not?" said the Papet.

"As for me," said Adélie without heat, "these things, they've never pleased me much."

"Nor me," said Ugolin. "But I'm young and my blood is strong——it's nature that wants it."

"Yes," said the Papet. "You should get these things out of the system, otherwise they bother you and interfere with your work."

Délie shook her head and showed little enthusiasm.

"Listen, Délie, I won't bore you by paying court in the usual way. I won't speak words of love to you; I don't know any. And I won't stop you from sleeping. And then look, if you stay on Saturdays I'll give you forty sous extra."

"Oh no!" said Délie shocked. "Oh no! It would be disgusting to be paid for that. But if you like, instead of giving me thirty sous a day, you could give me forty, and perhaps I'll stay, since on Saturday nights everybody's got something to do in the village and I never know what to do."

"Good," said the Papet. "Since you agree, we needn't bother to talk about it."

Adélie got up and took up the avid hunt for fluff.

"Come, Papet," said Ugolin. "I must talk to you. And afterwards I'll show you something. Come."

He led the old man to the ancient mulberry tree and made him sit on the little wall that encircled it.

"First, I have to tell you something. The life I live here is not rewarding. I work hard, and it brings nothing. Two bags of chick-peas, six baskets of apricots, twenty liters of oil, three barrels of wine, some almonds, some broken olives, a few dozen thrushes, a hundred kilos of dried figs, that's all. It's just pottering about . . . Altogether this year, I've made seven hundred and fifty francs . . . I would like to do a serious job."

"Bravo. You please me, because I've thought about that for you. I've got all the plans at home and I've calculated all the costs."

Ugolin seemed uneasy.

"And what is it, your plan?"

"It's to restore the old Soubeyran orchard on the whole Solitaire plateau, as it used to be in my father's time: two hundred fig trees, two hundred plum trees, two hundred apricot trees, two hundred peach trees, two hundred Princess almond trees. A thousand trees in twenty lines ten meters apart, and between the lines there will be rows of muscat grapes on wire: you'll walk between the walls of bunches, you'll see the sun through the grapes—and that, Galinette, will be a monument! It will be as beautiful as a church, and a true peasant won't enter it without making the sign of the cross!"

Ugolin, worried and ill at ease, said:

"And you think I could do that all alone? It'll take five men, five years, and a lot of money."

"Certainly! . . . I figure at least fifty thousand francs, but the profits will be enormous!"

"Not at all, Papet. I don't think so. First of all, you can hardly find any capable men, and then you would have to keep an eye on them and tell them what to do—it would be a great worry. And then the plums, the peaches, and even the apricots, you'll have to give them to the pigs every other year because there will be too many and you won't get ten sous a kilo . . . Because that's how it's been for three or four years; at Arles and Avignon they've had so much fruit that they've sent away boatloads of it that they didn't know what to do with . . . And then, at Gémenos, at Roquevaire, at Pont-de-l'Etoile, they've pulled up their orchards and put something else in their place . . . And since you want me to start on something I'll show you what I'd like to do—something I haven't told you about before."

He put his arm under the Papet's and led him to the back of the house.

CHAPTER 3

During his military service at Antibes Ugolin had had a very likable young fellow as a roommate, Attilio Tornabua, who told him: "I'm a peasant like you. I grow flowers."

This idea seemed so extravagant he thought it was a joke at first. But Attilio invited him to dinner with his father one Sunday, and Ugolin was dazzled.

At the table Aristotele Tornabua had told how he had arrived from Piedmont twenty years ago, with a loaf of bread and some onions in his haversack, and a pair of shoes hanging from his shoulder to save wear on them. And now he had a large farmhouse, as fine as a house in town, with blue curtains in all the windows and a varnished door; a dining room with a carved sideboard, and chairs with elastic cane seats. Madame Aristotele wore lace collars and cuffs, a gold necklace and sparkling earrings, and the maid was as fine as a lady. Attilio had two bicycles, two hunting guns, and a fishing boat, and at table they had eaten a whole leg of mutton and had drunk vintage wine! And all that by growing carnations.

That is why every evening at five, when they were off duty, Ugolin went with his comrade to work in the carnation fields, in order to learn; and on the day of his final discharge he secretly took thirty cuttings to Les Bastides. Without a word to the Papet, he had planted them behind Massacan, with all the care of a true florist.

He had then surrounded them with a hedge of rosemary to shelter them from possible gusts of the mistral, and especially to hide them from the sight of some lost hunter who might talk about them in the village.

He had covered them every evening with old blankets stretched on horizontal poles, under a thick layer of dried grass, and every morning he had drawn a dozen buckets of water from his well to water them one by one, with true love.

As they rounded the building Ugolin gestured triumphantly toward the little plantation.

The astonished Papet looked at the glowing flowers, then turned his head to his nephew, looked again at the flowers, and finally said:

"Is that what you amuse yourself with?"

Then Ugolin talked at length about Attilio's crops and about his fine house . . . The Papet grunted, shrugged his shoulders, and concluded:

"Say what you like, they're not real peasants."

But Ugolin cut about thirty open carnations, tied the bouquet with a wisp of raffia, folded it in a newspaper, and forced the Papet to take him to Aubagne in the bogie cart.

There, he resolutely entered a fine-looking florist's shop, tore off the newspaper, put the bouquet on the table, and said:

"What will you give me for them?"

The florist, who had a little white goatee and was quite bald, with a pince-nez, took the flowers in his hands, examined them, and said:

"These, they're fine!"

"They're Malmaisons," said Ugolin.

"Fine stems," replied the florist.

"What will you give me for them?"

"If you had come in February, I would certainly have gone up to fifty sous . . . But now, it's the end of the season . . ."

He examined the carnations again and smelled them.

"All the same, they're worth twenty sous. Do you agree?"

"I agree," said Ugolin. He winked at the Papet while the florist counted the flowers.

The old man thought:

"Twenty sous, that's the price of two kilos of potatoes, or a liter of wine . . . For a bouquet like that it's not half bad."

But the smiling florist said to Ugolin:

"Have you got ten francs?"

"Yes," said Ugolin, feeling in his pockets. The Papet did not understand. Why ten francs?

The florist took the ten-franc piece and gave a fifty-franc bill in exchange, which Ugolin put in his pocket.

On the road back, where the mule knew it was best to walk, the Papet was quiet, holding the reins slackly. Ugolin said:

"I want you to think about this: firstly, the cuttings, Attilio had thrown them away because they were a little past their prime. Secondly, I wasn't able to plant them before my liberation, so I had to plant them a good month too late. Thirdly, I didn't have any sheep manure, which is the delight of carnations. Fourthly . . ."

"Fourthly," said the Papet, "he gave you forty francs, and that proves you were right and shows what must be done. Since there are plenty of people who are stupid enough to buy flowers dearer than beefsteak, we must grow flowers. Why didn't you tell me about this before?"

"Because I wanted to try first . . . To see if the soil here was good enough . . . And then I wanted you to see them in flower so you could understand . . ."

"It wasn't the flowers that made me understand; it was the florist. Giddap, you brute! But it should be quite easy. You've got to know the tricks."

"Certainly. And I know them. Attilio showed me everything, and I worked with him nearly every Sunday, and often in the evenings. I made a list of the cures for all the diseases of flowers, and Attilio gave me the cuttings."

"How much money would it take to start on a large scale?"

Ugolin hesitated, blinked, shrugged his shoulders, and finally said:

"Fifteen thousand francs."

The Papet pushed back his felt hat, scratched his brow, shook his head, whipped the sleeping mule, and finally said:

"I'll give them to you."

"Papet, you're too good."

"Not all that good," said the old man. "The money's not for you. It's for the Soubeyrans. Those in the cemetery, and those still to come. Giddap, you brute!"

After a silence Ugolin replied:

"There's only one thing that bothers me!"

"What?"

"The water. One carnation plant drinks as much as a man. To water those thirty plants I tore the skin off my hands on the well rope."

"You could have a pump there," said the Papet.

"Yes, but if we were to water five hundred plants, the well would be dry by the end of four days . . ."

"That's a problem."

Thinking all the while, he whipped the mule, which responded with an asphyxiating series of farts.

"What a character!" said the Papet. "If this beast had a nose where its tail is, it wouldn't be able to live."

"Nor would we," said Ugolin; and continued immediately: "We'll have to make an enormous pond, with ditches to collect all the rain in the vallon."

"Is it at Massacan you want to plant?"

"Certainly," said Ugolin. "Up there it's sheltered from the wind, and it's the right soil for flowers . . . I've proved that to you."

"Well, good. I have an idea. What if we were to buy the field and the spring from Pique-Bouffigue at Les Romarins? It's three hundred meters up from you."

"Has it still got water, that spring? I used to hear my father talk about it, but he said it was dead."

"It must be more than half blocked. He doesn't grow anything, he drinks nothing but wine, and he never washes himself . . . But when I was young it was a fine little stream, and his father, Old Camoins, had cartloads full of vegetables . . . Perhaps with a few blows with a pickax . . ."

"D'you think he'd sell his farm?"

"Not the house, that's for sure. But perhaps the field and the spring. He's done nothing with it and never will. If we were to let him see the sous . . ."

Pique-Bouffigue was Marius Camoins, but for thirty years he had been called Pique-Bouffigue, because when he got out of the army he had taught the people of the village how to take care of blisters with an ordinary needle and a little piece of thread.

Since he had never been seen to work in living memory, it was astonishing that he knew exactly how to heal an injury due to work.

He explained that in order to escape a twenty-four-hour military march he had placed a trouser button in his shoe, under his heel, the evening before, and had thus procured a very fine blister; but a medical orderly, with this technique of needle and thread, had unfortunately put him on his feet in time for the next day's march.

Blisters were a professional malady among these peasants, whose main job was to lengthen the handles of their pickaxes. The remedy brought by the foremost idler of the village had been a great success, and its bearer merited not only great regard, but also his glorious surname.

He was big, bony, and lean. Careless of his person, he shaved with an old pair of scissors, so he always had a shiny black four-day beard, which made a pleasant contrast with his white hair.

He lived in the ancient house where he was born, at the bottom of a vallon in the hills, three hundred meters from Massacan, surrounded by a pine wood, the silence of solitude, the odor of resin, and the perfume of rosemary.

The pine wood sloped down both hillsides of the vallon and came to a stop at the bottom on the edge of a long field surrounded by a high fence that had been ruined by the passage of time.

The fence had formerly protected the crops against the nocturnal raids of rabbits, but now it was no more than rags and tatters of rusty wire netting attached to some blackish wooden posts. Nearly all of them leaned outwards or inwards, showing how the earth had eroded their feet.

This fence with its long gaps was unable to restrain the impetus of the garigue, and the field was invaded by rockrose, sheets of thistles, rosemary, and broom. Emerging from this undergrowth were thirty ancient olive trees; their dense branches were encumbered with dead twigs, and the thickets of suckers that encircled their invisible trunks testified to their abandonment.

At the end of the field the two pine woods came together again and rose to the edge of the sky, above a very ancient farmhouse, flanked by a shed with broken doors. A path left the mule track that ran along the side of the hill and led down to the house across a high undergrowth of rosemary . . .

In front of the facade there was a terrace of beaten earth bordered by a stone parapet in which were fixed some poles of black wood sustaining the ragged branches of a very old half-dead climbing vine . . . This was the farmhouse of Les Romarins, the solitary residence of Pique-Bouffigue.

At that time, nice boy scouts and likable campers had not yet started cooking their Sunday cutlets over the handfuls of crackling twigs that had scattered their sparks from St. Victoire to Mont Boron; immense pine woods still covered the long chain of mountains that bordered the Mediterranean, and it could be said without exaggeration that it was possible to walk all the way from Aix to Nice without passing under the sun.

Colonies of partridges hid under this cover, in the heaths, the gorse, and the scrub oaks, and rabbits prepared for roasting by feeding on thyme, and large red hares.

Then according to the season, flights of thrushes, swarms of starlings, flocks of whitetails, and the solitary woodcock would arrive; and in the high valleys there were herds of wild boars who in the winter sometimes came right up to the edge of the village.

That was why Pique-Bouffigue had renounced agriculture in order to devote all his activity to poaching. The clandestine sale of game to the hotels in Aubagne or Pichauris brought in much more than cultivating chick-peas or picking olives. He did not even have a vegetable garden, and it was said that he did not know the difference between a turnip and an artichoke. He bought all his vegetables and ate meat every day, like a summer visitor.

That meant he was a great deal happier than the rich people of Aubagne, who worried unduly about money. But this happiness was interrupted one day by a drama that carried the glory of Pique-Bouffigue to its summit—when the gendarmes were frequently seen in the village and the portrait of the proud poacher appeared in the two different papers taken by M. the curé and M. the mayor.

Six months earlier, a "stranger from outside" had come one day to settle in the village of Les Ombrées, on the other side of the hill.

He came from nobody knew where, but certainly from the north, because he had that ridiculous accent that suppressed the mute *e*, as in Parisian songs. Moreover, he never took off his big black hat because he feared the sun.

He was a tall man with thick heavy hands, a fat reddish face, and red eyelashes on his blue eyes. He had a strange name—Siméon.

He had bought a cabin on the hill just above Les Ombrées and lived there with an enormous wife of his breed, who cultivated vegetables in a little garden and fed five or six chickens.

This Siméon affected a great contempt for the natives, and they scowled at him.

Every year he took a hunting permit to justify his walks in the hills. But the gun was not his main weapon; in fact he set traps, snares, and very fine lime twigs around well-hidden watering places that he went to fill with water every day.

Twice a week he left for Marseille on a bicycle; he wore a plumber's blue overalls and fixed a big toolbox to his carrier, full of thrushes, rabbits, and partridges.

To the cover he attached an enormous tube-wrench and a brand-new copper tap.

That he should poach did not shock anybody. At Les Ombrées everybody did that, and the hills were immense. But it soon became clear that he robbed the traps of others. Of all thefts, that was the most odious. Two men from Les Ombrées having reproached him bloodily, returned all bloody themselves. For that reason, a dozen young fellows waited for him one fine evening in July on the footpath of the Baume Rouge and carried him back to his place stretched on a ladder the carpenter had made for him, singing a sort of canticle that ran in Provençal:

> You came here and you will leave us
> Farewell poor Carmentran . . .

Siméon's face was violet and twisted, his nostrils dilated unequally, his eyes squinting.

He did not leave Les Ombrées, but realized the full meaning of this ceremony, after the baker had told him while weighing his bread that it had simply been a kind of a warning.

He decided then to hunt much further away, on the other side of the Tête Rouge. It was thus that he encroached on the domain of Le Bastides that Pique-Bouffigue considered his own.

Soon he noticed that somebody had come to trap "his" rabbits and "his" partridges. He made a little inquiry at Les Bastides among those he thought might be interested parties.

The result was negative; but after a storm some days later he was able to follow the trail of a stranger on a footpath—footprints that were so big they certainly were not those of any foot in the village; such a megapod would have been famous long ago. So he concluded it must be a poacher from Aubagne or

Les Ombrées and thought, what a lot of nerve; nevertheless he respected the traps, according to tradition.

But a week later he had a fit of rage when he saw that the unknown had robbed his own traps!

He kept a careful watch and caught the man with the hat in the act in the gorges of Refresquière. Not in the least intimidated by the size of the thief, even though he didn't have his gun, Pique-Bouffigue abused him vigorously and demanded he restore all the traps that had disappeared, plus a hundred francs damages. The other made a pretense of humbly returning what he had just stolen and suddenly seized him by the throat.

Pique-Bouffigue, surprised and half-suffocated, received a good thrashing. His eyes were two blue-black bumps, and as he was trying to recover his strength the stranger tore off his bag, took the six traps it contained, and warned him never to come back to the hills. Pique-Bouffigue was stunned and stupefied and did not have the strength to reply to this abuse. He had to let him go without saying a word. He got home with some difficulty and stayed there for two days, dressing his wounds with herbs and preparing his vengeance in his bruised head.

The morning of the third day he felt he had recovered and was pleased to see that his face bore no trace of the brawl; he lunched off a fine onion and a good handful of almonds that he broke between two stones on the corner of the table, and he drank a big glass of wine. Then he gathered all his rabbit traps—he had a dozen of them—and went to set them on the hillsides all around Les Romarins. During this operation he repeated several times—as if to remind himself of something important—"There's only one thing I must do tomorrow evening, but I must do it." After that he returned home and took his twelve-calibre in his hands.

This gun was his luxury and his pride. He had bought it secondhand at a gunsmith's at Aubagne, at the fabulous price of 300 francs. It was a "hammerless," which he called the "nammerless." It fired a special brilliant yellow powder that burst all the other guns in the village, but didn't daunt the "nammerless."

He looked at it, weighed it, tried the bolt, closed it, and said:

"No, not this one. It's too well known."

He went up to the loft and came down again with a very old piston gun of his father's, a long, heavy muzzle-loader. He found the powder horn and the primers, cast a ball by melting a bit of lead tubing, and slowly chewed a ball of paper to make a wad. Finally, he carefully loaded the venerable weapon and hid it in the tall grandfather clock.

Then he took the "nammerless," unscrewed the sight, wrapped it in a piece of paper, and hid the little packet in a hole in the root of an olive tree inhabited by a colony of wasps capable of keeping away the unlikely curious visitor. Finally he left for Les Bastides, taking the "nammerless" by the strap.

He passed the baker first and was told he was kneading in the bakehouse.

Then he asked the baker's wife if she had a little tisane of four flowers because he had had terrible stomach cramps for two days. She sent him to the cleaning lady of the Republican Club who was famous for her mixture of herbs from the hill.

He stopped at the bakehouse and left his gun with the baker, asking him to give it to the postman the next day, to take to the gunsmith at Saint-Marcel to replace the sight he had lost on the hill.

"Oh, bad luck," said the baker, "he won't be able to take it for at least a week! What are you going to do without a gun for seven days?"

"I'll have to rest," said Pique-Bouffigue. "I don't know what I've got; my stomach's all upside-down, and my head is spinning! I ate some mushrooms the day before yesterday, perhaps it's that. Yet I know they were all right . . ."

"It does happen," said the baker, "that good mushrooms get poisonous when they grow where toadstools have been. They won't kill you, but they will upset you."

Next he went to the Republican Club and passed the *boules* game with unsteady gait; the players asked what was wrong and he described the suspect mushrooms. Meanwhile Philoxène forced him to drink a little glass of chartreuse to quiet the cramps that bent him double in midsentence. He left with the packet of herbs for the tisane under his arm.

The next morning at dawn he made a tour of his dozen traps; he had caught three rabbits, one of which was a big buck, still kicking and pulling at its broken legs. He finished it off with a blow behind the ears with the edge of his hand, and said with pleasure:

"This one will do!"

He looked at the rabbit and said these mysterious words to it in Provençal:

"Oh poor buck, it was a trap that caught you and now you are going to be the trap." He put it in the big wardrobe and then he took the hill track with his hands in his pockets.

He carried a snack in his game bag, with a bottle of wine and his little telescope; it was the old naval telescope he usually used to watch for the possible arrival of the gendarmes.

Slipping along the vallons and ravines, he got to the edge of the plateau of the Solitaire and settled between two blocks of rock behind a juniper tree, where he could look over the landscape on the side of Les Ombrées. From afar he could see an old man carrying a faggot of dead wood with difficulty, then a cart of woodsmen, then three youths bent forward under their big Tyrolean haversacks. But he had to wait nearly the whole day before his enemy appeared . . .

He arrived around five o'clock, under his big hat, along the bottom of the Refresquières valley, and climbed the length of the footpath that went obliquely up the rocky hillside, just under the feet of the watcher. The hillside stopped at the base of a rocky precipice, and all along the length of this wall there was a dense thicket of rockrose, turpentine trees, and junipers that Pique-Bouffigue knew well because he caught several dozen rabbits there every year.

Siméon penetrated under the high brushwood . . . Pique-Bouffigue lost sight of him, but watched the tops of the branches. He noted that the man stopped five times.

"Five traps," he thought. "Perhaps the very ones he stole from me!"

The enemy then crossed the vallon and made another tour on the opposite side; after a dozen stops he left toward Les Ombrées, at a peaceful stroller's pace.

When he had disappeared behind the ridge, Pique-Bouffigue waited a good while. Then having closed up his telescope he took the path down and retraced the stranger's first tour. He had no trouble finding the five rabbit traps and smiled with pity at the way they had been set.

"Holy Mother! And to think that perhaps they're mine! They would be ashamed, the poor things!"

He examined the immediate surroundings with his eyes and ears, then approached the widened base of a cleft in the precipice and slid into it feet first, pushing aside some big stones; finally he parted the rosemary and made sure that when lying flat on his belly he could see the position of one of the traps about fifteen meters away, a little to the right. Then he went to stand on this spot and observed with satisfaction that the curtain of junipers and rockroses made it almost impossible to see the opening of his hiding place. He cut some more branches at ground level, under the moss, and hid them at the bottom of his hole. Then he went home at nightfall across the deserted pine woods.

When he arrived at Les Romarins he closed the shutters and prepared a tomato omelette that filled the pan; he ate it with good appetite, but did not allow himself more than a single glass of wine. Then he took his little gourd and three-quarters filled it with coffee, and topped it up with eau-de-vie de marc. Finally he put the fine dead rabbit in his game bag, took his loaded old gun under his arm, blew out the lamp, and went out noiselessly under the stars.

First he placed the rabbit between the jaws of the trap that was set opposite his ambush and smiled at the thought that the sight of this capture would be his enemy's last joy. Then he made a soft bed of dried grass and pungent mint in the crevasse and passed a delicious night. Across the sonorous silence of the vallon, two distant lovesick owls responded to each other, green grasshoppers chirped in the lavender, a happy cricket made his silver cry vibrate, and Pique-Bouffigue floated in serene joy at the thought that everything was ready for an indispensable assassination—just, moral, and pleasant.

From time to time he regaled himself with a gulp from his gourd; then he reminded himself of all the details of the brawl, counted the blows he had received, caressed the ancient gun, and laughed very softly.

With the rising sun, at about four in the morning, the redoubtable Siméon appeared. He followed the little path and came straight toward the venerable arquebus. He made out the rabbit from afar; he hastened his step, all smiling under his big hat, and after a quick glance around he bent to open the trap . . . a low whistle sounded quite close by . . . Siméon raised himself suddenly, looked around him, and seemed to see something across the rosemary: a little black ring, surmounted by a wide-open eye, a red flash, a deafening explosion. First he bowed profoundly, then fell headfirst onto his brains, because the top of his skull had fallen behind him, into his hat.

Without deigning to approach his victim, the victor took the road back under a glorious dawn. After passing the Pas du Loup, he entered the great blanket of ivy that draped the rock ridge. He slid the ancient gun into a horizontal cleft between two layers of limestone behind the thick curtain of long drooping stems, and covered it with grit, earth, and moss. He completed this burial with a military salute at attention and went home. He locked the door, but instead of opening the shutters, he lit the paraffin lamp. Then, with hands joined above his head, he did a little dance—the dance of honor avenged—looking at his shadow leaping on the wall. Finally he reheated the remains of the coffee from his gourd, drank it, lay down, and fell into a peaceful sleep.

CHAPTER 4

Siméon's wife was not a very nervous person and was not overly concerned about his first night's absence; she thought he might be running from the gendarmes who had no doubt forced him to make an immense detour. But on the morning of the third day, she thought of the poacher of Les Bastides, whom Siméon had left for dead some days earlier—he had told her about the battle and had exaggerated a little. At the beginning of the afternoon she went to the rural policeman to report the disappearance of her husband.

He was taking part in a game of manille under the vine of the Café Chavin and replied that "he absolutely didn't care a damn about it." Since she refused to drop the matter, he ended by telling her that if he had a wife like her he would have disappeared a long time ago.

And so, preceded by her watchdog, she took to the hill track alone in search of her husband.

She had sometimes accompanied him on his expeditions, and perhaps she was guided by a wholly feminine intuition, because toward evening she took the fatal path, still behind the dog. Suddenly his tail shook; he penetrated the undergrowth barking, and joyfully brought her the hat. It still contained a piece of bone in the shape of a saucer, all hairy on one side; she did not bother to find the rest.

The gendarmes were alerted. Weeping, she told her story and gave them a complete description of the probable assassin, duly inflated by the account her husband had given her.

That was why the gendarmes, who had been looking for a giant, did not get to Pique-Bouffigue's house until the eighteenth day. They asked him to go with them and to bring his gun. He replied that his "nammerless" was still at the gunsmith's, where the postman had taken it the week before. They searched the whole farm and found nothing there but a dozen rabbit traps; Pique-Bouffigue declared with some emotion that he kept them as a souvenir of his poor father, but did not himself know how to set them.

All the same, they took him to the gendarmerie at Aubagne, where he was interrogated for a long time—a very long time—by a lieutenant. He denied guilt consistently, with perfect calm, and even gave a few amusing answers that made the officer laugh. But the moment he thought he was going to return home, the crafty inquisitor suddenly put a copper button on the table and demanded brusquely:

"And that? What's that?"

Pique-Bouffigue lowered his eyes to his coat and was unable to hide a start of rage, which did not escape the enemy. But he recovered quickly enough and said airily:

"Hullo! That's the missing button from my jacket! Did you find it in my house?"

"We found it," said one of the gendarmes, "in the little cave where the assassin hid himself!"

"Where is it, this cave?" he asked naively.

"You know that better than we do!"

That was how his portrait appeared in the newspapers, and he appeared before the judge in Aix-en-Provence.

He maintained his innocence calmly, right to the end, and succeeded in convincing his own lawyer, who had been appointed by the court, but whom he considered to be an agent of the law. He admitted only that the disastrous button belonged to him and that he had probably lost it while lying in wait for partridges the year before.

The people of Les Ombrées came to the witness box and painted a not very flattering picture of the victim; the people of Les Bastides, and the postman and the gunsmith, testified that Pique-Bouffigue did not have his gun at his disposal during the whole week of the crime. Moreover he had been seriously ill and had been seen rolling on the ground, with nose pinched and foam on his lips.

The affair was going quite well, but Pique-Bouffigue was uneasy when the prosecutor asked the jury "to look carefully at this brute's low forehead, his small cruel eyes with their ferocious glare, that prognathous jaw, those carnivorous teeth"; and was quite astonished to hear the magistrate "claim" the head that had just been described with such disgust, and beg the jury to give it to him, as if he wanted to take it away with him.

The smile of his counsel reassured him, but not for long.

In fact his counsel started by affirming that his client was clearly a degenerate, without family and without education, but with sweet and innocent manners, like most of the idiots of the village.

Next, he described the crime, which was even more horrible than the prosecutor had said: it was not an ordinary murder, but a veritable assassination—long premeditated, carried out in ambush, perpetrated on a trusting man in a totally cowardly manner in the silence of the hills, at the first glimmer of an innocent Provençal dawn . . . And then pointing a finger at the terrified Pique-Bouffigue the orator cried:

"You must condemn him to death! Yes, M. the prosecutor is right! Yes, a life must be paid for this crime—not just a derisory prison sentence! He must give his head!"

The despairing Pique-Bouffigue thought this man was betraying him, and like the prosecutor wanted to send him to the guillotine; he was about to rise and angrily protest, when the counsel, in a thundering voice, cried:

"*If* he were guilty! But he is not guilty, and we will show you!"

Pique-Bouffigue was unable to restrain a great burst of nervous laughter, and this had an excellent effect on the jury.

Now the counsel spoke with perfect scorn about the miserable copper button. He pointed to it, alone on the table of exhibits:

"There you see all that our accusers have been able to find. They want our head in exchange for a trouser button! Gentlemen of the jury, I will not insult you by continuing with this plea, because I'm sure you understand!"

The Provençal jurymen, who knew in what esteem trouser buttons were generally held (even if this one came from a jacket), shared this scorn of its value as proof, and refused to accord to the Advocate General the bloody head he demanded of them.

Pique-Bouffigue was acquitted and left triumphantly on the arm of his defence, who took him home at once for dinner.

The innocent ate well and drank better.

Then he asked:

"And so, now, it's finished?"

"Finished forever," said the valiant counsel.

"And if a witness should come forward who saw me?"

"That would be of no importance. An acquittal is definite. It's a thing that's been judged. You can't come back over it. And even if you were to declare publicly that it was you who killed this individual, neither the police nor the judge has the right to reconsider it."

"You're sure of that?" asked Pique-Bouffigue, totally moved.

"Absolutely sure."

The lawyer went to get a book from his library and read aloud an article of the code he had commented on.

Pique-Bouffigue wanted to see the article; although he couldn't read, he looked at it for a long time and finally said to the astonished counsel:

"That, for me, is the most beautiful of all, because I was quite content to have killed him, but it was hard for me not to say I had done it . . ."

When he returned to Les Bastides the next day, the mayor offered an aperitif of honor to the village innocent. But after Philoxène had pronounced some words of welcome and spoken about the unjust sufferings of the persecuted innocent, Pique-Bouffigue raised his hand and cried:

"Balls! It was me that killed him! Yes, it was me!" He beat his chest. "The counsel told me: Now I have permission to say so! Yes, it was me!"

"Idiot," said Philoxène, "we knew that! But don't shout like that—people will end by thinking you did it out of spite!"

Pique-Bouffigue told his story at length, and about his preparation of the ambush, which earned him sincere congratulations. Then, drunk with absinthe and pride, he walked the streets of the village, his eyes sparkling, his head high, triumphantly proclaiming his own glory; and when he went up the hill the solemn acknowledgments of the echoes could be heard far away.

His exploit, and his accounts of it, earned him a great reputation as a murderer; never again did a poacher from outside dare to venture on his territory, and he even gained the sympathy of the officers of the gendarmes who finally came to admire his style.

But on the other hand, the perfect success of his vengeance inflated him with exaggerated pride. It is a fact that when luck favors imbeciles, they quickly become unbearable; that is why he proudly lived alone on his little farm of Les Romarins, refusing entry to anybody, with his gun always on his shoulder.

CHAPTER 5

It was on a fine morning in June that Ugolin and the Papet ("properly" dressed, with hats) went to call on the recluse. They found him perched in an olive tree, and the Papet was really surprised to see him pruning a tree; but in fact he was cutting little straight branches to make snares.

They advanced up to the foot of the tree without the other appearing to notice their presence. The Papet raised his head and cried:

"Well then, Marius, things going well?"

"Why should you give a damn?" replied Pique-Bouffigue, continuing to snap his pruning shears.

The Papet was not the least disconcerted.

"Marius, why such a rude answer? Are you cross?"

"Neither cross, nor friendly," replied the poacher. "I don't give a damn for you, that's all. And you don't give a damn for me."

"Perhaps you don't give a damn for me," said the Papet, "but that's not how I feel about you, because I've come to see you."

"Since you've climbed up here, you must want to ask me for something."

"Quite right," said the Papet. "To ask you for something and to give you something!"

"I need *nothing*," said Pique-Bouffigue, "and it bores me when people talk to me, and it bores me more to talk."

Ugolin, already uneasy, blinked without a word. The Papet took a step back to get a better look at the face of the savage who had just climbed to a higher branch, and said calmly in a businesslike tone:

"Listen, Marius, I'll tell you in two words. If you want to sell me your property—not the house, nothing but the field and the hillside opposite—I'll give you the price you want. Look!"

He took five thousand-franc notes from his pocket, spread them fanwise, and brandished them over his head, saying:

"These are thousand-franc notes!"

For he thought the other had never seen any.

Pique-Bouffigue did not respond at once, but they heard him move about in the tree, and his face suddenly emerged from the leaves; it was red with fury.

"What's he trying to say?" he cried. "Who could imagine it? That I should sell my property? Hop it, bunch of pigs! Pack of Soubeyrans!"

"Marius," said the Papet, "don't shout like that, you'll choke yourself. And I'm talking civilly to you; don't insult the Soubeyrans because that could end badly!"

He spoke calmly, but had gone pale and his eyes gleamed with a black fire.

Ugolin tried to put things right.

"Papet, don't get cross, he didn't mean that seriously. He's in a bad temper, but it will pass . . ."

The furious poacher howled:

"And that red owl, why's he interfering? Go and blink somewhere else, because if I come down this tree, you'll see what I'll do to him, that Soubeyran . . ."

Then the Papet turned livid, and red flames of rage danced before his eyes. He hurled his walking stick far away, let his hat fly, took off his jacket and threw it on the grass; then with arms open and shoulders hunched, he said in a hoarse and panting voice:

"Come on then, come down! And make it fast. I'm in a hurry! Come down, ordure, rottenness, *assassin*!"

Ugolin bounded to the side; the poacher jumped across the branches, brandishing his pruning shears. The Papet, instead of drawing back, leaped forward and seized the ankles of the enemy, who fell flat on his belly behind him. Ugolin jumped and crushed the hand holding the shears with a blow of his heel. Then the Papet, who had not let go the ankles, threw himself backwards and rolled around. The body of Pique-Bouffigue turned five or six times; at each half-turn his nose or his chin hit the ground, and his bleeding hands grasped vainly at the brambles . . . At the last turn the Papet accelerated rapidly and let everything go; Pique-Bouffigue made a plunging flight of five or six meters with arms outstretched, his head scraped the ground and went through a clump of hawthorns at the foot of a large olive tree, which he struck heavily. The Papet rubbed his hands and went to pick up his jacket. Ugolin approached the vanquished poacher, stretched motionless on his belly. He gave him a little kick on the bottom but got no response. Then he turned him on his back and saw the lacerated face bleeding around a twisted nose.

The Papet approached.

"He mustn't die," said Ugolin.

"Why?" said the Papet. "He could have died falling from a tree. Let's carry him under the olive tree." They dragged him there, each pulling on a leg. His head bumped over the molehills . . .

They stretched him out on his belly under the tree, and placed the pruners at his side . . . The unfortunate man stayed flat on the grass, perfectly inert.

The Papet put on his jacket, fetched his hat lying on a dog rose, then his stick, and they went off, looking back from time to time.

Halfway to Massacan, Ugolin declared:

"So, the carnations are done for."

"That's a real pity," said the Papet. "It was a good spot . . ."

He took a few more steps, then stopped, pensive . . . He reflected a moment, looked around him, and said in a whisper:

"If he doesn't wake up, the heirs will surely auction the farm . . . I think there is still a sister at Peypin . . . We might be able to buy it for not very much . . ."

He looked thoughtfully at the sky, then the ground, and scratched it with the end of his stick . . . Ugolin waited, his hands in his pockets . . . Finally, he looked his nephew straight in the face, and whispered . . .

"What if we went back to finish him off?"

"No, no," said Ugolin, dismayed. "Perhaps somebody saw us . . . Come, Papet, come . . ."

He dragged the grim old man along, pulling heavily on his shoulder.

They descended to the village, to show themselves there, and proposed a game of *boules* to the butcher and the baker.

The Papet missed nothing, and Ugolin told remarkable jokes that he was the first to laugh at.

Toward six o'clock he said he had to go up home, because of the rabbits.

In fact he passed beyond Massacan and slid into the coppice leading to Les Romarins.

He saw from afar that the body was no longer under the olive tree . . . He crept up. Pique-Bouffigue was sitting with arms crossed on the terrace wall, swinging his head from left to right, then from right to left.

Ugolin withdrew noiselessly and ran to take the news to the Papet.

"We'll have to watch out," said the old man. "He is capable of firing his gun at us."

From that moment on they lived on the qui vive, keeping a loaded weapon ready at hand. Nothing happened in the first two days. But on the third, Ugolin saw the enemy appear at the top of the path that passed in front of the house on the way to the village. He was leaning on a stick, but was not armed.

Nevertheless, Ugolin went inside and watched events through a slit in the shutter.

Pique-Bouffigue went down the short steep rise. But instead of following it to the bottom of the valley in order to go up to the village, he took the perpendicular path that led to Massacan.

His nose was blue, between two puffed eyes, but he walked at a tranquil pace, and ran a pleased eye over the landscape.

He stopped in front of the house, and called:

"Oh Massacan!"

Ugolin was astonished. Massacan was the former owner, who had been dead ten years. Pique-Bouffigue waited a moment, looked around, then called again:

"Oh Massacan!"

Ugolin then saw his expression.

His bruised face was bright and smiling . . . Ugolin went out and approached the visitor.

"Oh, Pique-Bouffigue," he said, "how are things going?"

"Not too well," said the other, "not too well! But you, who are you?"

"Me, I'm Ugolin."

"Ugolin of the Soubeyrans?"

"Well, yes!" said Ugolin, stepping back a pace.

"How you've changed!" said Pique-Bouffigue. "I suppose you must be fifteen years old. Your mother is well?"

Ugolin—who was beginning to be afraid and did not dare tell him that she had been dead a good number of years—replied:

"She's fine!"

"Good!"

He passed his hand over his face and said:

"Just look at what I've done to myself!"

He pointed his finger at his aubergine nose and projected it toward Ugolin.

"Oh good heavens!" said Ugolin. "How did that happen to you?"

"I know *nothing* about it!" said Pique-Bouffigue forcefully. "Imagine, yesterday I climbed into an olive tree to cut branches, and the next thing I woke up on the ground all knocked out. I didn't mind that so much, but I was afraid I had had a stroke like my poor father. The first one is nothing, but the second . . ."

He shook his head and bit his lower lip, showing his unease.

"Massacan isn't there?"

"Oh no!" said Ugolin.

"Where is he?"

"In the cemetery."

"What's he gone to do down there?"

"He went there because he died," said Ugolin. "Ten years ago."

"Massacan is dead?" said Pique-Bouffigue pensively. ". . . That's amazing! Do you know what it can do, a stroke? It's not terrible that he's dead, but it's terrible not to remember it! Anyhow, there's something else. I was thinking of asking you to do me a favor: to go to the village for me . . . Because I would rather not be seen with this face I've got. Nobody gives a damn about me. So I want you to do an errand for me."

"I have to go to the village myself . . . What is it you want me to bring you?"

"Two bottles of wine, a big loaf of bread, and a whole sausage. I'm dying of hunger."

"Okay."

"You're a fine fellow," said Pique-Bouffigue. "Here are the sous."

He put a ten-franc note in his hand.

"Bring me back the change. I'll come back at noon."

He got up to go.

"Wait!" said Ugolin.

He went inside the house and came back with half a loaf and a small chunk of sausage.

"Take that while you're waiting!"

"Thank you," said Pique-Bouffigue. "Thank you."

He began to eat with astonishing voracity, turned his back, and went off.

The Papet heard Ugolin's account, pressed his lips, nodded his head several times, and said:

"He did that on purpose. It's so we won't suspect him. So he plays the simpleton, but perhaps he's less of one than we are."

"If you had seen him . . ." said Ugolin.

"Exactly, I want to see him. Go and do his errands quickly, and afterwards we'll go together."

They found him sitting on the terrace of the farmhouse. The Papet carried his gun on his shoulder, ready for anything.

Pique-Bouffigue recognized them perfectly well. He threw himself at the bottles, and positively wanted to clink glasses with them. He drank four glasses of wine, gulp by gulp, and sang, in an excruciating voice, an old Provençal carol: "lacambo mi fa maou."

They drew back, perplexed.

"In my opinion, he really has gone dotty!" said Ugolin.

"It's possible," said the Papet, "it's possible . . . a big blow on the head, that could turn the brain inside out like a pancake."

"So this might be the moment to offer him the five thousand francs again."

"Oh no!" cried the Papet. "If he really is simple, that might bring his memory back; if it's a comedy it's not worth the bother of talking to him about it— don't trust him! And don't go about alone anymore without your gun! He has already killed one man. No need for you to be the second and me the third . . . Don't trust him!"

After that day they kept guard, with the door barred and a loaded gun at the head of the bed.

CHAPTER 6

Meanwhile Ugolin fretted. His minuscule plantation yielded two more bouquets of flowers, which brought him fifty-one francs in Aubagne . . . This success broke his heart, and his chagrin was aggravated by a short letter from Attilio:

Oh Friend!
Have you decided? I have saved the cuttings for you. Ten thousand plants for two hundred furrows, not more. That's quite enough to make a profit of twelve thousand francs in a season. As soon as you write me I'll bring you them and come and explain.
Your friend
Attilio

"Twelve thousand francs!" said Ugolin. "This year I'm losing twelve thousand francs! How many twenty-franc pieces is that?"

The Papet reflected a moment, closed his eyes, moved his lips rapidly, counted on his fingers, and said at last:

"A big packet."

"That's so, and I don't want to lose this big packet. I've had enough. It's still not too late. Tomorrow I'm going on a trip around Gémenos. I'm sure to find some house to let, and a field, and some water. Down there you get everything you want. And so that's where we'll start the carnations."

The Papet frowned, and his eyes flashed.

"There indeed! Why, I'd rather not speak to you!"

"I'll explain . . ."

The Papet banged violently on the table.

"Be quiet! or talk about something else."

One never saw a Bastidian desert his village, except for the son of the Médérics, and the Testards. The young Médéric one could forgive, because he had finished school and had become a customs officer at Marseille; an altogether glorious profession since a customs officer wears a uniform and has the right to search everybody, even a curé; and moreover, nothing stops him from sleeping, neither ice, nor drought, nor hail, and everything ends with retirement, and no more work. It was not possible to have such a fine career while remaining at Les Bastides. But the Testards, who had gone elsewhere to till a less ungrateful soil, had thereby defamed their native soil and betrayed the honor of the village; when one passed by the ruins of their farm, one spat on the ground. Besides, what good was it to succeed in a "foreign" land? There were no friends to rejoice in your success, and you were not able to enjoy the comforting envy of your neighbors.

And then especially, the Soubeyrans regarded themselves rather as the lords of the village, guardians of its traditions and its secrets; Ugolin felt the profound indignation of the ensuing silence and was suddenly ashamed of having thought of deserting.

"And Le Plantier?" said the Papet, "wouldn't it be possible at Le Plantier?"

This was a remote little cave in the hills, enclosed by a wall of large stones, in which it was said a hermit had lived for a long time. Then it had served as a sheepfold, because a fine spring flowed there summer and winter.

"Certainly I thought of that . . . ," said Ugolin, "the spring is fine, but it's four hundred meters high; in winter there's hoarfrost every morning, and that's death for carnations . . . and then especially, don't forget it's still the property of Pique-Bouffigue!"

"That's true," said the Papet. "Then it has to be a reservoir. Let's try and make a big one near Massacan at the bottom of the vallon, with ditches to collect the rain . . . But we must know how big. He said ten thousand plants. Ask him how many liters per plant. And the price of the cuttings. Me, I can't write as well as I should at the moment because the aches have got to my hand."

Ugolin wrote a long letter to Attilio, fingers clenched on pen, tongue between teeth.

Some days later while pruning his peaches, he saw the Papet coming up, bringing him a letter from the village. It came from Antibes. It was the reply. They went to sit on the wall of the well.

Friend

I did not answer you immediately because my sister married Egidio, the one who chased her all the time. Now it's his right. As for the cuttings, naturally I'll make you a present of them. My father Monsieur Tornabua agrees. I didn't tell him you asked me the price. That would hurt him. They will be ready for you in April. Prepare the field, and especially the water. My father M. Tornabua says that for ten thousand plants you should have a reservoir of at least four hundred cubic meters. If you haven't got that absolutely certainly certainly certainly it's not worth the trouble of starting and not finishing. Do you understand properly? Four hundred meters. And not meters long. Cubes, the same as on the certificate of studies that I could never pass because of those meters, and now I use them to earn more sous than the teacher. That's life! Write to me again, but pay a little attention to your spelling! I didn't understand anything, I had to guess. I don't say this to annoy you. Me too, it happens to me not to understand a word well when somebody writes it: so, in its place I put another!

> *Your friend*
> *Attilio*

My sister told me to ask you if you still blink.

But this friendly joke did not even make Ugolin smile.

"Four hundred meters!" he said, ". . . I'm afraid that's a reservoir as big as the port of Marseille."

"But no! Don't fear! Do the calculation, then you'll know."

Ugolin scratched his head, perplexed . . .

"The calculation, when I think carefully I'll know how to do it. But what confuses me is the decimal point. I never know where to put it . . ."

The Papet smiled and said:

"Me, I know decimal points. Tonight at dinner I'll give you the answer."

The Papet knew how to do calculations, and decimal points did not frighten him; but because he had started from the premise that a cubic meter was ten liters, he declared that night that it would be enough to dig a hole four meters by four meters and three meters deep . . . Ugolin, having reflected, told him that that seemed to him to be too little.

The next day, at the café, they consulted Philoxène. He reflected in turn, then declared:

"Me, I don't know cubic meters very well. But it seems to me it must be bigger than a hectoliter. Much bigger . . . To my mind it's at least a hogshead!"

Luckily the old schoolmistress, in a black lace mantilla, passed by with her shopping basket. They stopped her. As soon as they had put the problem of the reservoir to her, this extraordinary woman, without even taking time to think, replied all in one breath that a cubic meter was a thousand liters; that a square reservoir ten meters per side and four meters deep was needed, which would mean removing four hundred thousand liters of earth, which weighed at least two kilograms per liter, that is, eight hundred thousand kilos, which would require a year and a half's work by a professional terrace builder. Finally, the lining of the interior, a quarter-meter thick and two hundred sixty square meters, would need sixty-five cubic meters of masonry at two tons a cubic meter, or one hundred thirty tons. Then as the church clock sounded half past six, at a trot she left them, stupefied by her virtuosity, and disconcerted by her results.

That evening at table, the Papet said:

"It's not possible, Galinette. It will be a three-year job."

"We could take on one or two workmen?"

"I thought of that, but I also think it doesn't rain enough there to fill such a big reservoir. That peak of Saint Esprit cuts the storms in two when they come from Sainte Victoire, and then the water falls elsewhere."

"I know," said Ugolin, "I know . . . we must think, we must go and look . . ."

He was very sad and blinked in a melancholy way, crunching his zucchini fritters.

For several weeks he did not talk any more about carnations, and he was preparing himself to write a desolate letter to Attilio, when Providence came to his aid.

On a tender October morning several people in their Sunday clothes were gathered on the terrace of Les Romarins. Anglade the Sage sat on the wall with Philoxène. His two sons examined the enormous stem of the climbing vine, arguing in stammers about its age.

Clarius, just come from Les Ombrées, looked at the abandoned olive trees, shaking his head . . . Finally, in front of the open window, there was a group of three: Casimir the blacksmith, Eliacin from the Tête Rouge, and Cabridan.

These three did not talk—they were watching with great interest a strange operation taking place in the kitchen.

Pique-Bouffigue was seated on a chair, his eyes wide open. The baker was holding him under the armpits. Pamphile was standing and energetically soaping his face, holding the shaving brush in one hand, and waving a large open razor in the air with the other. He said gaily:

"Above all don't budge, idiot. I'm starting!"

"Oh! It won't matter if you cut him," said the baker, "he's sure not to bleed!"

For Pique-Bouffigue was dead, dead for three days; but he had been propped up in a chair to have the last toilet carried out, because Pamphile had declared he was incapable of shaving a horizontal client.

Meanwhile, Ugolin and the Papet, also in their Sunday best, pretended to stroll in the vallon while awaiting the departure of the funeral procession.

From time to time Ugolin bent down, pulled up a plant, and examined the clod that came up with the root . . . The earth was brown, streaked with black humus, due to its having lain fallow so long. The Papet took a pinch of it, broke it between his fingers, and smelled it for a long time. Ugolin put some grains of it on his tongue and sucked them, as if appreciating a wine. Then they tackled the high undergrowth on the hillside, and climbed to the top of the slope that stopped at a bluff of white rock.

In fact they had been approaching the spring little by little, with several loitering detours, and had just arrived there. The trunk of an old fig tree stood there, bristling with several dead branches, but surrounded by verdant suckers. All this while the Papet pointed an index finger at the hillside opposite, which they pretended to look at:

"It's right here," said the Papet. "At the foot of the fig tree, there was a little well, just big enough for a man, about as tall as I am. It wasn't lined with stone; it had a semicircle of earth on one side, and rock on the other. And in the rock, near the bottom, there was a hole, quite round, like a five-franc piece. That was where the spring started, but it didn't come up to the top of the well. It had to be drawn with a bucket. Fat Camoins was no fool, and he saw that the level of the water was a bit higher than his field. So he dug a little trench and at the bottom ran a drain made out of bricks and tiles to the edge of the field; then he filled in the trench again and covered the well. That way the water went right to the bottom quite unseen."

Talking all the while, they descended across the prickly gorse and rockrose to a cluster of reeds that emerged from the undergrowth.

"This is where the drain discharged," said the Papet.

At the foot of the reeds there was some furze that came out from a patch of moss; they kept their eyes raised to the sky, as if they were interested in the buzzard that turned on high. The Papet murmured:

"Look around my foot . . . It squirts . . . The water is blocked up, but it's there . . . It wouldn't take much to . . ."

Ugolin in his turn walked on the moss, and his big shoe made the water spurt.

"When I think he allowed this fortune to be lost," he said, "I'm quite pleased I busted his face. He didn't just kill one man—he was a double murderer."

At the farmhouse four men came to place Pique-Bouffigue in his coffin. His face was so clean he was unrecognizable, and it clearly showed that his last toilet had been the first. As the carpenter was about to put the lid on the long box, the blacksmith intervened:

"Wait! One day when I was out hunting I met him, and we had a bite together. That was long before he went dotty. So then he showed me his hammerless and said to me: 'That's my only friend, and I want it buried with me.' "

"That would be stupid," said the baker, "to waste such a fine gun."

"And then, up there, what would he do with it?" said Pamphile. "Perhaps he would not be able to stop himself from shooting an angel in flight, and that wouldn't help to get his papers right!"

"Come on, come on," said the blacksmith, "no jokes. At a time like this I say we should give him the 'nammerless' since the wish of a dead man is sacred!"

He took the fine weapon and placed it under the right arm of the corpse, the barrel resting on the shoulder. Pique-Bouffigue had the air of going off to mount guard at the gates of Paradise.

It was while Pamphile was screwing down the lid that M. the curé arrived, preceded and accompanied by his choirboys.

The procession got organized behind the coffin, which six men carried on their shoulders. Along the length of the gorse and the flowers under the melancholy October sun, Pique-Bouffigue departed on his last journey, followed by about thirty peasants. When the coffin came over the pass and the village came into view, the knell could be heard tolling on the little bell of Les Bastides . . .

It was at this moment that Philoxène asked the baker:

"Did you see whether the gun was loaded?"

"No, I didn't think of it. You can't tell with a hammerless!"

But Eliacin called:

"Certainly it was loaded, with buckshot! When he came home he always loaded it with buckshot because of the wild boar that sometimes came during the night!"

"That could be dangerous . . . ," said the Papet.

"Especially," said the blacksmith, "since he had polished the trigger to make it more sensitive . . . He used to say that a gust of wind was enough to make it go off!"

This revelation ran the length of the procession.

Philoxène, who was walking behind the curé, turned to say:

"Perhaps there's a safety catch."

"That would surprise me!" said the blacksmith.

There was a little wavering in the ranks; behind the planks of the coffin, the barrel of the hammerless was pointed at them, just at the height of their faces

. . . After a few steps the funeral procession separated into two files, with a fairly large space between to allow the free passage of the buckshot after passing through the head of M. the curé, this saintly man who risked nothing worse than Paradise . . .

At the cemetery the Papet was grave and dignified, but several times he had to pinch Ugolin, who smiled without knowing it as he sang.

After the funeral there was the customary reunion at the club, where a little wine was drunk to the memory of the deceased. Ugolin and the Papet chatted with Anglade.

"So," said the Papet, "are you the one who inherits?"

"Oh no," said Anglade. "We were cousins, certainly, but rather distant. That's to say the mother of his father was first cousin to my grandfather. She was an Anglade girl."

"Does that give you the right to anything?"

"No. It's his sister who'll have everything."

"We're related too." said Casimir. "One-eyed Camoins, father of Big Camoins, who was father of Florette and Pique-Bouffigue—he married the sister of my grandfather. That makes us a little of the same blood. But naturally, it's Florette who inherits."

The Papet was stuffing his pipe and did not raise his eyes, but he asked:

"Do you think she's still living?"

"Why not?" said Anglade. "She's younger than you. I know her husband is dead . . . Somebody told me that at the Aubagne Fair five or six years ago. But she—I don't know . . . Women have a hard life!"

"And who is she, this woman?" asked Ugolin.

"Somebody the Papet knew well. Isn't that so, César?" The Papet felt in his pockets, looking for his matches. Anglade continued, almost in an undertone:

"She was Florette de Bérengère, Florette Camoins the beautiful."

"And where is she?" said Ugolin.

The Papet finished lighting his pipe and replied:

"At Crespin. Because she married Lionel, the blacksmith at Crespin."

Philoxène, who was pouring white wine at a neighboring table, turned his head toward the Papet and asked in an almost menacing tone:

"Who's talking about Crespin?"

Crespin was a very big village, with large communal lands contiguous with those of Les Bastides . . . In one of the books of the great Anatole France, somebody asks a minister, "Why do you fight so often with your neighbors?" The minister, most astonished, replies, "Who do you think we should fight with?" So Crespin was the hereditary enemy, and for all sorts of reasons. This dated very far back—perhaps (according to Philoxène) to the time of the Romans.

The first thing they quarrelled about was always the matter of hunting— that is to say poaching—which provided a handsome share of their nourishment for nothing.

Now once "those of Crespin" came with rare impudence to set their traps in the hills of Les Bastides. After a good number of brawls, the Bastidians got extremely angry. They organized a constant watch by a dozen of the wives and children, and every Crespinois caught hunting by four or five vigorous hearties was sent back to his family with an unrecognizable face. So somebody from Crespin, who was a deputy, nominated another Crespinois, who had returned from military service, to the rank of brigadier of the gendarmerie at Aubagne . . . This person, who had been thrashed by the Bastidians in his youth, did not leave the hills of Les Bastides again. In less than six months he served three summonses, but he was unable to prepare the fourth because he was found hanging from a mountain ash near La Baume de Ratepénades one day, and nobody ever knew who was responsible.

To avenge him the Crespinois set fire to the big pine wood of the Pas du Loup on the first day of a fine mistral, and it took thirty years to rebuild the forest . . .

Nevertheless, the war of the poachers cooled down in the course of time, because Crespin came to know prosperity thanks to the discovery of a lignite mine, and to a little irrigation canal cut through the good offices of the government. A rabbit or half a dozen thrushes no longer had the same nutritive importance. And so—this proves their nastiness—they found something else.

When they saw a bad cloud arrive they would fire shots from a cannon, and the hail that they had certainly deserved (because the Good Lord had sent it to them) came to ravage the meagre vines of Les Bastides . . . Finally there was the serious matter of the "fly."

The Crespin people no longer had many olive trees. They had sacrificed hundreds of them (another crime) to plant vines and had ceased to look after those that remained, so the olive fly attacked them. And if by bad luck the wind blew from the east at the moment of flowering the fly would be brought right up to Les Bastides, and half of the olive crop would be lost.

There was an interminable list of grievances, real but magnified and supplemented by tales carried from father to son. The Crespin people also had their list, and they usually said the people of Les Bastides belonged to a quasi-prehistoric race composed mainly of idiots, madmen, and murderers. In fact they looked like brothers, and under an outward appearance of good humor and Provençal joviality, they were equally jealous, suspicious, and secretive.

"We're talking about Crespin," said Anglade, "because we're talking about Florette's wedding . . ."

"Were you there yourself?"

"Certainly. I had come back from military service; that was nearly forty years ago."

"And I," said the Papet, "I was a good long way from here. I was in the military hospital in Africa . . . I came back nearly a year later, but my father told me about the battle."

The gigantic Eliacin approached and asked:

"What battle?"

"The battle of the wedding!"

The young ones formed a circle, glass in hand, and Anglade spoke:

"Florette Camoins was the marvel of the land. Rather pleased with herself, but truly beautiful. One evening she went to the fête at La Valentine with some other girls from here. And there she danced with this Lionel, who was big and strong with fine black moustaches . . . It was love at first sight, and about ten days later, after mass, M. the curé announced the marriage. It was like dynamite, and Florette's father and mother hung their heads and made themselves small. But she was first class—she came back, placed her hands on her hips, and looked all the world straight in the eye. And so M. the curé came to tell them to forget their quarrels. He said that the Good Lord had desired this marriage to give us the chance to make peace—that already M. the curé of Crespin had promised to have the hail cannon fire in the opposite direction, so that the hail would fall on Roquevaire. And besides, he said, the people of Crespin were our brothers—we should love them, and they would love us. In short, at least twenty came for the wedding, with their curé at the head. Our curé went to meet him, and they embraced each other. Afterwards he blessed the Crespin people. And then, at the wedding mass they both preached. My friends, everybody wept."

"Why?" asked Ugolin.

"Because it was beautiful!" cried Philoxène. "I was seven or eight years old, and I remember at the end of the mass everybody held hands. A very finely dressed lady from Crespin embraced me and said, 'Vive Les Bastides, where they make such beautiful children!' "

"Oh, Philoxène," said the carpenter, "are you sure it was you?"

Anglade continued:

"The Crespin people said that everything that had happened had been their fault. And we said it had been ours. In the end we agreed that we had been as bad as each other, and now everything was going well. We paired off; a boy from down there with one of our girls and vice versa . . . We began a great banquet in the plaza, at Big Camoins' expense, the father of the bride. There were six enormous hams, at least thirty legs of lamb, and fifty corn-fed chickens well stuffed with garlic and roasted on vine branches."

At this recital of the menu the gigantic Eliacin's lips curled up and his nose crinkled, and he opened his very small black eyes and stopped breathing.

Anglade continued:

"The people of Crespin had brought their wine: two barrels of 125 liters. It was fine to look at, but rather cheap and a little too light, so that one drank it like water . . . And so, old Médéric, who had a rather feeble head, asked—very nicely and even politely—what they did to make such a fine thin wine. In a flash a woman of Crespin said that as to our corn-fed chickens—she had thought they were starlings . . . Everyone wanted his say, and finally, one word after the other, somebody climbed on the table to fight, the table collapsed and it went like a house afire . . ."

"I climbed a tree," said Philoxène, "with Casimir . . . We saw everything."

"We had a fine time looking on," said Casimir. "The women were clawing at each other, the men were rolling on the ground. Everybody was shouting, and not a single kick on the butt was lost!"

"And the two curés who tried to separate them," said Anglade, "they would have done better not to get mixed up in it! Ours was laid out by a Crespinois with a great blow on the tonsure with a ham, and theirs received a flying chair; his head passed between the crossbars and he couldn't get it out . . . I nearly finished strangling a big shady character, all frizzy . . . I let him go and said, 'Get it now? Bugger off, you savage!' He breathed again and gave me a kick in the stomach, which brought the light wine right up into my nose; I wept like a lost soul and never saw him again. I quickly hid myself behind the acacia to cough and spit and wipe my eyes, and the last thing I saw was the old jalopy of Father Camoins taking the newlyweds off at a great gallop. And so, since that day it's been a lot worse than before with the Crespin people, and Florette—in no time at all she became more Crespinoise than Crespin!"

"With her character," said the Papet, "that wasn't much of a change for her!"

"I wrote to her officially," said Philoxène, "to inform her of the death of her brother. But she won't get my letter until tomorrow morning. If she's still living perhaps she'll come for the inheritance . . ."

"Is it sure she'll inherit?" said the baker.

Ugolin looked at the Papet, who made a scornful moue.

"She doesn't inherit much," he said.

"I agree with you," said Anglade. "Les Romarins doesn't seem to be worth much because Pique-Bouffigue never did anything to it. But at least the house should still be good. A few little repairs, a little paint, and it won't be bad. And then, fifty olive trees from before the war of '70 . . ."

"They're quite sick," said Ugolin, ". . . they're lost in misery . . ."

"If one went at them with a pick one could put them right again . . ."

"You'd have to work fast and with a big pickax . . ."

"About thirty almond trees," continued Anglade, "and two hectares of good land. Nearly all flat, at the bottom of the vallon."

"Yes," said the baker, "but it's a place that the rain can't find! We have a little field up there, a little beyond Les Romarins. We haven't cultivated it because of that . . . The storms—you hear them coming, you see them approaching . . . But as soon as the clouds hit the top of Saint Esprit, it cuts them in two, and the water falls on the other slope of the two hills and there's hardly more than four drops left for the vallon . . ."

"That's possible," said Anglade, "but what you might not know is that there's a spring at Pique-Bouffigue's place."

Ugolin blinked three times.

"There was a spring," said the Papet.

"I saw it," said Anglade. "It was fine; it made a little stream as big as a man's hand."

"I saw it too when I was small, hunting with my father," said Pamphile. "It seemed to me to be a real stream!"

"You must have been quite small," said the Papet, "and it must have been after a storm. Because I drank there, about forty years ago. It ran about as big as my finger. But it's disappeared since then."

"Do you think it could disappear, a spring like that?"

"I had a look at it this morning," said the Papet. "It was as dry as tinder . . . The truth is that Pique-Bouffigue was too lazy to bother with it, and it's blocked, and so it's found its way lower down and gone God knows where."

"If one dug a well?" said Casimir.

"You'd waste your time!" said the Papet. "That water must have come from the Depths. When the dirt made it impossible to come up, it made its way back to the Depths. Perhaps at thirty meters, perhaps at a hundred meters. I know the way springs are! They're like a pretty young girl. If you forget them, they go, and that's that."

"All the same," said the baker, "last year on the way under the ledge on the hillside, I saw a fig tree. That shows the water is not far off!"

"That proves that there was water there," said the Papet. "Once a fig tree's got going, it doesn't need anything. That one is at least a hundred years old!"

"All the same," said Philoxène, "since it grows shoots . . ."

The Papet cut in heavily.

"When you talk about aperitifs, I listen to you. But springs aren't your business. Pernod doesn't come from a spring. I tell you this, it won't ever come back. I tell you the olive trees are lost, that land is rotten with couch grass, and what little you could do there would all be taken by rabbits, badgers, and grasshoppers. You would have to plough to at least eighty centimeters and put up a fence with fifteen thousand francs worth of wire netting, and then you would be able to gather not more than four tomatoes, thirty potatoes, and fifty kilos of chickpeas; and you'd have to repair two kilometers of road to take them to the market."

"That's true," said Ugolin. "If you gave it to me for nothing, I wouldn't want it!"

CHAPTER 8

That same evening, eating a stew that was nearly black with Jacquez wine, they held council for a long time.

Ugolin wanted to go to Crespin and see Florette the next day.

"Not on your life," cried the Papet. "If you go and ask you'll show you want it and she'll give you a price that's three times too high. Besides, if Florette knew it was for us she'd say no . . ."

"Why?"

The Papet smiled a melancholy smile and said:

"Because. She's like that."

"So, what should we do?"

"Listen to my plan."

He started stuffing his pipe.

"In the first place, Florette never came back here. And then, when she was young, she liked money a lot. As she got older it got still worse. So she'll sell. Do you know a single family in the village that would like to buy that place? I'm talking about those who have something."

Ugolin thought a moment and said:

"No. I don't know anybody. Nearly everybody has too much land. Besides, nobody's going to leave the fields in the vallon and settle up there. No. But a stranger might come."

"And what will he come to do, this stranger?"

"Green vegetables, or perhaps even flowers! Like me! Because of the spring."

"Well, yes," said the Papet. "That's the point. Because of the spring. But if there were no spring, what would he want?"

"Nothing," said Ugolin. "Nothing. But it's there."

The Papet put his pipe in his mouth and smiled. Then he winked slyly and took his time lighting the tobacco. Finally he said in a whisper:

"It's already three-quarters blocked. And if, by *accident*, it should be blocked completely?"

Ugolin was perplexed, and asked:

"What kind of accident?"

"Suppose," said the Papet, "you were to pass near the spring with a bag of cement on your back. You slipped and fell, and the cement just blocked the hole! . . ."

Ugolin hesitated a second, then burst into laughter, saying:

"Bravo, Papet! We'll go and block it tomorrow! That's what must be done. It'll be an *accident*!"

But he suddenly became serious again:

"There's one snag," he said. "This spring, it's known . . . People have talked about it at the club . . ."

"Yes, but if strangers should come and visit the farm, nobody would tell them anything. We should get everything ready to go there tomorrow. Now, get the cement first. A sack will be enough. Then cut two or three big plugs out of hardwood. About as big as a bottle, but smaller at one end, and dry them well on the fire. Now let's talk about other matters: I'm going to write at once to Graffignette."

"Who's that?"

"You don't know her because she left before you were born. She was Marie d'Hortense, one of the Castelots of La Bermaine. Plump as a quail, with the face of an angel. She was called Graffignette because when the boys wanted to embrace her she would scratch their faces; she cut her nails to sharp points for the purpose. It was her glory, and M. the curé held her up as an example. But by scratching everybody she ended up an old maid, and when her parents died she became the maid of the curé of Mimet. And then, four or five years later, the pope sent the curé to Crespin, and she had to go with him . . ."

"Didn't she scratch him?"

"Oh! At her age there was hardly any more opportunity to scratch anyone

. . . And since she was a friend of Florette's, they saw a lot of each other . . .
I'm going to write to her at once."

"And if she's dead?"

"Now then!" said the Papet, "the people my age aren't all dead!"

"Not all," said Ugolin, "but many."

"That's true. Oh well, if she's dead the letter will come back to us . . ."

"How?"

"Because I'll put my address on the back."

Ugolin seemed worried.

"Aren't you afraid a letter with two addresses will confuse the postman?"

"My poor Ugolin, it's unbelievable how idiotic you can be. At the Post Office
they first look at the main address, on the same side as the stamp. And then if
the person has gone, or is dead, they turn the letter over and see the other address
and then send it back to you. And then we'll know whether Graffignette is not
there, or is dead!"

"But who puts on the stamp for sending the letter back?"

"Nobody," said the Papet, a little wearily. "There is no need for a stamp,
because in the end the first one you put on served no purpose when the letter
didn't arrive where you wanted. And so, at the Post Office . . ."

"Listen, Papet, don't bother to explain; I can't understand it at all but it's of
no importance. Write your letter and we'll find out what happens."

While the dumb woman cleared the table, they made the necessary preparations for their enterprise. They had to find the inkpot, then to add lukewarm
water and vinegar. The pen was rubbed with sand and put in working order.
Finally the letter was started, and there was a little discussion over every phrase,
on what to say and what not to say. Papet's writing was legible enough but he
hardly troubled himself with the spelling, and improved it without the least
prejudice.

Toward midnight it was finished, and he read the missive in a high voice.
Ugolin found it perfect, and he climbed up to Massacan under the stars with
a light step.

While waiting for the reply from Graffignette, they quickly went into action.

The Papet came to find him one morning at dawn. The evening before at
the club he had said that he was going to spend the day on the hill looking for
mushrooms, because it was the beginning of November. He carried two big

game bags with their straps crossed over his breast; one contained food, with the necks of two bottles sticking out, in the other were the tools.

Ugolin waited for him, while eating a salad of chick-peas and raw onions. On the table there were two conical plugs, cut from a holm oak branch and dried over the hot cinders in the fireplace.

"I think the smaller one will do it," said the Papet. "Take off your shoes and put on espadrilles. Have you got a drill?"

"I took it down there yesterday evening. It's hidden in the undergrowth with the hammer, the chisel, the big saw, and the little pickax."

He tied his laces tightly and went to take a half-filled sack, which he threw over his shoulder.

"That's the cement," he said, "the cement for the *accident*!"

They climbed up to Les Romarins in silence, under the cover of the pine wood.

The day broke a little hesitantly, under a colorless sunrise, with the silence disturbed only by the discreet "tchic" of the thrushes.

The Papet went to hide behind a bushy crag at the top of the little ledge of rock, just above the spring. From there he could look over the landscape and direct the work.

Ugolin first cut off all the shoots of the fig tree, then he attacked the roots of the stump. It took a very long time because to avoid making any noise, he could not wield the pickax vigorously; he dug in, pushing against the handle with his foot, and then using it as a lever; then he took out the broken-up earth with the trowel . . . He had not yet reached the tips of the roots, but as they descended toward the bottom of the spring the earth became more and more muddy. By ten o'clock he had dug a little semicircular well, which went down a meter and a half against the rock ledge.

He sweated great drops, not only because of the physical effort, but mainly for fear of being surprised. The heap of dirt filled two wheelbarrows, and it couldn't help but attract the attention of a passerby. Certainly nobody ever came to this vallon, but it would be just at a moment like this that the one stroller of the year would arrive.

From time to time the Papet murmured:

"Carry on, Galinette . . . There's nobody here, but hurry up."

"I'm doing all I can. But it's the roots. There's a sort of knot of them around the big ones."

He pushed and pulled the blade of the saw through the mud, which fortunately deadened the sound.

At last, about noon, after having thrown a dozen pieces of root on the dirt, he pulled at the last root; it resisted for a long time, and he could not use all his force at the bottom of the hole . . . So he attached a rope, strengthened the knot with wire, climbed up to the edge again, and pulled with powerful jerks. At the third jerk the root gave way and a jet of invisible water burst out under the dirt and set it dancing.

Ugolin was frantic; if the little well filled so quickly, how was he going to find the hole to push the plug in? He called softly, "Papet! Come quickly! The water's catching up on me!" The Papet came down without a word, but before he got there the level of the water stopped rising. Ugolin saw a little whirlpool halfway up the crumbling side of the well; this was where the water was going.

"I'll be damned!" said the Papet. "It's Old Camoins' little underground ditch . . . The water should come out below, there where the reeds are . . ."

"If somebody should pass by and see this flood we're sunk!" groaned Ugolin.

"Stop crying, Galinette. Cheer up; we'll find the hole . . . It's in the rock, just in front of you!"

The water became clearer and they could see the jet. Leaning on the palms of his hands on the edge of the well, Ugolin let himself down carefully.

"O Holy Mother! It's icy . . . I can't feel my feet anymore . . ."

The water now ran away faster than it came out, because it had unblocked the underground ditch, and the level slowly dropped.

He plunged his arms in up to the elbows and said: "I think the little plug will fit . . . It was this root that blocked it . . . There is still a bit inside . . ."

The Papet passed him the plug. He had to crouch to push it into the hole.

"Ayayay! It's terrible the way the butt is more sensitive than the feet! But it's going to be difficult to hit the plug, because of the water . . ."

"Hold it in place," said the Papet. "It will fall. But first fill the jug, so I can prepare the mortar."

He passed it to him at arm's length and Ugolin filled it.

After a minute the water had gone down just below the wooden plug, which was now surrounded by a wreath of little jets. At the third blow of the hammer they disappeared.

The Papet had already mixed the sand and cement with the gravel. They rammed this concrete into the bottom of the hole, up to just above the plug.

"Let's not put too much in!" said Ugolin. "Let's not forget that I'm the one who'll have to unplug the spring!"

The Papet climbed back onto the rock to resume his sentry duty. In the meantime Ugolin threw the dirt back into the little well, layer by layer, and crammed it in by dancing on it as if he were pressing grapes in a tub. Suddenly the Papet's face hung over the edge of the rock and whispered:

"Don't move! I hear a noise . . ."

"You do?"

"In the house . . ."

They listened: there was a long silence, then something creaked in the attic.

"It's the ghost of Pique-Bouffigue," said Ugolin laughing. "It's the rats . . . I saw them running on the roof yesterday morning. They're as big as rabbits."

They listened again for a moment. The house was dead, all the shutters closed. The silence was so profound they heard the call of the partridge carried on the wind. Finally the Papet whispered:

"Carry on."

Ugolin finished putting the dirt back; but as he expected, the well could not take all the earth that had been taken out because it was swollen. He took the surplus a little further away and made a little heap at the foot of the ledge. The Papet came down again and helped him replant the thyme and rockrose on the earth that had been denuded; the heap of earth received a thick layer of pine twigs.

"Now," said the Papet, "we must go down to the edge of the field and cut the canes, and especially remove the moss and rushes!"

The underground drain had worked, and two long pools of water shone on the edge of the field.

"That's bad!" said Ugolin. "If anybody saw that . . ."

"Pull up the canes, and let me fix that."

He went and pulled out one of the leaning fence posts, renewed its point with three blows of the axe, and pierced the bottoms of the pools with about a dozen holes. The water disappeared in a few minutes, and then he closed the holes with his heel and covered the moist soil with dead leaves. Then he tore up the big sheet of moss and dispersed the shreds in the undergrowth of the field. Meanwhile Ugolin had succeeded in pulling up a large number of reed roots resembling strings of little artichokes . . .

"It's terrible what's there. And there's still more besides!"

"We'll come back," said the Papet. "That'll do for today. The Angelus is ringing and we haven't eaten yet. I'm starving. Come on! Let's go!"

After having tied the roots of the fig tree and the reeds in faggots, they gathered their tools.

"We're going to eat on the hill?" asked Ugolin.

"It's not worth the trouble. Let's go to your place. We'll close the shutters and then we'll have a siesta!"

They went down to Massacan; the Papet, unencumbered, walked in front of Ugolin, who was loaded with the tools.

They closed the doors and windows and ate lengthily by lamplight, without a word. The faggots of roots burned on the hearth. From time to time they exchanged little bursts of smiles, as if they were celebrating the success of a first-rate farce.

CHAPTER 9

In the days that followed Ugolin got into the habit of returning to Les Romarins at the first light of dawn. He went up there without the least noise, with his ears cocked, carrying a saw, an axe, and a rope like somebody collecting wood, just in case.

First he would carefully examine the tomb of the spring; because water is a traitor! When you look for it you don't find it; when you try to stop it, it comes out somewhere else, as often as not. But every morning he saw that the operation had succeeded perfectly; no trace of humidity appeared on the surface of the ground, not a single shoot of the fig tree came up. They had done a really good job.

Next he went to the exit of the underground drain; sometimes he was unable even to find the place, and he laughed with pleasure and pride.

After these checks he set to work.

Around the olive trees, already hemmed in by nearly full-grown shoots, he sowed handfuls of thistle, rockrose, and clematis seeds. Then he judiciously pruned the brambles in order to encourage the growth of the best stems. He made cuttings at home of the sacrificed shoots, punctiliously watered them, and carefully planted them in a number of places where it was still possible to trace a passage. These accursed plants, surprised by so much amity, threw themselves into an assault on the stunted almond trees with an exuberant ferocity. He went so far as to attempt grafts on the brambles. They all succeeded at the first attempt. He was much amused by this singular work. He said to himself softly:

"I plug the springs, I plant brambles, I graft dog roses, I am the Devil's peasant!"

Before going home he took care of the old house. He broke the blisters in the roughcast with a stake pulled out from the vine and made two or three large patches fall down; then he threw stones on the roof to break some of the tiles . . .

Then, satisfied, he went down to Massacan for the season's work.

That is to say, he cut the wood for his fireplace, harvested some carrots, cauliflowers, and radishes, and pruned his few fruit trees; but without the least conviction, because he was thinking about his carnations. He waited with feverish impatience for news from Graffignette.

One morning in December, after descending from Les Romarins, he found the Papet seated under the mulberry tree. The old man, wrapped up in a long shepherd's cloak, was smoking his pipe under a pale and distant sun.

When he saw Ugolin arriving, he got up and waved a sheet of paper from afar.

Ugolin quickened his step and asked:

"Is that the reply?"

"And what do you want it to be?"

Ugolin looked to see if anybody was in view, then, fingers on hips and chin pointed, he stood and listened to his godfather, who had put on his glasses.

5th December, Feast of St. Sabas

My dear César,

You always do the most extraordinary things. After at least three dozen Christmases, you write to me about Florette. And imagine! The postman gave me your letter just the day she died, and I had come back to dress her. The voices of God are inscrutable. Imagine that! That is why I did not reply sooner. I thought she would not be able to leave much money, because her husband died five or six years ago, and she had lived quite well without doing anything. Meat every day, and vintage wine. But all the same there was her fine house and three hectares of meadows near Gémenos which were let to somebody down there. Which he did not seem to pay for. And then at Les Bastides, there is a very big piece of the hill where her grandfather kept goats. It is the vallon of Le Plantier where right at the bottom there is the hermit's cave with a fine

*little spring that the Good Lord had given to this saintly man whom the brig-
and Gaspard of Le Besse had killed for nothing, and which the great-
grandfather, instead of building a chapel, had closed with a big wall to make
a sheepfold with a door and a window and the goats and the billy goat and the
dogs drank at the spring of the Good Lord instead of the Saint. I am astonished
that the Good Lord allowed that to continue. But in spite of this fine water it
was no good, because there were not even three meters of cultivation.*

"I told you!" cried Ugolin.

The Papet continued:

*Finally, there is also that farm of her brother, which he left her, that great
murderer Pique-Bouffigue, who committed a crime that he confessed to everybody except M. the curé. How wicked he is. Now it is up there that he must
acquit himself. In the end the mercy of God is infinite, and it is possible that
he repented at the last moment; but frankly, if he is not in hell I ask myself
who does get sent there. Surely not me. Everything there will naturally go to
the son, who is called Jean Cadoret. He should be about thirty-five. He is a
tax collector, but I do not know where. The notary will surely find him, a tax
collector does not just get lost like that. He is married, and unfortunately, by
God's will, he is a hunchback. M. the curé said he will sell the land because he
does not want to be a peasant. When he comes here I will let you know. And
apropos, I hope you go to mass more often now. It is time, César. At your age,
one is at the gate of death, which comes in the night like a thief. I would be
content if you had told me that you had a good Easter this year. Like that you
will be all prepared inside. Florette died a good Christian death, which gave
pleasure to everybody. Give my good wishes to Finette, and to Claire of Les
Bouscarles, etc. . . . etc. . . . and when the hunchback comes I will write to
you . . .*

"Voilà," said the Papet. "I find it interesting, because that man isn't ever going
to set himself up here. Listen carefully: firstly, he is a tax collector. They're not
stupid, the tax collectors. They know perfectly well that it is easier to get money
out of my pocket than out of the ground. The ground is low and the cashier's
windows are high. And then, a fountain pen makes fewer blisters than a pickax.
Secondly, he is a hunchback; a peasant often becomes a hunchback, but it's rare
that a hunchback becomes a peasant."

"That's true," said Ugolin. "That's very good. There, we're lucky. And so, what are you going to do?"

"Wait."

"Aren't you afraid he'll sell all his property in one lot, to someone from Gémenos, or from Roquevaire?"

"That's not impossible; but if someone should buy the whole inheritance, he'd only keep what's good and he'd be glad to sell this farm again, and not expect much . . . if a peasant came to see it in the state that you've put it in the first thing he'd do would be to sit on the ground and weep."

"That's true," said Ugolin with the pride of an artist. "And in a month it will be even worse because the brush grows five centimeters a day . . ."

The Papet shouted with demoniac enthusiasm:

"And no water! No water! Nothing but a rotten little dried-up cistern!"

"There's only one thing I'm afraid of, I just thought about it last night . . ."

"What is it?"

"I'm afraid the spring may be marked on the notary's papers."

"Me too, I thought about that," said the Papet thoughtfully. "In the papers for my house the well is marked . . ."

They both reflected and the ticking of the tall grandfather clock emphasized their silence.

"Listen, Galinette . . . that spring, it's not old . . . I heard it said when I was small that it was One-eyed Camoins, father of Big Camoins, who found it."

"So," said Ugolin, "that's nearly a hundred years."

"Nearly. But the papers of notaries are still older than that. And since the farm has never been sold, I don't think the spring is on the papers."

"And if it had been declared at the time of an inheritance?"

"And why should they do that? It's never very smart to tell the government something they don't know! They always profit from it to raise the taxes! No, I don't think it's on the paper."

"But if the hunchback came here and somebody in the village told him about the spring?"

"I doubt that. The young ones don't know about it since that imbecile Pique-Bouffigue let it get lost at least twenty years ago, and you know very well that he put up that fence to keep people out . . . Those who know about it are those who've talked about it at the club and they also know that one hasn't got the right to meddle in other people's business. No, go on, all told, it will succeed.

There's nothing to do but to wait, and hope, and see what comes. Soon Marie will write to me again, when she's seen the young man . . . Because he must come to Crespin for his inheritance. And then perhaps we'll go and talk to him?"

He carefully folded the letter and put it back in his pocket. Then he was silent for a long moment while he relit his pipe. Finally he said despondently:

"Who would have thought that Florette would have a little hunchback? She was big, she was beautiful, she was as fresh as the dew."

"Did you know her well, Papet?"

"Oh yes! Very well. Too well, perhaps . . ."

Ugolin was about to ask more questions, but the Papet raised himself up with an effort and suddenly said:

"Let's go! I'm going down to the vineyard. I'm going to reprune it, because I left too much wood on it: it's like me, it's old, and I'm afraid that all that wood will wear it out . . . the old must help each other. See you this evening, Galinette. Rose has made us a polenta, and Claudius has given us a meter of black pudding!"

A month passed without news, and Ugolin got thinner every day. He continued his visits to Les Romarins but found nothing more to destroy and was unable to add anything. He thought:

"Why doesn't this Graffignette write? It's because she daren't tell us the property's been sold. One fine day somebody will see the spring on the papers, and they'll make it flow again. Perhaps they're people from Antibes and they'll grow carnations, and I'll go on growing chick-peas that are no more than two francs a kilo, because they make you fart all night . . ."

But one morning as he was hoeing his greens he saw the Papet's silhouette below, climbing up toward him on the steep path.

From afar the other cried:

"Don't hurry! All's well!"

He waited for him, and they went in silence to sit under the mulberry tree.

"So?" said Ugolin.

"So, listen."

He read Graffignette's letter in a low voice. It went thus:

9th January, Feast of St. Marcellin

My dear César,

Knock, and it will be opened to you. Write, and you will be answered. At last the hunchback has come. He has a fine face, but also a fine hump. These things always make me laugh. Especially because he is so big—they say his hump is false like a smuggler's. He has a redheaded wife, with heels so pointed that if she walked on you she would make holes in you. She is not of good family. But after all she could be a fine person. Do not judge if you do not wish to be judged. They stayed just one day and they ate at the Cheval Blanc (trout with white wine of Cassis, and a partridge with a bottle of Bordeaux wine). I won't talk about the cream puffs and the liqueurs, there's no end to that. Then they went to the notary to sign the papers, and now the notary has had notices put up to sell the house at Crespin and the meadow at Gémenos. That's how families end. M. the curé thinks after that they'll surely sell the property of Les Romarins that you spoke about. As soon as they put up the notice I'll let you know. They spent all that money in the town, but they did not stay afterwards. The maid of the Cheval Blanc told me that at the table his wife did nothing but laugh. Happy those who weep because they will be consoled. I asked M. the curé to send you his blessing. He did that immediately. And I send you an old kiss of good friendship.

"This letter," said the Papet, "ought to make you happy. I'm sure he'll put the farm up for auction, perhaps in a fortnight. Let's do what the spiders do; they don't tire themselves, they don't make a noise. They wait."

They waited more than two months.

Ugolin got ill from it, and the Papet started to show, if not his disquiet, at least his impatience. All the same it was bizarre that the hunchback, who had sold the house where he was born, did not decide to disembarrass himself of this abandoned farm. Perhaps he had forgotten it? In any case, Graffignette wrote a third letter to say that the curé had seen the notary, and the date of the sale was not yet fixed.

Ugolin did not go to Les Romarins so often anymore; it got on his nerves too much . . .

Nevertheless, he went up one Sunday morning with his gun on his shoulder, hoping for a blackbird or perhaps a rabbit . . . But he saw nothing.

In front of the farm the field had become a thicket, with a number of unmanaged trees emerging from it. There was nothing left between the clumps of brambles but passages as narrow as the footpaths. They had grown trunks as thick as a rake handle and fell in three-meter arcs above the bluish thistles that could be taken for artichokes.

Ugolin penetrated into a passage and thought for a moment—with some bitterness—about the extravagant vigor of these useless plants and the feeble health of those that brought in the money. The insolence of the dog roses around a pale and discouraged almond tree provided a thorny example. Truly, the Good Lord wanted to force us to work. He was just thinking he had achieved his object, and was congratulating himself on his astuteness, when he suddenly saw a footprint right in the middle of the path . . . He bent down to examine it.

It was not complete, but it was clearly a man's shoe . . . a sole without nails, a perfectly smooth sole, a leather sole . . . His heart suddenly beat faster—it was a town shoe!

With his poacher's science he examined the surroundings of the building, then the terrain. He found more footprints. Somebody had come, undoubtedly a man, a single man, who had gone round the farm several times and walked on the field . . . A great unease seized him. Perhaps it was a buyer, come to "visit" before signing the papers at the notary's. Or perhaps the hunchback himself, wanting to look over his inheritance.

But he did not see anybody. Besides, people would surely notice the hunchback coming by in the village. But what if he had come from the other side, across the hills? That was hardly possible—"foreigners" who wore shoes without nails did not know the paths across six or seven kilometers of garigue. So, what could explain those footprints? He decided to go and tell the Papet, but as he cast a last glance toward the farm, he seemed to hear a voice a long way off. He listened. It was certainly the voice of a man, encouraging a team in harness with shouts and cracks of a whip.

He said softly:

"It must be people gathering wood."

In fact only woodsmen were capable of risking their mules on such a tortuous and narrow path . . . In any case a cart was approaching, because he could now hear the noise of the iron-bound wheels ringing on the rocks and grinding as they crushed the gravel.

He ran to the hillside and hid in the gorse.

CHAPTER II

The entourage appeared.

Two mules were pulling a cart with great difficulty. The load, hidden under tarpaulins, was dangerously high. The muleteer advanced backward, pulling the first beast by the bridle, his raucous cries echoing in the vallon.

Behind the cart walked a man. From afar through the branches, he seemed immense and blond. When he came nearer Ugolin saw that he was of good height, but astride his neck was a little girl with golden curls with her hands crossed on the black hair of her mount.

Further behind them a tall, strawberry blonde woman appeared. Because of the slope she swayed as she walked, and her face was pale and rosy above an armful of flowering rosemary, which she pressed to her heart.

Ugolin was amazed and thought these people had lost their way. He was about to go and advise them to retrace their steps, when the man carrying the little girl on his back shouted to the muleteer:

"There it is! Stop on the road just above the house!" Then he took the path that descended obliquely to the farmhouse and went at a little gallop up to Pique-Bouffigue's ruined terrace with the little rider clinging to his hair and shouting with laughter.

He stopped and hoisted her above his head with his hands under her armpits and put her down in the rosemary in front of him.

Then Ugolin was horrified to see the hump that had served as a seat for the little girl: it was he, it was the hunchback, the heir, the owner!

He had come with his family, and this creaking cart was probably moving their furniture.

But he tried to reassure himself:

"After all, there's more than one hunchback on earth. Perhaps that one there is a friend of the heir. Hunchbacks seek each other's company. Perhaps the other one lent him the old house for the holidays?"

The man turned toward the pretty woman who had just come up and cried: "What do you think of it?"

She came forward looking delighted.

"Look!" cried the hunchback. "Will you look at these gigantic brambles! These inextricable olive trees, these arborescent rosemary bushes!"

"And these dog roses," said she, "has anybody ever seen any as beautiful as these?"

"It's Zola's Paradise!" cried the hunchback. "It's even more beautiful than the Paradise!"

Ugolin had never heard of Zola, and as for dog roses, he knew them only as "scratch-bottoms."

The hunchback took a number of steps in the undergrowth and suddenly he shouted:

"Aimée! Come and see these thistles!"

She ran and stopped near him, marvelling, with sighs of admiration.

"Don't touch them," said he. "I'll soon cut you a bouquet with scissors!"

He looked around him and said enthusiastically:

"And there are hundreds of them! It's enchanting! Ah! It will be hard for me to sacrifice them, but before I touch them I'll take photographs."

Ugolin listened to these insane declarations with amazement and bitterly regretted that he had taken so much trouble planting these horrors that so transported them with ecstasy.

"Let's go!" said the hunchback suddenly. "To work!"

When she turned, the woman saw the ruined facade of the house. She let the flowers fall to her feet, clasped her hands, and exclaimed with deep emotion:

"And that's the most beautiful of all!"

"Isn't it? I told you—it's all antique Provence, and it's not impossible that these decrepit walls were built by some Roman peasant!"

They stood in silence and looked. Then the man drew a shining object from his pocket and put it to his mouth, and Ugolin heard an astonishing music, that of a mouth organ, and suddenly the woman sang:

> I close my eyes, and see down there
> A humble retreat all white
> At the bottom of the wood . . .

It was a pure voice, surprisingly strong and sustained, and the echoes of the vallon responded to it with respect.

Ugolin, who had no ear for music, asked himself:

"What is it they're carrying in that cart?"

He got the answer at once, for the muleteer, who had stopped his cart just above the house, pulled at the tarpaulin and varnished furniture shone in the sun.

The hunchback drew a large rusty key from his pocket . . . He put it in the lock and the door opened with a heavy muffled creak . . .

The muleteer had already come down the path carrying a varnished table on his head, and the woman followed him into the house.

While she opened the shutters of the windows the two men came out again. The hunchback had taken off his jacket and had rolled up his shirtsleeves and followed the other to the cart.

Ugolin asked himself:

"Is it he, or somebody else?"

Then he remembered—Graffignette had indeed said that he was big and his wife was a redhead; but she had not said that she sang, nor that they had a little girl . . . And then, according to Graffignette, he was a tax collector in town. Would a tax collector go about on the hill, with furniture and a family? Maybe during the holidays, but not in March! But then, had he simply come to furnish the house, to get it ready for next summer? Surely that was it . . .

Was that good or bad?

On the one hand, it was bad, because if he was the real hunchback he would never sell the farm. But on the other hand, this man, whether he was the real one or another, was not a peasant! He would not stay the whole year, and one could rent the field from him and pretend to discover the spring . . . Since these people admired thistles they would be quite happy to have carnations around their house! It would give them pleasure to photograph them! . . . He ought to talk to them at once, get acquainted.

He hid his gun in the undergrowth and went toward the two men, who were unloading mattresses rolled in bundles.

Smiling, he called in his most cordial voice:

"Greetings, good day all!"

"Good day, monsieur," replied the hunchback. He seemed surprised.

"I was just asking myself," said Ugolin pleasantly, "whether you would refuse a helping hand!"

"Oh no!" replied the overjoyed muleteer. "There's one old chest in particular
that I didn't think we could carry down without taking apart."

"Yes, that was our problem," said the hunchback, "and I would be much
obliged if you would help us solve it!"

He had a fine deep voice, large dark brown eyes, and very white teeth, and
a lustrous black curl shone on his pale brow. Ugolin noticed the thickness of
his long, powerfully muscled arms.

"We'll do our best!" said Ugolin.

"I thank you a thousand times over for your help. You're from Aubagne?"

"No, I'm from Les Bastides. But I don't live there. My house is the last farm
you passed coming up here, just at the beginning of the vallon."

"So, we're going to be close neighbors."

"I'm called Ugolin, and even Ugolin de Zulma. Not because I belong to the
nobility," he added laughing. "It means my mother was called Zulma; and my
family name is Soubeyran."

He looked at the stranger, hoping that he would tell him his name in his
turn. But the muleteer was already on top of the cart, pushing a Provençal chest
with carved doors toward the back. Ugolin and the hunchback seized the two
feet, stepped back, and eased the chest down; its weight was considerable, and
Ugolin noted that despite his infirmity the hunchback was certainly as strong
as he was.

The three of them succeeded in carrying this monument of a bygone age
and getting it into the vast Provençal kitchen, which the woman and the little
girl were already very busy sweeping, after throwing Pique-Bouffigue's mildewed mattress out the window.

There remained some other souvenirs of the old poacher. On an immense
table made of thick beams there was a bottle half-full of black wine, on the
surface of which floated a whitish bloom; a plate of soup hardened and cracked
like clay in July; a half-loaf as hard as a paving stone; a glass marked with red
circles of evaporated watery wine.

On the wall there was kitchen equipment. A green jug in the sink, two chairs with the straw chewed by rats, and a big cupboard, old as the hills. The right-hand corner, which had lost its foot, rested on four bricks, and one of its doors hung at an angle. The tall Provençal clock, which had been stopped on the evening before the funeral, was covered with spiderwebs. But the hunchback declared that he found it very beautiful, that it was at least a hundred years old, and that it was probably a museum piece.

The men made about twenty journeys, carrying all kinds of furniture: a worm-eaten commode, a very fine bed of carved walnut, a night table in white-wood, a large bevelled mirror in a gilded wooden frame, a chandelier with crystal pendants, equipped with electric bulbs, a very big leather armchair, a number of rickety chairs; and then boxes full of books, a desk with bronze figurines, carpets rolled in bundles; they seemed immense to Ugolin, who had never seen anything but bedside mats of plaited straw. They then unloaded several bottle racks: mineral water with labels, and vintage wines with red and white wax.

"He's rich!" thought Ugolin. "It's him all right, it's the tax collector!"

Finally, under the last chests, he saw a large chest shaped like a coffin.

Ugolin wanted to lift it, but the muleteer laughed.

"Oh, that," he said, "it will take at least four men to carry it . . ."

"But how did you load it?"

"To load it," said the hunchback, "we first put the chest on the cart, then we put the tools in it one after the other; now we'll carry out the operation in reverse!"

"The tools?" thought Ugolin, "what tools?"

He climbed onto the vehicle and lifted the cover of the chest. He was astonished to see a large number of agricultural tools, all quite new: a two-pronged fork, another with four prongs, a spade, a pickax, a pitchfork, an axe, a hatchet, a sledgehammer, two rakes, a small two-handled saw, some small picks, two shovels, a scythe with its handle, two sickles . . .

There was also a fairly large bundle wrapped in a strong cloth and carefully tied.

"Those," said the hunchback, "are the pruners, the handsaw, the plane, the chisel, the hacksaw, etc. . . . I've got enough of those to make a fine little work-shop!"

He took the bundle away in his arms, while Ugolin followed him with an armful of pickaxes and shovels.

He was at the height of his anxiety, but an idea reassured him.

"He's a handyman. Townspeople are often like that. He's sure to want to make a little vegetable garden: four lettuces, three heads of celery, and a little chervil. Always planted too deep, and at the wrong time . . . I'll help him, and he'll rent the big field to me, perhaps for nothing!"

In the vast kitchen the singer adroitly opened the cases with a hammer and chisel and took out the utensils, which the little girl hung from nails fixed to the wall.

After the moving-in they took the beds up to the little rooms on the first floor; it was a long and difficult operation because of the tightness of the spiral staircase. Then the beautiful woman declared:

"My dear Jean, now you must rest a moment . . ."

"Gladly," said the hunchback, ". . . and what's more I think that the time has come to make a libation to Bacchus, or, if you prefer, that we deserve the pleasure of a drink!"

The three of them sat under the trellis while the singer drew the cork from a bottle of white wine gripped between her knees.

"Madame has an extraordinary voice," said Ugolin. "Even in church I've never heard singing like that!"

The hunchback smiled and said:

"She has astonished many others before you. She has sung the operas: *Lakmé*, *If I Were King*, *Manon* . . ."

Ugolin had never heard of these works, but his ignorance did not diminish his admiration.

"I bet," he said, "she has sung before the world!"

"Certainly! To halls filled to bursting."

He was not lying, but neglected to say that the halls were in Saigon, or Dakar, or provincial towns.

"That was several years ago," said the singer modestly. "Today I haven't got more than half a voice . . ."

"Half a voice? What could that be!"

"Admirable, unique!" cried the hunchback. "Her triumph was *Manon*. That's why we've given our little girl that name. Perhaps one day she will have the same talent."

The little girl smiled and lowered her eyes and swayed, while her mother filled the glasses all round.

The muleteer looked at the pine woods that mounted the successive ledges. He shook his head, and said:

"This is a fine place, all the same. The road is bad, but it's worth the difficulty. The air is fine—I can breathe!"

"The air is very good," said Ugolin. "It's cool, but it's good."

"As far as I'm concerned," said the hunchback, "it's a corner of an Earthly Paradise."

It was the moment to ask, but without showing too much interest.

"So that's why you've rented the old house!"

He smiled.

"I haven't rented it."

"You've bought it?"

"Not that either. Neither rented nor bought, but all the same I'm here in my house."

"You wouldn't by any chance be Jean de Florette?" said Ugolin shrewdly.

"It is quite true," said the hunchback, "that I'm called Jean, and that my mother was named Florette. But my name is Jean Cadoret."

"If you'd been born here, like your mother, you would be called Jean de Florette."

"Isn't that nice!" said the singer. "That would be a nice title for a song—or even a comic opera!"

"Then you knew my mother?" asked her husband.

"No," said Ugolin, "but I knew her brother, Marius, who was called Pique-Bouffigue—he was a good friend, and I used to do things for him in the village."

"I saw him only once, but that was a long time ago," said the hunchback. "He gave the impression of being unsociable, but I'm grateful to him for leaving this farm to my mother, who in turn left it to me!"

With all the evidence, Ugolin still had his doubts, but there was no getting away from it: he really was the heir, the owner, and he had no intention of selling his property, at least not for the time being . . .

The hunchback raised his glass very high and said with a certain solemnity:

"I drink to Mother Nature, to the fragrant hills, I drink to the cicadas, to the pine woods, to the breeze, to the rocks of thousands of years, I drink to the blue sky!"

Ugolin raised his glass in his turn, and responded more simply:

"To your health!"

As the three of them were drinking, they suddenly heard a great rattle of hooves and iron. The mules had had enough, turned the empty cart around, and rushed down the slope at a fast trot.

"Ah, the dirty beasts!" said the muleteer. "They do that to me every day! The smallest one's the most vicious! Excuse me, ladies and gents . . . see you tomorrow!"

He left at a gallop, hurling insults in pursuit of the empty vehicle, which bounded like a tiger on the reins of the terrified mules.

Ugolin thought:

"He said 'tomorrow.' Is he going to make another trip?"

He was dismayed at the thought, a second load of furniture would implant these people even more solidly.

The russet woman had refilled the glasses, then she sat on the ground, with her crossed hands pressing her calves, and her head leaning on her husband's knee.

The little girl threw old shoes, rugs, and all kinds of rubbish through the open window.

"Do you already know the property?" asked Ugolin.

"I'd been here just once," said the hunchback, "with my father more than twenty years ago. We crossed the hills from Crespin. But I came back last week to see what the house looked like now. Well, after twenty years I found all the footpaths!"

"You're a carrier pigeon," said his wife tenderly.

"It's a gift," said he. "I have a memory for places, an infallible memory."

He rubbed his hands joyfully.

"And so," said Ugolin, "you've come with your family to spend some time on holiday?"

"A holiday," said the hunchback, "that will last until I die."

And as Ugolin's eyes opened wide with anxiety, he continued forcefully:

"Yes, it's in the shade of these pine woods that I want to live, in the peace and joy of all the days the Lord grants me."

"Aren't you afraid the house will fall down on your head?"

"Not on your life! It's a lot more solid than it looks—and besides, I'm going to put it right again—tomorrow they're bringing the plaster and cement."

It was an overwhelming revelation. Perhaps somebody who talked of plaster, of cement, and of staying all his life, knew the secret of the spring? . . .

He had to settle the question at once. Casually he asked:

"You're probably right to move in here . . . But the water, what are you going to do about that?"

"My word, there's a cistern!"

"Yes, but it's rotten."

"I know. I examined it during my last visit. It's full to the brim with blackish water that smells very bad . . . But it's not incurable. It will be enough to empty it and put in some lumps of quicklime."

"That doesn't always work," said Ugolin. "It's been rotten for more than twenty years and the walls are encrusted . . ."

"I'll scrape them," said the hunchback tranquilly. "If necessary I'll line them with cement. There's only one thing that concerns me: is it big?"

"Oh no," said Ugolin. "It's small. In fact it's very small."

"Then I'll have to enlarge it," said the hunchback, as if it were a bagatelle.

"That's all!" said his wife, smiling with pleasure.

"In the meantime," said Ugolin, "don't drink that water, because you could catch typhoid, and maybe even something worse."

"You can imagine I've thought of that problem. I've brought some bottles of mineral water, just in case, until I know whether the water in the spring is drinkable."

At the terrible word "spring" Ugolin felt his heart beating, and he blinked vigorously, as if dazzled. Then he put on an astonished air and said:

"A spring? What spring? Where is it?"

"I haven't seen it yet, but it's shown on a copy of the land registry that the notary gave me. I'll show you the document, and you may be able to tell me about it." He went into the house.

"That's it," thought Ugolin. "What a catastrophe. If he has the paper there's not much anyone can do about it. Whatever happens, I know nothing and I've seen nothing."

Aimée filled his glass again, and said:

"It's lucky that we have a neighbor like you!"

"And me," said Ugolin, "I'm glad you'll be here, because I've been quite alone up to now. It's not that I'm bored, because I've got a lot of work to do.

But all the same, it's nice to have neighbors because one can help them . . . If somebody's ill, or there's a fire, one can lend a helping hand . . . It's quite natural . . ."

He blinked more than ever and his red eyelashes beat frantically.

The hunchback returned and unfolded a land registry map; he pushed back the glasses to spread it on the table.

"These maps," said Ugolin, "they embarrass me very much—to tell the truth, I don't understand them at all!"

"Look," said the hunchback. "You see this little circle here? It means a well, or a spring . . ."

"And the house, where is it marked?"

"Here. That one. So the spring is about two kilometers away, at the end of a vallon called the vallon of Le Plantier."

Ugolin breathed deeply and blinked three times. He was unable to restrain a burst of laughter.

"Ah!" said he, "if it's Le Plantier you're talking about, I know it! It's on the other side of the hill . . . At the end of the valley, it goes up a lot, and at the top there's a cave, and in the cave there's the spring. It's very fine water but it doesn't run any bigger than my thumb."

"Are you listening, Aimée?"

"I'm listening," she said. "I hope it's not too far from here."

"My word," said Ugolin, "it's a good hour's walk."

"They're bringing me a donkey tomorrow, and all kinds of construction materials," said the hunchback, "and the little donkey will be enough to go there once a week."

"It will be our Sunday walk," said Aimée.

"Rather a long walk," said Ugolin. "But if you like walking on the hill . . ."

"As a matter of fact," said the hunchback, "we adore it."

"At the moment," said Ugolin, "there's a woodcutter and his wife living in the sheepfold at the cave . . . They're Piedmontese. The wife's named Baptistine. She's rather a witch. She knows all the plants. But all the same they're good people. Everything is very clean and well arranged . . . But if that bothers you, you can make them go . . ."

"God forbid!" said the hunchback. "If this cave is enough for them, I'm not the one to drive them out. We'll visit them soon, because the question of water is important."

"Certainly," said Ugolin. "But there's no need for you to hurry, because I have my well. At the moment it's giving quite enough, and for two or three weeks you can come and get two or three watering cans a day."

"There," said the hunchback, "a generous offer that I accept with all my heart until we get organized. Thank you, and your good health, my neighbor!"

"Your health, Mister Tax Collector!" said Ugolin smiling.

"Ho ho! How you're talking! No, I wasn't a tax collector, but a clerk in the tax office. It's not a very pleasant job and to tell the truth it's very boring, especially for a man like me."

He was nice, this hunchback, but not very modest.

"Are you wondering, dear neighbor, why an intellectual like me should decide to settle down here?"

"Well, yes," said Ugolin, shaking his head. "I did wonder!"

"Well, look: after having worked hard—I mean intellectual work—after meditating a long time and *philosophizing*, I came to the irrefutable conclusion that the only possible happiness was to be a man of Nature. I need air, I need space to crystallize my thoughts. I am more interested in what is true, pure, free—in a word, *authentic*, and I came here to cultivate the *authentic*. I hope you understand me?"

"Yes," said Ugolin. "Of course."

"I want to live in communion with Nature. I want to eat the vegetables of my garden, the oil of my olive trees, to suck the fresh eggs of my chickens, to get drunk on the wine of my vines, and as far as possible to eat the bread I make with my wheat."

"You know," said Ugolin, "that will not be soon! These olive trees, they've gone wild, and it will take three years to get them right again. The vine here will do well but you still must count on three years. Your chickens—you'll eat the eggs if the foxes don't eat the chickens. And the vegetables in the garden— they won't be very big without water . . ."

"We'll see," said the hunchback with a superior smile. "I know you can't get anything done without time and work. But thanks to the little inheritance— which I owe to the benevolent avarice of my mother—we have enough to hold on for at least three years. And in three years . . ."

He smiled mysteriously and kept silent.

"Yes, in three years! . . ." said the singer.

She shook her head with a triumphant air.

"What will there be in three years?" said Ugolin.

"We have vast projects!" said the hunchback, caressing his wife's hair. "But it's not the time to tell you about them. I'll talk to you about them one of these days: and as to that, there's something I want to ask you. Will it be possible for me to rent or buy the fields north of ours?"

For a moment Ugolin was breathless . . .

"You know you've got more than twelve thousand meters?"

"Twelve thousand eight hundred," said the hunchback, ". . . it's not enough, or rather one day it won't be enough, and I want to be sure in advance of at least a hectare more. Would you be so kind as to think about it?"

"I'll ask in the village," said Ugolin. "I think your cousin, he's the baker . . . I'll ask him."

"Thank you."

"But won't you need some workers to cultivate two hectares?"

"Certainly, I'll need two. And here are the workers, look!"

He opened his hands wide, and showed them: they were big and long, but fine and white, with nearly transparent nails.

Then he got up, smiling.

"I must tell you your kindness gave me a very pleasant surprise. As a matter of fact my mother, who was born here, told me very often that the peasants of Les Bastides were real savages, who very foolishly detested the people of Crespin. I see with pleasure that you are one exception, and I am thankful that I met you. But please don't announce our arrival in the village: they'll learn about it soon enough."

"You'll be bound to go there to get your bread!"

"We'll get provisions at Ruissatel. Of course it's a little bit farther, but there are some civilized people there . . . Thanks again; but now I must provide for the most immediate needs. Aimée, what time is it?"

She looked at her gold wristwatch.

"Just ten o'clock," she said.

"We haven't a moment to lose. While you put things in order and get lunch ready, I'll start on the roof. Excuse me, my dear neighbor. This first day is particularly important and I must get to work at once!"

He got up and shook Ugolin's hand, saying:

"Thank you for your generous help, and I beg you to think of my neighborly friendship. To work!"

He went into the house and soon his head and shoulders reappeared on the roof, in a clatter of broken tiles.

"Look," he said gaily, "a real battlefield. Do you suppose these stones were put on the tiles to stop them being blown off by the mistral?"

"Probably so," said Ugolin.

"They must have been put there rather roughly," said the hunchback, "or perhaps they were thrown from below . . . Many of the tiles are broken . . . Fortunately the ones on the stable seem to be in good condition and it will be child's play to transfer them."

"Above all," cried the fair-haired woman, "don't damage your hands!"

"I've got what I need!"

He drew a pair of ancient leather gloves from his pocket.

"Careful of scorpions!" cried Ugolin. "There are lots of them under the tiles."

"Thanks for the warning," replied the hunchback, who had just hoisted himself onto the roof. "What I'm going to do now is just for the time being because I haven't got cement or lime. But all the same, it will be enough to shelter us from the spring rain!"

"Oh well, good luck," said Ugolin.

"We haven't missed any of that," replied the hunchback.

With his hands gloved and his arms crossed, he advanced the whole length of the tiled ridge like a tightrope walker.

CHAPTER *12*

Ugolin ran to look for the Papet. He finally found him in his vineyard in the vallon. Seated on a stool that he carried about with him, he was busy restretching the wires for supporting the vine shoots that were already sprouting.

He raised his head at the sound of his nephew's running.

Ugolin was out of breath. He looked around first, then said in a low voice:

"The hunchback has arrived. With his wife and daughter. All their furniture. They're moving in."

"Good," said the Papet. "Go and find my game bag down there, in the turpentine tree, and let's eat a little. I forgot lunch."

Ugolin sat in the bottom of a furrow; the Papet sat on his stool and broke the bread and cut slices of sausage, while his nephew uncorked the bottle and filled the glass.

"So what kind of person is he, this man?"

Ugolin hesitated a moment and replied:

"He's a typical town hunchback," as if he were speaking of a well-known species.

"Much of a townsman?"

"Completely! They're nice enough, both of them, but they say incredible things. He thought nothing was more beautiful than the thistles, and wanted to photograph them; and his wife, she was full of emotion just looking at the scratch-bottoms. And they said the farm was a paradise!"

"So you've spoken to them?"

Ugolin's mouth was full and he had trouble talking:

"I helped them unload their furniture, and we drank a bottle of white wine."

"They reckon on staying a long time up there?"

"Until he dies. That's what he told me."

"Is he sick?"

"Oh, not at all! He has the arms of a blacksmith. He brought a cartload of pickaxes, picks, rakes, shovels, and he wants to be a peasant."

"He told you that?"

"Oh yes. He even told me that his twelve thousand meters were not enough—he wants another hectare. And he wants to buy the baker's field. He said he had 'vast projects!'"

"So," said the Papet, "did he know about the spring?"

"No!" said Ugolin. "I assure you, no! He knows about the spring at Le Plantier, which is marked on his papers, but ours is not there. I brought the subject of water into the conversation several times. He said they would go to Le Plantier for drinking water. And he's going to enlarge the cistern."

"Galinette, listen! Never trust a hunchback! They're always smarter than we are! That spring—it would have been quite natural for his mother to talk to him about it! Don't forget he comes from Crespin, and he distrusts us! He may be an innocent from town, but all the same, he's not talking about working two hectares with a cistern! And what does he want to plant?"

"Vegetables, vines, wheat, and above all, he said, he's going to 'cultivate the orthentic!' Orthentics everywhere! What are they?"

"It must be a plant that grows in books . . . I can tell that without going any further."

"He said, 'We must be modern!'"

"I bet you ten francs he talked to you about the 'system.'"

"What's that?"

"It's a town expression—it means that everything our elders taught us must be tossed into the air because it's not modern, and that now miracles have been invented . . ."

"Perhaps it's true?"

"It's pure rubbish," said the Papet. "Twenty years ago I used to go and work every day with a big shot from Marseille who had set himself up near Gémenos with machines, with winches, and above all with Ideas. Ah, that man—he talked about the system! He talked about it so well I nearly ended up by believing him! So he made us plant five hectares of black beans, which he'd bought at the Colonial Exhibition, and we put sacks of powdered chemical fertilizer on them that costs more than tobacco snuff—tobacco snuff wasn't part of the drill! . . . Those beans, they grew at an unbelievable rate. They grew a meter a week! At the end of the month they were higher than the canes and they floated up there in the air! It took a billhook to get inside. And in the end what did they produce? Shade! Not a pod, not a bean. At the end of a year the gentleman packed his bags and said to us, 'My friends, I have learned my lesson, and I'm returning to the city. But if you ever see another one like me heading this way, tell him from me that there are three ways of ruining yourself: women, gambling, and agriculture. Agriculture is the quickest, and moreover the least enjoyable! Farewell!' And he was gone. These orthentics of your hunchback's are probably something like that. They'll not come to anything and he'll get discouraged, but it will still make us lose time . . ."

"At least a year," said Ugolin worriedly.

"If he knows about the spring, two years, maybe three. Because with water he'll always be pushing along little by little by little . . . These people from town, sometimes some of them persist until their money runs out . . . But if he doesn't know about the spring we'll see him gone by next May . . ."

"That could work out," said Ugolin. "I could begin digging up the field in October . . . But three years—that would be a disaster . . ."

"Galinette, you mustn't always think the worst. I tell you some day or another you'll see that cart coming back to move the furniture in the opposite direction . . . As for us, we'll analyze the situation and prepare our plan.

"Now that I think about it, I bet he doesn't know about the spring, but Anglade or Casimir, who are his relations, might end up telling him about it . . . That's my biggest fear."

"You have nothing to worry about there. His mother warned him about Les Bastides; they'll buy their bread at Ruissatel, and he asked me not to say that he was from Crespin."

"But that's exactly what we will say!" cried the Papet joyfully. "We'll say it's somebody from Crespin who's bought the farm, but without mentioning Florette and without giving his name! And you must do little things for him. When people move in they always need something. Give him a helping hand, lend him my mule, or perhaps any tools he hasn't got, and be especially gracious to his wife: two handfuls of almonds, a pair of thrushes, a basket of figs . . . That way, he'll sell the farm to you when he goes, rather than somebody else!"

"I've already started," said Ugolin. "I told him he could get drinking water from my well. A watering can a day. But I didn't do it for the reason you said."

"What was the reason then?"

Ugolin looked embarrassed: his eyes fluttered, his eyelids batted three times, then, as if to excuse uncalled-for generosity, he said very quickly:

"You see, if they had drunk the water from their cistern all three of them would be dead for sure, and that would be a nuisance. To have plugged the spring was not criminal: that was for the carnations. But if people died as a result, well, we mightn't talk about it, but we'd think about it."

The Papet smiled gently, then, moved with a sort of tenderness, he said:

"You're the living image of your poor mother. She worried unduly about others all the time! After all you did the right thing, because if the whole family died, who knows who would come in their place. In the end it's better to have him than a real peasant . . ."

"And I'll start right away to discourage him. I'll tell him the olive trees are finished, the ground is rotten with twitch grass, the grasshoppers eat everything, it never rains at Les Romarins, the cistern will always be too small, in the winter it freezes up every morning, the mistral . . ."

"Quiet! Quiet!" cried the Papet. "You're taking the wrong tack! Remember that even in people's heads it's easier to go down than up! Tell him the orthentics are terrific, that he'll never lack rain, that he should start right away on his vast projects. Nudge him in the direction he's going to fall."

"That should be easy since he's already leaning in the wrong direction without any help. But I would like you to come and see him yourself, and see what you think of him . . ."

The Papet reflected a moment, stuffing his pipe.

"No," he said, "no. It would be better if he didn't know me. One day that could be useful to us."

CHAPTER *13*

When Ugolin went back to his house at about three o'clock, he heard the harmonica from afar; he found the musician seated under the mulberry tree of Massacan, between two brand new watering cans.

"Greetings, neighbor!" said the hunchback. "You see that I've hardly waited to take advantage of your generosity!"

"You've done the right thing, but there was no need for you to wait for me. Just help yourself!"

"Since it's the first time . . . Besides, I haven't been wasting my time, I've been getting to know this admirable landscape."

He pointed to the valley that stretched to the sea at the foot of the distant chain of Marseille-Veyre.

"Upon my word," said Ugolin, "I know hardly anything about landscapes. That one's good because it's big, so you can see what weather it's bringing . . ."

Talking all the time, he let the bucket down to the bottom of the well. They heard it hit the surface of the water: Ugolin seized the chain and shook it three or four times.

"You must always do that," he said, "otherwise the bucket floats and you pull it up empty."

A rattling noise came up from the well, then a brief glug-glug.

"That's it! It's tipped over. It's gone down."

He pulled on the chain for a long time, and emptied the shining water into a watering can.

Then he asked:

"How's your roof?"

"Good enough, but there's no doubt some tiles are missing, and I forgot to ask the muleteer to bring some. What bothers me is that they'll be new, and short, and that they'll spoil the beauty of the whole picture . . ."

"You hardly see a roof!" said Ugolin.

"You're right," said the hunchback. "But all the same . . . All the same . . ."

Ugolin emptied a second bucketful into the watering can.

"There," he said. "Now help yourself, because I've had some slips in the shed for three days and I must plant them before evening!"

The hunchback was profusely grateful. He drew another three buckets of water, then left, balancing the two watering cans.

Ten minutes later, as he was planting out his tomatoes in front of his house, Ugolin heard the muleteer's cart; with great difficulty and with great shouts it climbed the hairpin bends that rose toward him. A little donkey was harnessed in front of two mules. The load was covered with a green canvas, and behind everything else were tethered two fine goats, braking with their four feet and half strangled by their halters.

The whip cracked and the muleteer shouted, and when the cart arrived at the open space in front of the farmhouse the animals stopped to take a breather, and the driver drew an immense greyish handkerchief from his pocket to wipe the sweat from his brow.

Ugolin came forward.

"Hi, buddy! More furniture?"

"Some," said the muleteer. "But it's mainly crates of books, crates of crockery, and big trunks full of linen and clothes."

"And some tools?"

"Not many. A crate of windowpanes, some pots of paint, and a little pump."

Ugolin twitched immediately.

"And what's he going to pump?"

"It'll be for the cistern."

That was plausible, Ugolin thought:

"If he knew about the spring, he'd have no need of the pump. But perhaps he doesn't know that it will flow by itself. In any case, I'll go and see where he puts that pump!"

"Let's go!" said the muleteer. "I must get down again soon. My wife is about to give me a child! Giddap, you brutes!"

The next morning the cart reappeared.

"Ho ho!" said Ugolin, "this is starting to be alarming."

It seemed to him indeed that such a large accumulation of riches would root this hunchback of ill fortune forever.

This time the carrier paused five or six times during the climb before stopping for a breather on the little level.

The load on the vehicle, invisible under its cover, flattened the springs.

"This time," said the muleteer, "I don't know if I'll make it to the top. I've got two hundred kilos of cement piping and three hundred kilos of wire netting!"

He pointed at the cover undulating over the great rolls . . . .

"What does he want to do?"

"Make a fence . . . I'll have to come back again tomorrow to bring more stuff, with six bags of plaster from Aubagne . . .

"He must be quite rich," said Ugolin.

"I don't know if he's rich, but he always pays well."

"D'you think he'll stay up there a long time?"

"I don't know anything about that," said the muleteer. "D'you know what he's asked me for? Old tiles, as long as sixty centimeters, even if they're a bit broken! You can't find them like that . . . I'm afraid he's a bit dotty in his way."

"You know," said Ugolin by way of an excuse, "that he's a townsman."

"So'm I," said the muleteer proudly (he lived in a distant suburb), "I'm a townsman, but that doesn't make me dotty! On the contrary! By the way— it's a boy!"

"Which boy?"

"My little one, that I told you about yesterday, it's a boy! He weighs four and a half kilos!"

"I congratulate you, and bravo for your wife!"

"He's named Bruno, after his godfather, Ernestine's brother. Terrific chap. Drinks ten liters of wine a day. And in the evening he's as fresh as he was in the morning. I should tell you he is a blacksmith. Terrific! And so . . ."

Fortunately the second mule bit the tail of the first, who responded with a kick and shot off suddenly.

"O Blessed Virgin," said the muleteer; he leaped forward, cracking his whip and shouting insults at the aggressor.

Ugolin watched them go, and suddenly a phrase from the conversation hit him. Five minutes afterward, as usual. The carter had spoken of "great cement pipes"! What could the hunchback be planning to do with these pipes? Pipes are for carrying water. What water? He was terrified. Once again the Papet had been right—the hunchback knew about the existence of the spring and was going to put in pipes to irrigate two hectares. That was what the "vast projects" were! Then he reasoned: the hunchback was rather pretentious, but nice enough. He didn't look like a liar . . . But looks weren't everything . . . And then, he came from Crespin. Could one trust someone from Crespin?

He remained fixed, with his arms swinging and his mouth open, now looking at the horizon; now at the tips of his shoes. Finally he decided that it would be reasonable to wait for the carter to come back before despairing, and he returned to his slips.

Toward noon the empty cart reappeared. He stopped it on its way.

"What are they, these pipes you've been taking to him?"

"Cement pipes."

"Big?"

"You can put a finger inside."

"Are there a lot of them?"

"Thirty meters, perhaps forty."

"And what are they for, these pipes?"

"Usually they're for water."

At this Ugolin, quite unnerved, cried:

"But there isn't any water there!"

"Perhaps it's for the cistern . . . To take the rainwater that runs on the road down to the cistern?"

"He told you that?"

"No. He didn't tell me anything. But it seems pretty obvious! Not that I give a damn. Giddap! So long, buddy . . ."

The cart took to the slope.

"Thirty meters, maybe forty! That costs a fortune . . . You don't spend money like that for nothing! He certainly made a sucker out of me!"

He went on planting cloves of garlic, which he buried with the toe of his shoe.

"Perhaps he came over the hills one day, after he knew that he'd inherit . . . He stayed out of sight and watched us plugging . . . For the moment he's acting as if he knows nothing. And then one fine day he'll say to me: 'Oh neighbor! Come and have a little look at what I've found!' And he'll make me look at a stream running like a fireman's hose. And on top of all that he'll suddenly pick up the wooden plug and say to me: 'Who pushed this plug in? Who was it who wanted to steal my spring? You're the last of those swine, and I'm going to turn you over to the gendarmes!' That'll be the last straw!"

He planted some more cloves, and said in a whisper:

"No, no! I'm imagining things. It's much simpler than that: his mother told him about the spring, he'll go and unplug it, and he'll never go away.

"With water, and with that land, if you plant a tomato stake, you'll sleep in the shade a week later! He's going to grow strawberries like lanterns, and cucumbers like cartwheels, olives as big as apricots, and vast incredible projects. And as for the carnations, they're finished!"

He raked a few strokes and then said suddenly:

"I must go and see those pipes. It would be better to know at once."

He dropped the handle of the rake and ran toward his stable, where the Papet's mule slept on its feet.

CHAPTER *14*

Jean Cadoret's ideas were fanciful, but he devoted indomitable energy to them, and detailed attention. The force and the endurance of his dreams were sometimes maniacal.

His handbook on roofing and plumbing lay on the ridge of the roof. With trowel in hand, feet bare, and an eye half-closed by wasp-stings, he was fixing the old tiles.

From time to time he leaned over the edge of the gutter and let down a jam jar on a string for his daughter to fill with mortar.

Despite the ridiculous inadequacy of these means, he had already put more than half the tiles in place, and was glorying in his work like everyone who discovers the interest and pleasure of working with his hands.

As he was trying once more to count how many tiles were missing, he saw the skeleton of an immense mule arriving on the path, carrying a pack of two large esparto grass pouches. Ugolin followed this starving animal; he stopped it in front of the terrace and shouted gaily:

"Greetings, good day, Monsieur Jean!"

"Greetings!" said the hunchback.

"Look at this!" said Ugolin.

From one of the pouches of the pack he drew some long Provençal tiles that seemed quite old but intact.

"Where did you get those tiles?"

"Here," said Ugolin. "I've had them in a corner of the stable for years, and after what you told me yesterday I thought they would please you, so I've brought them to you!"

"A second gesture of friendship that I won't forget!" said the hunchback.

He came down quickly from the roof and went to take his hand. Then they both arranged the tiles at the foot of the wall.

During these comings and goings Ugolin looked around for the pipes. He found them neatly stacked in the roofless stable next to the rolls of wire netting . . .

The hunchback then invited him to drink a jug of white wine; he accepted without ceremony and they went to sit under the trellis.

"I've been thinking," said Ugolin, "about the problem of your water. You could use the tank for a little watering, only it will dry up quickly and your roof isn't very big. But when it rains, a lot of water collects up there on the road; if you had pipes, cement pipes, quite big ones, you could make a little conduit from up there to the water tank, and it would be filled all the time!"

"What a good idea!" cried the hunchback. "And the pipes—that's exactly what I got this morning!"

"That's a bit of luck!" said Ugolin. "But what were you planning on doing with them?"

"That," said the hunchback with a mysterious smile, "is still a big secret . . ."

("That it is," thought Ugolin. "Surely he knows about the spring . . . It looks odd, his talking about 'a big secret' . . . Oh, he's making a fool of me that's for sure! . . .")

But he tried to smile amiably.

The woman came out of the house with a bottle and two glasses. On a tray, like in a café. Ugolin stood up to greet her. She was all smiles, and pretty, and clean; her golden hair emerged from a scarf knotted with two little horns in front, as pretty as a hat; she wore a long apron going up to her shoulders and drawn in by a belt. This garment, of a very light blue, was bordered with pale yellow lace.

"Excuse me," she said, "for appearing in these clothes; but I still have a lot of work to do in the house and just the simple cleaning will take at least another week!"

Ugolin didn't understand these excuses at all, because the knotted scarf and the apron seemed to him to be the height of elegance.

He greeted her and drew several handfuls of almonds from his pockets and threw them on the table.

"I've brought some almonds for the little girl!" he said.

"How nice of you!" said Aimée. "You've given us a lot of pleasure! Manon!" she cried, "go and find the nutcracker!"

"No need to do that," said Ugolin. "They are Princesses: you can crack them with two fingers."

Little Manon ran up to them. Ugolin tried to caress her golden curls; she jumped backward, folding her arms across her breast, and ran to hide her face under the sumptuous apron.

"You must excuse her," said her mother. "She is a little wild because she doesn't know you yet!"

He was boiling with impatience and anxiety. How to get back to those pipes? He summoned his courage and said straight out:

"I saw a big load on the way to you. Are you going to mend the fence?"

"Oh yes; a rather special fence—it's going to go 0.60 meters underground."

"Ha ha!" said Ugolin. "You're afraid the rabbits are going to come and eat your vegetables?"

The hunchback raised a finger, assumed a mysterious air, and said:

"You're getting very warm! You're only wrong about the direction of the rabbits!"

Ugolin puckered his eyebrows, blinked three times rapidly, and said:

"I don't understand."

The hunchback looked at his wife.

"Shall I tell him?"

"If you want! Why not?"

"Very well!"

He went into the house.

Ugolin thought:

"'The direction of the rabbits'? What's he trying to say? In any case he said the pipes were a great secret. And this woman who's always smiling, I'm sure she doesn't give a damn for me. And the little girl who keeps away from me as if I were a ferocious beast . . . And on top of that I don't understand anything, they're too smart for me . . ."

The hunchback reappeared with a brochure in his hand. He sat down comfortably with his elbows on the table and his chin between his hands.

"I've already told you," he said, "that I'm planning some pretty large-scale projects."

"Vast projects."

"That's it, and I'm going to show them to you today." He took on the tone of a lecturer.

"What attracts me here is first of all my love of nature. But although I don't lack money at present, I have a family to feed, and I must assure my little daughter's future; that's why the philosopher in me has had to reconcile his desire for the natural life with his obligation to make a fortune."

Ugolin noted only the last words of this discourse. He intended to "make a fortune." Make a fortune at Les Romarins! With what? Surely not with half-dead olive trees, nor those dying almond trees; nor with the vegetation, nor the wheat, nor the wine. So he knows about the spring and he probably wants to plant carnations!

That was why, as a desperate counterattack, he said:

"You know that here, flowers, even if you had a fine spring . . ."

"What flowers?" said the hunchback with a surprised look. "Do you think I hope to make a fortune selling dog roses and thistles? And what spring? You know the only one I've got is a good long way from here!"

He seemed to be sincere. But Ugolin said to him:

"And the pipes? What do you want those pipes for? What is the big secret?"

The orator continued:

"You're right to think that I'm not talking about something trivial, that I've given the subject serious thought, and I've worked out all the details. My plan is this . . ."

His wife smiled proudly, but said nothing.

"First I'm going to grow a number of small household crops: leeks, tomatoes, potatoes, chervil . . . That will be easy."

("That's what you think," thought Ugolin. But he approved enthusiastically.)

"Nothing easier."

"An hour's work a day," said the hunchback.

"When the vegetable garden's been planted, you'll need only half an hour."

"That's rather what I hope."

"But," said Aimée, "the water tank is really small: what would we do if we didn't have enough water to irrigate?"

"Goodness," said Ugolin smiling, "your vegetables would be smaller. But what perfume! And what taste!"

"So much the better!" said the hunchback. "What I'm looking for is not quantity; it's quality!"

Ugolin assumed a convinced look.

"Oh! as to quality, you'll have it!"

"So that question is settled."

With a simple gesture, like sweeping the table, he dismissed the question of feeding his whole family, and continued:

"After these household crops I'll have to produce the more important crops necessary for the massive breeding of the rabbit!"

"Massive?" said Ugolin. "What do you mean, massive? Do you mean big rabbits?"

"No!" cried Aimée. "We mean many hundreds of rabbits a month, and then many thousands!"

"Aimée," said her husband, "let's not exaggerate. No daydreams; let's stay within the bounds of common sense."

He opened his brochure at a double page and put a chart under Ugolin's eyes, the columns all black with figures.

"Look at these!"

Ugolin looked, knit his eyebrows twice, and declared:

"I don't understand this at all. Naturally, I know very well how to read; but these numbers, they muddle me."

"Well then," said the hunchback, "I understand them very well and I'll tell you what they mean: they mean that from a single pair of rabbits a *modern* breeder can get, at the end of the third year, a monthly production of five hundred rabbits. At least that's what the specialist says."

Ugolin blinked three times rapidly and wondered for a moment whether the hunchback was joking. But he saw a grave face, the face of a city technician. He thought of the Papet's advice: "push him in the direction he's going to fall." So, blinking all the time, he assumed the role of a dazzled admirer and said:

"That's terrific! Five hundred rabbits a month!"

"That astonishes you," said the hunchback. "But you've seen rabbits and surely you've bred them?"

"I always have about six of them."

"Oh well, in spite of your experience, you don't seem to me to have a very clear idea of the fecundity of these rodents. This technician"—he brandished the brochure—"says that a rearing that exceeds five thousand head is likely to become a public danger, because starting with a thousand males and five thousand females the breeder will find himself submerged under a flood of thirty thousand rabbits after the first month; this will exceed two hundred thousand after six months, and two million a month by the tenth! An entire province, perhaps an entire country, would be reduced to famine and death."

Ugolin regarded this malevolent magician with raised eyebrows. He saw his fields of beans and chick-peas devastated, while enraged rabbits swarmed up his trouser legs . . .

"You think so?" he said.

"Australia!" said Aimée suddenly. "Tell him about Australia!"

"Indeed," said the hunchback, resuming the tone of a lecturer, "this unhappy continent, fourteen times bigger than France, very nearly perished because of a single pair of rabbits brought in by an immigrant. These rodents razed the fields and meadows, and in order to save the country it was necessary to construct an electrified fence two thousand kilometers long! Now they continue to multiply in the uninhabited part of the island. The race is enormous and when there isn't enough grass they know how to climb up the trees!"

"Up the trees?" said Ugolin, incredulous but scared.

"Yes, monsieur, and they nibble up entire forests."

"Is that the kind of rabbit you want to bring here?"

"No, fortunately not. Besides, I think the strength and harmfulness of this race is due to the Australian climate; here, in two or three generations, they will certainly become more like our field rabbits, though noticeably bigger than them."

"Fortunately!" said Ugolin. "So, you plan to raise five hundred a month?"

"Oh no, no!" said the hunchback, in the tone of one who does not daydream. "No. One must be modern in all things. Within limits! The figures the technician suggests are no doubt exact. But they're nothing more than figures, and reality will give the lie to them. However, you will agree that if I reduce these forecasts to a quarter, I'll be quite safe. So I reckon to get a hundred and twenty-five to a hundred and fifty rabbits a month in two years and I'll keep my breed to that figure."

"Why?" said Aimée plaintively, ". . . you told me at least two hundred and fifty!"

He put his hand tenderly on his wife's shoulder, and said, smiling:

"Women, my dear neighbor, have all the qualities except good sense! My dear friend, one must master one's enthusiasm while holding the reins of Reason in both hands. We will keep only six males and about a hundred females, which will assure us of fifteen hundred births a year, which will be quite enough!"

"Certainly," said Ugolin. "Even that will be quite a good job . . . Even clearing the cages—that doesn't happen by itself!"

The hunchback looked triumphant and said:

"Oh yes, it will—it will happen by itself!"

"How?"

"Do wild rabbits need their territory cleaned?"

"That's true," said Ugolin. "But they're not in cages."

"There you are!" cried the hunchback. "The great mistake of breeders is the cage. And the cage, dear sir, is the System."

("Bravo," thought Ugolin, "he said it. That'll please the Papet.")

"And the most absurd system because it's keeping rabbits in captivity that causes all their diseases . . . And besides, what did King Louis XI do when he wanted to reduce a cardinal to a skeleton? He put him in a cage! History tells us that!"

History had not told Ugolin that, and he could not see any connection between a cardinal, a king, a skeleton, and rabbits; but the hunchback continued:

"I'm going to establish a big park and I'm going to start Modern breeding, breeding in fresh air!"

"Bravo," said Ugolin. "That's an interesting idea!"

Then he thought it might be shrewd to mention a few harmless difficulties now so that later he could say, "I told you so," when things failed.

"Have you thought about foxes?"

"Are there many of them here?"

"Not bad, not a bad number of them. There's no shortage of them."

"You forget the fence!" said Aimée. "It will be nearly two meters high! Galvanized!"

"Oh! So!" said Ugolin, reassured, "two meters! Galvanized!"

"Don't you believe it!" said the hunchback severely, "don't you believe it! A fox will easily clear a fence of two meters! But, but, I've provided for artificial burrows, underground of course, with entries made of cement pipes!"

Ugolin's heart trembled with joy. ("That's the pipes!")

"Pipes," continued the hunchback, "with a diameter that would let a rabbit through but would be *less* than the head of a fox! The carnivore will not be able to enlarge the entry to get in, and my rabbits will scoff at him in complete security."

"That," said Ugolin, "is another good idea!"

"And d'you know what I'll be doing all that time?" said the hunchback slyly.

"Yes, what will you be doing?" said Aimée.

"Well, I'll simply put my bed in front of the window of our room, and on fine moonlit nights, while these disappointed gluttons scrape their noses against the cement entrances, I'll suddenly smash their necks with my father's old sixteen-calibre, cruelly loaded with buckshot; and the sale of fox skins will be added to the profits we'll already be getting from the rabbit skins!"

The little girl clapped her hands. Aimée was radiant, and said:

"I'll have the first five skins to make a tippet!"

"No, not the first!" said the hunchback with great authority. "We must wait until midwinter to have furs with thick well-set hair!"

"That's so," said Ugolin. "The best are those at the end of December!"

"So they're promised for the end of December! But not before."

"That's all very well," said Ugolin, "but what are these rabbits going to eat?"

"I've been expecting you to ask that! And you're right to ask because it's obviously the most important question! Well, my dear neighbor, here's my answer. First of all I'm going to sow some sainfoin and clover in the paddock they're going to live in, which will enrich the natural grass of this terrain. My daughter and her mother will go for a walk in the hills twice a day and bring back armfuls of herbs to perfume the flesh. But above all, above all—and this is the great novelty and the real key to my success—I have *this*!"

He felt in the pocket of his waistcoat and drew out four large seeds of a brilliant blackness. He presented them in his cupped hand to Ugolin, who examined them and said:

"They're watermelon seeds?"

"Oh no!" said the hunchback with a mysterious smile. "Oh no!"

"Then," said Ugolin, "are they orthentics?"

The hunchback took some time and said in a deep voice:

"Authentics? Certainly. They're perfectly authentic seeds of *Cucurbita melanospora*, which come from Asia."

"Is that what they call them there?"

"No, that's their scientific name, their native name, which means gourd, or pumpkin, with black seeds . . . This plant, my dear neighbor, grows with magical rapidity! In tropical climates after the rainy season, its rampant stems grow thirty to forty centimeters a day! Obviously we're not in a tropical climate . . ."

"Fortunately!" said Aimée.

"And properly speaking we haven't got a rainy season . . ."

"You know," said Ugolin, "it rains a lot here all the same . . . Not very often, but when it falls it really falls!"

"I'll give you the figures," said the hunchback.

He drew a notebook with a black oilcloth cover from his pocket.

"According to the statistics for the last fifty years, established by the scientists at the observatory at Marseille, the rainfall of our region reaches fifty-two centimeters a year. That's to say, if the bottom of this valley were impermeable and surrounded by a wall, it would be entirely covered at the end of the year with a lake of a uniform depth of fifty-two centimeters, and at the end of five years the table in our kitchen would be floating and grazing the ceiling!"

Ugolin, completely overwhelmed, declared:

"I wouldn't doubt that!"

"The figures are there!" said the hunchback. "It's true the fifty-two centimeters include the winter rains, which are of no interest to us. But look what the heavens will provide during the months of growth: April, six days of rain; May, five days; June, four days; July, two days; August, three; September, six days; October, six days."

"I agree," said Ugolin, "exactly that."

"However," replied the hunchback, "we mustn't deceive ourselves. Sometimes the rain is capricious and there won't be enough for this generous *cucurbitacae* to give us its full yield. So I'm not hoping for a tropical growth. No. I won't even say twenty-five centimeters, we may not exceed fifteen."

"Always the pessimist!" said Aimée.

"One should be," affirmed the hunchback, "when one wishes to be spared from a painful disillusionment. It's not a game, my dear Aimée. Imagine that we're condemned to return to the hell of town life in three years' time unless we're successful before then. So I say fifteen centimeters, which is still very good."

"And then," said Ugolin, "fifteen centimeters a day will be a nuisance . . . At the end of six months you'll have to go right up to the village to cut the pumpkins! And if the branches are all knitted together you'll never get out!"

"Perfect reasoning!"

"But then," said Aimée plaintively, "we won't have a hundred kilos of melons a plant?"

"A hundred kilos?" said Ugolin, stupefied.

"Yes," said the hunchback. "That's the normal yield. Good sense tells us that here, even with attentive care, our average won't be more than fifty or sixty kilos . . ."

"That'll be magnificent anyhow!" said Ugolin. "But you've only got four seeds . . ."

"They're very difficult to get. I owe these to the friendship of a sailor from Marseille . . . I'll plant them under shelter and look after them like the apple of my eye . . . That way it will be possible for me to study their behavior before undertaking the large-scale planting. In five or six months they'll give me a good hundred pumpkins at least—that's enough seeds to sow a hectare. That's what we'll do next year. In eighteen months we'll have the harvest, and the beginning of the massive culture! You can't arrange this kind of enterprise at short notice; you have to count on three years before it really gets going. We can hold out until then!"

He had spoken with such great confidence that Ugolin was disconcerted. Three years!

("Fortunately," he thought, "he doesn't know about the spring!")

"Well, my neighbor, what do you think of that?"

"It's very interesting!" said Ugolin. "But these pumpkins, are they good to eat?"

"Delicious!" said the hunchback, as if he ate them every day. "What's more, the rind is so hard, and so perfectly impermeable, that it's possible to keep them for several years without the flesh being changed; the melon stays as fresh and nourishing as the day it was picked!"

"It's a pity," said Ugolin, "that one can't let the peasants know about them."

"Oh yes!" said Aimée, "it's a great pity!"

"What can you do," said Ugolin sadly, "the rest of us, we've got hardly any books . . . We get taught by our old people, so we get stuck with the System. Ah! the System, it's terrible . . ."

"At last," said the charmed hunchback, "there's a true peasant who agrees! Well, since you are capable of understanding, I'll give you some seeds; today I've only got these four, but in six months the problem won't be to find seeds, but to stop their sprouting!"

"So," said Ugolin, "if you can't stop either the rabbits or the melons, I wonder where we're going!"

"To riches!" said the hunchback, "and I want you to know that in recognition of your spontaneous kindness, I'm going to take you there with me!"

"He deserves it," said Aimée.

She poured two big glasses of wine.

"In connection with that," said Ugolin, "I've thought about your business with the baker's field, and in the end I said nothing to him."

"Why?"

"Because yesterday at the club, they were talking about you. They know who you are, you know . . ."

"Who told them that?"

"That I don't know . . . In the villages people look, they talk . . . Well, an old man told me about the battle at your mother's wedding . . ."

"My father often told me about that," said the hunchback, "but he always laughed during the telling."

"Oh well, these people, you can never make them laugh. That the prettiest girl in the village should go off with somebody from Crespin has always been treason for them . . ."

"How mean!" said Aimée scornfully.

"Such a stupid grudge," said the hunchback, "proves that she had reason a thousand times over to quit that bunch of bumpkins that I never intended to visit; I've already told you that."

Aimée was pale with anger.

"It's a great honor my husband has done them to come and live here. Tell them that from me."

"What can you do, they're like that . . . But they won't try and do you any harm . . . If you say nothing to them, they'll leave you in peace. But as for the field, I'll try and rent it, saying it's for me, and I'll pass it on to you. And then I've thought of something else. Ruissatel is a long way for provisions. So, if it's any help to you, I've got Délie who comes three times a week to do my house . . . You've only got to give me a list and she'll bring back everything you want!"

"My dear neighbor," said the hunchback, "once more I accept your generous offer, because at the moment we must finish our moving in and we haven't got any time to lose. But I assure you that when the time comes I'll show my gratitude in more than words."

CHAPTER 15

Ugolin ran to the village. The Papet was ending a game of *boules* on the esplanade. After long reflection, with his left hand supported on his stick, he aimed magnificently and, amid the cheers of the onlookers, his ball rolled to a stop on the target, giving his side the winning point.

But Ugolin did not say a word in front of all these people. He went to drink an aperitif afterward with the players, and this took a good hour even though he had winked at the Papet, who had judged it unwise to leave too soon. Then they went up the hill, talking about one thing and another until they reached the Soubeyran house. When the door was closed, and they had made sure the old deaf and dumb woman was occupied grating the cheese for the soup, and they had sat at the table with a bottle of wine in front of them, the Papet lit his pipe and asked:

"Anything new?"

"Yes, good news and bad news. First, the vast projects, that's large-scale breeding of rabbits out in the open inside a wire fence."

"Very good. He's got a book?"

"Yes, he let me see it. It's quite full of figures. They show that if you start with two rabbits, you'll have more than a thousand at the end of six months. And if you let them go on, it's perdition: that's how they ate up Australia."

"I know about that," said the Papet. "But I didn't see it in a book, it was in a newspaper . . . With a fountain pen it's easy to make rabbits multiply. One night at La Valentine I even saw an artiste make four of them come out of a top hat."

"He said he wanted to limit himself. Not more than a hundred and fifty a month."

The Papet sneered:

"Bravo! Bravo!"

"He's going to feed them with Chinese pumpkins that have wooden rinds. He said they grow as fast as a snake coming out of a hole, and each plant produces at least a hundred kilos of pumpkins, but he's going to be satisfied with fifty."

"Galinette, are you sure you're not exaggerating a little?"

"Oh, not at all! I'm telling you what he said."

"Could he have been fooling you?"

"For a few moments I wondered. But then not—he's serious. This morning a great load of fencing, posts, and cement came up. And the messenger told me he wasn't done."

"Ah well, all that pleases me a lot, because the Good Lord made him to measure for us. In six months he'll be gone."

"Ah well, there you deceive yourself. I told you I had good news and bad news. The bad news is that he's going to take three years over it. He said to his wife: we're condemned to go back to town if we don't succeed within three years. That's what he said."

"What he said and what he'll do are certainly not the same thing."

"Perhaps, but it shows he's got the money. You know he sold the house and property at Gémenos? You know he's had an inheritance?"

"Galinette, the money from an inheritance is no good. It won't stick to the fingers . . . If he starts buying cement! Ideas and cement take you a long way . . . Before six months he'll start going hungry . . . With six thousand francs we'll be rid of him . . . And until then it will be amusing to see him getting tangled up with his melons—we must be patient . . ."

"Papet, I would like you to come and see him to explain things because there are times when I don't understand anything!"

"I've already told you no! But all the same, since I'm curious, I'll make myself a little hiding place in the pine wood to watch things from a distance . . . That will be for my entertainment."

At this moment the door opened and the dumb woman directed a large number of mysterious signs toward the Papet. The Papet nodded yes.

"She says the food's all ready."

And as the dumb woman lightly waved her two open hands he translated:

"It's little birds in the pan . . ."

"You're right," said Ugolin, "I already smell the beautiful smell."

At the same time, at the table under the paraffin lamp, the hunchback was saying gravely:

"Our judgments are always too hasty, and souls are truly separated when love does not unite them. I was wrong in my reckoning of that man. You see, when he helped me move the furniture the first day I attributed his generosity to peasant curiosity, and I even thought I saw a sort of hostility in his smile. Mea culpa! First he gave us the precious water from his well without my asking. Today he thought of bringing us those tiles, which saved me a long and expensive journey to Aubagne. Yes, this man, weighed down by work without respite—because his poor fields are really well tended although the earth seems ungrateful—this man came to offer his services to a neighbor he did not know. And even what he told us about those imbeciles in the village is witness of his sympathy, and moreover, a proof of the delicacy of his character—he refuses to espouse their stupidity. Besides, he lives alone, his farm is nearly as isolated as ours, and I have the impression he hardly ever visits them."

"He didn't appeal to me very much," said Aimée timidly.

"Because he's ugly! Because he's gauche and rustic . . . But under a cover of coarseness there is often a pure soul . . ."

"I know that perfectly well," said Aimée. "I'll try to remember that. In any case he frightens this little one . . . He wanted to caress her hair and she howled."

"Manon, you astonish me. Don't you like the nice peasant?"

"He's nasty," said the little girl. "He makes my skin go cold. He's a toad!"

"Manon," said the hunchback gravely, "it's your thoughts that are nasty. This gentleman gave us the tiles we were missing, so every time it rains we should recognize it and give him a little thanks."

CHAPTER *16*

On Sunday afternoon Ugolin went to the village to play *boules* as usual. It was a long and pleasant game. He played with Ange and the Papet against the baker, the butcher, and Pamphile. Philoxène was detained in his bar and only joined them from time to time, to measure the distances when they were disputed.

Before a gallery of some consequence—with Cabridan, Anglade, and the blacksmith conspicuous in the forefront, providing the essential commentary—they won the first round and the replay. This called for aperitifs, to which the commentators were invited.

Many of the people there had seen the arrival of the hunchback and the journeys of the wagoner from afar. But nobody talked about it, "because one doesn't stick one's nose into other people's affairs." Ugolin made the first move.

"Up there," he said, "a queer chap has turned up with all his household goods."

"I saw the cart going up," said Pamphile. "I saw it at least three times!"

"And I saw it four times," said Eliacin.

"Has he rented the farm?" asked Philoxène.

"No," said Ugolin. "He bought it. At least, that's what he told me."

"He's a peasant?"

"No. He's a hunchback."

"Poor chap!" said Pamphile.

"Has he been there a long time?" asked the baker.

"A week."

"I've not seen him yet. Where does he go for his bread?"

"To Ruissatel," said Ugolin. "He buys everything at Ruissatel." The baker was annoyed.

"Why? Is he afraid my bread will poison him?"

"Certainly not . . . The truth is, he doesn't want to come to the village."

He paused, blinked, and said:

"He's from Crespin."

"Ayayay!" said the blacksmith. "That's not a recommendation."

"Perhaps he's a spy," said Cabridan.

"And what do you want him to spy on?" cried Philoxène. "Do you think he's come to count your chick-peas?"

The wily Pamphile added:

"But then, if he were a spy he wouldn't say he was from Crespin!"

"And he'd come to the village to find things out!"

"And he does exactly the opposite!" said the Papet. "Go on, go on, that's all nonsense. They're not all bad at Crespin!"

"What did he do down there?"

"He wrote things down in the office of the tax collector."

There was a silence, then Cabridan, opening frightened rabbit's eyes, said:

"Perhaps he's going to make new taxes for us?"

"Oh no, no," said the Papet. "Taxes aren't done like that!"

"Has he got a family?" asked the baker.

"Yes, a wife and a little girl."

"Do you think he'll stay a long time?"

"He didn't tell me. In any case, he's repairing the house."

"He's doing it alone?" asked Casimir.

"Yes, with gloves."

"It should be done well!" said Philoxène.

"He does what he can."

"So, he's got no money?"

"How do you expect me to know that? We've talked two or three times for five minutes."

"All the same," said Ange, "a hunchback who comes from Crespin, and stays hidden on the hillside—I'm suspicious."

"Why should you be suspicious?" replied Philoxène. "He stays up there, he isn't harming anybody!"

"Bah!" said the Papet, "there's nothing to do but leave him in peace, he doesn't want anything from us!"

CHAPTER *17*

On the thirtieth of March the roof of the house was good as new, the shed had a new roof, the doors and windows had been refitted, with all the glass in place. The shutters were repainted a light green, and the facade, adequately replastered with lime, shone white in the sun. Finally, the rotten poles of the trellis were replaced with red and black trunks of young pine trees, and the once disheveled vine branches now formed a verdant ceiling over the restored terrace.

To celebrate the end of this work, and especially to obtain other congratulations besides those of his own family, Jean Cadoret invited Ugolin to drink a glass of champagne.

He arrived about six in the evening. When he turned into the dale and saw the house, he opened his eyes wide and stopped for some moments. The hunchback watched him from afar, smiling. At ten meters Ugolin stopped again, looked for a long time, and shook his head.

"Well? What do you think of it?"

"If I had known I was coming to a house like this I'd have put on my Sunday clothes!"

Aimée had just come out, in a rose pink dress, two thick tresses of auburn hair crowning her pale face; little Manon was sitting on a swing attached to a low branch of an olive tree, with her blue espadrilles pointed forward and a blade of fennel in her mouth.

Finally he saw the fine hand pump installed on the wooden cover of the cistern, and a rubber hose rolled around a big wooden bobbin: Ugolin reckoned it was thirty meters long and cost at least a hundred francs.

He did not recognize the kitchen. It was animated by the grandfather clock, restored to newness with beeswax, and all lit up by the whiteness of the walls and enriched by the glint of copper. He admired the gilded chains of a large hanging paraffin lamp with a blue glass shade surrounded by a circle of useless but luxurious electric lamps. When he went upstairs he was amazed to see that the husband did not sleep with his wife—they had separate rooms, the way rich people did. This diabolical hunchback surely had a lot of money, he knew how to work with his hands, and his confidence in the eventual success of his enterprise seemed justified in Ugolin's eyes, by this first achievement . . . He left to see the Papet in a very worried mood.

The next morning Jean Cadoret started his pioneer work.

He got up before dawn without making a sound. He went downstairs with his shoes in his hand in order not to wake his wife and daughter. He blew on the embers to heat his coffee and then left to work on the furthest side of the field.

Before attacking the first wild shrub, he made a little speech to himself in the breaking dawn, invoking the need to feed his family; then, in honor of all the plants he was going to kill, he played a little tune on the mouth organ, noble and sad, while the day dawned . . .

His first days were not very successful. Because of his clumsiness the hatchet, the billhook, and the saw cost him a great deal of effort, and he was not able to sharpen the edge of the scythe by hammering it on the small anvil. Moreover, when he thrust the great blade before him the point dug into the ground; if he had not seen mowers attacking swathes with perfect ease during his childhood, he would have discarded this absurd tool. But he thought and he persevered. He tried lifting the point slightly, and he learned how to pivot his body, and in less than a week he was able to handle the instrument like a professional.

In the same way he learned the movements that raised the pickax to a good height and planted it a good distance, with correct and measured effort. No doubt this style and this efficiency were due to his peasant heredity. Perhaps also to the fact that manual work (whatever the demagogues may say) does not demand a veritable genius, since it is more difficult to extract a square root than a gorse root.

He cut the giant brambles and the thorny broom with the long-handled billhook. Then he scythed the thistles, and pulled out the rockrose and the rosemary with two hands . . . Finally he pulled this dead foliage with a fork and rake up to the pine woods on the sides, followed by the she-donkey and the goats who chose to pasture on thistles and wild thyme.

About eight o'clock he hung the scythe on an olive tree, laid out his tools, and played a hunting horn refrain on his mouth organ. Then his wife and daughter arrived carrying his breakfast, because he stayed at his place of work for his breakfast, like a peasant . . . It was a real feast: hard-boiled eggs, anchovies, cold meat, thick slices of bread, and a big glass of red wine.

Then, after some chatter and a little music, everybody went back to work. The father took up his scythe and his fork, the mother returned to her housework, and the little girl looked after her goats.

At noon Aimée laid the table under the trellis, singing all the while, but the hunchback did not give himself more than half an hour for this meal and returned to work until nightfall.

Then at the owls' first cries he came home to the big kitchen, exhausted but smiling. His little girl was covering pages with writing at the end of the table, while her mother laid the plates around a bouquet of wild flowers. He washed and combed twigs, thyme leaves, and scraps of bark out of his hair.

Then he sat close to the lamp and searched under the skin on his fingers for the day's thorns with a needle sterilized in the candle flame, while his attentive daughter uttered little cries of pain and suddenly pulled the big hands to her lips to kiss the wounded fingers.

During dinner he explained once more the long-matured plans that were so quickly going to make their fortune, and especially the little one's—they could almost see the pieces of gold spinning on the table. After dessert she sat on a cushion clasping her father's calves and resting her curls on his knee while he played old peasant songs and antique Provençal Christmas carols on his mouth organ. Sometimes Aimée sang with an admirable soprano voice, and her husband accompanied her; in the moonlit pine wood the owls made their distant responses.

During the first weeks Aimée was worried by her husband's overwork, and he himself feared for a moment that he would not be able to keep up his effort. But he soon saw that his strength grew every day, and that the air of the hills was making a new man of him . . .

For the first time in his life he had great pleasure in living. His mother had been born on this lonely farm. In her youth she had gathered the almonds of these almond trees, and dried her sheets on the grass under these olive trees that her forefathers had planted two or three centuries ago . . . He loved these pine woods, these junipers, these turpentine trees, the cuckoos in the morning, the sparrow hawks at midday, and the owls in the evening; and while he dug his land under the flights of the swallows, he reflected that none of these living creatures knew that he was a hunchback.

Every two or three days, on his way back from poaching, Ugolin passed Les Romarins. He always left a present: a partridge, two or three thrushes, some savory herbs cut at Les Escaouprès. Sometimes he would even unload his gun and put it down on the grass; then he would sit down under an olive tree, put the little anvil on the ground, and hammer the blade of the scythe for a long time under Monsieur Jean's attentive eyes.

At the end of a fortnight the field was really clean. The olive trees, rid of their suckers and dead branches, had resumed their tree-shapes, and the brush-wood had been pushed up to the foot of the hillside.

One evening Jean announced to his family that the next day was going to be a great day, the first day of the actual agricultural project, because he was going to start digging up the ground, and this would soon be followed by the planting.

At dawn they were silently breakfasting together in the kitchen when little Manon appeared at the top of the steps, very sleepy, but smiling; she had dressed noiselessly and had come to take part in the ceremony.

He spoke to them gravely:

"The work I'm going to start today will be long and painful. It will certainly last many months, but we don't need all the tillable area at once. For the moment it will be enough to have three hundred square meters for the vegetable garden and six or seven hundred square meters for the little meadow in the rabbit park. According to Ugolin I should easily be able to dig up forty square meters a day."

"It's like a problem!" said Manon. "But I don't yet know how to do square meters and I don't understand them at all . . ."

"I'll show them to you on the ground and you'll understand at once! So I'll need about twelve days to get the vegetable garden ready for planting, and about three weeks for the little meadow. Then I'll have all winter to dig up the field where I plan to have a big plantation of gourds and corn. I think it's a reasonable and workable plan, if Providence will allow me to stay in good health as it has up to now. Let's go!"

They went out. The sunrise was glowing in the pine woods and all along the crests of the hills on the east.

They stopped in silence at the edge of the field.

The mother and daughter listened to the father's prayer with their heads bowed and their hands clasped. He lifted his face and asked the heavens to bless the work he was about to commence. As he pronounced the last word he heard stones rattling on the mule road, then a whip cracked, and they saw Ugolin's back advancing. He was pulling the mule by the bridle, while the creaking cart jolted over the pebbles.

The hunchback thought his neighbor was going to look for wood. But the cart left the hill track and came down toward the farm. On the cart lay a long plough.

"Greetings, neighbor!" said the hunchback. "Where are you going then with that plough?"

"To you!" said Ugolin. While he unhitched the mule, he continued: "I thought to myself that with the pickax you'd be at it for three months and it would break your constitution; while we could do all the work with the plough, even for next year's gourds. That will be good for the earth and we'll finish this evening!"

The hunchback turned a radiant face to his wife.

"Aimée, the prayer was not in vain. Here's the reply from Heaven!"

Ugolin was thus promoted to the first rank among the instruments of Providence. In fact his intentions were not really angelic.

First of all, he was following the Papet's advice: gain the friendship of the neighbor in order to buy the farm one day at a better price. And then he feared the pickax would go astray on the side where the spring was and bring some revealing signs of humidity into the light of day—his presence and his advice could avoid such a misfortune. Next, he thought that in accelerating the execution of an absurd plan, the end of it would be seen sooner. Finally, he burned with the desire to appraise this land, to measure the depth of it, to know its suppleness, to smell its odor; and on top of this, this labor would be, more than anything, a preparation for his future work.

Moreover, to these base reasons was added an obscure remorse that acted without his knowing it, and he said to himself: "I'm helping him, I'm doing him good. I know his business won't succeed, but all the same it's a good deed and the Good Lord will take it into account for me."

Because of the future carnations, and to embellish the "good deed," he spared neither his time nor his trouble; the work lasted one long day.

Under a thick layer of humus the earth was brown, a powder of dead roots and rotten leaves that made up a rich compost. Not a single stone: generations of serfs and peasants had gathered them up, and they formed the warrens that bordered the bottom of the field. This earth was so deep that the plough would be drowned without the small guide wheel to arrest the plunge of the share.

Ugolin held firmly to the plough-stock; he looked at the large dark band of earth that rose up the length of the shining ploughshare before falling to the side of the furrow, and thought:

"All that, it's full of pieces of gold that ask only to be picked up."

They lunched under the big olive tree: anchovies, sausage, partridge with cabbage, crêpes, and three bottles of vintage wine that caused the first furrows of the afternoon to be rather twisted.

In the evening, drinking a big glass of dry white wine, Ugolin declared:

"Now, Monsieur Jean, we must leave this land quiet for a fortnight so that it can get a little sun and taste the dew . . . But that would delay planting the vegetable garden. Where do you want to make the garden? And the park for the rabbits?"

The position of the park was tormenting Ugolin. If the breeder installed thirty little subterranean cement buildings at the bottom of the vallon it would take a month to demolish them and get the earth ready for planting carnations. It was therefore necessary to dig the burrows on the hillside; but not on the right, where the imprisoned spring lay.

"You understand, Monsieur Jean, at the bottom of the valley, it will make you lose a lot of arable land. And then you mustn't forget that rabbits piss a lot. It's a good idea to make their burrows out of cement; but if there isn't any outflow they'll die like flies. So if I were in your place I would dig the burrows on the side of the hill; with four holes in the bottom of the cement, so they'll stay dry. So, the burrows should be on the hillside. But which of the two? Certainly not the right; it is on the north. No sun, and it will get the mistral, while the one on the left is in broad daylight and protected from the wind. What do you think?"

Jean Cadoret found his reasoning excellent, and Ugolin, to make quite sure, declared that he would come the next day and help plant the stakes.

Then they chose a fairly long terrace for the vegetable garden, the vallon being reserved for the miraculous gourds. Finally, after clinking glasses for the last time, Ugolin put the mule between the shafts again, and the plough on the cart, and followed the cart in the light of the moon.

They watched him going, on the track bordered with rosemary and flowers. His hands were in his pockets, and he was dancing.

From that day Aimée considered him a saint; but the little girl never let him touch her. Besides, he never tried again; he was afraid to.

Monsieur Jean started ("let's be methodical") on the freshly worked earth with the installation of the vegetable garden.

On the hillside of Les Romarins the Papet had fitted up his observatory, which he could reach by a detour under a forest of gorse. It was a lookout, a sort of hut made of branches, such as is used in hunting partridges. Between two juniper trees, and behind a curtain of clematis pierced with two openings, he sat on a sack of dried grass that allayed the hardness of a lump of stone below it, and he leaned his back against the trunk of a pine tree, with a gun at his side to justify his presence in case of surprise.

He came to sit there nearly every day about four o'clock, and treated himself to the strange ways of the amateur. That evening at the table he commented on them.

"Galinette, he's put the tomatoes on the north, in the shade of the pine wood. Even if they produce any fruit they'll never ripen. It's been seven days since he sowed the chick-peas. He pushed them in with a stick and they haven't come out yet. I'll be amazed if he'll eat half a salad bowl of them. He's planted the onions around a big olive tree. Perhaps that will look pretty if he lets them go to seed. And the potatoes, he's buried them a few centimeters deep! If this ninny is counting on feeding his family with that, there'll be nothing left of them but skin and bone!"

The "ninny" next sowed the clover and sainfoin on the site of the rabbit park. The Papet didn't find much to say, except that the moon was not right, and besides the sower didn't know how to fan out the seeds.

"He doesn't sow them, he throws them! That'll make them come out in bunches like Médéric's bald spots. But in the end it won't matter because, without watering there'll be nothing but grass! When I look at him working I want to laugh sometimes, but on the other hand it makes me sick, and I often want to go down and take the tools out of his hands and show him what to do."

"Oh, Papet," said Ugolin, "don't excite yourself like that! Let him do it his way. It may not be any good, but it's best for us!"

After the planting of the vegetable garden, Ugolin was invited to the sowing of the four black seeds. The planter had dug four holes at the foot of the wall that went along the terrace and filled them with humus enriched with the manure of the she-ass. The buried seeds were liberally watered, and little Manon, blushing with pride, was entrusted with the mission of watering them every evening—one little watering can for each plant.

"In a fortnight," said Monsieur Jean, "they will be above the wall and they'll start climbing the trellis."

The next day he tackled the installation of the rabbit park.

The Papet did not have much to do to his vineyard and often came to his observation post. He saw the hunchback beginning the trench that was to receive the bottom of the wire fencing.

With his arms bare, but his hump hidden under an old flowered waistcoat, he let his miner's pickax fly and then he shovelled up the spoil with a narrow coal shovel.

From time to time he rested under an olive tree. Then he pulled his mouth organ from his pocket and played Provençal songs like "Magali" or "Misé Babet," or mysterious music that sounded like church music. His wife, who was sweeping the terrace under the trellis, or stretching her washing on the rosemary, often sang to the tune of the distant mouth organ; and sometimes with tunes that were merry and staccato, the little girl danced barefoot on the spring grass with her arms raised like an amphora above her head.

The Papet listened and looked, vaguely moved, and thought:

"They really are artistes . . . They would be very successful at charity concerts on saints' days, or in a circus . . . But this imbecile who digs like a curé is wasting his time and his money on work that will never do him any good . . ."

The Papet had calculated the length of the enclosure: certainly more than a hundred meters. He had estimated that the poor man would not get to the end of such a job in less than six months of daily work, but he soon saw that in spite of the artistic interludes the trench advanced five or six meters a day, and that the digger would finish in less than six weeks. He consoled himself with the thought that this possible small success was of no great importance because the failure of the "massive" breeding was inevitable. But Ugolin seemed to be discouraged.

"Papet," he said, "this hunchback frightens me. He's planted everything haphazard, and it grows. His crazy gourds are up to my knees. His enclosure is nearly finished. And instead of getting thin, he's getting fat . . . If he succeeds a little this year he's bound to continue . . ."

The Papet shrugged his shoulders and did not answer. Ugolin tried to evaluate the hunchback's inheritance, and his expenses, to get an idea of how much longer he could hold out . . . Or he would calculate the fabulous sums the "ninny" made him lose every day, and jot the sums down on the table . . .

He forgot to eat, while Monsieur Jean, highly satisfied with his work, showed a marvellous appetite, a clear complexion, bright eyes, and a great zest for life, which he expressed every night with a mouth organ concert.

But one day while he was handling the lever of the pump to water the vegetable garden, he heard a strange gurgling from the bottom of the cistern, and at the same time Manon, who held the little copper water nozzle in the middle of the garden, cried: "It's not running anymore."

He lit the candle in the lantern and let it down into the cistern at the end of a string: the hose was touching the surface of the water, which was no more than a thin layer in the lowest corner of the reservoir.

He was not disturbed.

"I expected it!" he said. "I thought we still had one or two days' watering, but I expected it, and if it doesn't rain tonight, we'll think about it tomorrow."

CHAPTER *19*

In the afternoon at about four o'clock Ugolin was hard at work hoeing his chick-peas, when he saw a charming expedition coming down the road from Les Romarins.

The little girl was astride the ass, between two great cans. Behind her marched her father; a sort of shelf was attached to his shoulders by two leather slings and poised on his hump, which was protected by a cushion. On the shelf was a great demijohn of thirty liters, attached to his brow by a wide strap. He leaned on a long pilgrim's staff and appeared to be tremendously merry.

Behind him came his wife in the shade of a large straw hat with the brim bent becomingly under a muslin scarf. She stopped every three steps to cut the wildflowers that bordered the path.

"My greetings to the family!" said Ugolin. "You're going on an excursion?"

"Eh, yes! On an excursion—or rather a reconnaissance—a reconnaissance that has, moreover, something to do with precisely what I owe you."

Ugolin understood nothing of this fine talk the hunchback was treating himself to.

"This is what I want to say: since we've been here you have generously supplied us with two cans of drinking water a day. Now I've noticed that the level of your well has begun to fall, and summer has come, and the sky doesn't appear to be disposed to give us the rain it owes us. We are therefore going to the spring at Le Plantier to provision ourselves with drinking water. As this will be our first visit I call it a 'reconnaissance' in the military sense of the word, which I have also used in the sense of recognition to make an allusion to my gratitude. Do you understand?"

"Certainly," said Ugolin. "I understand you're going to Le Plantier, and I'd have understood even without your telling me, just by seeing that big jar on your back, and these cans and these jugs. Unfortunately I can't go with you because I must hoe my chick-peas. They don't need watering—that does them more harm than good—but they need to be scratched at the foot so they can profit from the morning dew. That's what pleases them most. I've neglected them a bit, and now look, some of them don't look well, and I'm trying to revive them . . ."

"I understand that," said Monsieur Jean, "and all the better because my discretion about your well isn't the only reason for this expedition—my cistern is empty. But I'm not very worried about it because I can promise you—and I promise myself—it will rain tomorrow, or the day after at the latest."

"And how can you do that? Do you know it by your rheumatism?"

"Fortunately I haven't got that, but I have shown you the statistics of the observatory! The sky, which owed us six days of rain in May, gave us only three; since the first of June it should have rained twice; we haven't had any. Therefore we have a credit of five days of rain. It's quite an extraordinary deficit in the celestial accounts, and the debt will certainly be honored tomorrow or the day after! Against that promise, show me the shortest way to Le Plantier."

"No," said Ugolin, "not the shortest, because you'll get lost. I'll show you the easiest. Go down to the bottom of the vallon there under our feet, and then, instead of going up the other side toward the village, turn right, and continue: the cave is at the end of the track, above the gully at the end of the vallon."

Aimée asked:

"Are there any flowers on these hills?"

"If you mean roses or carnations, I can guarantee there aren't any . . ."

"She means field flowers, wildflowers."

"I've never noticed them—I notice the thorns more—but they're bound to be there."

"Thank you."

They went down the incline, with Ugolin regretting having pronounced the word *carnation*, because it was part of his secret.

The vallon was bordered by two sheer drops of bluish rock and was more a large gorge than a vallon.

The track stretched along the bottom under the cliff on the right. On the left was a long series of terraced fields, supported by dry stone walls a meter high.

Those nearest the village were still cultivated. There were some well-kept vineyards, barley in the blade, and long rows of chick-peas under olive or plum trees. But as the vallon rose toward the hills the gardens were replaced by rough yellowish grass, groups of turpentine trees, young pines, and big bushes of eglantine. Here and there were plum trees prickly with black dead branches and some old fig trees suffocated by their suckers.

Little by little, the vallon became narrower. At the end of an hour's walk, there were no more fields to be seen, and the vallon became a deep gorge with oblique sides that widened in stages as they mounted to the empty blue sky. It had been carved thousands of years ago by storm torrents, and there was nothing to see but a few pine trees leaning over the narrow passage, which looked like a miniature canyon. An undergrowth of rosemary, broom, and lentisk had closed over the track, which was now barely visible through their branches; they had to open a passage by pushing the branches back with hands and knees, being careful not to let the big springy brooms go suddenly, lest they strike the face of the one following.

The she-ass seemed quite at ease, but she stopped from time to time to pluck admirable golden thistles for which Aimée contested in vain. The little girl sang "Magali," and her father had let the bridle loose in order to throw stones into the bushes. This made blackbirds as black as crows burst forth, amidst peals of laughter.

The she-ass had just disappeared behind a bend in the gorge, when the little girl's voice rang out, multiplied by echoes:

"Papa! Come and look."

They went forward: above a steep and stony ravine a wall of large bare stones seemed to be embedded in the base of a high rock face.

"It's truly very beautiful," said Jean, "and I envy the people who live in this place. If I didn't have my fortune to make, I would offer them our farm in exchange for their place!"

Then up there the head of a man appeared above the undergrowth. He had put his open hand over his eyes to watch them coming up: it was Giuseppe, the woodcutter. Next, a grand lady dressed in black: it was Baptistine.

Ten years earlier in a little village in Piedmont, Baptistine had married Giuseppe, who was apprenticed to his father. But instead of setting himself up at once in a thatched cottage and producing a brood of infants, Giuseppe, who was an adventurous spirit who had no wish to die poor, had kissed the brow of his young bride as they left the little church, and had left for France, where woodcutters—so it was said—ate meat every day. Two years later he sent for his virginal beloved.

He came to the railway station at Aubagne to wait for her arrival on a train that had jolted along for thirty hours. He wore a fine pair of maroon corduroy trousers held up by a wide blue belt, a shirt with large red squares separated by thick black lines, and a handsome green corduroy jacket. A glossy curly forelock emerged from a flat hat on the back of his head; his eyebrows were shining and his moustache was as long and as bushy as King Victor Emmanuel's. On his feet—supreme luxury—he wore a pair of shoes of real leather, as beautiful as a soldier's, and the platform resounded to the magnificent ring of the nails in them.

They exchanged scarcely a word because of all the people passing by who had no need to know their secrets, and they set off on the road, loaded with bundles and packets.

Giuseppe walked in front, and suddenly turned to the right to take the path up the hills. At the end of an hour they stopped in front of a dry stone wall that closed off the entry of a cave at the foot of a sheer drop of blue rock, high above a wild ravine. There was a door in the wall, and a little window on either side.

He entered first and opened the shutters.

In a corner was the bed covered with a thick blanket of yellow wool on a frame of strong holm-oak branches barely stripped of bark, under a copper crucifix shining in a patch of sunshine. Along the limestone wall there were some stools, two chests decorated with large nailheads, and a tin alarm clock on the lid of an old kneading trough.

On the left, near the door, in the corner where the wall joined the rock, there was a hearth, with a red plaster mantel marked with deep fingerprints. Against the wall on the right, suspended from thick wooden pegs, there were pruning hatchets, billhooks, and two big axes with narrow curved blades protected by leather muzzles.

Baptistine gazed with astonishment and joy at their wild love nest.

Giuseppe raised a finger and said:

"Don't make a sound: listen!"

They heard a sort of twittering of birds, and from time to time a light ringing sound. He took her by the hand and led her to the bottom of the cave. There, under a mossy chink in the rock, was a little pool full to the brim with clear water.

"The spring!" he said.

The water ran along a furrow that went through the wall on the right.

He made her sit on the bed.

"Baptistine, my darling, this is where I've lived for two years. I don't know who the master of this old sheepfold is—nobody has ever asked me for anything. I came here because it was convenient for my work, and besides, it saved money. But I have the money to buy a house in the village: look."

He went and plunged his arms in a hole in the rock and pulled out a small narrow canvas bag, like a tube. He took one end of it and shook it over the blanket, and some pieces of gold fell out. Baptistine clasped her hands in ecstasy.

"There are sixty-two of these," said Giuseppe. "I made them with the blows of my axe, and now they're yours. I didn't buy the house, because it's the wife who should choose. So, this is what I say to you: if you want to, we'll live here until you have the first sickness. Then at that moment you will go and choose a house in the village. There, that's my idea. But if this cave doesn't please you . . ."

"Oh, Giuseppe," said Baptistine, "for me it is the palace of a king. It's a cave, and for me this cave is a palace of gold and marble. But don't say any more. I've been your fiancée for five years and your virgin wife for two years . . . Come quickly, so that I may be married."

And she tore off her dress, and she gnawed at his mouth, and they stayed in this palace; they stayed all these years because the morning sickness had never wanted to come.

That day Giuseppe had not gone to work because he had to plant vegetables in the little vegetable garden put in by shepherds in front of the cave in bygone days.

In the course of more than a century the shepherds had built a dry stone wall on the steep slope, then they had filled it from behind with earth, with earth they had gathered here and there on the hill and had carried back night after night in a sack, sometimes even, the legend says, in their hats. It was thus they had made a sort of long pool of fertile earth behind the retaining wall, which, with the manure from their goats, gave them vegetables, tomatoes, the fruit of a few plum trees, three fig trees, and an apricot tree.

Giuseppe greeted the arrivals warmly, and Baptistine smiled. They could hear the bells of his goats but could not see them because of the height of the coppice. From time to time a dog yapped in the underbrush.

She came forward and said, in a bizarre language made up of a few French words mixed with Provençal and Piedmontese:

"I'm sure you've come to look for water!"

Jean Cadoret had been clerk in the tax collector's office in a suburb of Marseille, and the fey Aimée had sung operas in Italian—but without exactly understanding them.

On the other hand, Giuseppe spoke a French that was on a par with the hunchback's Italian. By gesturing and making faces, they were able to have a conversation, while the she-ass browsed, and the little girl chased magnificent butterflies with her hat.

Jean Cadoret explained that he had come to look for drinking water because the water in his cistern was bad, and added that his mother had left him this cave and the land around it. At this great tears suddenly sprang from Baptistine's eyes. She raised her arms to the skies and invoked the Madonna, then threw herself on her knees in front of him and poured forth weeping supplications. She had understood that the proprietor of the palace had come to live there himself, and they had to give up the place.

The astonished hunchback looked at Giuseppe, who explained the meaning of these demonstrations. Then he took her hands and raised her and said solemnly—looking for the words in his brand of Italian:

"I haven't come to live in this sheepfold. You can stay here as long as you like."

These words, which made no sense in any language, were nevertheless understood by the Piedmontese, who profited from them immediately to invoke the Madonna anew, weeping with gratitude. Then she seized the hand of the master and kissed it furiously.

Manon had abandoned the butterflies to witness this interesting scene. Baptistine called her Angel of Heaven, called the blessings of the Virgin on her head, and declared that if ever Manon were hungry she would give her liver and her eyes, which did not astonish anybody—because nobody understood this promise, except Giuseppe, who had already heard it many times.

Then they all went up to the cave, and the enchanted Aimée admired its comfort and cleanliness while her husband looked at the beautiful spring and listened to its little music.

Giuseppe went to fetch the cans on the donkey and filled them with a saucepan and a funnel. Then he showed the hunchback the pipes made of reeds that led the water from the spring to the vegetable garden.

During this time Baptistine had sat Aimée down in front of a table as heavy as a billiard table on a big block of wood, like those that support anvils.

She offered her dried figs, almonds, hazelnuts, and sugared polenta crêpes, warmed up on a hot stone and sprinkled with aniseed.

When they left at about five o'clock they first had to catch the she-ass and the two goats who had got in touch with Baptistine's flock, and had already made themselves part of it. It was rather a long chase.

Giuseppe was determined to accompany the family and hoisted a little thirty-liter barrel on his shoulder because he did not have a bigger one, while Baptistine carried two glazed clay jugs, and Aimée a fine watering can.

The hunchback made a small calculation: fifty liters on the she-ass, thirty liters on Giuseppe's shoulder, thirty liters on his hump, that made a hundred and ten liters already, to which he should add about fifteen liters carried by the women.

"A hundred and twenty-five liters," he said, "of course it's not much. But it will enable us to wait for the first rain . . ."

"Perhaps," said Giuseppe. "Perhaps . . ."

He made them take a shortcut that followed the side of the hill above the vallon.

Jean Cadoret seemed happy. He made jokes, and thanked the Good Lord for having accorded him the hump, whose use at last he understood. All the same, he stopped several times on the route, on the pretext of admiring the landscape, but in fact to rest his bruised back by leaning the heavy shelf against a rock.

On the way, Ugolin rushed forward laughing and wanted to carry Aimée's watering can to the farm.

When they arrived at the vegetable garden, Monsieur Jean had an unpleasant surprise: many plants were bending their heads, others seemed faded. The large leaves along the stalks of the four Asiatic gourds had begun to wilt.

"But a little while ago everything was fine! What's happened?"

"An afternoon's happened," said Ugolin. "Didn't you feel that suffocating heat between four and five o'clock? It was the wind from Africa, and it's only just dropped. But if we could give them a little water it'll be nothing."

Everybody started watering the plants. To the great joy of the spectators this seemed to have immediate results. Next they drank two bottles of wine, and then at nightfall Giuseppe and Baptistine took leave of their new friends.

"Our Master," said Giuseppe, "tomorrow I can't help you because I'm going to work for three days at Pichauris . . ."

"Don't worry," said Jean. "The cistern is not completely empty, and it will certainly rain within a few days."

Baptistine kissed everybody's hands, then she said in her gibberish:

"I know a good prayer for the rain. I'll say it three times before I go to bed."

She called again for the blessings of the Heavens on the admirable family, with a Piedmontese formula that it would be wise not to abuse, since the Madonna herself is incapable of resisting it.

That evening at the table Jean Cadoret said to his wife:

"If we had a spring like that there'd be no problem . . . But don't think I'm discouraged. Even if our crops don't entirely succeed this year we still have enough money to continue the enterprise. We'll trust to statistics and Providence."

He took his mouth organ, and said:

"And now Manon will sing: 'Alouette, gentille alouette . . .'"

Baptistine's prayer had the desired effect, because the statistics kept their promise and watered the fields four times, and replenished the cistern. The Asiatic pumpkins flourished on the trellis, little Manon grew visibly, and in six weeks the rabbit park was finished: Monsieur Jean played better than ever on the mouth organ, and poor Ugolin, seated on the ground under the mulberry tree, flailed his chick-peas . . .

One morning he saw Monsieur Jean tackle a little carpentry job.

He very adroitly made four rabbit cages with the crates used for the moving in, with wire mesh doors fitted to them. Then he placed them in the shed, whose double doors he had repaired.

"Look," he said to Ugolin, "the beginning of our farming. Tomorrow I'm going to look for our breeding animals: one male and three females, and we're going to bring them up in these cages until the birth of the first litters. It will be easy for us to feed them with the grass we'll find on the hill. I reckon on about twenty births between now and the end of July. So I'll buy some bags of coarse flour at the mill at Ruissatel to supplement their rations of greenstuffs. Toward the beginning of November we will have other broods. I'll install the whole menagerie in the rabbit park, and the black pumpkins will start ripening. So, that will be the great Adventure!"

CHAPTER *20*

The next morning about seven o'clock Jean Cadoret left his farm, dressed in town clothes. Under a black bowler hat he was perfectly groomed, and in his hand he held a cane with a silver handle.

In front of the stable Aimée and Manon were very busy brushing the hooves of the she-ass who waited peacefully under her pack loaded with two boxes pierced by small round holes. Ugolin was on his way back from the hills dragging a long dead branch, with the handle of a big basket full of snails hanging from his arms.

He left the path on the hillside and came down toward the farm.

"Greetings!" said the hunchback. "As you see, I'm going to Aubagne. Is there anything you'd like me to get you?"

"For the moment I don't need anything, but thanks all the same. Are you going to look for more seeds?"

"Better than that! I'm going to fetch my breeders! That's why I want to ask you to do something for me. Since I'll be away all day, I'd be grateful if you'd call on my wife and make sure all's well."

"Count on me!" said Ugolin. "I'll come by about eleven o'clock, and I'll come back this evening. I'd be interested to see your first rabbits!"

"Well then, until this evening!"

He went off, followed by the she-ass, and the pine wood was astonished to see a bowler hat go by.

Ugolin returned before noon, smiling and obliging, and asked the fair Aimée if she needed anything. She asked him to split a knotted log that she could not get to the end of; he took the axe and split a dozen and carefully arranged them on the woodpile.

He came back about six o'clock, at the same moment that the black bowler reappeared behind the she-ass, above the arch of a big sack of bran that leaned against the two boxes suspended from the pack.

They carried the load into the shed and put it down in front of the rabbit cages, which were already well supplied with greens. Under the eyes of his family the breeder delicately loosened the cover of a box with the help of scissors, raised it, and brought out three red rabbits, about as big as large rats, one after the other.

"You understand," he said, "I took very young females who have not yet been pregnant. If you want to create a new breed, that's the first condition."

These virgins went into the same cage without any difficulty and disappeared at once under the edible greens.

"And now, the male! Manon, go and close the door, because the animal is surprisingly vigorous, and he could get away from us."

Ugolin smiled.

"Don't worry," he said, "he won't escape from me! Undo the ropes and lift the lid, just a little . . ."

But as soon as he plunged his hand into the narrow opening, the box was shaken by sudden shocks, mingled with a violent scratching of claws. Ugolin seemed astonished, and cried:

"O Holy Mother of God! Is it a hare?"

"No," said the hunchback, smiling. "No. It's a cross between the Flemish Giant and the Ram of Charentes . . ."

He cast an inexplicable wink at his wife, talking all the time.

Ugolin reached in up to the elbow, and the invisible struggle became so furious that little Manon recoiled.

"There it is!" said Ugolin suddenly. "I've got the hind legs! Let go the lid!"

And then he pulled a reddish brown animal from the box. The animal was not yet finished; with its head down, it shortened and extended itself with such violent jolts that Ugolin's arms shuddered. Manon jumped backward, and Aimée's mouth was round with amazement. Ugolin lifted it to the level of his eyes, and cried:

"But what is it? It's got the hair of a dog, the feet of a hare, and the ears of a donkey! I've never seen the like of it!"

The hunchback's eyes shone with joy and pride; his wife hung on his arms, struck with wonder at the strangeness of the animal.

"And where did you find this?"

Jean Cadoret seemed to hesitate a moment, and replied:

"From one of my friends."

"Did it cost you a lot?"

"Oh yes. A great deal."

"It's a curiosity," said Ugolin. "But its defect is that it's very thin. It looks like a hairy skeleton . . . With a beast like that there's nothing to eat, except maybe the ears!"

"It's a breeder," said the hunchback. "It's not very young anymore, but it's still strong, as you saw! Put it in its cage—the one with a padlock!"

The operation was successful, and the male immediately calmed down and started eating; he put his two hind legs on an acacia branch and pulled off the leaves with jerky movements of his head.

"He eats like a dog," said Ugolin. "And he's got a wicked look! I bet a bit of meat wouldn't frighten him!"

"Perhaps you're exaggerating a bit," said Aimée.

"Yes, I'm exaggerating, but there's some truth in it. In any case, don't put the little rabbits with him, because I guarantee that tomorrow morning there'd be nothing left but the bones!"

After a drink of white wine he left reassured.

The choice of this gangling skeletal male seemed to him an irreparable folly.

"He's nuts," he told the Papet. "Imagine the phantom of a dead hare with the temper of a hundred years!"

"What breed?"

He tried to describe it, but succeeded only after a crisis of mad laughter that frightened the deaf-mute who thought he was dying.

That night before going to bed Jean Cadoret went to sit on his wife's bed.

"Aimée, I've got a secret to tell you."

"Oh, that's nice!" she said. "I adore secrets. Is it about Ugolin?"

"No, about the rabbit. The male."

"It's not a rabbit, I doubt that! Oh, I had a good look at its eyes! And besides, he'll never fit in a casserole! Tell me quickly what it is!"

"It's a rabbit, but not an ordinary rabbit!"

He whispered:

"It's a rabbit from Australia!"

"Is he going to climb trees?"

"Perhaps he's capable of it, but I don't want to find out. This one will stay captive. But the cross with the European rabbits promises very fine litters."

"You should tell that to Ugolin. It's sure to interest him!"

"I've told you it's a secret. Nobody must know it . . . It's against the law to introduce these Australians into France!"

"But who sold it to you?"

"A breeder, who bought it from a smuggler . . . He had created a breed and then wanted to get rid of this animal because its presence in his place could be very expensive. He sold it to me for a hundred francs. Here we're not risking much. And besides, I plan to sacrifice it as soon as we've got the stock of the new breed, the prodigious breed that all the breeders of France will one day call the breed of Les Romarins."

It was a fortnight before a little hope reanimated poor Ugolin. After several torrid days he saw the caravan passing by loaded with cans—the cistern was empty, and the hunchback was worried . . . After they had gone by, Ugolin ran to Les Romarins. The leaves of the tomatoes had started to crumple, those of the corn were stiff, those of the pumpkins were hanging soft as rags, and the sainfoin in the park had started to yellow . . .

He picked some leaves and took them to the Papet, who rolled them in a ball, smelled them, and chewed them.

"Galinette," he said, "if we have some more fine days they won't be able to save the corn and the vegetable garden and the sainfoin with their cans . . ."

To their great satisfaction the heat continued at its finest, and the caravan went by four times a day . . . The tomatoes bowed their heads, and the corn turned pale; everything dried out more and more rapidly, and Monsieur Jean confided his worries to Ugolin, who was falsely touched.

"I ask myself," he told him, "if I shouldn't sacrifice half my vegetables, and some of the sainfoin."

"That would be a great pity," said Ugolin, ". . . why not try to hold out for three or four more days? In the end the rain will come . . ."

The hunchback took this advice, and two days later the pair of accomplices thought the game was won. But that night as the Papet was sleeping peacefully he was awakened by the pain in his hip that never deceived him. He got up hastily and ran to the window quite naked and pushed open the shutters. In the dull light of dawn, he saw a pearly white curtain approaching . . . He licked his forefinger and raised it to the sky; a breeze from the sea came through the thickness of the downpour, the first drops of a rainstorm rang on the tiles of the old house and stuck to the boar's hairs that covered his chest.

"It won't last," he said. "Just enough for my vineyard, but not enough for the vegetables or the meadow. Anyhow, it's too late; his business is already done for."

At the same moment Ugolin was in his nightshirt on the doorstep of his house; he saw the storm ripping leaves from the mulberry tree and started talking to himself.

"Ugolin, what do you say now?"

"I say it could be a disaster . . . It must come from Baptistine's prayer. If it rains like that all day there'll be enough to bring the dead back to life . . ."

During this time Jean Cadoret was floundering about in the mud in spouting espadrilles, with a lantern in hand under a postman's hood, building little dams to direct the streams of rain onto his crops. His wife and daughter helped him at this game, turbaned with dishcloths, and Manon laughed convulsively when the rainwater ran down her back under her dress.

About eight o'clock the storm subsided, but a dense and heavy rain continued to feed the little streams that coiled about in grooves and furrows. They had to disconnect the hose that carried water from the roof to the cistern because it ran over into the kitchen.

In three weeks there were three nightly falls of rain. And so the four Asiatic pumpkins climbed the trellis and mixed their lighter green with the vines. The sainfoin and the clover abounded to form a little meadow, a little humped in places as the Papet had foreseen, but dense and thick and dark green . . . The triumph was the vegetable garden; the carrots were pushed up by their own vigor and backed out of the earth, and the tomatoes, which had overtaken their props, let their green summits fall and float in the evening wind.

Ugolin, discouraged by this triumph, made his report to the Papet, who mounted up to his lookout, pensive and peevish. From afar he saw the huge chick-peas, the tunnel of pumpkins, the bushy tomatoes.

He came back fairly content.

"All that," he said, "is gone in foliage that gives nothing but shade. If he dried those plants in the sun he could stuff mattresses with them, or they could do as a litter for his donkey; and as for the tomatoes, he won't gather a kilo!"

Nevertheless, a dismayed Ugolin came three days later to tell him that one could see enormous fruits glowing across this barely penetrable thicket . . . and the new potatoes were three weeks ahead of Ugolin's, whose land was exhausted by a century of harvests . . . Finally, the chick-peas, although sown out of season, revealed themselves as royal as those that were the glory of Cabridan.

Nearly every morning Monsieur Jean descended to Ruissatel with the donkey loaded with tomatoes and brought back provisions and a little money.

He often offered a basketful of vegetables in gratitude to Ugolin, who took them to the Papet's house. The first evening, the deaf-mute clasped her hands before the fleshy tomatoes, the tender blond chick-peas, the smooth potatoes with their fragile skins; she uttered squeaks of admiration and congratulated Ugolin on such fine success with signs and little barks.

Behind their fixed smiles the two men felt a painful peasant jealousy boil in their hearts, and the Papet brutally sent her back to the kitchen, quite astonished.

Ugolin was sombre; he did not dare admit that the amateur criticized the peasant methods more and more freely and gave advice with an authority that seemed justified by his success.

CHAPTER 22

The enclosure of the park advanced more quickly than the Papet had foreseen; the trench was completed in two months; putting up the wire fence took only two weeks, but the construction of the four burrows was not finished until the end of September.

The breeders had produced their first litters, and on a fine October morning all the rabbits were let loose in the park.

Ugolin was invited to this ceremony and was astonished by the size and vitality of the offspring of the old "phantom." They were red like foxes and jumped like hares. Their mothers browsed peacefully on the clover and sainfoin, but the father, who had been the last to be released, went to the middle of the park. He sat on his bottom, cocked his long ears, and slowly grimaced with his pendulous lips; then suddenly he hurled himself against the fence, and was bounced back like a ball. At the fourth reverse he gave up and disappeared into a burrow.

"Look!" said Monsieur Jean triumphantly. "The first breeders are in service . . . Now all that's left to see is if the Asiatic pumpkins will live up to my hopes!"

They were already bigger than oranges. There were about twelve hundred of them; they reproduced on wire mesh attached to the trellis, which was shored up with a number of supplementary posts in anticipation of their heavy maturity: but how to judge their ripeness? The hardness of the rind made testing impossible . . .

It was Ugolin who solved the problem.

"They'll be ripe when they don't grow anymore!" he said.

At the end of November they reached the size of watermelons; Monsieur

Jean decided to sacrifice one without waiting any longer. This called for another ceremony, at which Ugolin presided.

It took a pruning shears to cut the stalk; then the exotic gourd was divided into two hemispheres with a serrated knife that had been carefully cleaned with sand.

A filamentous flesh, white as milk, surrounded a ring of brilliant black seeds. Ugolin cut a slice, and everyone wanted to taste it.

"That's not the taste of pumpkin," said Ugolin.

Monsieur Jean reflected a moment.

"It's like watermelon without sugar . . . It's fresh. A light perfume, indefinable . . . But delicious!"

"We should see whether the rabbits like it," said Ugolin, "and if it gives them the runs."

The experiment was done at once; they prepared a paste by mixing bran with the white flesh. The rabbits regaled themselves on it without any bad effects.

Aimée then made fritters from a recipe in the booklet; they were a great success. Ugolin admitted that the strange gourd had great qualities and declared that he was going to plant it himself.

"So much for the second step!" said Monsieur Jean. "We're on the right road!"

"You have succeeded!"

"Not yet! I'm still a long way from that! But there's no doubt about it, we're off to a good start!"

"The start, the start," said the Papet. "It's easy to start . . . But afterward, you've got to finish!"

But his nephew was pessimistic. The conclusion he drew from these successes was that the hunchback was protected.

"Papet," he said, "there's never been so much rain in the summer . . . I think the Good Lord gave him the rain to take the place of that spring we buried alive . . ."

"Fool, fool, fool," said the Papet.

"Secondly, they don't miss the town at all; on the contrary! They've never been so happy. He kills himself working, and he gets fat. His wife sings like a nightingale, the little one has grown the width of a hand. She has beautiful big calves. She eats all day, she dances, she swings on the swing . . . Go on! he's no idiot . . . It's true he takes you in a bit, and you can't always understand what he says; but his vegetable garden, it's succeeded, his rabbit park, he's made it; his carnival rabbit has produced superb little ones, and his wooden pumpkins aren't imagination: with four plants he's going to pick two hundred kilos, and they're as good for people as they are for animals. In the beginning I laughed all right; but now I'm afraid, and I think he'll never leave!"

"But no, no!" said the Papet. "All that, it won't last! He's succeeded with four plants because he could water them; but if he wanted to plant five hundred, half of them would die in July and the rest would produce pumpkins no bigger than almonds!

"Second, if he succeeds in raising fifty rabbits, I put ten of them down to disease, seven or eight to the buzzards, the same for the weasels, and at the first drought there'll be no more grass on the hillside, and he'll have to buy food for the ones that are left, and he'll be selling rabbits that cost him three francs for a hundred sous; and when the sous end, he'll go."

CHAPTER 24

One evening when the little girl was sleeping Jean Cadoret went to sit on his wife's bed.

"Aimée, I've done my accounts. Of the 13,682 francs inheritance there's not much left because I've risked everything on the enterprise that should make us rich; but I can tell you today that I have certainly won back part of it. All our expenses have been paid, and the most difficult part is done. I'll put the rest of our money in your hands—1123 francs. This amount will be enough for us to live on for a whole year, even if we had no other resources. Now, we don't pay rent, we don't need expensive clothes, we've got plenty of vegetables, and in three months I hope to start selling the rabbits . . ."

"And besides," she said, "we could sell my necklace if necessary. I've always been told that it's worth at least ten thousand francs."

"Sell it? Never!" he cried. "Your necklace is a family jewel, and it should stay in the family. I'd rather walk barefoot! I refuse to tolerate such sacrilege. Besides, there's no need: while our situation isn't brilliant, it is perfectly healthy, and I promise you that in a year our projects will be under way . . . Let me explain . . ."

"My dear husband," said Aimée, "I don't need any explanations to know that at your side we aren't risking anything. If you'd told me that we only had a sou left, I'd have believed you, of course, but it would have made me laugh. But I must ask you one thing—the tiring work is done, you have far fewer worries, and it's beginning to get cold at night. So it seems to me that it would be quite natural that you should come and sleep close to me."

She blushed suddenly and hid her face under the sheet; but it wasn't necessary, because her husband had blown out the candle.

The autumn was peaceful and pleasant.

The gourds were picked and lined up on shelves put up in the kitchen because of the rats in the shed. The farmer sawed up three of them every morning for the soup and the rabbit food, and washed the black seeds before putting them in a glass bottle in the cupboard . . . Then the family left for the hill to get the grass.

The father carried a big roll of jute sacking on his shoulder, and in the pockets of the she-donkey's pack there were several empty bags, a scythe, a sickle, and the lunch.

The goats formed the advance guard, followed by the cries and stones Manon threw at them, and all along the rocky escarpment she listened for the echoes of bursts of laughter and the little tunes on the mouth organ.

The she-ass followed, stopping at thistles from time to time; then, lightly propelled by her master's stick, she would set off again nonchalantly, her mouth bristling with flowers.

During the first days it was not necessary to go very far; but little by little they had to climb up to the distant vallons of the high plateaux, where the late wild grasses were still feebly green.

There they would meet Baptistine guarding her little flock and picking medicinal plants. She would help them fill their sacks. About half past eight they would lunch with great appetite, sitting in a circle at the foot of a rock, and then go down the long slopes again.

The sacks, swollen with grass, were tied on the she-ass in a great dome that swayed at every step; and nothing could be seen of Jean Cadoret but his legs, as he moved off under a veritable haystack, with songs emerging from it.

In December the olives were picked. The old trees, rid of their suckers and dead branches—but pruned a little haphazardly by the goats—had responded to care so long forgotten, and yielded thirty-five liters of oil, for the honest miller of Bramafan had been so moved by the kindness, and the hunch, of Monsieur Jean that he did not cheat more than ten percent.

The vegetable garden continued to prosper; the well-nourished rabbits, lacking neither air nor sun, multiplied—not at an Australian pace, but the first litters provided forty, the second eighteen, and the third about thirty.

The breeder organized a pleasant chase in the rabbit park every week. While the ever-hungry rabbits were gathered around a big pile of grass brought down from the hills, he closed the entry to the burrows; then the family, dancing, shouting, and applauding, tried to hem those individuals that had just reached stewing age into a corner.

They were isolated in the cages for eight days, where they were fed on choice herbs and a rich paste of pumpkin and bran.

Every Saturday at daybreak the breeder left for Aubagne. The she-ass had on her sides two flat wooden boxes containing five or six fine-looking rabbits, and sometimes she carried a hamper of vegetables as well. He followed her, switch in hand, in his grey jacket, striped trousers, and buttoned boots. He was highly pleased with himself, and under his arm he held a little plank on which he had painted in fine blue letters "Product of Les Romarins."

His bowler hat soon became known in the market, and sometimes the peasants burst out laughing on seeing him standing among his cages under his notice board attached to the trunk of a plane tree. His neighbor, a large saleswoman, noticed that he was incapable of resisting the haggling of the buyers, and offered to sell his produce for him, an offer that he thankfully accepted. During this time he would go to listen to mass at seven o'clock, then he would buy a comic paper for Manon and read it himself until the end of the sale, leaning against the plane tree. Then, richer by fifteen, perhaps twenty francs, he would return toward the hills astride the she-ass, the empty cages under his arms and his buttoned boots hanging comically from the ends of his striped trousers.

The family thus lived in some comfort, and the woman did not have a single care.

Aimée, always carefully dressed, with her hair well arranged, attended to the household work like a lady who happened to be taking her maid's place. The good air had improved her looks, and she sang when she woke up in the morning.

Little Manon was approaching her tenth year. She was all golden, with sea blue eyes too big for her face, and hair so thick that her mother could hardly extract the oak leaves, pine needles, or bramble twigs from it without a pair of scissors.

The wind of the hills, the friendship of the trees, and the silence of the lonely places had fashioned her into a little wild animal, as light and lively as a fox. Her great love was Baptistine, whom she admired like somebody from a fairy story, and the Piedmontese adored her. Every morning they watched their goats together on the plateaux of the garigue. Baptistine taught her how to look after animals, the art of setting traps, and the thousand secrets of the hills; at first she did this in incomprehensible French, illustrated with gestures and grimaces; but after some weeks the little girl was able to understand, and then to speak, the rough patois of Piedmont. She would go down to Les Romarins mounted on the galloping she-ass, uttering cries of victory; and in the pouches of the pack she brought wild food: bloodred mushrooms, big pine kernels, spongy morels, snails fed on thyme, and blackbirds perfumed with myrtle, or thrushes gorged on juniper berries.

At first she was a little ashamed when she threw dead birds on the table, and refused to eat them.

One evening her father gravely declared, while sliding a row of lard-covered ortolans from a skewer:

"One always gets soft about the misfortunes of little birds, because they fly and go tweet-tweet. But remember they are ferocious animals that massacre minute living creatures in order to eat them . . .

"And as for old maids who weep for innocent blackbirds or kind finches, I've noticed they never weep when they see a lamb cutlet; even when they see them on burning charcoal, it's the cutlet that does the weeping!"

And he started to chew a piece of toast, golden with the sizzling grease of fat ortolans. She took one in her turn, and her tender scruples faded away.

The fare was not always so succulent, but her father refused to notice that.

"Mother Nature," he said, "always nourishes her children. I've never had so much pleasure eating. Our temporary poverty has forced us for some time to eat nothing but the produce of the season, and especially the wild produce that comes from the earth of the Good Lord with no fertilizer other than natural humus. What's more, it's fortunate that I've given up my three daily cups of coffee. For one thing, I appreciate the Sunday mocha so much the more, for another I sleep much better, and lastly the sage tea that gives me such pleasure when I get up has very great medicinal virtues . . . I owe my perfect health to this new regime.

"As for town air, it's the cause of the most terrible diseases. When I think of those unfortunates who live piled up one on the other, surrounded by infernal noise, and go and sit in foul-smelling offices every morning, and consider themselves the better people, well, I sneer!"

And he sneered, and Manon burst out laughing.

She did not talk much in the house; she preferred to listen to her father, whom she admired in everything, and for whom she cherished a special tenderness because of his infirmity. At the table, she looked after his glass and his plate. It was for him that she chose the biggest thrush, the finest figs, the best mushrooms, and when he came back from the fields, she knelt before him to unlace his heavy peasant boots.

Her great joy was the rainy days in winter, because then the family hardly left the house. In front of the hearth, where the faggots of broom crackled under resinous logs, he told her the history of France, read poems, or played Molière's comedies, changing his voice for each character. Then, between lessons they gave concerts, since he had bought her a little mouth organ at Aubagne.

Manon played "Magali," or "Misé Babet," and her father embroidered marvellous variations around the theme of the song.

Giuseppe the woodsman often left to work for a week in the ravines of the Pilon du Roi, or on the slopes of the Baou de Bertagno. Then Baptistine would come, followed by her goats and her black dog. She brought a hamper of vegetables, or two jugs of water from the spring, or a long resinous log. It was, she said, to pay her rent. Monsieur Jean accepted these presents with hearty thanks because a refusal would break her heart, and she spent the day with them. With Manon acting as interpreter, she taught Aimée the art of making rough cheeses with the curdled blue milk of the garigues, pressed in rush strainers the way Virgil's goatherds did it; or little round cheeses encrusted with savory herbs, or onion tarts, or basil soup.

At noon she lunched with the family, but it was always impossible to make her sit at the table. She ate sitting at the corner of the hearth, her plate on her knees, from time to time bursting into unexpected laughter, or a fervent benediction. In the evening she made her adieus. Then Monsieur Jean barred her passage, locked the door with the key, and put the key in his pocket. After dinner he took the mouth organ and made her sing old Piedmontese songs, and Aimée sang duets with her, and Manon danced barefoot on the table. In the solitary farmhouse of the hills there was a great joy in life, much tenderness, and much hope.

Ugolin often came to visit his neighbor and made his report to the Papet.

"Papet, I'm afraid . . . His business is going quite well . . . And that life, it doesn't displease him . . . It shows his grandfather was a peasant . . . If he's satisfied with about forty rabbits, and about fifty pumpkin plants, I'm sure he could easily live there for twenty years . . ."

"Patience, patience. Courage is fine. But this is a man who reads books and has ambition . . . That can take you really far, Galinette, and that's what will sink him."

CHAPTER 26

One evening after dinner Jean Cadoret said to his wife:

"Tomorrow's Sunday. We must dress nicely because we're all three going to mass at Les Bastides to thank the Lord for what He's done for us."

"After what our friend told us about those people, I would prefer to go to the other village, to Ruissatel."

"Definitely not! We mustn't give the impression we're hiding ourselves. I don't owe anything to anybody, I'm not afraid of anybody, and I've decided to show them."

They dressed "nicely." Aimée, under a feathered hat, was squeezed into a canary yellow tailored suit; with a blue thistle boutonniere, a gilded bag in her hand, and swaying a little on Louis XV heels of astonishing height, she was visible from two hundred meters.

Little Manon looked really pretty, and pleased with herself to be so. Her shining blonde curls emerged from a broad-brimmed blue sun hat; her patent leather pumps, her taut white socks, her pink satin dress, and above all a sky blue sash tied around her waist with a bow at the back, gave an impression of luxury and elegance. As for her father, lightly strangled by a collar that hid his Adam's apple, he wore a grey jacket, a gold-colored waistcoat, a mouse grey bowler hat, pearl grey gloves, and he elegantly wielded a silver-handled black cane.

When Ugolin saw them pass he would not have recognized them except for their number. He approached them, amazed.

"You're going down to town?"

"No. We're going to mass in the village."

Ugolin did not know how to reply and said foolishly:

"It's true it's Sunday! . . . I never know what day it is! So! Good mass and good return . . ."

He watched them go down the path.

"Hang it! It's unbelievable that people like that don't live in town. If he weren't a hunchback you'd think he was the prefect . . . It's a good thing for me he's disguised himself as a stranger; nobody will talk to him."

Their arrival at the town square was quite an event. Several peasants who did not know of their existence asked the others who these people were. The Papet replied to Médéric de Barbaraou:

"He's a gentleman from town who's come to be a peasant."

"That's not possible!" said Médéric. "You must mean he's going to take on workers?"

"Not at all," said the Papet. "He wants to be a peasant like you and me. Except that he puts on gloves for digging!"

Médéric looked fixedly at the hunchback and burst out laughing.

Jean Cadoret went red with anger and humiliation because he thought the other was laughing at his hump; clenching his teeth, he ran a disdainful eye around him. As the newcomers made the turn of the square they encountered nothing but amused smiles. The women commented on Aimée's toilette, her watch-chain, her brooch, her rings . . . All through the mass people looked at them. M. the curé was really very old; cataract obliged him to wear reading glasses, and false teeth frequently impeded his elocution. He did not notice the presence of his new parishioners. They were sitting in the back row (because the hunchback preferred people to see his face), but faces were turned toward them continuously; he thought he read mockery in them and responded with defiant stares . . .

On leaving, Aimée stopped at the butcher, who stayed open on Sundays because it was his big day for sales. Claudius served them amiably. The Papet watched the family from a distance and noted with pleasure that he did not engage them in conversation because the customers were arriving in crowds and he had a lot to do.

"Anyhow," he thought, "Claudius has spent a long time in town . . . The hills hardly interest him, and he's sure to know nothing about the spring."

They went next to the baker's, where the peasants stood aside to let them through with whispers that Jean took to be hostile, and the baker's wife weighed the bread in perfect silence. Finally, they passed by the area where the stalwart souls who did not go to mass were finishing a game of *boules*.

He passed in front of them with great dignity, affecting not to see anyone.

"It's Ugolin's neighbor," said Pamphile.

Philoxène declared:

"He hasn't got a low opinion of himself."

The family turned their backs on them and took the path that went down to the vallon by a fairly steep slope. Cabridan chose just this moment to shoot at Pamphile's ball, which had just touched the target.

He studied it for a long time, made three jumps, and missed it as usual; but his own ball, bouncing off the round head of a buried rock, took flight over the holm oak on the side of the path, plunged down the vallon, and hit the back of the hunchback walking in the rear. Mad with rage, Jean picked up the dangerous projectile and threw it with all his strength toward the players, who could not see him. Fortunately Cabridan, who had come running to look for his property, had the presence of mind to jump aside, because the ball passed at the height of his head before landing up at the top, on the foot of Bernard the mason. Bernard, with his ankle in both hands, danced on his other foot, while Cabridan shouted in Provençal:

"So, not enough to be a hunchback, do you have to be a madman as well?"

Jean Cadoret did not deign to reply to these insults, which his family did not understand. They continued down the path, but he turned round from time to time, as if he feared the arrival of another projectile.

"My mother was right," he said. "They're brutes, savages, and I'm ashamed to be vaguely related to them."

At the same moment Philoxène was lecturing the King of the Chick-Pea.

"You, I've never seen you hit a ball, and you are foolish enough to shoot. If you had hit that man on the head, you could have killed him outright."

"And the little one?" said Pamphile. "If you had killed the little one?"

"But I didn't hit anyone!" cried Cabridan.

"And I tell you that he got the ball on his hump!" cried the blacksmith. "I was on the side of the path. I saw it!"

"That can't have done him any harm!" retorted the Papet. "Might even straighten him out!"

This flash of wit was a great success.

"In any case," replied Cabridan, "everybody knows I didn't do it on purpose. Besides, he's not dead, because he's gone."

Arriving at the Massacan field, they found Ugolin watering two rows of onions. The hunchback recounted the drama.

Aimée was deeply moved and declared:

"They wanted to kill my husband!"

"I don't think so, Madame Aimée . . . They're a little wild, you know, but not to that extent . . . I think it was an accident. It was just something that happened."

"Would you swear to that?" cried Monsieur Jean.

"Swear it? No. Obviously I can't swear to it, because I didn't see it. But I believe it was an accident. Probably."

In the spring the great works were started again, but Ugolin did not renew the offer of his labor. He excused himself, saying that the owner of the mule had made him dig up some land on the other side of the village to plant a little vineyard; he added that the field at Les Romarins did not need much work because it had been done the previous year and the earth had had a good rest. Monsieur Jean did not see him again for three weeks.

All cheered up by the winter, he took the pick and marked out the furrows.

In spite of the sale of the rabbits he had to cut into his savings to buy bran. He had no more than 720 francs left . . . He resolved to devote half of it to buying and transporting four cartloads of manure through the intermediary of the fat saleslady in Aubagne, whose son was a guard corporal at the stable of the barracks of the hussars. Digging in this precious fertilizer cost him three days' work; then one fine morning he planted the seeds of the Asiatic pumpkin.

"At a hundred kilos a plant," he said, " we can expect twenty to twenty-five tons of pumpkins; according to my principle of 'safety first,' I won't count on more than half of that, which will be quite enough, because the book talks of eight tons of mash a year. Now we'll move on to corn."

He planted ten kilos of it in the upper field, saying: "One seed always gives an ear of four hundred to four hundred and fifty seeds, and sometimes two ears. Theoretically one can count on an average yield of four hundred times the sowing. I'll admit three hundred times, which is prudent. So we'll have at least three tons of corn. The most difficult thing obviously will be to find and transport fifty or sixty kilos of greens a day. But the problem won't arise until the farming reaches its maximum, that's to say in eighteen months. By then

we'll be earning enough money to assure ourselves of the services of some Piedmontese, perhaps even our friend Giuseppe, who's going to be a precious assistant for us."

"He won't want that," said Manon. "He's too proud. He likes his great axe.
He says grass is women's work. But next year I'll be twelve years old. So I and
Baptistine and the she-ass, we'll be able to do it very well. And if you buy an-
other she-ass, we'll fill the shed for you."

The April rains greatly exceeded the promises of the statistics; the wind from
the sea brought long, conveniently spaced nocturnal rainfalls, the seeds grew
in a few days, and the young plants greened.

Ugolin said to the Papet one evening:

"These rains in the night are a blessing. The hunchback's pumpkins have
started and the corn is superb. Things have started well for him."

"Too well," said the Papet. "Nine days of rain in April—that's not good:

> If it rains for Saint Paterne
> Summer will dry your cistern."

May was just as generous. The cistern was always full, and every evening fine
clouds rose from the sea. Ugolin, in spite of the vigor of his own crops, was no
longer master of his tics, and he blinked like an owl at midnight.

"Galinette," said the Papet, "don't let yourself be deluded:

> If it rains on the Ascension
> All your work will go to perdition."

In June the nocturnal rains continued, and under the bright sun of the long
days dark green branches thrust themselves out on all sides with magical rapidity, and covered themselves with flowers . . . Then, toward the beginning
of July, the little pumpkins came up from the bursting flowers . . . There were
hundreds of them, swelling under the eyes of the family; the corn plants, as
high as a man, shook their white tufts, and the twilight breeze whispered in
the long leaves . . .

The rain had made the hills fertile, and wild plants, high and thickset as
corn, invaded the vallons. The well-fed rabbits multiplied in six weeks and
whole families could be seen coming out of the burrows. The breeder went to
look for Ugolin to show him the spectacle; the man of carnations was dismayed,
and unable to hide his agitation.

"What's bothering you?" asked Aimée.

He hesitated, blinked three times, and said with an effort:

"All this is magnificent, and that's why I'm a little bothered, because summer hasn't yet started this year . . ."

"You're a real pessimist, my dear neighbor," cried Monsieur Jean. "It's the third of July, the cistern is overflowing, and in a month, at most, all danger will be past, because we can count on the August storms!"

"That's true," said Ugolin. "That's true. It's because I easily worry too much on your account that I see everything black! It would be unfortunate if such a glowing success should founder at the last moment!"

"After all," he said to the Papet, "the Good Lord is against us. The damned hunchback has all the water he wants; that water has mildewed my chick-peas, and your vineyard has got the rot in a big way. His pumpkins have swollen as if the angel Bouffareou had blown inside them . . . He's going to make a fortune and he's never going to leave!"

"Don't worry," said the Papet. "He's had the luck of a wet spring, but that's the sign of a fiery summer. I tell you, at the end of July all those plants will be as yellow as ripe corn, and the corn leaves will sing like cicadas . . .

> If it rains in June,
> You will chew your fist soon."

The old peasant and his wise saws were right.

It was on the fifth of July that the delayed summer set in with brutal suddenness. The cicadas, which had been timid until then, started chirping frantically in the olive trees, and an enormous sun mounted straight up the zenith like a balloon of fire.

At noon the pine trees cast round shades at their feet. The earth began to give off transparent bluish wreaths of smoke, and the vegetation immediately grew excited. The field of corn grew several centimeters every night, the pumpkins attached themselves to the trunks of the olive trees as if they were going to climb up them. Their fruits were already bigger than small melons.

"Look at that," explained the planter, "the secret of tropical vegetation; after the insistent and penetrating rain, a big burst of sunshine stimulates the branches and leaves, thus accelerating the metabolism. This marvellous system of alternation has set in this summer, and it's clear that Providence has decided to reward us for our efforts."

But after the third day of sunshine he noticed that the leaves were starting to lose their brightness; some of them hung backward, as if fatigued. It was high time to use the cistern.

That evening in front of Ugolin, who had come for news, he laid out his plan.

"The cistern is full to the brim. It contains a dozen cubic meters. I'll need three for watering, and I'll have to water every other day. So the cistern assures me eight days of peace."

"I agree," said Ugolin, "but it may not rain in eight days' time."

"Foreseen!" said Monsieur Jean. "That's why, starting tomorrow, we're going to start trips to Le Plantier. A hundred liters a trip, four trips a day. That's to say, in eight days we'll have put thirty-two hundred liters in the cistern, which gives us two more days, that is ten days in all."

"Ten days, that's fine," said Ugolin, "but at this time of year you never know."

"You're right. I've also foreseen the worst. If in ten days the sky continues to betray me, I'll sacrifice part of the harvest, and I'll hire your mule. It can certainly carry fifty-liter tanks. So if we made five trips a day we could provide a cubic meter a day for the cistern, which would be enough to wait for the next rain."

"You've thought of everything," said Ugolin.

"I hope," said Monsieur Jean, "that it won't come to that."

The next day after dawn he had a pleasant surprise: in the east the sky seemed to be thick. He decided to postpone the departure for the spring and work in the vegetable garden. But toward eight o'clock the sun pierced the clouds and soon dispersed them to the four corners of the sky. And the cicadas chirped and a sparkling day got under way.

They made three trips to the spring, that is, six hours of walking on a path of uneven rocks or rolling pebbles.

On the last trip, toward seven in the evening, he saw with pride that the carefully marked water level in the cistern had gone up by fifteen centimeters.

Meanwhile, Manon slept at the table; his wife laughingly complained of being unable to get up without help when she bent down in front of the hearth;

and he himself felt little flashes of pain in the nape of his neck. He declared that it was good healthy fatigue. Nevertheless he left alone after dawn behind the she-ass, carrying a pick, a fairly large S-shaped iron hook, two meters of strong cord, and a billhook . . .

All along the path from the spring he cut to ground level all the prickly branches that caught at him on the way, pushed aside the rolling stones, broke up the projecting rocks they stumbled on, and filled in a number of holes.

In addition he arranged a halfway halt under a shady pine tree. After having removed the scrub at the foot of the tree, he set up seats in the form of little dolmens. Finally he hung the iron S on a low branch; thus he could hang the heavy demijohn by its reed handle, detach the strap that held it to his forehead, sit for a moment in the shade, and then put it back on its shelf without help and without any effort.

The path was long; on the way back from this journey he did not bring back more than eighty liters of water, but he was able to announce to his family that the track had become a "boulevard," and thanks to the resting place he had set up, the transport of the precious liquid was going to be no more than a healthy promenade.

Meanwhile the summer burnt continuously, pitilessly, and despite four daily journeys the cistern lowered rapidly . . . The grass on the hills was yellow, there was nothing more left for feeding his rabbits than about twenty pumpkins, a little barley, and very little money. So he left one morning before daybreak to take a dozen rabbits to the saleslady and came back toward eight with a bag of barley and some bottles of wine. The women were returning from the spring. He took off his jacket and put on his espadrilles, and left with them. Manon sheltered under a broad-brimmed straw hat, Aimée carried a pink sunshade with a gilded handle.

These trips for water lasted ten days; when fatigue overtook them he comforted himself with big glasses of wine, and he always took a bottle of it under the cans on the she-ass's pack.

In the evening at the table he reread the statistics in a loud voice, as if to force the skies to obey them, and every night he thought he could hear the sound of rain. He would dash to the window and push back the shutters; the stars shone, cruelly—it had not rained except in his dream . . .

On the eighth day he saw that despite all their efforts the cistern contained no more than one watering . . . So when the women had gone to bed, he went off with the she-ass, lantern in hand.

He came back with Giuseppe, who had sacrificed two hours of his precious sleep on the night after a woodsman's hard day.

They brought back a hundred and twenty liters of water.

They found little Manon in her nightgown. She had heard her father going and was waiting seated on the doorstep, looking at the flying sparks of the fireflies. Giuseppe went to examine the crops by the light of the moon. He pulled up the leaves and crushed them between his palms.

"Our Master," he said, "they're suffering . . . Half of them will have to be sacrificed, because if it doesn't rain in four days, you're going to lose everything."

"But it has to rain!" cried the hunchback.

"Not tomorrow," said the woodsman. "Look at the moon!"

"I've already got half a meter of water in the cistern. With five trips a day I've got six before me! It will rain, because the rain is two weeks late!"

"I know, I know, but it's not a good season. It's gone badly . . . You'll have to abandon half of the plants, because I can't help you!"

He lowered his eyes and added:

"Tomorrow I have to go with five other woodsmen. We have signed a contract with an entrepreneur, and I'm in charge of the team. It's in the Var, near Le Muy. They're waiting for me tomorrow morning at the railway station at Aubagne. It's a four-week job. So I'll be down there up to the twenty-fifth of August, but on the twenty-sixth I'll come. In the meantime you must lose half, otherwise you'll lose all!"

"I know, I know, you're right . . ."

"But if the sun continues, I'll come with Enzo and Giacomo on the twenty-sixth, and we'll refill the cistern."

It was a reassuring promise, and he knew it would be kept; but the obstinacy of Providence in refusing him the rain that was due to him had discouraged him. He addressed prayers to Providence appealing more to justice than to kindness, sounding more like final demands, but they evoked no response. Aimée sang no more, and seemed increasingly careworn.

One morning he asked her:

"How much money have we got left?"

"Very little," she said. "About a hundred francs. But we've got some provisions . . ."

"With ten or twelve francs we could hire Ugolin's mule for two or three days.

"I'll go and ask him for it this evening . . . Besides, it's not impossible that he'll lend it to me for nothing . . . With that beast, we'll be saved . . ."

He went again with his shelf on his hump; he talked gaily with his daughter, played the mouth organ, and stopped regularly at the resting place; he attached the demijohn to the S, rubbed the cramps in his calves, and drank a big glass of wine. After four expeditions and an hour of watering, he went to Massacan; he found no one but Délie.

"Ugolin is in the village," she said, "and he won't be back until after dinner, but late . . ."

"That's a nuisance," said the hunchback.

"I can give him a message when I see him."

"Oh well, if you see him, ask him if he could rent his mule to me from tomorrow . . ."

CHAPTER 28

That evening at the table at old Anglade's place his son Josias, who was called the "the senior twin" because he was bigger than his brother, said:

"Oh, father! I think the hunchback from Crespin's gone mad."

"He spoke to you?"

"No, but while I was digging the little vineyard I saw him go by seven or eight times on the track to Le Plantier, with the donkey, his wife, and his little girl, and all of them were carrying cans and jugs . . ."

"The wife had a pink sunshade," said Josias, "and he was carrying a big demijohn on his hump, and that made him look as if he was bending over."

"According to what they say," replied Anglade, "he wants to grow gourds from America, but they're dying because of the drought."

"And why does he go so far for his water? . . . According to what Aunt Fine told me there's some kind of spring near his house."

His father shrugged his shoulders, and replied:

"Aunt Fine was talking about antediluvian times! I used to know that spring too, but it must have got lost."

"It appears," replied Josias, "that César Soubeyran . . ."

Anglade frowned and spoke severely:

"It appears that it doesn't appear at all. César does what he wants, and we do what we want! Bérarde, give us a little more soup. At the table, when one doesn't eat, one talks. And when one talks, one always talks too much!"

At the same moment Ugolin and the Papet were sitting down to the table . . . They had returned from the aperitif at the club, where there had been a long talk about the drought, which had lived up to their worst fears. The water from the fountain assured the harvest in the vegetable gardens, but the crops in the vallons were seriously jeopardized. The Papet said:

"Did you hear what Anglade said?

> If it doesn't rain for Saint Anne,
> There's no hope until Saint Jane."

Saint Anne was today, and Saint Jane will be in three months."

"So," said Ugolin, "my apricots are going to dry up . . ."

"Oh yes! and my vineyard's not going to fill two hogsheads. But we've got one consolation with our little bit of bad luck. The affairs of your neighbor are not going well! This morning, while they were gone, I went on a little tour of his pumpkins. They haven't got enough water, and in spite of his killing himself they'll be dead in a week!"

"He told me he was going to sacrifice half of them."

"That's not a bad idea, but the other half will be lost all the same. He needs at least a thousand liters a day. How much do you think he can carry, with the she-ass, a woman and a half, a parasol, and a hump? Another eight days of sun and he will be finished."

At that moment Délie knocked on the window.

"The hunchbacked gentleman came," she said. "He said to say he wants to rent the mule for tomorrow. There you are! Good night!"

"He's beginning to understand," sneered the Papet.

"He talked to me about that some days ago. If the drought continued he was going to rent the mule from us."

"And what did you say?"

"Nothing."

He hesitated a moment, and added timidly:

"But if he asks me, it will be difficult to refuse."

The astonished old man replied:

"But you can't say yes to him! If you go there with the mule, you'll save him. The mule can carry five hundred liters a day!"

Ugolin looked at him for a moment, then dropped his eyes again.

"Don't say that, because . . ."

He was silent.

The Papet frowned.

"Because what?"

Ugolin batted his eyelids, sniffled, and shrugged his shoulders.

"I don't know how to tell you . . . Things go through my head."

He coughed under the icy gaze of the old man.

"You understand—you told me I should become his friend. I managed it pretty well and succeeded, and it's even lasted nearly two years . . . Only, little by little, on his side too, we've become friends. By calling him Monsieur Jean, by, by drinking white wine . . ."

The astonished Papet glared, and cried:

"What d'you want, imbecile—carnations or friends? What an idiot! It seems to me I can hear your poor mother talking!"

He looked at his nephew grimly and said:

"When you start strangling the cat you have to finish it."

They ate their bacon soup without a word, but with a lot of noise . . . Then the deaf-mute brought four cutlets on polenta.

"So you will agree to go and help him with the mule, and carry a jar on your back?"

"That's not what I wanted to say, not that . . . I wanted to say that if he asks me I would not be surprised if I went. So I would prefer to go away."

"Where?"

"To Attilio's. At the moment I haven't got much to do here. Délie can pick my apricots and you could get Anglade to take them to Aubagne. If I go and spend ten days at Antibes, I could help them. That would please them, and it would do me good with the carnations. I'll choose my cuttings, he'll tell me where I can sell . . . That's important, you understand?"

"It's a good idea. I agree completely. I'll give you some money, and you'll go tomorrow morning. You're right; it would be better for you to get out. Because if it's you who refuses the mule, he might get angry with you, and we'll risk his selling the farm to someone else. Agreed. You'll leave early tomorrow. Agreed."

They ate slowly, and the tall grandfather clock emphasized the silence. Ugolin did not dare raise his eyes again. As he folded his napkin the Papet spoke:

"I know what you're thinking. You're unhappy at the idea that you could save him. But I tell you the opposite. I tell you it's for his good. And you even told me one day—if he has a success this year, even a small one, he'll go on, and next year he'll start again, and that'll be a misfortune all his life, until he dies of work. But if all the plants die standing, he'll understand, and with the money

I'm kindly going to give him to buy his farm, he can go back and set himself up in town. That'll be much better for him. Even if it were not a question of carnations I wouldn't lend him the mule, because if you don't help him, you're helping him. Look, here's fifty francs. Go to bed, and tomorrow morning scram for the station at Aubagne and don't come back!"

"Listen, Papet, I'll go and dress down there and come back and sleep here, because he's capable of coming to see me at four in the morning . . . And so . . ."

"So you're a great trouble to me. Get going, scram and hurry back."

The next morning about seven Monsieur Jean presented himself at Massacan. He knocked at the door in vain, then on the shutters, and went down to Ugolin's fields. He found nobody, but as he started going back to his place he saw Délie arriving from the village. He waited for her.

"Do you know where Ugolin is?"

"His godfather's just told me he's gone!"

"To Aubagne?"

"Yes, to catch the train. He's gone to a friend to help with the harvest . . ."

"When'll he come back?"

"I don't know."

"And the mule? Do you know where it is?"

"The godfather told me he let it to somebody from Les Ombrées until the grape harvest."

"Are there any others in the village?"

"I know four or five," said Délie, "but they're all scratching the fields because of the drought . . . Perhaps I could find one. I'll ask this afternoon, but you know, they don't like letting their animals, and I don't promise anything . . ."

The family took to the path to Le Plantier again with their cans and their jugs and the bottle of wine. They walked all day, on their growing shadows.

On their last return in the evening he watered half the crop. Turning the pump handle all the time with his head buzzing and his feet burning, he resolved to go to Aubagne the next day and take a dozen rabbits to the market. Then he would pawn his wife's necklace at Mont-de-Piété, and buy a mule . . . Thus the remaining crop would be saved, and he could envisage rearing thirty or forty rabbits a month. That would be an excellent beginning. He calculated the weight of the gourds he was going to get, then the number of bags of corn, then the amount of barley he could buy with the resale of the mule in October. No, nothing was lost. Moreover, on the way to the spring he would conserve his strength by riding the powerful beast while Manon rode the she-ass . . . He was smiling at this pleasing image when the fatal gurgling in the hose attached to the pump broke into his reverie . . . The cistern was empty.

At first he was upset, then he shrugged his shoulders. "Doesn't matter," he said, "tomorrow I'll have a mule . . ."

He went out. Manon ran up to him, afraid . . .

"Papa, it's not running at all!"

"I know, I know," he said gaily. "But from tomorrow we can wait for the rain!"

"How?"

"Come! I'll show you at the table."

As he spoke of future rides, Manon clapped her hands and laughed with pleasure; but Aimée's smile was constrained. She asked:

"Does a mule cost a lot?"

"It's certainly much dearer than a she-ass! I'm thinking of finding one at Aubagne between four and five hundred francs . . . This money won't be lost, because at the end of September I'll sell the mule again, and perhaps"—he shook his raised forefinger—"at a profit! But this operation forces me to ask you to make a sacrifice. A momentary sacrifice. I should say a 'separation.' Yes. It concerns your necklace."

Aimée looked uneasy, and Manon, as if terrified by an act of sacrilege, said in a low voice:

"You're going to sell Maman's necklace?"

"But no! I said 'a momentary separation.' What I mean is I'll deposit the jewel at Mont-de-Piété, which is a sort of official bank. It's the government, you understand? There's no risk! And on this security they'll lend me at least two thousand francs: the three emeralds are well worth it. So, I'll buy a very fine mule; in two months I'll sell it again, and certainly at a profit, because it will thrive in the air of the hills; I'll bring back the two thousand francs, and they'll give back the necklace."

"Oh good!" said Manon, reassured. "Since Maman never puts it on, that will hardly deprive her! Isn't that so, Maman?"

"Certainly, my darling . . . But now it's nine o'clock and we've got a lot to do tomorrow morning . . . Let's go to bed!"

She lit the three candles and blew out the lamp while he barred the door, then, each carrying a little flame, they climbed the wooden stairs.

As soon as he sat on his bed she knelt down to undo the laces of his heavy boots.

He was exhausted by the day's walking, but full of hope and new calculations.

"That's what I should have done right away," he said. "It's true one couldn't imagine such a dreadful drought . . . But after all, it's not too late . . ."

She raised her eyes to him, wet with tears. He was surprised.

"Is it so hard for you to be parted from your necklace?"

She replied with a little shrug of her shoulders and lowered her head . . .

"My darling, I understand your attachment to this very fine family jewel, but I repeat, it will not be lost! This loan is indispensable, and to tell the truth it's my last and only hope. The cistern is empty, and if the rain doesn't get here three days from now, my plants will be ruined . . . I didn't tell you that we have some debts so that you wouldn't worry. Yes, I owe three hundred and fifty francs to the miller at Ruissatel, about a hundred francs to the ironmonger at Aubagne, and about the same for two cartloads of manure. If the mule doesn't save the harvest we won't go back to zero, we'll go to less than zero!"

She suddenly burst into tears, hid her face in her hands, and murmured:

"It's there already . . ."

He did not understand at once.

"What are you saying?"

"The necklace . . . I've already taken it to Mont-de-Piété . . ."

"When?"

"Last month."

"But why?"

"Because I didn't have any more money . . . I should have told you . . . But I wanted to spare you the worry . . . You've bought a lot of things . . . books, tools, manure . . ."

Lowering her eyes, she added:

"And then, for some time we've drunk a lot of wine . . . So, I pawned the necklace . . ."

"That may be!" he said. "But shouldn't there be quite a lot left?"

"They didn't lend me more than a hundred francs . . . The emeralds were false . . ."

"False? That's not possible!"

"I showed them to a jeweller . . . He said the same thing at first glance."

He was amazed and indignant.

"A family jewel of such importance! It's unbelievable that in your family . . ."

As for the family, she thought bitterly of the leader of the Argentinian orchestra who had once offered her this "jewel" when she sang Manon and Lakmé at the Opera of Curepipe . . .

She wept at his feet. He raised her tenderly.

"Calm yourself," he said. " . . . Nothing is irreparable . . . Our situation is not as desperate as I told you just now . . . What you did was well done . . . It was I who was wrong not to restrain my expenses, and to let you worry . . . Now go and sleep and don't worry . . . I will think, and I'll certainly find a solution to my problem. You know you can have confidence in me. Come, my darling."

He took her to bed, undressed her, and tucked her in like a child.

He returned to his room, crushed. Although the window was opened wide, the white flame of the candle burned straight up. The stars shone cruelly, a tepid silence immobilized the pines. He closed the shutters on the hostile night, went back to sit on his bed, and slowly rubbed his swollen ankles.

What to do? He resolved to conserve no more than a dozen plants, and a row of corn for the next year's seeds. Perhaps he could pay his debts with the remaining rabbits, or at least part of them? In any case, he felt defeated and ridiculous . . . Perhaps he had better go back to town and get back behind a cashier's window? No, never! Never would he admit his failure before Ugolin, before his wife, before his daughter . . .

He knelt against his bed and prayed for a long time, with a sudden access of piety that was not disinterested and was addressed to Heaven only to ask for help.

Elbows on the blanket and hands joined, he felt the stiffness of the nape of his neck, and the ridiculous weight of his wounded hump, and the ache in his legs from the poison of his fatigue. It was a prayer without words; he heard the heavy beating of his heart, and the rush of his blood in his ears. He slid slowly into sleep, and his pathetic dream began again; he heard the distant roll of thunder, the light tinkle of raindrops on the roof, the hiss of water in the gutter; but he knew well it was a dream, as usual, and refused to wake up; the thunder rumbled nearer, and he saw little Manon fleeing under the heavy rain, pursued by flashes of lightning, calling to him for help . . . He opened his eyes: the lightning illuminated his room, and there she stood on the doorstep in her long white chemise. She stretched her arms toward him and her radiant face shone with tears.

"Papa, listen!"

The torrential storm spluttered on the tiles, a marvellous music mounted the wooden stairs—the rhythmic song of falling water reawakening echoes in the empty vaults of the cistern.

She leaped into his arms and rubbed her tears on his prickly cheek . . . Aimée entered, and they went to the window and leaned their heads under the downpour. The lightning revealed the pine woods across a thousand diamonds . . . He hugged them both to the sound of the rain. Aimée trembled, and the little girl let out wild shouts in a rage of victory and happiness.

At the break of day Jean Cadoret walked about his fields in an ancient hooded cape, barefoot in the beating rain.

He was not alone in this cape. Between two buttons there emerged a big bush of golden hair above the face of his daughter.

The plants were already straightening out their leaves, and they unfolded as one looked at them.

Even those he had abandoned a week ago seemed to take heart again.

"There!" he said. "At the moment when all seems lost, all is saved . . . The cistern is running over, the farm has made a new start, the hills are growing green again. In four days we'll have so much grass we won't know what to do with it, and thanks to the slope of the burrows, the rabbits haven't suffered. Besides, we're at the beginning of August. Not even counting the seven days of rain that the skies still owe us, and which I will pass as irrecoverable debts, the statistics promise us at least four days of rain, which will be plenty to last to autumn. But let's not go to sleep in blind confidence, and let's get ready to face twenty-four days of drought, that is until Giuseppe comes back with his companions who will be here on the twenty-sixth of August. To work!"

They left for Le Plantier, but without worry and without haste; this drudgery was no more than a precaution, very probably unnecessary.

Thanks to the storm, which had deeply penetrated the earth, and thanks to the provision of the cistern, the striped green pumpkins grew round in the shade of their leaves, the ears of corn swelled vigorously, and the refreshed grass of the hills sufficed for the feeding of the rabbits.

Meanwhile the flaming August sun rose each morning in an empty sky and sucked up the very light mist that floated above the grass and the plants; toward noon everything was dry, and the friable earth powdered under Monsieur Jean's steps. He therefore decided to change his methods, and pour two liters of water at the foot of each cucurbitaceous plant every morning; then to slow down the evaporation, he covered them with scraps of sacking, an old tablecloth, bed sheets, blankets, newspapers, the doors of the shed laid on four stones, and large branches of holm oak or pine. When the Papet (who watched the operation) saw the display for the first time he wept with laughter. He was wrong, because as long as there was water in the cistern the plants so protected continued to prosper.

On the tenth day, the worried hunchback again started doing Certificate of Study problems: "Given that a cistern still contains six cubic meters of water, and that the owner is obliged to dispense two cubic meters every other day; that on the other hand he can transport to it every day . . . etc. etc. . . ."

He concluded that to hold out until the twenty-sixth of August he must use Baptistine, Aimée, and Manon, and do seven journeys a day, that is, twelve hours of walking. Then, since it was impossible to impose on these women a program that would frighten an Alpine Chasseur, he persuaded himself that it was absurd to envisage such a long drought, and he changed the conditions of the problem to ameliorate the solution: he decided therefore that the rain would come to his rescue on the twentieth of August. Until then the women would not accompany him more than twice a day, and would thus have time to occupy themselves with the household, the watering, and the rabbits. And if the skies refused the rain he could wait until the arrival of the woodsmen.

He therefore took up his forced marches again . . . The cistern went down every day, but Giuseppe would come, and his plants would be saved . . .

One morning as he arrived at Le Plantier with the empty cans, with Manon astride the she-ass playing the mouth organ, he met with the hand of Fate in Baptistine's cave.

She was sitting on her bed, blanched, haggard, dumb. Before her stood a man, doubtless a woodsman, wiping her brow with a damp cloth, talking softly in Piedmontese. In the corner was another man, cap in hand, a giant with a hairy beard, immobile as a statue.

Jean Cadoret could not understand what the Piedmontese was saying, but the little girl flung herself at Baptistine and held her in her arms, wailing . . .

The giant then came out, made a sign to the hunchback to follow him, and explained with difficulty.

He was dead, the great Giuseppe, the fine woodsman of the hills. Down there, in a forest in the Var, a great twisted holm oak, with a rotten trunk that could not be seen, had fallen at the first blow of the axe, and Giuseppe had jumped back too late . . . A branch, not a very big one, had struck him on the nape of the neck and broken the little bones of the neck . . .

While they were taking him to the hospital he had understood that he was going to die; he was able to tell them to go and tell his wife, and then to commend her to his friend "il mousou gobo."

And since Jean Cadoret did not understand, and asked who Monsieur Gobo was, the woodsman pulled his neck into his raised shoulders and pointed at him . . .

Manon stayed all day with Baptistine, while the woodsmen helped her father for the first journey; the giant who was called Giacomo carried a barrel of fifty liters, the second, Enzo, was distressed not to have more than two large demijohns at his disposal. Jean Cadoret made four journeys. At the fourth he wanted to bring Baptistine to Les Romarins. But she shook her head. She did not weep, she did not talk, she did not move. Manon was exhausted and slept on a straw pallet, and did not even hear the voice of her old friend when she started to sing a strange Piedmontese chant at midnight—perhaps an improvisation of her own—which spoke of love and death.

The next morning Baptistine seemed to be in a trance; she prepared a cup of coffee, saying she was going to look for Giuseppe because she must bury him in the corner of the cave, not too far from the fireplace, so that he should not get cold, and against the rock so that nobody could walk above him, God forbid! Then she took two handfuls of pieces of gold from the crevice, to pay the railway, to go to Le Muy, and for a fine cart to bring Giuseppe back; but the woodsmen, who had slept in the sheepfold, declared that the contractor had done everything that had to be done, and that poor Giuseppe would arrive the next day at the church at Les Bastides in a fine black car that went with a motor. She insisted on leaving at once for the final rendezvous and passed the night sitting on the steps of the church, between her two companions.

The next morning Monsieur Jean, after two journeys to the spring, went with his family to attend the funeral of his friend. Without a word he coldly acknowledged Philoxène, Pamphile, Anglade, and Casimir, who represented the population of the village.

The old curé celebrated the mass, praised the fortitude and courage of the deceased—whom he had never met—and gave him absolution with all simplicity. After the short ceremony at the cemetery, the Italians embraced the widow at length and left for the plateaux of Les Ombrées, where another job awaited them, while the Cadoret family took Baptistine to Les Romarins.

CHAPTER 29

Ugolin returned from Antibes, carrying a large, carefully tied parcel under each arm. They were cuttings prepared by Attilio to provide the flowers for the following season.

He had bought a fine checked cap and shoes that creaked at every step.

The Papet was smoking his pipe, seated on the steps in front of his door.

Ugolin pushed the door with his elbow, closed it with his foot, and said: "So?"

"So," said the Papet, "we had a great storm the day after you left. At just the wrong time. He had good luck."

"Oh shit!" said Ugolin. "But I'm not surprised that you give me bad news. It's my fault, I realized on the train."

"You realized what?"

"That I was wrong to bring the cuttings. It's like when you buy the crib before the little one's arrived. It brings bad luck."

"I don't understand," said the Papet, "how it is possible to make it rain last week by bringing the cuttings this morning. And besides, the news is not all bad, because he's not yet saved. Giuseppe is dead, the Italian woman is no good at anything anymore, and I'm full of hope."

"What bothers me," said Ugolin, "is that he's going to ask me for the mule!"

"You'll tell him the truth. We start the grape harvest tomorrow . . . As for your apricots, they were not very big, but there were hardly any at the market, and Anglade sold them for you at a good price."

CHAPTER 30

Baptistine was sitting in the cinders on the edge of the hearth. Mute as a statue, eyes blank, face frozen. Manon clung to her, caressing her hard leathery hand and whispering incomprehensible Piedmontese words. Her mother had gone alone on the exhausting task of gathering grass, and the black dog watched the goats on the hillside. Monsieur Jean went to the spring, but stopped at Massacan to ask for Ugolin's help.

He found him as he was leaving the farm. After double-locking the door he hid the key under the stone doorstep for Délie.

"At last," said Monsieur Jean," you've come back!"

"Um—yes!" said Ugolin, "for my godfather's grape harvest . . . it's the biggest job of the year . . . are things going well for you?"

"Unfortunately no! And during your absence we've had a hard time of it! I was quite convinced everything was lost . . . A very fine storm saved us, but only for the time being, alas, because this abominable drought is hanging on. I've got no more than one watering in my cistern and I must water tonight . . ."

"It's a really rotten year," said Ugolin. ". . . Everybody's suffering, and even the vines . . . The grapes are all wrinkled, like the ones they put in brioches . . . We have to hurry to gather them, and we're starting this morning . . ."

With an effort he said:

"If it hadn't been for that, I'd have lent you the mule . . . But at the moment it's not possible . . ."

"Perhaps in two or three days . . . ?"

"Oh no," said Ugolin sadly. ". . . After my godfather's grapes are in, the mule has to do the carpenter's, then Casimir the blacksmith's; that's what's done every year; it's what we always do . . . It lasts over a week . . . Oh yes! At least ten days . . . But you know, with these great heat waves, we're bound to have some fine storms! . . . It's the season."

He looked at the sky, and added:

"I would not be surprised if tonight . . ."

"God hear you!" said Monsieur Jean.

He went off behind the she-ass, to the sound of his empty cans and the ring of his hobnailed boots on the stones.

After an exhausting day he put what was left of the water in the cistern on the best pumpkins and the finest rows of corn.

"We're prepared for two days," he said. "If we succeed in doing seven trips a day, we'll still have two days' respite because we will have transported fourteen hundred liters of water, which is nearly enough for a watering. Now Ugolin told me this morning that the storm season starts today or tomorrow. For today he was wrong, because the stars are shining more cruelly than ever . . . But I've got confidence in his forecast. Besides, something tells me the rain isn't far away. Let's go to bed, and get ready for what will surely be a decisive battle."

Toward five in the morning he was half-awakened by the passage of a heavily loaded cart, which seemed to be rolling on the road in the vallon, making the windows rattle.

"I wonder what that is? Woodsmen?"

He rubbed his eyes, sat up on the bed, and listened: thunder was rolling on Sainte Baume in distant but powerful rumblings.

He leaped up and ran to open the window. At the end of the vallon a flash of lightning briefly illuminated the silent dawn.

He pulled on his trousers and shoes in haste while his womenfolk knotted scarves on their heads and put smocks on over their nightdresses . . .

As they went down the stairs the rumblings came closer.

"It was inevitable," he said in a voice trembling with joy. ". . . It's not a present the sky is giving us. Ugolin foretold it. It's the normal weather of the season!"

They went out. The dawn was still clear above their heads, but an immense black cliff of clouds mounted in the north, illuminated by rapid and trembling flashes of lightning.

"A fine storm!" he said. "Perhaps it won't last long, but it'll fill the cistern in five minutes."

They climbed up the side of the hill, the better to see the arrival of the rescuing clouds . . . Manon held her father's hand and laughed.

On the right the red sun of the breaking day emerged from the pine woods, hardly veiled by the swirls of mist preceding the storm.

The black front advanced continuously, now torn by lightning that overturned dazzling dead trees, throwing their roots in the air. Jean laughed and applauded like a child. The exciting smell of the storm descended from the sky, but seemed to rise from the earth and envelop them in an invisible cloud . . . A wind came up, running like a river on the violet heath . . . Suddenly he brought his hand to his forehead.

"There it is!" he said. "The first drop!"

Manon put out the palm of her little hand:

"Me too! Me too!"

She licked the great drops of rain.

On their right the storm suddenly pushed out a violet tentacle to meet the yellowing sun. On La Tête Rouge and on Garlaban the strokes of thunder followed each other, and the high drums of rock replied drily with their echoes as if shaken by explosions . . . A gust of wind charged with horizontal rain set the pine woods shivering. Aimée was afraid.

"I think," she said, "we'd better go in."

"Oh no," he said. "I want to receive this gift that Providence has finally accorded us full on my face!"

He kneeled in the grass and recited an act of grace.

It was while he was praying that the sea of clouds reached the high reef of Saint Esprit, five hundred meters from them, and opened up as if split by the headland of an island. The two halves of the storm went off each on its side, while a long white triangle remained immobile over their heads.

He got up openmouthed and stared at the incomprehensible betrayal that was taking place. Beyond the hilltops in other parts of the vallon the rain was falling, illuminated by flashes of lightning, while the furious wind splattered derisively on their faces.

He gritted his teeth and forced a smile.

"So!" he said. "There's a curious phenomenon that doesn't mend matters for us . . . Let's go in."

Manon wept noiselessly; he took her hand and went down toward the farm-house . . . But suddenly he stopped, pushed the little girl away, and leaped onto a rock with his face raised to the sky. Then, in a powerful and desperate voice, he shouted:

"I'm a HUNCHBACK! Don't you know that I AM A HUNCHBACK? You think it's easy?"

The women ran to his feet in tears.

He trumpeted his hands and shouted again across the rumblings of thunder:

"IS THERE NOBODY UP THERE?"

While the echoes prolonged his cry of revolt, he went down again toward the terrified women, put his hands on their shoulders, and returned slowly to the house.

Aimée prepared a cup of coffee, and he drank it, caressing his kneeling daughter's hair.

He said suddenly:

"I've just been a little ridiculous, but I'm not discouraged. This storm is a presage of others that won't be so extravagantly cruel. Perhaps soon, perhaps this evening, perhaps tonight. While we wait, let's go to Le Plantier!"

They went back under a blinding sun. With grim energy, sustained by a quarter bottle of wine, he was able to fulfil his program; but at the table that evening nobody said a word, and he had to force the women to take a little food.

CHAPTER *31*

Pamphile the carpenter had spent the afternoon waiting for partridges in a lookout of myrtles on the edge of the escarpment of La Garette, and had seen the little cortege behind the she-ass pass several times . . .

When he returned home he found his great Amélie serving a stew, already salivating. She thought her husband seemed worried, and as she filled her own plate with the saddle and liver of a hill rabbit, she said:

"What's got you?"

"Me?"

"Yes, you. You look like you're worried about something."

"It's not worry. It's ideas . . . A thing I've seen that bothers me . . ."

"What thing?"

"Oh well, this afternoon I was at the lookout, and within five hours I saw the hunchback of Les Romarins passing at least six times, all along the hillside to Le Plantier . . . He went up to the cave and came back with a big jar on his hump . . . And besides, he had an ass with cans, and then two women and a little girl carrying jugs."

Amélie slid two rabbit thighs onto his plate, and asked:

"And so?"

"They went to look for water at the cave of Le Plantier in order to water a forest of pumpkins, which I saw at his place as I passed. But it's terrible, with all the heat, to march like convicts!"

"But who's forcing them to do it?"

"The pumpkins," said Pamphile. "With this sun, they might die."

"That shows," said Amélie, "that he's planned his business badly."

"Perhaps. But I know that he has a spring near him."

"And why does he look for water so far away?"

"Because he doesn't know."

"Can't he see the spring?"

"It looks as if it's been blocked . . . And perhaps it didn't get blocked by itself."

Amélie frowned.

"And who blocked it?"

"I know nothing," said Pamphile prudently.

Then he added in a half-whisper:

"Perhaps the Soubeyrans know."

"Now, now!" said Amélie, "you shouldn't say things like that!"

"I'm not saying it to anybody else, but I find that . . ."

"Pamphile, you get nothing out of putting your nose in other people's business. To start with, this hunchback is from Crespin. The baker said so the other day. You know what they're like, these people from Crespin."

Pamphile shrugged his shoulders.

"All that's just stories; they're like everybody else."

"Oh, you think so? The first time he came to the village he tried to kill Cabridan by throwing a ball at him!"

"But that's not true! I was there! It was he, poor chap, who got the ball on his hump! And so . . ."

"And so don't stick your nose in other people's business. You need to have clients . . . It's not a hunchback from Crespin who's going to give you work."

She finished serving the stew and took her place at the table.

"As a matter of fact," she said, "the Papet came. He wants you to repair his mule's manger."

"Is it urgent?"

"With him it's always urgent—but he pays cash!"

"Good," said Pamphile. "I'll go tomorrow morning."

That night the hunchback slept like an animal, and it was a sleepy little Manon who woke up the house when the sun had already come out from the pine woods . . .

He was distressed at having lost three hours, and dressed hastily without taking the time to open the shutters, and ran downstairs . . . As soon as he opened the door he was frozen on the doorstep by a strange sensation; it seemed to him he could not breathe anymore, that he was at the door of an oven. At the same time a light wind sighed, and he saw the year's weak shoots trembling at the tops of the leafless olive trees. He stepped onto the terrace and looked at the sky. Not a cloud, but the sunlight seemed yellowed and troubled, and the wind that brushed his face seemed to burn. He called his wife. She opened the window.

"Aimée, have I got a fever, or is it the wind that's burning my face?" She woke up completely and held her face into the breeze.

"My God!" she said, "is it a fire?"

He smelled the air, then walked away from the house and looked at it from all sides. He saw no smoke, and the only perceptible odor was that of pine resin.

"No . . . It's much worse; it's the sirocco . . . It's the wind from Africa . . ."

She came down in haste.

"That's the limit," he said. "That's the final betrayal, the donkey's kick of fate! Well, no! I won't give in, I won't bow to iniquity! This atrocious wind's not going to last all day, but it could do us a lot of harm before the evening. It's a matter of hours. Everybody to the water at once!"

As he bridled the she-ass and put on the packsaddle he said:

"I'm going to work as fast as I can. You won't be able to keep up with me, but make as many trips as you can and pour all the water that you bring at the foot of the plants without waiting."

He took a half-loaf, a cheese, and put two bottles of wine on the pack, under the cans. Then with a stick under his arm he went off at a great pace behind the she-ass, eating his snack.

The strange reddish light turned the shadows a hazy black, like a fog. The burning wind flowed on without gusts; there was not a birdsong, not a cicada. When he finished eating he drank half a bottle of wine, then he whipped the she-ass with his stick and followed her at a trot up to Le Plantier.

On his way back he met the three women; without stopping, he said to them as he passed:

"It's a matter of life or death!"

Aimée was frightened by his feverishness, and Manon said to her mother:

"Maman, he'll get sick . . ."

"It's quite possible . . . But there's nothing I can do."

He made four complete trips in the morning alone. Toward noon the poor she-ass was trembling on her feet and he had to allow her half an hour's rest. While Manon and Baptistine rubbed her down and offered her grass, he sucked two eggs and drank a bottle of wine, to encourage sweating, he said. The watered plants, protected by their steaming covers, seemed not to have suffered . . . He went off cheered up, already proclaiming victory with surprising volubility. The baleful wind sighed continuously. It now let fall a very fine reddish dust that stuck to the sweat on his face; and the heavy heat sapped the strength from his legs. On the return journey, overcome by the weight of the water, he hung on to the tail of the animal and walked like an automaton muttering insults under his breath to Fate, Providence, and the Sahara. Little Manon wept; on the way his wife offered him a hat, but he pushed it back without interrupting his litany, and continued his staggering course, drunk with sun, fatigue, and wine . . .

There were a number of peasants working in the hills.

At the bottom of the vallon Ugolin was harvesting grapes with the Papet, the deaf-mute, and two urchins from the village. From afar he could see "poor Monsieur Jean" making his journeys.

"Papet, he'll kill himself!"

The Papet, shears in hand, said gravely:

"He can always be a tax collector, but the poor she-ass, she can't . . . It's her I'm worried about!"

Eliacin was repairing the stone retaining walls that supported his fields. Because of a turn in the vallon he saw only one part of the journey; at each passage he stopped hammering for a moment and watched the event as if it were a new spectacle . . . He laughed heartily, shrugged his shoulders, or slapped his thigh, repeating in a loud voice: "Poor fool! Poor, poor fool!"

Pamphile, who was mowing a little field of black wheat, watched this folly for the whole afternoon . . . But about five o'clock, when he saw the unfortunate man running like a maniac, he said:

"Why, he's ready to drop, I don't want to see that . . ."

He took the gun he had hidden in the undergrowth, went over the crest of the hill, and plunged down toward Les Ombrées.

It was nine o'clock in the evening when he put the limping she-ass back in the stable and came into the kitchen. The table had been laid around the lamp. Baptistine snored noisily on the bottom step of the stairs. Aimée slept on the cane armchair, her bare feet on the tiles and her head falling back against the wall. Manon was waiting, her eyes circled blue in a face no bigger than a fist.

At the door he said: "We've won. The plants have held. We've won!" Aimée opened her eyes and got up. Manon led him by the hand to his place and made him sit down.

His face was dark red, contracted by a grimace that exposed his teeth. He breathed through his open mouth and stretched a trembling hand to pour a glass of wine; but suddenly his eyes closed and he fell forward with his chin on his plate and his arms hanging down straight under the table. His wife and daughter, in tears, stretched him on the floor, then on a mattress that they brought down from a bedroom.

The awakened Baptistine approached him and looked at him for a long time. He was lying on his side, and his rapid breathing was like a dog's after a chase on a very hot day. His face had suddenly got emaciated, the features drawn, and there was sweat on the temples. The Piedmontese smelled him, then said some words to Manon, who translated:

"She says it's the sun. The bad sun today."

Baptistine spoke again.

"She says she's going to 'drive out the sun.' She says that if the sun isn't driven out he'll be dead the day after tomorrow.

"She says she knows how to do it."

In the meantime the Piedmontese had gone to take a glass from the sink; she filled it with water from the jug, pronouncing incantatory words in a loud voice all the while. Then she bowed before the hearth, pushed aside the ashes, and with a blow of the shovel detached a glowing ember from a log, as big as a nut. She took this with the end of the tongs.

Then she got up and approached the lifeless prone body; with eyes closed she pronounced some more phrases, which the girl could not understand. Finally she placed the glass full of water on the sick man's forehead, and murmuring all the time, she suddenly plunged the glowing ember in it; the vapor hissed furiously in white wreaths.

"The sun is leaving him," she said. ". . . Did you see? The sun has just gone!"

Aimée wept with a trembling mouth. Little Manon gazed at her father, gravely, and without apparent emotion, and suddenly his face cleared; his breathing slowed and at the end of a minute he let out a long sigh.

"There it is," said Baptistine. "The sun has gone. But he's done himself harm. He won't speak for three days. Now I'm going to look for herbs to make a tisane."

She took a lantern and went out into the night.

It was the morning of the third day before he opened his lackluster eyes. His wife spoke to him softly without getting any response. His face was very pale, and the fever had subsided. She succeeded in making him drink the herbal tisane. Then he made a sort of grimace, which could have been a smile, and went peacefully to sleep again. When she heard his regular breathing, poor Aimée crossed her arms on the table, laid her forehead on them, and went to sleep herself.

During this time Baptistine gathered dried grass on the hillsides for the starving rabbits as she minded the goats; and Manon, her left arm stretched out to balance her full jug, came back from the spring, where she had gone three times a day with the she-ass, in order to look after eight pumpkin plants that she was trying to save from disaster . . .

On the evening of the fourth day he woke up, and Baptistine administered a new tisane. He tried to talk, but could not articulate a word. The terrified Aimée could not restrain her tears, but the Piedmontese gave her to understand that she had nothing to fear, he would soon speak.

In fact he recovered his spirits in the morning and insisted on trying to get up, but his legs were unable to carry him and he fell sitting on the straw pallet . . . Then he managed a feeble smile and said:

"What happened to me?"

"Sunstroke," said Aimée. "But thanks to Baptistine you've been saved."

She kissed his hand and wept. Manon came in and asked him in the most natural tone:

"Are you feeling better, Papa?"

"Yes," he said. "But there's a day lost!"

They did not dare tell him the truth. Baptistine brought a plate of boiled vegetables sprinkled with a spoonful of rice. He ate slowly and looked at them one by one. Then he wanted to go up to his room, which he managed to do by leaning against the wall . . . They helped him to stretch out on his bed; then he asked:

"Haven't the pumpkins suffered a lot?"

"A little," said Manon. "But the hot wind has died, and the best ones are left."

"We'll see," he said. "We'll see. Thank you."

He went to sleep holding his wife's hand.

Manon made another journey to the spring, then she wept in her bed, thinking of the terrible disappointment he was going to have the next day when he learned how long he had slept and suddenly found himself facing disaster. She would have wept all night if the kind sleep of her youth had not slowly relaxed her.

He got up very early, without waking the two sleepers; carefully, fearing another catastrophe, he lingered in the kitchen, preparing a cup of coffee on some crackling twigs.

But while he was drinking in little pensive sips, he heard something like a burst of distant laughter coming from the cistern. He went to lift the wooden cover; a thin trickle of water was running from the descending hose . . .

He ran to open the shutters: day was breaking, and little grey streaks of rain were falling. A strong emotion brought tears to his eyes; he knelt down to thank Heaven and the skies. Then, bareheaded, he went out into the rain.

It was not very strong, but for all that it made a strange noise on the leaves of corn, a resonant drumming sound.

He advanced on the muddy earth; the corn was white and the drops rang on the parchment leaves.

It seemed to him that his breast had suddenly tightened. He went into the field and seized fistfuls of leaves; they crackled between his fingers. The corn was dead. . . . A burst of wind crossed the little white forest and made it whisper. Then he smiled bitterly and said in a loud voice:

"Midas, King Midas, has the ears of an ass."

With slow steps he went toward the pumpkins.

In bringing the rain, the night wind had dispersed the covers spread over the brushwood, and the old newspapers attached to the olive trees; on the hillside, an old sheet full of holes hung sadly . . .

The large yellow-stained leaves of the pumpkins were soft and withered; their long branches, convulsed by the heat and tangled by the wind, were as dry as bundles of vine shoots.

Nevertheless they bore hundreds of fruits, which were already bigger than oranges, but would never grow any bigger.

They also were lost. As he walked with lowered eyes in the midst of this disaster, he did not see the rich foliage caught up in the branches of the old olive tree . . . He bent down, gathered a dead pumpkin, weighed it in his hand, then broke the hard rind between two stones; he saw a greenish stringy pulp.

He smelled it, then tasted it. It was hard and rather bitter.

"Perhaps," he said. ". . . After all, they eat lettuce well enough and it's more bitter than this . . ."

He went toward the rabbit park.

At the sound of his steps the young red-and-white rabbits rushed out of the burrows and threw themselves against the fence. They pressed against the netting and watched him come . . .

He was astonished at their number because he had never seen them all together.

There were about fifty of them, of all sizes and ages. The old male, thin and starving, stayed behind alone in the middle of the close-cropped park.

He threw a piece of the pumpkin toward him; the Australian approached it without haste while his progeny waited in a semicircle a good distance away.

He turned over the piece of pumpkin and plunged his nose twice into the pulp. Then he stared fixedly at his feeder and drew back his lips as if to laugh.

Suddenly he turned his back and ran toward the bottom of the park. He cleared the fencing with a prodigious jump and disappeared in the corn.

"He too!" he said stupidly.

He slowly walked the length of the park, hands in pockets. The crowd of starvelings followed him all the length of the fencing.

Behind the closed shutters the awakened women looked at him, cheek to cheek, mute and overcome. Then, when they saw him approaching the house they went down to wait for him in the kitchen.

He was calm.

"How long did I sleep?"

Aimée shrugged her shoulders and replied with sincerity:

"I don't know anymore."

"Six days," said Manon. "It is six days since the night you fell asleep at the table . . ."

"There!" he said. "These six days have ruined two years of hope and of work. The corn is dead, the pumpkins are dead . . ."

"Not all," cried Manon. "Didn't you see the big olive tree?"

She took him by the hand. He followed her.

As they crossed the devastated area she explained:

"I did what Giuseppe told me. I looked for the biggest ones. They were down there at the end, by the olive tree. You understand, Maman was looking after you, Baptistine had bad feet; I had to go to the spring quite alone with the she-ass . . . So I didn't waste water on the others . . ."

They approached the tree; when he raised his eyes he saw a tall mass of foliage. With the little girl's daily watering, and with the violent heat of the sirocco, the plants had covered the old tree in six days. Now its silvery branches were hardly visible under the curtain of dazzling green leaves that were as big as a man's hand. But there was no fruit to be seen. She parted two plants and pulled her father toward the black trunk. He raised his head.

Against the walls of the cone of leaves the white-striped fruits, round like little watermelons, were suspended in tiers.

"Hundred and thirteen," she said. "I've counted them."

He took her by her shoulders and looked for a long time into her blue eyes.

"We should have had ten times more," he said. "But these are very precious. They are the proof, the decisive proof . . . Little girl, you have given me the most beautiful Christmas tree."

He kissed her forehead, smiled, and said:

"Come. Let's make a little music!"

During these terrible days Ugolin made the Papet's wine; but every morning at dawn he went back up to Massacan to water his beloved cuttings with several buckets of water drawn from the well. But he did not even take the time to go into his house; tormented by an obscure remorse, he was afraid of encountering Monsieur Jean in the midst of disaster—he was quite willing to strangle the cat, but he did not want to look at it.

Early one morning while Ugolin was racking the wine the Papet went up to his lookout post; he came back in a lively mood.

"Galinette," he said, "it's time to go there. It looks like a battlefield. All the rags have been blown away, the pumpkins are in corkscrews, and the corn is as white as paper. And as for him, I haven't seen him . . . He doesn't have to die, poor chap . . . of sickness or despair . . . Offer him six thousand francs—perhaps seven . . . But bargain with him! . . . And go quicky, before anybody else gets there. And take a couple of bottles of the new wine. There's nothing better for sickness . . ."

Ugolin went out in the rain with a basket hanging from his elbow. From afar he saw the bed sheet, then the newspapers and the damp rags. Nobody in the field. He went down toward the gourds . . . The long interlacing creepers crackled under his feet. He pulled one up and examined the roots.

"Done for," he said, "it's done for!"

Then he went to rub some corn leaves. Again he said, "Done for."

The rabbits followed him behind the wire netting. He looked at them for a moment and said:

"How thin they are!"

He sighed, and murmured:

"In the end it had to be like this for him to understand."

He approached the house noiselessly, as if visiting someone gravely ill, but when he had taken ten steps it seemed to him he heard music . . . He went forward again and stopped. Mouth organs were playing a Christmas carol, the "March of the Kings."

"I wonder," he said, "whether I'm not going mad! Or whether he is!"

He waited until the end of the hymn of joy and knocked on a shutter . . .

Monsieur Jean appeared at the door, mouth organ in hand. He was pale and thin, but neither his look nor his voice was that of a defeated man.

"Good day, neighbor! The wine harvest is done?"

"Yes, Monsieur Jean! The wine is drawn, all that's left is to drink it! There's hardly any, but it's good and strong . . . I've brought you a couple of bottles. It's not quite ready yet, but it's already good!"

"We'll taste it at once! Aimée, bring the glasses!"

They went to sit in the kitchen, and Ugolin put the bottles on the table.

"So," said Monsieur Jean, "you've seen the disaster?"

Ugolin looked at the devastated field and shook his head.

"Yes . . . It's the same with me, my vegetable garden has dried up . . . The sirocco has killed many harvests."

"My husband," said Aimée, "has had so much trouble he nearly died of sunstroke!"

Filling two glasses to the top, Monsieur Jean smiled and said:

"It was Baptistine who cured me, with a burning charcoal in a glass of water. At least, that's what my wife tells me. Your good health!"

They clinked glasses.

"It's the only way," said Ugolin, "to drive the sun out of the head. But you have to know the magic words, otherwise it doesn't work!"

"Baptistine knows them," said Manon. "And she even told me she would teach them to me!"

"That'll be a fine present!" said Ugolin. "Only, they'll say you're a witch! Your health!"

They clinked glasses and Monsieur Jean, having drunk half his glass with great satisfaction, declared:

"My dear neighbor, your wine is delicious, but my business is unsuccessful!

I could blame the injustice of the heavens, or the exceptional weather, but I prefer to attribute my setback to my own stupidity, to my lack of good sense . . . This has been a cruel lesson, but it won't be lost."

He drank the rest of the wine.

Ugolin waited impatiently for the rest.

"I thought I was very clever and very careful, whereas to be honest I never saw to the heart of the problem; that's to say, the whole problem was water."

"Certainly," approved Ugolin. "Without water, your business can't succeed."

"That's obvious. The only possible excuse is that I didn't know the power of that cape of rock so wrongly called the Saint Esprit—actually it is diabolic. Well, that's past history. Look what I intend to do now."

He filled his glass again and continued:

"First, liquidate three-quarters of my rabbits. We haven't harvested enough to feed them properly—and on the other hand we really need a little ready cash." ("That's good," said Ugolin to himself.) "Moreover, I haven't got the time to occupy myself with breeding because of the work I'm going to undertake as soon as I get my strength back. Because, before I do anything else, I'm going to dig a well."

"Ayayay!" thought Ugolin, ". . . I can't say I like that . . ."

He asked:

"Whereabouts?"

"I haven't decided yet; a divining rod will show me."

Ugolin trembled:

"You're a dowser?"

"Not exactly. But I possess a very precious manual, which I'm going to study very closely and when I've mastered the rod I'm pretty certain to find water in this vallon. Oh! I'm not asking for a subterranean river! No! A trickle of water no thicker than my wrist will be quite enough. After all the disappointments I've had, I hope Providence will not refuse me this recompense."

He was sure of himself again, and almost merry.

"D'you know how to dig wells?"

"My word, I intend to succeed. After all, a well—it's no more than a hole! Mine won't be more than twelve meters deep, and as soon as it's finished, even if I don't find a drop of water, my problem will be solved."

He smiled with a Machiavellian air.

"But how?" said Aimée. "What use is a well without water?"

He replied triumphantly:

"It can serve as a cistern! A well of twelve meters depth and two meters diameter—quite modest dimensions—contains exactly forty-three cubic meters. If I dig it at the bottom of the vallon I can conduct all the water that runs down both hillsides to it by means of ditches . . . The spring rains will be enough to fill it . . . Thus, in the first days of summer we'll have a reserve of fifty-five cubic meters at our disposal, thanks to the well and our cistern, which will assure us of eighteen waterings, that's to say thirty-six days without the least worry."

"Thirty-six days are fine," said Ugolin, ". . . but we've seen longer droughts than that."

"You forget," replied the well-digger triumphantly, "that during these thirty-six days we'll have time to transport a good dozen cubic meters without wearing ourselves out, which will assure us of at least eight days more!"

The wine in him had started to flare up. With forefinger raised, he cried:

"Where have you seen an uninterrupted drought of forty-four days? In the Sahara perhaps! In the middle of the Gobi desert perhaps! But here, in spite of the peak of Saint Esprit, it is mathematically IMPOSSIBLE!"

Then he laughed, beating the table with the flat of his hand, and said:

"Problem solved! Let's drink."

He filled his glass again and swallowed it in one gulp.

Ugolin left, disconcerted.

The Papet waited for him in the Soubeyran house.

Ugolin gave him an account of his visit and the conversation. The old man could not hide his disappointment and anxiety.

"In what you've told me, there's only one good thing—that he's taken to red wine. It's always like that with people who want to do too much and get their strength from wine. By the end of six months they're not good for much. But the divining rod is tiresome . . ."

"Are you afraid he'll find the secret in his book?"

"Not on your life . . . It's not a secret, it's more a question of nerves. It will be most extraordinary if he should happen exactly on the spring . . . But once he gets started, he might end up hiring a real water diviner."

"And you think he might get one to come? . . ."

"There's one at Les Ombrées. If he came up to Les Romarins looking like an idiot with his piece of wood he'd get straight to the spring in five minutes, and he'd tell you the depth, and how many liters a day . . ."

Ugolin trembled.

"Is he always at Les Ombrées?"

"Yes, he's always there, but fortunately in the cemetery."

"So much the better!" said Ugolin.

"Yes, so much the better . . . Has he got any money left?"

"He said he had hardly any left . . . But when it comes to money, you never know with these people . . ."

"If he has only twenty francs left," said the Papet, "he'll go to Aubagne, he'll ask for a diviner, and they'll tell him about five or six . . . Fortunately nearly all of them are incompetent . . . But if he should happen on a good one?" He shook his head pensively. Ugolin, pale and short of breath, blinked desperately.

For a whole fortnight Ugolin was busy with the first ploughing, transporting manure to the vineyard and the orchard, and then with pruning his fruit trees. Nevertheless he did make two visits to Les Romarins, but did not find Monsieur Jean, who was in Aubagne.

Indeed, the absentee was busy "regulating his financial situation," that is to say, finding a little money . . . He sold about fifty rabbits, keeping only two males and six females; he disposed of his watch and his signet ring at Mont-de-Piété, and sold a number of books—a dictionary, *The Marvels of Science*, and *The History of the Consulat and the Empire* by M. Adolphe Thiers, and a silver saltcellar.

He was thus able to put a hundred and sixty francs together; with the seventy francs that Aimée had so carefully guarded, he had two hundred and thirty francs—not for paying his debts (which were more than seven hundred francs with the miller at Ruissatel and the hardware merchant at Aubagne), but for buying bread and wine.

"As for the rest," he said to his wife, "we will have oil because our olive trees are full; we have a hundred *cucurbita* and a little harvest of chick-peas that survived the drought thanks to Manon, a sack of almonds, goats' milk, little cheeses from Baptistine, some rabbits, and the resources of the hills—mushrooms, wild salads, and especially game . . . That will be our diet for at least six months . . . It's austere, but healthy, and we know what success is waiting at the end of it!"

"What worries me," said Aimée, "is that we don't have any more shoes . . . The journeys to the spring have ruined five or six pairs. You've got nothing left but your patent leather boots."

"They will do for going to Aubagne . . . Here I much prefer to walk bare-foot."

CHAPTER *34*

One morning when Ugolin was gathering wood in the hills, with a rope round his waist and a hatchet on his shoulder, he saw from afar a strange cortege enacting some kind of ceremony in the middle of the vallon.

The hunchback, holding a diviner's rod in both hands, was walking with slow and measured paces, with his face raised to the sky. His wife followed silently. Behind her the little girl, with a grave and strained air, preceded the she-ass, accompanied by two goats. The strange group was going up the bottom of the vallon. Suddenly the water diviner stopped and his followers stood still. The rod had just bent up toward his chin. He took two steps backward, then two steps forward, and stopped again. Aimée came forward and planted a stick in the ground. Then they resumed their solemn march.

"That," murmured Ugolin, "is very worrying indeed. If he's got the right kind of nerves he may find the spring. Especially if it's not deep. O Holy Mother, Holy Mother!"

In the afternoon Manon came down from the top of Saint Esprit with the she-ass and the goats. When she crossed the mule track she stopped and called to her father, who was walking slowly with his eyes closed, holding the branches of the magic instrument.

"Papa, come and look!"

"What is it?"

"Some black painting on a rock."

She was crouching at the side of the track, near a flat stone on which an arrow was crudely painted apparently pointing to the farmhouse.

"It's still not quite dry," she said, showing the tip of her forefinger. "What is it?"

"Perhaps," he said, "this arrow marks a route for hikers, although I've never seen any of them around here . . . Did anybody come by this morning?"

"I don't think so. I was up there in the pine wood, I didn't see anybody."

He reflected, perplexed . . . Perhaps this arrow was some sort of mute aggression, to point out to rare passersby the house of the enemy from Crespin. Then he thought this was hardly possible, and he must not let himself give in to persecution mania. Besides, the arrow did not exactly point to the house, but rather to the hillside opposite, on the east.

"Perhaps it's a direction indicator," he said, ". . . no doubt for the army, or the Waters and Forests Department . . ."

In the evening Ugolin saw another arrow as he came down from the hills with a faggot of dead wood, fifty meters above the house; it did not point in the same direction as the other, but almost at a right angle to it.

"Oh, Monsieur Jean! Are you the one who painted that?"

Monsieur Jean came up to meet him, saying:

"Do you think I have nothing to do all day! There's another one down there, pointing to the east. This one's pointing nearly south . . . Most likely they're reference marks for the cartographers, or for the people from the land registry."

"I'm more inclined to think," said Ugolin, "they're marks for hiking societies. There are yellow ones on the path from Garlaban and blue ones on Les Refresquières . . . That could mean that we're going to see the Sunday idiots coming . . . And on the way they'll steal my plums or my apricots, according to the season! As for me, all the arrows that I find—over they go!"

He lifted the big stone with difficulty and deposited it upside down in the broom.

They went down toward the farmhouse.

"So," said Ugolin, "it talks, that rod?"

"Well, yes!" said Monsieur Jean. "I even find it too chatty. According to what it says there should be at least four major places for water in the vallon. At the bottom of the vallon, naturally."

Ugolin breathed.

"Yes," he said. "The water follows the slopes . . ."

"But I must do some experiments before choosing the best place for the well, and the most convenient. I will certainly have it fixed tomorrow . . ."

The next morning, very early, Ugolin went to check his traps in the vallon. He found a fine big partridge and decided to go and offer it to Aimée and see how things were getting on.

As he approached Les Romarins he heard the ring of a pickax, then he saw the hunchback at work.

He was up to his knees in a round hole in the middle of the field, handling a miner's pickax.

His wife and daughter were seated near him on a small volcano of spoil. Near them was a bag of esparto grass and a bottle of wine capped with a glass. He had started on the well.

Ugolin advanced, smiling, and saluted the sweet Aimée and offered her the partridge, while the miner emerged from his hole.

Ugolin saw that his feet were bare—thin, white, bony feet. He walked as if he were walking on eggs, with his big toes comically pricked up.

Ugolin's look did not escape him.

"I've been training myself since yesterday," he said, "to walk barefoot. You might ask why. Oh well, firstly, because shoes are very dear. So I want to get used to doing without them and I'm taking my first steps here, to give myself a horny sole, as strong as the best leather, and more supple . . . On the other hand, since I want to be a man of Nature, these ridiculous covers already seem to me to be perfectly useless. It's a great pleasure to walk barefoot, and it seems to me that the subterranean currents of our Mother Earth penetrate my body better, to revitalize and rejuvenate it!"

"And so," said Ugolin, "is this the right spot?"

"Exactly!" said the radiant hunchback. "Right here, when I passed with the rod in my hand above the center of the hole, the instrument literally jumped out of my hands."

"It was impressive!" said Aimée. "It made two turns above it, and hop!"

"It flew!" said Manon. "Like a bird!"

"I'm also very happy," he said, "that the rod chose this place because it's the lowest in the vallon, and if by chance I don't find water here, it will be easy for me to make furrows for the rain to converge here. Furthermore, it is right in the middle of my fields; when I put my pump on the edge—or perhaps a little windmill—I will only have to move my little sluice gates to make sure of my waterings, while I play the mouth organ on a chaise longue!"

Ugolin calculated that they were a hundred meters from the spring, and nearly fifty meters to the left.

"If the rod jumped," he said, "then that's where you must dig! But what about the depth?"

"Eight meters fifty," said the hunchback simply.

"You've measured it?"

"Obviously!"

"How?"

"By the method of little pebbles. An assistant puts them in the left hand of the operator one by one . . . Each pebble as big as a hazelnut signifies one meter, and the smaller pebbles one-half meter. It's a well-established convention among water diviners. Well, at the eighth pebble the rod shivered; when a small pebble was added it started trembling. Another small pebble, everything stopped. So, eight meters fifty."

This scientifically alluring explanation, this mysterious "convention," made a big impression on Ugolin, especially since the hunchback spoke of the maneuvers as if he were dealing with something as natural and as well known as the culture of chick-peas or the planting out of onions.

"Eight meters fifty," said Ugolin, "that's a lot of work all the same."

"Certainly, certainly, but see for yourself: in two days we're already at sixty centimeters; it's therefore not unreasonable to estimate an average advance of thirty centimeters a day, so a well of twelve meters won't take me more than forty days!"

Meanwhile, Aimée had jumped into the hole and was filling the bag with dirt using a little copper shovel from the fireplace. Ugolin thought it was ridiculous, but nevertheless, this work of ants, pursued for weeks and months, would perhaps achieve its aim.

"Obviously," continued Monsieur Jean, "we must take into account the nature of the terrain we're going to encounter. We could have some very painful surprises. The subsoil of this vallon is certainly made up of many different layers. First the arable soil, which I've just gone through. Beneath that we probably have gravel, then, I'm sure, some sand (the rod told me that). This won't present any difficulty. But let's not forget"—he looked at Ugolin fixedly and pointed a forefinger toward the escarpments of Saint Esprit—"let's not forget that we're in the middle of Jurassic Cretacean of the second epoch of the Quaternary! Oh yes, the Cretacean! That is, at a certain depth, we're going to find a pretty hard layer of white rock in the stratigraphy. If the water runs on top of this rock, we'll be there in a fortnight. But if it passes under the Quaternary layer it will take six months' work, perhaps more. That's the truth. So what! 'Labor improbus omnia vincit,' which means 'with work you achieve everything!' Let's get going!"

He jumped into the hole.

Under the mulberry tree at Massacan, face to face astride a bench, Ugolin and the Papet were flattening large green olives with light mallet blows; they were preparing "a jar of broken olives." Meanwhile a lugubrious Ugolin was reporting to the Papet.

"What frightens me is that he's a scientist. That's like saying he's a simpleton, but it's frightening how intelligent he is. He told me everything that was under the earth, and at the bottom there's the Quaternary, which is very hard. But perhaps he won't have to make a hole in it because the water is on top of the Quaternary."

"Galinette," said the Papet, "don't worry about it. That's all words. I tell you he'll find nothing at the bottom of the vallon. But the most serious thing is that if he has the strength to finish it he'll have one more cistern, and that's important because it's a reasonable idea. Mark my words, it will surely end in a mess; but it will take two or three years, and right now I can't see what we can do about it. Our only hope is that he'll be discouraged when he hits the rock. Let's wait."

CHAPTER 35

Autumn brought setting suns that draped the distant escarpments in red, and refreshing breezes that bore off the swallows and carried in the thrushes from the Alps.

Ugolin finished his provision of wood for the winter . . . Every morning he passed by on the path that dominated Les Romarins, pulling the mule by the bridle, and shouted a friendly "good day." After the fifth day he saw no more than the face of the hunchback, who replied to him from ground level. Two days later the fair Aimée was seated on the pile of spoil; she was knitting, and when the bag rose to the rim of the hole she seized it by the ears, emptied it, and let it fall back into the well.

"It's getting on," he thought. ". . . He's arrived at the gravel . . . But after that?"

The next week he heard the pick from afar; it rang hard, and at times it clinked.

"There it is. He's hit the rock!"

There was now a three-legged derrick above the well, supporting a pulley, and a double rope plunged into the hole.

Aimée arrived carrying a tray, just like one in a café, with half a loaf, a glass, and two little cheeses. Manon clutched a bottle to her heart. She ran lightly on bare feet.

He went down toward the work in progress.

"So," he said gaily, "do I see that things are going well?"

"Yes," she said. "But it's getting more difficult."

She pointed to pieces of bluish rock in the spoil. He picked one up, examined it, and said:

"It's hard."

"Yes, it's hard," said the voice of the hunchback, and his gloved hands appeared on the rim of the hole . . .

He climbed the last rungs of the rope ladder and came to sit on the spoil. He was as thin as a Pierrot, and white with powdered stone, but sweat had traced furrows on this makeup exposing a red-brown skin. His feet were still bare and his legs trembled.

"Four meters twenty!" he said. "I've gone through the gravel and I've arrived at the white rock. It rings like granite. It's the Quaternary I told you about."

He took off his broken-seamed gloves, pulled a grubby handkerchief from his pocket, and wiped his forehead.

He took four steps to sit on the slope of the pile of earth. His daughter went toward him with a bottle in her hand. The hunchback took it to his lips and lifted the bottom to the sky. Ugolin looked at the angular Adam's apple shuddering on the thin and wrinkled neck.

The drinker let out a great sigh, laughed, and said:

"Now I understand the thirst of ditchdiggers! That really does a lot of good!"

He began to eat slowly.

Ugolin looked at his trembling hands and his thin legs streaked with scratches, and suddenly he was sure this man was going to die. He knelt in front of him and sat on his heels.

"Monsieur Jean, I must speak to you frankly. Perhaps you'll say I'm mixing myself in things that don't concern me. So much the worse. But it's out of good friendship."

The hunchback raised his eyes, surprised:

"That's an interesting preamble."

"Perhaps," said Ugolin, who did not understand *preamble*, "perhaps. The truth is, I'm worried about you. Monsieur Jean, you're wasting your time and your health here. It worries me to see you get thinner every day. The work you've done these last two and a half years is unbelievable, it's madness, it's murder! You haven't got the hands for it, you haven't got the constitution for it . . . You'll never get to the end of this well, and even if you find water, that won't mend matters, because you'd need a river for all that corn and those pumpkins. And your rabbits—that might succeed for a while, but the first time one of them catches swollen belly the whole park will be wiped out. All this, it's not your métier, and that's the truth!"

Little Manon looked at him severely, but Monsieur Jean heard him out, smiling amicably.

"Go on," he said, "you interest me."

Ugolin was taken aback for a moment, then continued forcefully:

"A man like you should be in town. I can understand that you don't want to stay a tax collector, taking money from others, because you've got a good heart . . . But with some guidance you could become a schoolteacher, or a postal clerk, or keep a tobacco shop. Or even in an office of a big town hall where they get a lot of money for doing nothing. I see you all clean and tidy with collar and cuffs in a fine house with a mat in front of the door, a letter box in the hall, and lampposts on the stairs. That's the right thing for you. While if you stay here you'll get thinner and thinner. I can see quite well you've got no more money. That's no disgrace, but you miss it. So you eat snails, rabbits, mushrooms, and dandelions. That's not food for a worker. It gets to you so you're obliged to drink too much wine; and you'll end by dying. And then what will become of Madame Aimée and the little one? They're already not very strong, and haven't been for some time. You don't see it, but I've noticed it . . . I know very well it's none of my business, but it bothers me, it grieves me, and I'm just telling you what I think . . ."

"It's proof of good friendship," said the hunchback, "and I thank you for it . . Your arguments aren't all valid, but on the whole you're right. It is very probable that if I persist in piercing several meters of living rock with this pick I'll lose the best of my strength and perhaps my health. Moreover, I was wrong to impose a regime of austerity on my family. I renounce that now, because I have another solution all ready. It doesn't please me, but it seems unavoidable."

He took some time to wipe his lips, looked around him, and asked brusquely:

"In your opinion, how much is this farm worth?"

Ugolin trembled and blinked.

"To let or to sell?"

"To sell, of course."

Manon stepped forward and cried:

"No! No!"

"Wait a moment," said her father.

Ugolin's eyelashes beat rapidly. He thought, "There it is, I've won. I must tell him a good price, but all the same not too dear!"

He replied:

"I've never thought about it, but we could discuss it. It's a very nice place, isn't it? And besides, the house is well organized. But it's a bit far for a country house. And for a peasant, you can't do much without water . . ."

"With a second cistern," said Monsieur Jean, "it would be a lot better."

"That's true," said Ugolin. "Much better."

He reflected for a moment, looked at the house, and said:

"Seven thousand francs?"

"Is that your last price?"

Ugolin hesitated again. His heart beat, his tics pulled his face in every direction.

"I might even find somebody who'd take it for eight thousand. I'll see."

Little Manon stamped her foot and cried again:

"No! Papa, I don't want it!"

"Calm down," said her father. "We're talking then of eight thousand francs. I agree to this figure."

Ugolin wondered whether he should get up and shake his hand to conclude the business.

"No!" cried Manon. "No!"

Aimée advanced, very pale.

"Look, Jean, you're not going to . . ."

"Silence," said Monsieur Jean. "I said this price seemed reasonable to me because it allows me to ask our notary in Crespin for a loan of four thousand francs on first mortgage."

"That means you're not selling it?" said Aimée.

"Not on your life! I would never sell the farm where my mother was born and where I hope to finish my days after I've made my fortune."

Great tears of joy sprang from the little girl's eyes while half a dozen grimaces crossed Ugolin's blemished face.

"With the four thousand francs the notary will advance, it will be possible to live quite well until our eventual success. It will be possible to buy a mule, and above all, above all, to buy miners' tools, and some kilos of powder to pulverize this cursed rock without wearing me out; our first year of breeding will enable me to pay back the mortgage, and the trick will be worked! That's my plan."

Then the little girl burst out laughing, drew her mouth organ from her bodice, and blew joyful arpeggios in Ugolin's face.

He coughed, and asked:

"Are you going to dynamite, Monsieur Jean?"

"As much as it takes to go down twelve meters."

"Do you know how to do it?"

"I've got the *Miner's Manual*!"

"Be careful not to start an explosion of statistics again! They've smacked your hand, those statistics; and dynamite is far more dangerous!"

"This danger," said Monsieur Jean with great authority, "is inversely proportional to the intelligence of the manipulator. And since I've been talking for twenty minutes, I think another glass of nectar would be a pleasant conclusion to this discourse!"

Ugolin departed, puzzled.

"There!" he said. "I wanted to do him a kindness, and I fell on my nose . . . I'm the one who gave him the idea of four thousand francs . . . I mustn't tell the Papet that. I'll tell him he thought of it by himself. This mortgage, I think it won't do us any good. It's always wrong to talk."

The old man was sitting on his doorstep sharpening stakes for his garden.

"So?"

"Oh, his well's getting on. Only he hasn't got a sou left and he walks barefoot, and his daughter too."

"People who walk barefoot eat nothing," said the Papet.

"I don't know what he eats, but anyway he's still drinking wine and he's as thin as a praying mantis and he digs like a convict."

"That's all pretty good for us . . ."

"Wait! He told me he's going to have four thousand francs because he knows a notary in Crespin who'll give him a mortgage. Is that possible?"

The Papet seemed startled.

"Ho ho!" he said, getting up, "d'you know what a mortgage is?"

"It means that the notary lends money to people who have a little property because that gives him confidence that they're not dishonest, that they're men of their word."

"What word? First the notary makes him sign *papers with stamps on them*, and if he doesn't return the money on the day that's marked, the notary takes all his property. Don't you remember the Cascavels?"

"Was that for a mortgage?"

"Naturally."

It was a terrible story. When Old Man Cascavel died, his sons, who weren't very responsible, took out a mortgage on the farm, to make some rather pretentious repairs. As might be expected it was their wives who wanted to put on a display of their wealth. Then they had bad harvests, and the gentlemen of the mortgage sold all their property, and now the Cascavel sons, instead of breathing the breezes of the hills, walk all day in the sewers of Marseille carrying their boots and a lantern in their hands.

"That's what they are, mortgages, and they always end like that!"

The Papet thought for a moment, then his face cleared.

"Galinette," he said at last, "that's both bad and good. The bad is that if he has four thousand francs, he'll buy a mule, and next summer his business will succeed. Not as much as he imagines, but enough to encourage him. On the other hand, I know he has debts at the mill, at least seven hundred francs . . . As for the mule, I bet you anything the horse dealer in Aubagne will charge him a thousand francs for some sorry nag that's been bought back from the slaughterhouse. That leaves twenty-three hundred francs. Deduct five hundred francs for the chisels, the fuses, and the contraband powder . . . That leaves eighteen hundred francs. He'll buy shoes, and, above all, wine, because he can't go without it anymore. Then he'll need bran and coarse flour for his rabbits before they start bringing in anything. I tell you in a year he'll have just enough left to pay the interest on the mortgage; but it's possible that the lender could give him a renewal for a year, and then I don't know where things would go.

"But on the other hand, since he's a man who's had hardly any luck, lots of things could happen. Firstly, since he's done everything he could to make himself sick, he could die, or perhaps get so thin that he won't be able to get out of bed for six months. Secondly, if he goes in for explosives, gunpowder and wine won't go well together, and a cartridge might blow up in his face. Thirdly, if the rabbits get swollen belly he'll be ruined in a week. In any case, it's the mortgage that's master of the situation. I'm going to give him a mortgage. If he succeeds, he'll reimburse me and pay me interest. If things go wrong, we'll have the farm."

"You're deep, Papet. There's no other way to put it, you're deep."

"I'm deep because I've got the money. Go and see him at once: tell him you have an old uncle who'll give him the mortgage of four thousand francs, at a low interest. He's got nothing to do but present himself in three days to the notary in Aubagne, at 8, cours Barthèlemy, with his papers. I won't be there, because I'm ill. He's only got to sign and the lawyer will give him the money."

Ugolin was deeply moved and looked at his Papet with great gratitude.

"All the same, it's fine to have a Papet like you . . . There! I must kiss you."

But the Papet pushed him away, and said:

"Let's not waste our time on nonsense. Go quickly, in case he's already left for Crespin."

Thus it was that Monsieur Jean returned from Aubagne one November afternoon, blessing dear Ugolin.

In front of him walked the she-ass, loaded with tools, provisions, espadrilles, and linen. But his joy was not unmixed, and he never stopped looking to both sides with visible anxiety. In fact he was carrying a dozen sticks of dynamite in his haversack, and two little packets of detonators in his waistcoat pockets, and a Bickford fuse wound round his waist, under his shirt. He had no right at all to transport these dangerous materials, illicitly bought from a carrier burdened with family, who had himself stolen them from a workyard. Nevertheless, he dared to stop at the miller's on the way to pick up a sack of bran and pay his debts and drink two glasses of white wine.

In the evening after dinner he studied his miner's manual for a long time. He read twice, in a loud voice, the three pages that described in detail the loading of a mine. The author laid stress on the dangers of the detonator, which had to be applied delicately to the end of the fuse with WOODEN tweezers, and then on the dangers of tamping the explosive, which also demanded a great deal of sensitivity and the employment of a round WOODEN rod.

He was very excited by the possession of these explosives, as children generally are, and proudly manipulated the yellow sausages whose magical power was at his disposal.

"I'm nearly certain," he said to Aimée, "that the first explosion will be good because I'll dig a hole of nearly a meter, and I won't hesitate to put in six cartridges."

"Papa," said Manon, "you should first try with a little mine. Very little . . ."

"My darling, a little bomb can kill a man as well as a big one, if he is imprudent enough to tamp it roughly, or if he goes down to the bottom of the well to light a fuse that's too short. As for me, I'm going to take such minute precautions they'll make an expert laugh. But first of all, there won't be an expert there to look at me, and besides, I don't care if I'm ridiculous. Safety first."

"What are you going to do?" asked Manon.

"Well, quite simply, I'm going to use a fuse eight meters long, leading to the edge of the well. Thus I won't risk falling off the ladder when I climb up after lighting the fuse. This length of fuse will force us to wait at least eight minutes. We'll go and sit some distance away, under the bushy tree, and we'll hear a magnificent explosion. The earth will tremble, and perhaps we'll see some stones bursting out, but they won't touch us because they'll be pointed straight upward by the walls of the well, like bullets in a gun."

"That'll be lovely," said Manon. "But when you go to light the fuse, that's what'll be dangerous!"

"So little dangerous," he replied, "that it will be you who'll light it!"

It took him two whole days to drill the hole to a depth of nearly a meter with a small pick and then with the crowbar. He finished it in the evening by the light of a lantern because the last days of autumn were really short. Then he declared:

"Tomorrow, perhaps before noon, we'll see the water of the hills surging through the ripped-open rock, a hundred times more precious than gold!"

The day broke cold but clear. Robin redbreasts called each other under the rosemary bushes on the hillsides, the close-cropped grass in the rabbit park was powdered with white frost, which was immediately blotted out by the first rays of the sun.

He prepared his mine with ceremonious slowness. First, he made the tweezers by joining two short wooden rods with a wire ring passing through their ends. Then he ordered a terrified Manon to retreat at least twenty paces, and applied the capsule of the detonator to the Bickford fuse. Then with his haversack on his back he slowly descended to the bottom of the well, while his daughter held firmly to the free end of the fuse. Finally he slid the cartridges one by one to the bottom of the mine hole, suspended on a string to avoid shock on arrival at the bottom . . . He sent down five; then he opened the paraffined paper case of the sixth, introduced the detonator, tied the envelope around the fuse again, and let the cartridge down on top of the other five. He observed with pleasure that there were thirty centimeters left for packing the tamping. He poured some sand into the hole, then some fine gravel, and then he molded sausages of clay and pushed them in with the end of his hardwood stick. He rammed the last sausage carefully, pressing lightly . . . Finally, he climbed up again toward his daughter's face, which was leaning toward him between two long vertical cascades of golden curls.

"We're ready!" he said.

He attached the end of the long fuse to one of the legs of the derrick. Then he handed a box of matches to Manon.

"The honor is yours!" he said.

Gravely she brought the little flame to the end of the fuse. It crackled feebly and threw off a thin jet of smoke.

"Go and call your mother. She should be here in case the water suddenly gushes out."

Ugolin was stretching a string between two stakes to align his tomato plants when a powerful explosion made him tremble.

"There it is!" he said. "He's started the dynamite. Who knows what that will lead to?"

He tied the string to the stake thoughtfully . . . He blinked three times, looked at the empty sky, and took the path to Les Romarins.

There was nobody in the field; light smoke still issued from the well. He approached, smelled the bitter odor of the powder, and made out a small pile of rock splinters at the bottom.

"For all the noise," he said, "it hasn't accomplished much! After all, the water hasn't come out, and he isn't dead. But then, where is he?"

He went toward the house.

Jean Cadoret was sitting on a chair with his head bent down to his chest; Manon was kneeling in front of him, in tears. Behind him, Baptistine was applying a poultice of herbs to the nape of his neck.

Ugolin entered:

"An accident?"

"He got a stone on his neck," said little Manon.

The hunchback, without lifting his head, whispered:

"It was my fault . . . I ran to the well in the hope of seeing the water gushing out, and a stone, which must have gone very high, fell on the back of my head . . ."

"Since you're talking," said Ugolin, "it can't be very serious . . ."

"I hope not . . ."

"There's a hole," said Baptistine, "but not very big."

"Perhaps," said Ugolin, "you didn't tamp hard enough . . . So then, instead of splitting the rock, the bomb went off like a cannon, and that could throw a stone a hundred meters high."

Aimée gave the wounded man a cup of coffee. He raised his head painfully and tried to drink; but the cup escaped him and his head tumbled backward . . . He remained with his face upturned; a groan escaped from his open mouth . . .

Ugolin jumped to take him by the shoulders.

"It's weakness," he said, ". . . it's natural . . . It'll pass."

Manon, horrified and pale as death, supported her father's neck. His closed eyes seemed to sink into their sockets . . . Aimée sobbed . . .

Ugolin ran upstairs to take a pillow and a mattress from one of the bedrooms and put them on the table; with great care they stretched the wounded man on it on his right-hand side, because of the hump.

"Go quickly and find a doctor," said Aimée. "Quickly, we've got the money . . ."

"I'll go and ask the mayor to telephone the doctor at Les Ombrées—he knows how to do it. He'll be here in about an hour, but not before . . ."

Aimée tried to force a spoon containing some white wine between her husband's clenched teeth.

Ugolin ran to the village.

During the afternoon the three women stayed with the recumbent man. He was immobile, but his breathing was rapid and short and his sallow face was contorted by a sort of rictus . . . From time to time Baptistine bathed the dressing with a cool tea and Aimée softly wiped the hollow cheeks.

Ugolin reappeared about five o'clock; night was falling.

"The doctor was not at home, but he's just returned. He left Les Ombrées on his motorcycle and he'll be here in half an hour, perhaps sooner."

"Does he know the road?" asked Aimée.

"Oh yes! It was he who came here to verify the death of Pique-Bouffigue!"

Without a word Manon lit the lantern, took her cape, and ran to wait in the little clearing at Massacan.

The doctor did not arrive until about seven o'clock, and because of the state of the track, he left his motorcycle leaning against the mulberry tree.

He was a big strong man with a thick blond moustache; he wore a black felt hat and a black overcoat and carried a leather briefcase.

Manon told him about the accident. He took big strides, and she trotted to follow him.

She spoke very quickly:

"Not a very big stone . . . a flat stone, no bigger than my hand—that won't be anything, will it? Papa is very strong . . . He's not like everybody else, because his back is a little round, even very round . . . But he was born like that, and it doesn't bother him at all . . . He's never tired, and he has very good health . . . He's very gay . . . It's not serious, is it?"

"We must see," said the doctor. ". . . If he doesn't talk, if he doesn't reply, it's because there's something . . . The nape of the neck—that could be serious . . ."

"I think he's sleeping," said Manon. "He's worked a lot recently . . . It would be natural for him to sleep. It's already happened to him to sleep at the table . . . Besides, he came back to the house quite alone . . . He leaned on me a little, but not much . . . He walks very well . . . He's not going to die, is he?"

"No, no! . . . One doesn't die so easily," said the doctor. ". . . But all the same, it could be serious, and we'll do everything that has to be done."

As they entered the kitchen Baptistine was on her knees, praying; Aimée was softly wiping the pallid face with a scrap of muslin.

She whispered:

"He tried to talk just now and ground his teeth . . . But he hasn't moved since a moment ago . . ."

The doctor took the wounded man's wrist and felt the pulse for a long time, then he took a wooden stethoscope from his case. The sight of this apparatus worried Ugolin and reassured Manon; science was coming to her father's aid. The doctor listened for a long time in a profound silence emphasized by the ticking of the grandfather clock.

Finally, he took a little mirror and held it for a moment in front of the pinched nostrils.

Baptistine kneeled and started praying in a whisper. The doctor took the fatal stone from Manon's hands and examined it. Then he unrolled the dressing and uncovered a red wound in the hollow of the nape of the neck; it was hardly two centimeters long, on a violet swelling.

Then he took a pair of long shining tweezers . . . Manon gritted her teeth and closed her eyes. When she opened them she saw a little splinter of limestone on the end of the tweezers, red with blood and no bigger than a fingernail.

"The stone is not very big," said the doctor, "but it has a fine cutting point. Because of the shape of his back, his vertebrae are more vulnerable, more fragile. There's no doubt, he did not suffer much in going where we all have to go . . ."

Aimée looked at him stupidly. Baptistine mumbled Piedmontese prayers . . .

Manon, who did not understand, softly seized the hanging hand of her father, to put it on the table. She felt the weight of death. Seized by an animal fear, she pulled her hands to her chest and drew away, her back to the wall. Then Ugolin crossed himself, walked around the funeral table on tiptoe, and stopped the pendulum of the grandfather clock with the tip of his forefinger.

Outside in the falling night an owl called. The doctor closed his case, saying words that were useless except to fill the horrible silence.

"He did not suffer . . . He certainly did not understand the gravity of the wound . . . Even if I had come sooner, there would have been nothing to do, nothing . . . I understand your grief, but I must tell you it is the destiny of all of us . . . And if you have faith, think that you will see him again in Heaven, delivered from the cruelties of this life . . ."

Ugolin did not listen to him. In the yellow light of the petrol lamp, he looked at the valiant corpse, forever immobile, the black lock on his pallid forehead, the thin smile on his pale lips. A strange grief gripped his side, and he trembled with dread, while great tears sprang from his eyes . . . Stepping backward, he reached the door, and in the penumbra of the night, with the owls calling, he took flight.

All the length of the village road he spoke in a loud voice:

"I told him it was dangerous . . . It's not my fault, I have nothing to do with it . . . He looked hard for it, his misfortune . . . It's the books that killed him . . . He thought he knew everything, and now look at the result . . . If he'd listened to me the other day, this wouldn't have happened . . . I have a clear conscience . . ."

But he wept all the time, without knowing why.

He arrived at the Papet's house out of breath and stopped for a moment to wipe his face with his shirt-sleeve before opening the door.

The table was laid under the lamp.

While he waited for his nephew, the Papet, with his hat on his head, had started a bottle of white wine and was reading the *Parochial Bulletin*, which delighted him. That was why he was laughing noisily when Ugolin entered.

"Papet, I've just stopped the grandfather clock in Monsieur Jean's house."

His voice sounded like a toy flute. His eyelids beat rapidly and made the tears fall onto a grimacing smile.

The Papet got up, astonished.

"And is that why you're crying?"

"I don't know. I'm not doing it on purpose. It's nervous . . . It's not me who's crying, it's my eyes . . ."

"After all, it's not your fault—it's the weakness from your poor mother. Are you sure he's dead? And what of?"

"The explosion," said Ugolin. "The first explosion."

He recounted the events in a low voice, and his tears never stopped flowing. The Papet, irritated, filled a glass of white wine.

"Take it, idiot."

Then, while Ugolin drank in long drafts:

"And the carnations. Do they still interest you, the carnations?"

"Oh yes, they interest me! And on the one hand I'm very pleased. There, see! They've stopped. Come on, let's eat . . . Let's eat."

He took his place at the table and the Papet went to open the door to the kitchen.

"Wipe your eyes—she may hear nothing, but she sees everything."

He sat down in his turn. The mute placed the soup tureen in the middle of the table and left.

"Galinette, I feel sorry for him, too. I'm glad he didn't suffer; but there's no question, it was his fate . . . That man, if he'd stayed a tax collector he could have lived fat to a hundred years . . . It's the books that killed him. May the Good Lord receive him!"

He served a big plate of soup and some slices of bread.

"Now's the time to keep our eyes open. We're in a good position because we hold the mortgage . . . But somebody could come along . . . a little cousin that he didn't even know—or a relative of his wife's—or an envious person from Crespin—or another idiot from town, who'd have the idea of planting coffee or sugarcane. So they'd make proposals, the notary would put up notices . . . Notaries' notices find fools as far as Pampelune . . . What we have to do is buy the farm right away, with the help of the mortgage, and buy it without any ill-feeling. So eat in peace, and then go back there and keep the vigil with those women. Since you have the weakness of weeping, go and weep with them! At least that will be of some use . . ."

The funeral took place two days later.

On the horizon the low end-November sun cast only grey shadows, as long as those of a summer evening. A light, cold breeze ran through the shivering olive trees, and the thrushes darted about in the turpentine trees.

Casimir and Pamphile had finished making the coffin during the night and came to help Ugolin place the body in it while the women got dressed in their rooms. They loaded the long box on the Papet's cart. Baptistine put two armfuls of wild everlasting with a strong odor of honey on it, and Jean de Florette departed for the field of rest under a swarm of bees, to the distant sound of the bell.

The wife and daughter hid their faces burnt by the night's tears under mourning veils that Pamphile had brought. Baptistine, all black, supported Aimée. Manon walked straight and stiff like a little soldier in an absurd frozen dream. Ugolin led the mule by the bridle, kicking away the stones on the road.

At the funeral mass the women saw people they did not know: Ange the fountaineer, Claudius the butcher, Cabridan, who bitterly regretted the episode of the ball, old Anglade, pale and trembling between his twins.

When they left the church Philoxène went to join the little cortege, bowler hat in hand; but the Papet stayed at home.

At the cemetery Casimir and Pamphile, each holding an end of the rope, let the coffin down to the bottom of the grave. The little girl, solemn and calm, let a sprig of rosemary fall on it. Her mother, as if absent under her veil, did not move.

Baptistine divided the everlasting and the bees between the tombs of her master and of Giuseppe.

Then the mayor greeted Aimée and told her he regretted not having known her husband, and that the community would take care of the cost of the funeral; when Aimée asked in a toneless voice whom she should pay for the coffin, Pamphile went up to her and whispered that it had been paid for by someone from Crespin.

As they went up again toward the village, Casimir said:

"If that man had not been forced to dig a well, he wouldn't be dead now."

And he looked Ugolin straight in the face.

Pamphile said, with an indifferent air:

"If he had had a spring, he wouldn't have dug a well."

Then he raised his eyes toward the black silhouettes walking in front of them.

"What are they going to do now?"

"I don't know," said Ugolin. "They must have relatives . . . And then, they can always sell the farm . . ."

"And you," said Casimir, putting on a friendly air, "perhaps you will be charitable enough to buy it from them?"

"That depends. What do you think it's worth?"

"Not very much," said the carpenter. "In any case, it's not worth the death of a man."

CHAPTER 38

Ugolin took the prostrate women back to Les Romarins on the funeral cart. He left them around the fire, after having vainly offered his services, while Baptistine boiled tisanes. Worn out himself by two nights of vigil, he went to sleep at Massacan.

The crackling of a faggot of wood awoke him in the evening. The Papet was warming his sore bones with his back to the fireplace. The cloth was laid on the table.

"Oh, how well you've done!" said Ugolin. "I'm dying of hunger but I don't know if I'd have the strength to go to the village!"

"Well, let's eat and talk, it's time."

He took the earthenware pot containing a sputtering roast chicken from the corner of the fire.

Both of them were pensive, as on the evening of a battle. The Papet took the bird by one wing and said:

"Pull!"

Ugolin took the other wing and pulled, and the breast came away from the chicken.

The Papet cut his part into little pieces because of his bad teeth. It was Ugolin who spoke first.

"So, what are we going to do now?"

"We'll see the woman tomorrow morning, we'll explain the mortgage to her, and we'll buy the farm from her."

"Don't you think we should wait a bit?"

"Wait? Why?"

"At the cemetery some of them gave us funny looks."

"And so? What does that matter? I can give them a funny look too."

"Yes, but what are they going to say if we jump on the inheritance right away?"

"They'll say what they like. I don't meddle in other people's business and I'll never let them meddle in mine."

"You know, Pamphile said some things that I didn't like."

"What does it matter what Pamphile said? If windmills could talk they'd say the same things he did."

"And Casimir made digs at me too."

The Papet's face suddenly darkened.

"Casimir stole part of his sister's inheritance, the sister who's in Marseille. Yes, the green jug full of pieces of gold, it's he who kept them without saying a word to anybody. So, the next time he makes a dig at you, tell him good day to the green jug. We'll go and see the widow tomorrow morning."

They ate in silence for a moment. Then Ugolin drank a glass of wine and continued:

"Listen, Papet, if we make the women go at once, that'll make talk. The men I don't mind. But the village women, you know them. Nothing will stop them from spitting on the ground after we pass by."

The Papet thought for a moment, then drank in his turn.

"Galinette, you might be right there. But, so, what do you want to do?"

"Well, as for the carnations, we're in no hurry; we've got until the end of March before we have to plant the cuttings . . . So I think we should buy the farm immediately, but tell them to stay as long as they want. That won't stop us from starting the digging, laying out the furrows, and getting everything ready . . . By March they will have gone of their own accord and nobody will be able to say a word to us."

"Are you sure they'll go?"

"And what d'you want these women to do, alone on that hill? . . . They'll die of fear in the night . . . They surely haven't got the strength to carry on with that folly of the rabbits . . . Then, when they've gone, we'll unplug the spring."

"And if they stay?" said the Papet. "With fifteen hundred francs, the goats, and the garden, they could dig themselves in for two or three years!"

"I thought of that," said Ugolin. "If they stay, I will always live at Massacan, and that will make me a sort of caretaker of the land. And besides, the women could do very good work with the carnations—watering, gathering, making bouquets. They could work for me and they wouldn't cost me very much."

"Ha ha!" said the Papet with admiration. "That's what you've got in your head!"

"Not exactly, but something like that."

The Papet thought for a moment, fork in the air, then smiled, winked, and said:

"Without even counting that the woman is still beautiful . . . She'll get bored on the hill . . ."

Ugolin blushed slightly.

"Be quiet, Papet. I've never thought of that, especially not now, with the poor man hardly cold in his grave."

CHAPTER 39

At eight in the morning the slight opening of the shutters did not let more than a ray of light into the kitchen of the solitary farmhouse. Baptistine was kneeling in front of the fireplace, lighting the wood fire.

Near the window Aimée, disfigured by tears, was trying to sew black material, and little Manon was sitting immobile on her father's low chair. Under her disordered hair she gazed vacantly at the wall. Between her hands, which rested on her knees, there were two mouth organs. Only the light crackling of the fire pierced the silence, because Manon had not wanted to start the grandfather clock again.

Footsteps approached on the terrace, then two shadows passed in front of the slit in the shutter and there was a discreet knock at the door. Manon shuddered and got up. Baptistine cried:

"What is it?"

The door turned on protesting hinges and Ugolin appeared. He was in his Sunday clothes, as he had been on the day of the funeral. Behind him came an old man with a whitening moustache, perfectly clean, carrying a black felt hat in his hand. It was the Papet, whom they had never seen.

"Madame Jean," said Ugolin, "forgive us for coming like this to trouble you, but it's in your interest."

Little Manon took a step backward and looked at them with her habitual distrust.

"What interest?" she asked curtly.

"Mademoiselle," said the Papet, "you are very young, and you don't know yet that after misfortune there come troubles . . . When a person dies, there is inevitably the question of the inheritance, and the tax collector will certainly demand money from you."

"And unfortunately," said Ugolin, "I know that you haven't got any left, because Monsieur Jean told me."

Aimée, her shoulders hunched, murmured:

"I have eleven hundred francs left . . ."

"You have no need to tell that to anybody. But you also have this house, and the fields, and the vallon of Le Plantier. It's your inheritance. That has some value . . . People from the government will come and tell you: 'That is worth a lot and you owe me a lot!'"

"So," said Manon brusquely, "must we pay because my father is dead?"

"Well, yes," said Ugolin. "It's unjust, but it's like that."

"And besides," said the Papet, "I know that your husband took out a mortgage on this farm . . ."

"My God! I didn't think of that!" cried Aimée. "That notary lent him four thousand francs!"

"It will have to be paid back," said the Papet.

"But how?"

"Since we have nothing," said Manon drily, "we'll simply not pay it back."

"Poor child!" cried the mother. "Don't forget that your father's signature is on that paper! Everything, I'll sell everything, even our bread, even . . ."

But she could not continue, and burst into tears.

"Madame," said the Papet, "don't be distressed about this question of money. I can arrange it."

"That's why," said Ugolin, "I said 'in your interest' a moment ago. It's because this gentleman is going to save you!"

Aimée lifted her head, Manon came forward.

The Papet spoke with habitual authority.

"You have no need to sell everything, and especially not your bread! I know that notary and I'll go and talk to him. Instead of taking your money, he'll give you some! Naturally you'll be obliged to sell something. You'll keep Le Plantier, which is valuable because it's big. Besides, it's all cultivated. It grows superb melons! With an extraordinary perfume! And then you have that spring! It's a property, Le Plantier! Moreover, you'll keep all your furniture, all your belongings. But the farm, unfortunately you'll have to sell it."

"No," cried Manon. "No! Never! Maman, don't say yes. I don't want you to! . . ."

She threw herself on her mother and held her in her arms.

"If we're forced to . . . ," she murmured.

"But why can't we sell Le Plantier . . . Won't that be just as good?"

"No," said the Papet. "It's not the same. For Le Plantier you'd have to take time, put announcements in the newspapers . . . And then you'd have to pay interest on the mortgage, and reimburse the capital. And if you couldn't, the notary would put everything up for auction: Le Plantier, the farm, the furniture . . . Not many people would come, because it's a long way from everywhere . . . And in the end it wouldn't sell for much, and you'd leave without a sou. While as for me, I will make you an honest proposition. I will buy the farm at once for the price of eight thousand francs. That will mean that you pay the four thousand to the notary, plus the expenses, and you'll have at least three thousand left."

"It's I who said eight thousand," said Ugolin, "because that was poor Monsieur Jean's idea . . . He told me that one day in front of the little one. He said: 'It's worth seven or eight thousand.'"

The Papet pretended to be annoyed.

"Seven or eight? So why did you tell me eight? When one says seven or eight, it means one will accept seven!"

"Naturally," said Ugolin, "but now that the women are alone, somebody must consider their interests! Since you've accepted eight, it's eight. Isn't that true, Madame Jean? Don't you let it go, what's said is said!"

"It's quite true," said Aimée, "that my husband spoke to me about seven or eight thousand. But he didn't intend to sell."

"Intention," said the Papet, "is one thing. But when a person doesn't have any choice, intention no longer counts for much. Nor did I have any intention of buying. But when I saw that you would be forced to sell, then I was forced to buy. Is it agreed?"

"No!" cried Manon. ". . . Maman, don't answer! Maman!"

She threw herself sobbing at her mother's knees.

"Maman, I don't want to go. No, I don't want to! You're not going to leave him alone in the cemetery? Maman!"

Ugolin got up quickly, moved by this despair.

"Don't cry, little one, don't cry. Listen to me. This gentleman is buying the farm, but he already has lands, and besides, he's too old to work much. So he's buying it so he can rent it to me. Yes, me, I don't want the hill to come and eat up all the work that poor Monsieur Jean put into the field. I want to cultivate the field. It's next to mine. So I'll stay at Massacan, and you can stay here as long as you want."

"That," said the Papet, "is his business. That doesn't concern me."

"Will you do that?" asked Aimée, trembling.

"Yes, I'll do that . . . You stay here at your place, and I will never come in without knocking at the door, because for me it will always be Monsieur Jean's house."

To his own surprise, he pronounced these words with real emotion, and tears sprang to his eyes. The Papet looked at him with astonishment, and asked himself if he should admire his talent an actor or deplore this imbecile sentimentality; but the little girl got up again and murmured: "Thank you . . . thank you . . . thank you . . ."

Then Baptistine got up and called for the immediate intercession of the Blessed Virgin, to assure the generous Ugolin a considerable fortune, a long full life, and many healthy children.

They descended one morning to Aubagne, across the beloved hills. Aimée had put on deep mourning again and a widow's veil. The little girl's golden curls lightened her black dress. The Papet waited for them on the promenade in front of the notary's house.

The man of law was agreeable and declared that the price of eight thousand francs was more than reasonable.

"If these lands had water," he said, "they would certainly be worth double . . . But as there is no more than one cistern, and the building is very old, and a long way from everything, I think I am justified in saying that the buyer has shown himself to be generous."

The Papet smiled a debonair smile, to show that this generosity was quite natural for him, and there was no need to be surprised.

The notary declared that the mortgage would be paid off immediately, and that with interest and expenses deducted, there remained to Mme. the widow Cadoret the sum of 3880 francs, which the buyer would pay to her—for obscure notarial reasons—"out of the sight of the undersigned notary"; at which the Papet thought it necessary to stand up and turn his back to the man of law in order to hand over to the widow Cadoret the sum that was due to her—honestly "out of sight."

After the signatures were exchanged, they went out the door together, but the Papet immediately took leave of the sellers, with the pretext of a visit to an old friend. In fact, it displeased him to go through town at the side of this woman draped in crêpe and this little girl whose tearless despair was already not that of a child.

CHAPTER *41*

That evening, with all the shutters closed and the door barred, they had a big dinner, a deluxe dinner to celebrate their success.

There were two tins of sardines in tomato sauce (the mute nursed a cut hand), some pork-butcher's ravioli, and a fine leg of mutton. The Papet had brought these riches from Aubagne, because purchases of such importance could not be made in the village—where it would make talk. And on the table there were two bottles clothed in dust; as he drew their corks without the slightest jolt, the Papet asked:

"D'you know what it is, this wine?"

"A Jacquez?"

"Yes, it's a Jacquez from the vineyard that my father planted at Passe-Temps."

"Ayayay!" said Ugolin. "So it's as old as I am!"

"Exactly!" said the Papet. "The year of your birth thirty bottles were set aside for you. It was drunk for your first communion, and I'm keeping the others for your marriage. But today's a feast—Les Romarins is ours and perhaps it's a fortune."

"Certainly it's a fortune! So, how do we start?"

They looked at each other, smiling and proudly masticating this nourishment of townspeople.

The Papet slowly filled their glasses and they clinked before drinking the black wine of their native hills; its harshness enchanted their palates.

The feast proceeded without a word being spoken, because it was pleasant and stimulating to hear the golden bread crackling in their jaws, and their looks were enough to express their delight.

But after the ravioli they had to wait for the mutton, which the mute had not put on the spit until the last moment. So they exchanged some approving belches, and then the Papet spoke:

"Galinette," he said, "yesterday you told me we would unplug the spring when they had gone. Well, you were wrong. That's where we'll start, and we'll start at once."

"Why?"

"Because I've been thinking, and I'm a little worried. This water, it's been plugged at least three years. And what if it has found another way? And if it's lost for good?"

"O Holy Mother!" said Ugolin, terrified. "Don't say things like that to me, you'll stop the ravioli in my stomach!"

"Wait. I don't think it'll be lost. But it's sure to have found another way. Now listen to my reasoning . . . It took its first way quite naturally because it was the easiest. We plug it. Good. Then it looks for another, but that doesn't please it as much, because it took it out of vexation, and if we give it the first one again, I'm sure it'll come back. D'you understand me?"

"Certainly," said Ugolin. "It's like Antoine."

"What about Antoine?"

"He wanted Rosalie de Clarisse, and then suddenly she married the postman. So when he saw she was, so to speak, plugged, he took a girl from Aubagne. But as soon as Rosalie became a widow, he divorced his wife and took Rosalie, whom the Good Lord had unplugged."

"That's it," said the Papet, "that's it. But, remember, his divorce took some time. And with us it's going to be the same thing. Behind our plug there should be a lot of silt, some gravel, and perhaps some roots. Because when it doesn't flow it gets choked up . . . So, we'll have to wait a month or two before the water comes to us in full. That's why I tell you—let's unplug it tomorrow!"

"I wanted to wait until they'd gone, because there's a good chance that when they see the water they'll feel terribly sick . . ."

"Perhaps, but when we've gotten everything ready and paid out all the money and the water doesn't flow immediately, that'll make us even more sick. So, let's go tomorrow. Don't worry. We'll provide them with a little diversion and perhaps they'll be proud to see that the poor hunchback wasn't deluding himself after all. Here's the mutton."

They arrived at Les Romarins at seven in the morning, at sunrise. Ugolin carried a long crowbar and a pickax, and had a shovel on his shoulder.

The Papet brought a trowel and chisels in his heavy haversack, and carried a quarrier's hammer in his hand.

On the terrace of the house Baptistine was busy milking the impatient goats. The shutters on the first floor were still closed.

They put their tools down under the big olive tree, and then the Papet took out his watch on the end of a silver chain; he seemed to set the watch, and started walking on the field with slow and measured steps, with his eyes on the sky. Meanwhile Ugolin sat under a pine tree devouring a snack.

Ten minutes later little Manon appeared at the door. She was dressed in black and was holding a fine Asiatic white-streaked pumpkin to her breast. Behind her appeared Aimée in her mourning veil. She was carrying a big bouquet of rosemary and flowers.

The little girl looked for a moment at the Papet's exercises, while he pretended to be in a medium's trance. Then they both approached Ugolin, who got up awkwardly to greet them.

"Are you looking for water already?" said Aimée.

"Well, yes. Trying."

"Why don't you finish my husband's well?"

"I'm afraid that would bring us misfortune . . . It's better to let it stay just as he left it."

"D'you think you'll find a spring?" asked Manon.

"There has to be one here somewhere, because your father said so. When he said something, it was never stupid. He was a learned man . . ."

"D'you plan to grow pumpkins, like him?"

"Oh, no!" said Ugolin. "He was much more intelligent than me, and yet he didn't succeed . . ."

"If it hadn't been for that stone," said Manon, "he would have done everything he said. That's for sure . . . The pumpkins were marvellous . . . When I gave some pumpkin to the rabbits, they threw themselves at it. They adored it. Papa was right . . . If he'd had water . . ."

But she could not continue. Her chin trembled. Two great tears sprang from her eyes . . . She ran off suddenly.

Aimée asked: "Is M. the curé the one who has the key to the cemetery?"

"Yes," said Ugolin. "But the blacksmith has another. You only have to take it when you go by."

"Thank you."

She left, stumbling in the grass, toward the gold-and-black orphan clutching her offering to her breast.

"The flowers I can understand," said Ugolin, "but what are they going to do with that pumpkin?"

The Papet interrupted his reflections with a low whistle. He signalled to him to come quickly.

"Let's take advantage of their absence!" he said. "Bring the tools quickly!"

It took longer than they thought. Three years earlier Ugolin had rammed the earth too well, for fear of a leak and a resurrection of the fig tree. He dug for two hours, cutting a narrow trench long enough to permit the use of the pick and shovel . . . At last he raised his head with a radiant smile and threw the pick down beside the hole.

"Give me the iron bar!"

He raised the heavy steel bar with two hands and let it fall between his feet. A hard shock arrested the descent of the point. Ugolin winked at the Papet— he had just reached the cement. Then he struck with all his strength with machinelike regularity, and the bar vibrated and rang in his hands. He passed the chips of concrete to the Papet and the old man climbed a few steps up the hillside and scattered them around the bushes of broom.

Suddenly Ugolin said, "It's moist," then, "Here's the plug!" He crouched down at the bottom of the hole, and said, "It won't budge!"

"That holm oak," said the Papet, "it lasts a thousand years!"

"It's swollen. I'll never be able to pull it out! I'll have to break the rock around it . . ."

The Papet passed him the hammer and chisel and repeated blows rang for a long time.

Suddenly the Papet said:

"Look, they're coming back. No, the woman is alone. The little one isn't there . . . Go on, go on . . ."

Aimée went toward the house; lost in her revived despair, she seemed to hear nothing and see nothing.

Ugolin suddenly threw down the hammer and chisel.

"This time I'll have it."

He bent down and said:

"There it is!"

He jumped up onto the side of the trench and started laughing noiselessly. The Papet took the wooden plug and threw it far away and leaned down; at the bottom of the hole a powerful jet of water as big as a man's arm sprang from the rock and disappeared under a swirling eddy that hollowed out the wall of earth and gravel.

"It's grown," said Ugolin, "there must be a lot behind it."

Meanwhile, on the edge of the little escarpment, twenty meters from them, the broom parted cautiously, and Manon's face appeared; immobile and pale, her eyes wide open, she looked at the two leaning men, without knowing what they were looking at.

The water rose continuously and noiselessly toward Ugolin's smile. He murmured:

"The carnations, Papet . . . Fifteen thousand francs a year . . . The carnations . . . It's a fortune that's bubbling up . . . Look! Look! . . . It will run to the carnations . . . Look!"

Old Camoins' ditch was blocked; suddenly the hole overflowed and the little revived stream bounded down the slope in blue-and-white coils. . . Then Ugolin burst out laughing, threw his cap in the air, and started dancing with arms outstretched . . . But a long piercing cry rose from the other side of the broom, a desperate cry, strident and monotonous, that echoed across the pine woods and suddenly surrounded them.

Ugolin froze.

"What's that?" he said.

"It's a hare, just taken by a buzzard."

They raised their heads. The grey sky was empty. Ugolin climbed up to the little escarpment. The silence returned. He saw nothing. He shrugged his shoulders and climbed down again near the stream; then both of them looked for a long time at the course of the bubbling water, exchanging winks and radiant smiles.

It was Baptistine who found Manon three hours later . . . She was huddled up under some junipers at the bottom of a ravine, pale and silent, her teeth clenched. The Piedmontese crouched beside her and softly spoke rough words to her, caressing her like a sick animal. Then she spoke to her of her mother, and Manon followed her submissively; but when they arrived at the top, they saw the silver thread of the stream down below, across the pine wood. Then the little girl hid her eyes with both her hands and fell sobbing on her knees . . . Baptistine folded her in her arms, murmuring prayers, and took her to the house.

The joyful accomplices had gone to lunch in the village in the big Soubeyran house.

Ugolin's joy was so great and so profound that he stammered like one of Anglade's twins. Delivered from all worry, he devoured the long-simmered daube (the mute had got up twice in the night to look at it) while the Papet smiled with pleasure and munched the little tubes of greasy fat, which his astute tongue easily gathered to his remaining teeth. They drank a lot; then, after the coffee and the marc, Ugolin insisted on preparing a letter for Attilio. It was a song of triumph that needed more than an hour's thought and discussion. At last, the stamp stuck down and the letter placed in the box, they went up again to Les Romarins.

As they passed in front of Massacan, Ugolin ran behind the house and pulled up two carnation plants with their balls of earth; he carried one in each hand, and the flowers swayed in the sun . . .

The Papet regarded the house with its half-opened shutters for a long time, and said:

"I think they must be asleep, or there's nobody there."

"All the better!" said Ugolin. "To work! Look at the spring! It's running even stronger than this morning!"

He dug two holes and lodged the plants in them; then he watered them well with a zinc mug.

In the meantime the Papet had gone down to the farmhouse and knocked on the door. No response. He put his face to the glass and did not see anybody. Then he inspected the shed and went back up to his nephew.

"They must be up on the hill," he said. "They've taken the she-ass and the goats . . ."

But Ugolin wasn't listening. He looked in the distance and said:

"Look, what's that coming along there?"

He showed the Papet a group that appeared to be approaching them by the hill track.

"There are two mules . . . ," said the Papet.

"And two men, and a woman . . . I think it's Baptistine . . ."

In fact it was she, with Enzo and Giacomo. On the mule packs there were two woodsmen's sledges.

They fastened the mules to olive trees while Baptistine opened the door with the key.

"What's happening?" asked the Papet.

She explained: "The little one does not want to come back here. It upsets her nerves, it will end by her losing her mind. So the lady has decided to go and live in the cave of Le Plantier. That way, they'll be living in their own place. So Giuseppe's friends have come to help with the move. We've made two journeys, two. And then tomorrow I'll catch the rabbits to take them to the market. And then I'll come from time to time to gather Monsieur Jean's pumpkins. Alas, the poor man was right, never in his life did he do anything stupid, except to die. But now he's with the Good Lord, and up there he sees us and talks with Giuseppe. And Le Plantier is better for the little one, and for the lady (poor thing, may the Madonna bless her), and it's better for the goats, and it's better for the she-ass, and it's better for everybody. And that spring, the Madonna sent it for Monsieur Jean, but four days too late, because too many people were praying to her, often for foolish things, but there it is, that upsets her, and then everything can go wrong. After all, what's done is done. This is the last journey, and I'll give you the key, because it's yours."

She took it from a hole in her skirt, then, gravely and slowly, she handed him her master's key, as if it were that of a city, and took three steps back, and bowed deeply.

During these explanations the woodsmen were loading the last pieces of furniture on the sledges: the chest, the commode, with the boxes and bundles of books between the legs of the table pointing skywards.

On the mule packs there were pallets, mattresses, two bedsteads, and two night tables; but to avoid a third trip the men carried the boxes on their heads, protected by cushions. Baptistine had run a cord through the handles of seven or eight casseroles and made a belt of this strange chaplet; with her left arm she clutched the mechanism of the grandfather clock, and her hand steadied the long box of light wood on her right shoulder. Finally, held by a big ribbon around her neck, the gilded pendulum hung down to her flat buttocks, beating the seconds at each step.

They departed with a great rumbling of the sledges on the pebbles, and the heretical Angelus of the tintinnabulating casseroles.

Never had music seemed so beautiful to the Papet. With the key in his hand, he followed the liberating departure with his eyes for a long time, then went up again toward Ugolin, to give him the symbol of his power. He saw him kneeling at the edge of the stream. He had girdled his red ringlets with a crown of white carnations and held his mug full of water to the sky. It looked to the Papet like he was saying grace and was about to take a drink; instead the Papet poured the water over Ugolin's head, saying solemnly:

"In the name of the Father, the Son, and the Holy Ghost, I baptize you King of the Carnations!"

Manon of the Springs

CHAPTER *I*

Attilio was on his way as soon as he heard the good news. He came from Antibes to direct the first work himself.

He arrived on a glistening motorcycle that banged like a gun, trailing a long cloud of blue smoke.

He was big, wide-shouldered, and handsome as a Roman prince. He spoke a patois that was not easy to understand and a passable French that often employed two adjectives, one on top of the other.

In front of the spring he crossed himself and looked at it flowing for a long time. He declared it was beautifully clear, then drank a glass of it as carefully as a professional taster, and pronounced it deliciously fresh.

Next, with his watch and a bucket, he did a number of experiments, and finally said:

"You've got at least forty meters a day. Cubed! . . . At Antibes that much water would cost the likes of us three thousand francs a year! For a farm with two workers you've got three times more than you need!"

Ugolin and the Papet looked at each other and laughed with pleasure. Then they took a walk in the field. Ugolin dug up a little clod, and Attilio broke it in his hand, looked at it, and smelled it.

"It's nice and fat," he said. "It'll make big flowers. But the first job is to pull up all the olive trees."

"All?" said the Papet, astonished.

"All. Those trees eat everything. You can keep the four big ones down there in front of the house. But the others must go. And then these pines that come down the hillside, they must be cut back at least thirty meters. And then I imagine you've got rabbits here?"

"Yes," said the Papet uneasily. "There are quite a few here. That fence over there used to be a rabbit park . . . About two dozen escaped and set up house with the wild ones . . ."

"Too bad!" said Attilio. "You'll have to have a fence all round the field, with the bottom buried at least fifty centimeters. Otherwise it's no use talking about carnations. A rabbit to a flower grower is like a wolf to a shepherd. If just one gets into the field he'll treat himself to a supper worth three hundred francs, and he'll leave without paying!"

"Agreed," said the Papet. "We'll buy the fencing."

"Make a note of it!" said Attilio.

"No," said the Papet, "if I write it down I'll forget it and perhaps I'll lose the notebook."

Attilio smiled and said:

"M. Tornabua, my father, said the same thing. After that you'll have to plough to a depth of sixty centimeters; eighty would be better, but here sixty will be enough."

"We'll dig down to eighty," said the Papet. "Isn't that so, Galinette?"

"I'll see to that," said Ugolin. "We'll have to borrow another mule. Plough each furrow three times, then the shovel and the pickax. Twelve hours a day—that doesn't bother me."

"You'll have my mule, and Anglade's, and Eliacin's hinny," said the Papet. "I'll take care of it."

"We'll have to harness the hinny in front," said Ugolin. "He's smaller than the other two. If we put him in the middle, when the first one pulls he'll be lifted from the ground and dance in the air, and he'll worry."

The deaf-and-dumb woman served them a rich luncheon in the Papet's fine house. Attilio, excited by the Jacquez wine, waxed poetical about his trade; he became tender about the fragility of the cuttings, the infinite richness of the colors of the Malmaison carnation, the length of the stems of the "Remontant de Nice." Then he fulminated against the red spider, castigated the Mexican louse, and criticized the director of the auction at Antibes, who shamefully favored the Italians (for Attilio was born in France and his father M. Tornabua had long since been naturalized).

Then he drew a long list of things that were needed from his pocket.

"First, four thousand sixty-centimeter sticks. You need three or four per plant. No need to buy them, you can make them yourselves."

"That'll be my job," said the Papet.

"Next, you'll need to make stakes and crosspieces to support the straw matting."

"We can do them, too."

"Then you'll have to order the straw matting to cover the flowers at night. It's made with rushes from the Camargue, and you'll need at least a thousand francs worth . . . Then, fifty bobbins of cotton thread, and chemical fertilizer, insecticides, and two sulfate sprayers. I figure altogether it will cost seven or eight thousand francs."

Ugolin looked at the Papet, fearing that the statement of such a sum would not be well received, but the old man said simply:

"We've got the sulfate sprayers."

"So, Papet, do you agree that he should order all those things for us?"

"That would be very kind of him, because we don't know where to buy them!"

As he straddled his sputtering motorcycle the handsome Attilio declared:

"Do what I've told you . . . I'll come back in three months to lay out the beds and I'll bring you the cuttings, all ready to bed out. It's M. Tornabua, my father, who's giving them to you, because you've helped us so much."

It was quite easy to push back the pine woods; a team of woodsmen undertook the job in exchange for half the trees cut down; of course it was necessary to keep an eye on them since they might cut down both hillsides, right up to the top of the hill, to increase their share of the wood; yes, that's what woodsmen are like.

The olive trees were pulled up next.

They were centenarians several times over, and their roots formed enormous tangles.

It took five weeks with pickaxes, hatchets, and a block and tackle to get to the end of this job and fill in the three- and four-meter craters that were left.

All during this work Ugolin suffered from a bad conscience. He offered twenty small candles to Saint Dominique to obtain pardon for his crime and promised to care devotedly for the four trees that had been spared.

Then they had to fill in the well of "poor Monsieur Jean." Ugolin spent two long days throwing the spoil back into the hole and was moved to think of the man who had come to such a bad end extracting all this earth. But he was too interested in his project to be moved for long. After the deep ploughing, the digging with the pickax took him six weeks, from dawn to dusk. He left the field unable to raise his head and shoulders until the Papet had rubbed him with eau-de-vie perfumed with spikes of lavender. Then they started on the fencing; but the wire netting of the rabbit park provided less than half of it, and they had to buy the rest at Aubagne for nine hundred francs; the iron posts and the cement cost seven hundred eighty francs, which the Papet paid without hesitation.

Attilio came back in May. He praised the work that had been done and directed the installation of the first beds. These were narrow flat strips surrounded by a little wall of earth, like minuscule rice fields.

Attilio traced the straight lines with string and Ugolin shaped the earth. The Papet, who had made himself some knee-pads from a pair of old shoes, followed behind him and finicked over the work with a small pickax and a trowel, humming an unrecognizable love song all the time. Every once in a while he said:

"I'm enjoying this!"

After the last counsels, Attilio took Ugolin to Marseille.

The Papet could not hide his fear when he saw the last of the Soubeyrans straddle the luggage rack of a machine that could (according to Attilio) exceed a speed of forty kilometers an hour. But Ugolin, clinging to his friend's waist, reassured him with a triumphant wink.

They went to see M. Trémelat, an "expéditeur," that is, a flower broker, who was Attilio's contact in Marseille.

The wholesale dealer, who was fat, smiling, and garrulous, promised that if Ugolin's carnations were good he would buy his entire crop at the market price (which in any case he fixed himself).

As to transport, all Ugolin had to do was entrust the reed baskets to the messenger at Aubagne on Tuesday, Thursday, and Saturday before four in the morning.

Ugolin spared no pains; from dawn to dusk, and sometimes even by lantern light, he was with his carnations. The Papet helped him patiently, with the easy and the exacting jobs, like the spraying or the cutting and gathering in bundles. In spite of two frosts, which were, however, not very hard, his first crop was a fine success; he was able to repay his godfather and still have a hundred and twenty beautiful louis for himself, for M. Trémelat had agreed to pay him in gold, for a small percentage. There was only one dark spot in the picture—in spite of the efforts of the Papet, and of Délie, M. Trémelat maintained that the bundles were so poorly prepared that his own workers were obliged to do them again. If that was the best they could do, it would be better to send the flowers loose, but he would pay five percent less. Ugolin was forced to let it go at that, but the thought of the five percent that he was losing nagged at him continually. In the meantime the Papet tried to compose the ideal bundle, according to his own taste, but it was not M. Trémelat's taste.

CHAPTER **2**

It caused a lot of talk in the village . . . Hunters who used to take the other slope of Saint Esprit to go toward the plateaux now seemed to have a preference for the road by Les Romarins, in order to get a look at the farm on the way.

It was rumored that Ugolin had made hundreds and thousands; the messenger from Aubagne confided to Philoxène that just for his part, carrying three large baskets of flowers to Trémelat et Cie three times a week, he had received more than six hundred francs. Sometimes he took four baskets—and once even five! Everybody tried to calculate the relation between the cost of the transport and the value of the merchandise. They came to staggering conclusions, but for all of that, they underestimated the real state of affairs.

The second year was a triumph.

Two big frosts had devastated the fields on the Côte d'Azur, and the price of carnations tripled. By a celestial caprice the frost did not reach Marseille, and Ugolin's flowers hardly suffered at all.

Attilio came on a wobbling truck to announce the marvellous catastrophe and took an entire crop of flowers to the market at Antibes. M. Trémelat uttered joyous cries and came right up to Les Romarins to bid higher. He did not bring up the question of the elegance of the bundles, nor the regrettable five percent.

After a long discussion, in the course of which the broker rose up three times and cried "robbers!," it was agreed that he should have half the harvest, the other half being reserved for Attilio, but that he should pay for the flowers at the going price of the auction at Antibes, where agents fought with thousand-franc notes to buy carnations that had been given to the goats the previous year. Thus it was that Ugolin was able one evening to line up 260 pieces of gold on the table.

The big problem of the peasant has always been picking a hiding place; Ugolin was rather pleased with the solution he had found.

Above the rickety little chest in his kitchen he nailed a big piece of yellowish cardboard, on which he had traced, in uneven letters, a discouraging inscription:

ATTENTION, BURGLAR!

Don't waste your time looking for money. It is not here.
It is in the bank, in the middle of Aubagne, next door
to the gendarmerie. 12, cour Voltaire.
There is nothing you can do.

This was a ruse he judged to be infallible. In fact the treasure was buried under a large stone in the corner of the hearth, a meter away from the fire. In addition, to lend the sign a little more credence, he frequently played a comedy for Délie's benefit, "because the women, they gossip!" Every time M. Trémelat came he said:

"I won't be around tomorrow morning because I have to go put the money in the bank at Aubagne. There aren't any good hiding places. I always put everything in the bank—that way I can relax!"

Meanwhile, his appearance did not change—on the contrary! Completely absorbed in his passion, he would never have gone to the village for the Saturday evening session at the club if the Papet had not forced him to shave and dress up from time to time. During the games of lotto or manille he would go out at least once to assure himself that the stars were still there. He constantly feared a cold spell, or a frost, or a strong mistral that could carry away the straw mats. Above all he feared the return of the old giant rabbit—that he would jump over the fence, as he had already done, and with his ass's jaw cut down two or three beds . . .

Moreover, the conversations bothered him.

One Sunday Philoxène asked him:

"What gave you the idea of growing flowers?"

"It was when I was in military service at Antibes. I saw the peasants growing them. I looked a bit, and I thought they would do well here . . ."

"Carnations," said old Anglade, "they do well everywhere, provided there's no frost . . ."

"And especially," said Casimir, "you need a lot of water . . . No end of water . . . He was lucky to find the spring again."

"That's what the poor hunchback was looking for," said Pamphile. "I saw him with his divining rod . . . He had a mysterious look, like a wizard . . . And he passed by right next to it . . ."

"You make a good profit?" asked Cabridan.

"That depends," said the Papet. "It depends on the day . . ."

"The biggest profits are on the holidays," said Ugolin. "Christmas is best . . . And then Mardi Gras, and Easter . . . Easter is very good!"

"And the Dead?" asked Pamphile. "Is there much profit from the Dead?"

"Not bad . . . The Dead aren't bad. They give a pretty good return."

"That depends on the dead," said Casimir. "Some leave a big inheritance; and then others reach up from the grave to drag you down . . ."

And as Casimir burst out laughing, the Papet said brusquely:

"Well then? Are we playing or aren't we?"

No, the kind Monsieur Jean never came back to haunt Ugolin . . . Indeed he was a long way from his thoughts, always occupied and filled as they were by the present.

The massacre of the olive trees had enlarged the vallon. A sheet of bright flowers undulated at the slightest breeze, and at the foot of the hillside there shone a little round pond—fed by the underground stream—with water that lay smooth, then rippled out in a short narrow cascade . . . Jean de Florette had really departed forever for another kingdom. Nothing remained of his passing and his long misfortune, or very little: in an olive tree near the house two rings from which a swing used to hang were now rusted by passing seasons; and during the nights of the mistral a mouth organ hidden high up in the gutter played a little tune.

In the meantime Manon and her mother and the old Piedmontese woman were living together in the cave at Le Plantier, in the fragrant solitudes of the garigue.

Aimée had not touched anything in Baptistine's strange palace, but had furnished the sheepfold that occupied the other half of the cave.

In order to fertilize his garden, Giuseppe had scraped off the thick layer of sheep manure that had accumulated and dried over a century of pasturage, and the floor was now covered with a fine carpet of reddish moss, stained with dark green lichens. The furniture from Les Romarins was arranged along the walls and the side of the cave, as in a secondhand shop.

The handsome dressing table shone between two trunks, opposite the Venetian mirror attached to the strata of bluish limestone; and the useless chandelier, suspended with a plaited wire from a long stalactite, swayed every time the ancient door was opened. The beds stood end to end under the sloping rock, from which there hung a double curtain, yellow with little flowers, which opened like the curtain of an Italian theatre. Finally, between the two beds stood the tall grandfather clock. Little Manon had put it back together, and she polished the varnish and the brasswork nearly every day, but she had never wound it up, and the two gilded hands always marked the fatal hour of her father's death.

With the four thousand francs from the sale, Aimée had paid for the plot at the cemetery and for the tombstone. She still had two five-hundred-franc notes sewn into the lining of her corset, a dozen louis, and a handful of silver. She had put the coins in a little bag and had hidden this "treasure" in a cleft in the rock at the head of her bed.

Her husband's death had disturbed her reason. She certainly was not mad, and from six in the morning, after placing a flower before her husband's photograph, she did her housework very energetically, and prepared a lunch as before; but in the afternoon she sometimes sat for hours with her back to the wall in front of the cave without saying a word, with her gaze lost in the distance. At other times she walked on the deserted plateau of the Plan de l'Aigle, dressed in the remains of several opera costumes, gathering flowers and singing Werther or Lakmé.

During the second year she started talking almost continually, in a low voice, smiling and making faces. The subjects she talked about were surprising. Often it was the question of the commandant. He was a very fine man, always polite and obliging, but his wife, who had a little moustache, was unbearably coarse. She had caused a real scandal, and they had been obliged to leave Saigon. The commandant had wept over it. There was also the director of the theatre of Tananarive, a real twerp who never kept his promises and dropped people like old shoes; whereas the secretary general of the Gaité Lyrique, dear Armand, behaved like a gentleman, and "I wouldn't be here if he hadn't died, because he wanted me to sing Manon at the Paris Opera. I did get in, thanks to Victor, but in the chorus."

Baptistine nodded her head without understanding anything, and Manon thought these gentlemen must have been friends of her father's, but she did not ask questions.

Recently her mother had acquired a mania for writing letters to people who lived in Paris or Marseille, and she went herself to post these letters at Les Ombrées; but she complained every now and then about never getting any replies, saying, "As for Armand, that's just like him! But I'm surprised at Victor . . . It's not like him! But then, perhaps he's dead, he too . . . But all the same I'll keep on . . ."

And she went back to her writing table.

Manon had stretched a network of wire against the wall that closed off the cave, and the ledge that prolonged it—and every year in the spring she planted the black seeds. The Asiatic pumpkins hid the stones and the rock under a thick curtain of foliage until the middle of autumn, and six boxes with wire netting sheltered a dozen rabbits. Manon put her whole heart into this breeding, whose constant success justified her father's vain hopes. Every month she entrusted four or five rabbits of fine appearance and good weight, nourished all year on the Asiatic pumpkins, to Monsieur Jean's fat saleswoman. These pumpkins were so prolific that in the autumn Baptistine went to the market at Aubagne to sell as many as the she-ass could carry.

Because of the strangeness of the fruit it was not easy in the beginning; people regarded the heavy balls of green wood with suspicion, and a clown suggested to Baptistine that they team up to start a factory for cup-and-ball games. But the fat saleswoman took them up and launched the Asiatic fritters, which her daughter made on the spot in an immense frying pan on the chestnut-seller's brazier . . .

Baptistine had become quite old, and her face was shrunken under her white hair. She hardly spoke anymore, but worked ceaselessly like a machine.

It was she who kept up the little vegetable garden, which she was able to water profusely, thanks to the inexhaustible spring.

Every morning and every evening she milked the dozen goats. With the bluish milk of the hills she made little cheeses encrusted with savory herbs in the manner of the shepherds of Banon. She plaited round baskets with split reeds and rushes for a basket maker in Aubagne, and in the evening she sorted out the aromatic herbs that Manon brought back from her walks in the hills.

There were faggots of fennel, bundles of thyme, wild pepper, and pungent mint, and especially bunches of rue—a fairly rare plant that was illegal to sell because it was used in preparing a devilish tisane that caused abortions. The goats knew rue well and never touched it, unless they were carrying a malformed kid that was not worth finishing.

These little dealings supplemented the clandestine sale of game caught in snares, and the resources of the hills allowed the three women to live without worrying about tomorrow.

From time to time they received visits from Enzo and Giacomo; when their work brought them to the forest of Les Ombrées, or to the woods of Pichauris, they came to lunch in the cave on Sundays. As soon as they arrived they deposited a couple of hampers of pine nuts or mushrooms on the kitchen table, and four or five bottles of wine in a haversack, and a great packet of a dozen cutlets wrapped in coarse yellow paper. Then they hung their fine blue jackets on the wall, and their green hats and their red scarves, and took off their Sunday shoes. Barefoot, they took the sheaths off Giuseppe's axes to prepare a supply of wood, and Baptistine was happy to hear the sound of the curved blades of the great axes being revived. Next they did a number of heavy jobs, like mending the road where it washed away in places by storms. It was they who constructed the log shelter for the goats and built the little pond for the vegetable garden. After lunch, seated in the shade of the rock face, they sang Piedmontese songs; Manon accompanied them on the sacred mouth organ, and Baptistine smiled through her tears. When they departed in the evening they turned round two or three times with arms raised in distant farewells, but something remained of their presence—a sense of security, the certitude that in case of misfortune or danger these two huge males would come running at their first call . . .

Manon had just turned fifteen, but she was big for her age. With her mother's help, she made her clothes from the old theatrical costumes. Time had not spared the colors, but the rich materials had kept their strength; that was why the little shepherdess ran about the heath in gowns of soft-hued brocade and boleros of faded silk, and why, under the rain, she wore the operatic Manon's golden-fringed hood.

From these sumptuous rags emerged her brown arms, scratched by broom and hawthorn, and her long muscled legs, often blackened by running about in the burnt woods where the herbs were richest and where little processions of hooded morels could sometimes be found without looking. Her thick mane of hair, gilded by the sun and dried by the wind, was cut at the shoulders. Her sea-blue eyes shone behind curls that hid her brow, and all her face had that vivid radiance that is retained by ripe nectarines for only a day, but glows for three or four years on the smooth cheeks of young girls.

Enzo, who was forty and claimed to know life, often said to her: "Madonina, another year and you'll be so beautiful it will be frightening." And Giacomo said to her one day: "If you go into town, for pity's sake wear dark glasses, otherwise you'll set the town on fire!"

She was proud of these compliments from these men, and laughed with pleasure.

An hour after dawn every morning, when Baptistine had milked the goats, Manon went off with her stick in her hand, shouting the piercing cry of all shepherds: "Bilibili! Bililibili!" The flock would leave at a gallop, followed by the she-ass and the black dog.

On the she-ass's pack there was a bag, tied in the middle with a strap. It contained pruning shears, a sickle, a little pick for digging up flying ants, some string for tying herbs, half a loaf of bread, a goat cheese, a tin mug, and two or three books, taken haphazard from her father's precious box.

A little strapless bag was attached to her belt. There she kept her treasures: a tortoiseshell comb with a silver mount, a golden louis wrapped in paper, a piece of agate found on the hill, a small pair of tweezers (possibly made of gold) for extracting thorns, the two mouth organs of the happy days, and, in a wallet softened by time, a picture of the Blessed Virgin, and a half-effaced photograph of her father's handsome face.

Pushing the flock before her, she first made a tour of the traps she had set the evening before. When a light mistral was blowing, bringing flights of whitetails with it, she set her traps at the base of little pyramids of flat stones she had built on the edge of the escarpments to lure the birds from the wind . . . If there was a strong mistral, bending the pine trees, she would go down to the bottoms of the gorges and place her devices at the foot of the sheer drops under the turpentine trees and myrtles; but when the weather was calm she placed her traps on the plateaux, near sheepfolds or ruined farm hovels, around old dying fruit trees.

When she got to her destination she gathered herbs and plants and stuffed them in the bag on the back of the she-ass; then, if the weather was fine, she always went to the same place.

It was on the steep hillside of the vallon of Refresquières. A long wide terrace of rock stretched between two ravines, covered with thyme, juniper trees, and rosemary. Protected from the mistral by the ledge of blue rock that supported the higher plateau, it overlooked the bottom of the verdant valley above a sheer drop of fifty meters and could be reached only by very narrow paths leading from the bottom of the ravines.

On it there stood a very old mountain ash, whose roots doubtless plunged down an invisible crevasse. Mutilated by lightning, bristling with stumps like a parrot's comb, it stretched a long leafy branch over the flat rock, as smooth as a mirror.

On the side of the trunk opposite this branch, there was an enormous hump. Manon loved this tree, because one day when they were gathering grass for the rabbits, her father, seeing it some distance away, had said gaily:

"Heh heh! There's a colleague whom the skies haven't spared; but it hasn't lost heart and its last branch is greening valiantly! Let's pay it a visit and present our compliments."

They climbed up to the foot of the tree, the hunchback greeted it pleasantly, then they filled their bags with sorb apples . . . As they left he laughed; then, after a last look, he said:

"You could say that was my statue in wood!"

Manon spent some hours on the floor of rock. Keeping an eye on her goats, which Bicou never let stray too far, she ate her bread and cheese, combed her hair for a long time, and read, it did not matter what: *Robinson Crusoe*, the *Maxims* of La Rochefoucauld, the *Adventures of an Urchin in Paris*, Brunot's *Grammar*, the *Iliad*, or the illustrated newspapers of her childhood.

Sometimes, in the margins or on the endpapers, there were notes in the paternal hand. She would kiss the dear writing and look at the fierce distant crest of Saint Esprit, the cloud-ripping reef that had ruined him.

She had never returned to Les Romarins, but her thoughts turned to it ceaselessly. Then, she would take the mouth organ—the bigger one—and play the tunes he had taught her . . . Often it was the fugue of "Frère Jacques," accompanied by the echo of the Pas du Loup. According to the distance and the wind, the responses of the echo fell so exactly that one could imagine a human presence. With her eyes closed she imagined he was down there, hidden in the lush growths of ivy, and that he was pleased with the progress she had made.

From the height of her observatory she saw the rare passersby on the hills coming from a distance. She hid herself under the broom or scrambled up to the plateau by the path to Cabrettes and saw without being seen the stratagems of some thieves from Les Ombrées whose names she did not know, or people from Les Bastides, like Pamphile or Casimir whom she got to know at her father's funeral. Sometimes too, but rarely, she saw hunters wearing leather leggings and feathers in their hats, pushing dogs with long ears before them. These people were fine, but a nuisance because their dogs got caught in the rabbit traps, while their masters would fire doubles at a warbler, and salvos at a thrush, and make so much noise the game disappeared for eight days after they had gone through.

Town, for her, was Aubagne. She went there nearly every week, modestly hidden in a cape of her father's, her hair under a blue scarf. Behind her walked the she-ass with an enormous bundle that did not weigh much because it contained nothing more than aromatic plants she was taking to the herbalist, or baskets of woven reeds.

When she entered Aubagne, all the noise of the big market under the plane trees deafened and frightened her . . . It seemed to her that the mixed cries of the saleswomen, the frenetic bell of a stall-keeper, the shouts of a game merchant through a megaphone were a prelude to a general battle, and she hastened her steps . . . Nevertheless, she had to go through this uproar to deliver the baskets to the salesman, whose shop was no more than a wooden booth under a plane tree.

Then, leaving the she-ass in the herbalist's street she went to hear the eight o'clock mass, like her father, and she prayed for him. Next she had to go to the heart of the town to do her shopping, to buy the bread, the sugar, the coffee, the paraffin, the salt, the pepper, the soap . . .

The narrow streets oppressed her. One saw nothing but strips of sky with no glimpse of the sun; one could not forecast the weather for the next five minutes, and the air was thick with insupportable odors . . . From afar the shepherdess of lavender, resins, and junipers could smell the salted food, the cheeses, the sulfurous fumes of coal, the stinking breezes from the gutters flowing along the pavements, and especially the lewd and lugubrious odor of the townspeople, bustling like ants and brushing against her on the narrow thresholds of the shops.

Moreover, they looked at her often—without malice, but with an interest that sometimes made her blush; and there were youths who mocked her or threw compliments in passing . . . And one day in the baker's there was even a little old man with a musty face who said in a loud voice, "Look at this little one! I could eat her!" She took flight from this cannibal, clutching two great burning loaves to her heart . . .

No, she would never live in this anthill, she would remain a shepherdess all her life, and if one day she married, it would be to a very rich young man whom she would meet in the hills, a forest owner who lived in a château on the slopes of the Baou de Bertagno, or on the shoulder of the Pilon du Roi; he would give work to the dear woodsmen; he would buy Les Romarins again, and then they would put all the furniture back in its place and spend the summer months there. But first, on the very first day, they would plug forever that perfidious spring that had favored Ugolin. Then they would finish the well of her father's misfortune; and the water he had vainly sought would gush forth through the vanquished rock, right up to the sky.

In the village, life continued, monotonous and peaceful, at least on the surface, in spite of the arrival of two new personages.

The old curé, gone to a rest home, had been replaced by a priest about forty years old, born on a farm in the Gard. Former chaplain of the Legion, he wore a narrow Légion d'Honneur ribbon on his soutane for having gone to hear the confessions of the dying under enemy fire, and he suffered severe war wounds in silence. That was why the bishop had sent him to rest in this little village in the hills.

On his large pink face there shone a beautiful smile, but as Casimir said, he didn't "make fun of virtue," nor did he refrain in his sermons from strong denunciations of the unbelief, the selfishness, and the avarice of his parishioners. The bigoted old women and the Sunday school children—who enjoyed being bullied—adored him, and the men liked him too because he was the son of a peasant and talked to them in the gentle language of Provence.

Moreover, the old schoolmistress had retired and gone to live with her daughter, who kept a grocery shop "in town," that is to say in a quarter where one professed to be able "to watch the world go by." That is why the end of September saw the arrival of a young *instituteur*—the teacher.

It was due to Philoxène's complaints that they had finally obtained a male teacher, capable of disciplining the "big ones," and preparing them for the certificate of studies.

His name was Bernard Olivier. Twenty-five years old, dark, with big eyes the color of roasted coffee, wide shoulders, an assured step, and hair on the back of his hands. Unfortunately without a moustache—shaved like a statue; fortunately his voice was deep and musical and his teeth sparkling. Old Anglade thought it would be necessary to keep an eye on the young girls, even his own, a confirmed virgin twenty-five years old.

At the club he was welcomed with a drink in his honor.

Philoxène delivered a kindly welcoming speech, then the teacher declared that he was very glad to begin his teaching in this village with its salubrious air and friendly population, and in these hills that were very interesting to him since he was keen on mineralogy. The entire municipal council learned that day that the "Massif of Les Bastides" contained rare rocks, and that the young savant planned to do research there on the bauxites and lignites. He added that he played a fair game of *boules*, and of checkers, that he was not married, but lived with his mother, a widow since his birth. His name was immediately put down for the Republican Club, and he challenged all comers to a game of *boules*. Casimir was at once delegated as champion of the village; and the teacher, without the least tact, made him "kiss his fanny" in twenty minutes. Philoxène declared:

"He's quite a fellow!"

Casimir, without the slightest rancor, stated solemnly:

"With a young fellow of that quality they're bound to pass the certificate of studies."

His mother—a townswoman of fifty years—was really very young for her age, younger than Nathalie who was only thirty-five.

And besides, she was a flirt, with her hair always done well, and even a little powdered. In the beginning this was not well received. But one afternoon when the old grannies were knitting on the wall of the esplanade she went off without ceremony to sit with them and put up the hems of a dozen quite new dusters. The grannies spoke nothing but Provençal among themselves.

When Léonie (one of the Castelots, a little deaf) asked who this lady was, it was the lady who replied in the same language:

"Me? I'm the mother of the teacher, and very glad to have come to live in this village, because it reminds me of mine. I'm from Lachau, in the Drôme. My father grew peaches and lavender and I often took my turn with the sickle . . ."

That evening among their families the grannies reported that the mother of the "essituteur" was a marvel—intelligent, beautiful, and decent, and she spoke the patois as easily as French. The only thing she could be reproached with was that in order to say "perhaps" she said "beleou" instead of "bessai." But say what you like, the Drôme was in the North . . .

At the end of a week, since the gossips persisted in calling her "Madame l'essitutrice," she declared:

"I am not a teacher, and my name is Magali."

Only Sidonie, the doyenne, who had a lot of cheek, dared to take her up on this authorization right away. The others were very proud to have it, but only gradually became bold enough to call her Magali, and for the first time a "foreigner" was naturalized as a Bastidienne, in front of whom one could talk freely.

On Thursdays and Sundays the "essituteur" left early in the morning for the hills, with a fine leather bag on his shoulder. He explained to the club that he was going to collect samples of minerals to make a little museum at the school.

In the beginning, since his bag seemed to be well filled, they thought this story was no more than a pretext for setting traps for thrushes. Then, when they saw that his mother still bought thrushes from the poachers in the village and that he really did bring back stones and splinters of rocks, his explanation was accepted; all the more since the baker told them that the spirited young man carried a pound loaf, half a sausage, a goat cheese, and a bottle of wine in his bag for his breakfast on the hill.

Moreover, he soon got into the habit of coming for his evening aperitif to the terrace of Philoxène's café and became an important member of the daily council that met there under the chairmanship of the mayor. Since they never went to mass, the new curé called them "the band of unbelievers." They were the baker, the butcher, the blacksmith, the Papet, the carpenter, Ange the fountaineer, and M. Belloiseau.

M. Belloiseau, who called himself a former notary, had in fact been the head clerk in an important office in Marseille. He was tall and thin, with a slightly ridiculous distinction. His greying beard, cut to a point, was the object of much care. He always wore a grey jacket, of wool in the winter, under a bowler hat, and of alpaca in the summer, under a panama hat. Since he claimed that this straw, plaited in the tropics, was perfectly impermeable, he was frequently asked to prove it, and then he would fill it at once with water from the fountain. This was why this marvellous headgear, truly impermeable, but sorely tried by the humidity of these experiences, changed in shape and size according to the time and the season—so much so that after a long game of *boules* in the sun it was necessary to water it for quite a while to separate it from the scalp of its owner.

M. Belloiseau had been in the habit of spending his vacations in the village. He had been a summer visitor during these years, with the acerbic Mme. Belloiseau. Then age had come. Mme. Belloiseau had departed to vituperate in Purgatory, and a very sprightly M. Belloiseau had retired and decided to stay in his little house until his death. His house faced the square four steps from the café, on the corner of the narrow street that led to the club. The ground floor was taken up by an old cellar. Outside stairs, with stone steps hollowed by time, led to a little terrace in front of the apartment.

He was looked after by Célestine, whom he had brought from the city. Rather plump, with fine teeth and black eyes, she was hardly thirty. She was a "maid of all work," and in fact she did do everything, to the despair of M. the curé and the joy of the youths of the village.

M. Belloiseau's conversation, nourished by philosophical remarks and bawdy subjects, was all the more pleasant as he was perfectly deaf (Philoxène maintained that his eardrums were made of sausage skin) and gave random answers to the questions he was unable to hear.

Ugolin also came there from time to time, at the insistence of the Papet, who said:

"In the first place, you should see people a little, otherwise you'll become a savage and end up with a beard. Secondly, they know you've got some sous now, and you don't want it to look as if you've abandoned your friends. Go down at six o'clock once a week, or even twice, and have an aperitif before coming to dinner with me . . ."

The meetings of the unbelievers—who had no need to be summoned—always followed the same agenda.

Philoxène first read a number of articles from the newspaper in a loud voice. They discussed local politics, the price of vegetables, wine, tools. When there was an interesting crime, the one who was reading would put the newspaper on the table in order to have his hands free for gestures; thus he would strangle the woman living on her private income, stab the lover of the unfaithful spouse, or stretch out the hanged man's long tongue . . .

Then they talked of everything and nothing, and sometimes even about "other people's business," but by means of discreet allusions that neither the teacher nor M. Belloiseau could understand . . . For example, when the baker said one evening: "Some families are really on good terms with each other," it was because Petoffi had just gone by, and he was suspected of being the father of his sister-in-law's child.

Then, about six o'clock, in the summer when they had the heart, they would go and play a game of *boules* at the club, after drawing straws to choose up teams.

CHAPTER 5

One morning Manon, stretched face down under the mountain ash with her fists under her chin, was reading *The Gold Seekers of Alaska*. The April sun was not yet very high on the horizon and the silence was so pure she could hear the goats browsing. The faithful Bicou growled, pricked his ears, and raised his nose, and Manon saw a man twenty meters below her going along the scree under the escarpment. He walked slowly, looking at the ground as if he were looking for something lost. Suddenly he bent down and picked up a fairly large pebble. He examined it for a moment, then put it on a rock, drew a shining little hammer from his pocket, and with a sharp blow broke the stone into several splinters.

Then he took a big magnifying glass from his haversack and examined the fragments one by one.

Manon looked at him, most interested. She thought: "Perhaps he's looking for gold!"

He put a splinter in his pocket, after having marked it with a big pencil; then he resumed his walk on the scree.

He soon reached the ravine that cut into the escarpment, but instead of going down, he came up toward the mountain ash . . .

Manon hid her book under a juniper bush, got up noiselessly, and ran to talk to her dog in a whisper, pointing her finger at the ground. Bicou sat down on his tail. Then she ran toward a pine tree whose thick branches were nearly impenetrable, clasped the trunk, and disappeared into the foliage, while a great squirrel fled up to the top of the tree.

She had often climbed this tree to gather pinecones containing sweet nuts; she stopped in a central fork formed by three large branches and waited.

The seeker for gold climbed toward her; he could certainly have distinguished something through the thickness of the foliage if he had known she was there; but he walked slowly, looking at the ground at his feet.

When he got to the tree he stopped and listened; he had just heard a little bell sounding. He looked around and saw a big she-kid looking at him with great curiosity, a bouquet of white flowers at the end of her muzzle. He went toward her, and the vigilant Bicou darted up to defend the goat, growling as he showed his fangs.

The prospector took a step toward him, but the dog did not step back, and yapped furiously.

"Heh heh! You're afraid I'll steal your goats?"

The rest of the flock formed a semicircle behind their shaggy guardian and looked at the intruder, but the she-ass advanced peaceably toward him, until she could give him a nudge in the side with her muzzle. Then she pulled her long lip back on her yellow teeth and gave him, with eyes half-closed, a very beautiful she-assinine smile.

"Ha ha!" he said, "you want to be fondled!"

He softly scratched the rough grey silk between the two ears . . . But after a few moments, the she-ass plunged her nostrils under his arm and nibbled at his fine leather bag. He pushed her back gently.

"So, caresses aren't enough for you! You want to lunch with me! Wait a bit, we'll try . . . But where is your shepherd?"

He looked around him again. The dog had gathered the goats together and taken them away from the enemy.

The young man whistled, then called on two notes:

"Ho . . . ho . . ."

The echo from a distant slope replied.

Then he went to the foot of the pine tree and put his bag on the carpet of dried twigs. He sat with his back against the trunk of the tree, took off his beret, and unbuckled his lunch. First he took his bottle of wine and leaned it against a stone; then he took out a silver-plated mug, and a Bologna sausage. The she-ass watched his doings with great interest. Her globulous eyes, as big as plums, shone through long sandy lashes. When she saw the sausage she suddenly stretched her neck to smell it.

"No, it's not for you," said the young man. "And besides, I should tell you that dishonest butchers sometimes put donkey in the sausage. So, beware!"

He cut a slice of bread and offered it to the she-ass on his open palm.

Manon looked at this stratagem. She thought:

"He may be from town, but all the same he knows how to give donkeys something to eat . . ."

She could see no more of the young man than shining waves of very black hair, the white nape of his neck, and forearms gilded by the sun.

He now tried to cut slices of the sausage, pushing back the quivering nostrils with his elbow all the while. Manon laughed silently; the prospector would certainly not be able to have his lunch if the beast stayed with him.

Fortunately Bicou suddenly appeared. Having seen the goats safe, he bounded back with his tongue hanging out to recover the traitress who had repudiated the flock for a piece of bread.

He started dancing around her, biting playfully at her front legs to avoid kicks. She turned round quickly to repulse him, but the wheeling aggressor really knew his business.

After seven or eight kicks, the sole effect of which was a spurt of sand on the prospector's bread, the she-ass had to submit, and she went off at a gallop toward the distant bells of the flock. Then Bicou, watching the tree all the time, yapped, then wept, to call his dear mistress. The young man thought this discourse was addressed to him and started on his lunch with great appetite.

Getting no response, the dog, tormented by the weight of his responsibilities, suddenly made an about-face and hurried off toward his duties.

Manon heard the bread cracking between the jaws of the mysterious seeker of gold . . . He might stay there for half an hour, but this prospect did not alarm her. From her lookout she could see the flock at a distance, circled from time to time by the dog; and below, through the branches, she spied on the solitude of an unknown, who was decent and young, who spoke to beasts with a voice that was male and gentle, and who had laughed so amiably when the she-ass pushed her muzzle under his arm . . .

She thought:

"Papa was a seeker for water, this one is a seeker for gold . . . Perhaps he won't have any more luck, but anyway, he's looking for something . . ."

At the end of a quarter of an hour the luncher drank a big glass of wine, gathered his utensils, and got up and stretched himself with a sigh of pleasure.

Then, with the bag over his shoulder, he went off toward the flock, looking on all sides. Bicou came again to repel him. The young man whistled, then called, as if he wanted to talk to the shepherd. In vain . . . He retraced his steps, took the path to La Garette, and disappeared in the distance under the pine wood.

Manon came down from her tree, but as she jumped to the ground she saw something shining in the grass. It was the knife of the adventurer. A fine knife with four blades, supplemented with a spike, a corkscrew, a nail file, and a tiny pair of scissors. She looked at it for a long time and thought that the young man would come back and look for it . . . Regretfully she placed it in full view on a stone; but when she got away from it, she saw that the nickel shone very brightly.

She said to herself:

"The first person to come by will surely put it in his pocket."

She retraced her steps, hesitated a moment, then picked up her find.

"If he comes back I'll see him and I'll give it to him. If he doesn't come back, too bad for him!"

As the schoolmaster continued his prospecting in the pine wood, he saw an old peasant dressed in rags, gathering wild asparagus. His hair and his shaggy beard were white but his wrinkles were black.

"Greetings, sir!" said the teacher.

The other man raised two big blue eyes and smiled a timid sort of smile.

"Greetings!"

"They're doing well, the asparagus?"

"Not bad. They're a little late, but they're fine."

"And that flock over there, is it yours?"

"Oh no," said the old man. "I've only got two goats, and my wife looks after them . . . I don't come from here. I'm from Les Ombrées . . . That flock belongs to the girl of the springs."

"What springs?"

"The little springs in the hills," said the old man. "She looks after them; she cleans them . . . She makes little basins with clay, nice and clean . . . Since I don't know her name, I call her the girl of the springs, otherwise I wouldn't know what to say . . . She's nice. The other day she gave me a cheese. Without asking, because I never ask for anything."

"Is she a girl from Les Ombrées?"

"No, certainly not."

"So, she's from Les Bastides?"

"I don't know. I don't think so. She's not from Les Bastides. I haven't asked her, I never ask!"

Then, looking at the neck of the bottle protruding from the bag, he repeated:

"I never ask for anything!"

The teacher understood at once that, without ever asking, the proud old man always accepted, and made him a present of the wine that was left. The old man did not even take the time to thank him, but mouthed the bottle like a trumpet, while the generous donor laughingly took the path that plunged down the vallon.

That evening, about six o'clock, the unbelievers were in place on the terrace of the café, around a game of manille led in a masterful manner by the Philoxène-Belloiseau team, who cruelly mauled Casimir and Claudius the butcher. Sitting astride their chairs, the Papet, Ugolin, Pamphile, Ange, and the baker silently appraised the sly tricks and the cheating, but uttered cries of woe at the fall of a cleaned-out manillon.

The teacher arrived at the end of the game, but was careful not to open his mouth before the last trick, which M. Belloiseau announced with a wild shout as he laid the trump card down on the table.

"They've been so crushed," said Philoxène as he got up, "that it would be a shame to make them pay the round . . . They've suffered too much. It's my round!"

The teacher took a place beside M. Belloiseau.

"Well, my dear Bernard," said the notary, "what did you do today?"

"This afternoon I corrected my pupils' exercise books and prepared my class for tomorrow. But this morning I went for a long walk on the hill and I brought back several extremely rare calcareous crystals. Apropos, gentlemen, who is the girl of the springs?"

"The girl of the springs?" said Philoxène, pouring a Pernod. "You saw that in a book?"

"Not at all! I met a poor old man from Les Ombrées who told me that up there there's a girl who looks after the little springs in the hills."

"I have noticed," said the baker, "that somebody's fixed up the Font du Rigaou and it runs twice as fast as before."

"The Laurier too, it's been cleaned and tended," said the butcher. "But I thought it was the woodsmen."

"Or shepherds," said the Papet. "They need them for their animals . . ."

"Well, according to the good old man, it's a shepherdess."

"And what's she like, this shepherdess?" asked Pamphile.

"I didn't see her," said the teacher. "I only saw her flock."

"Sheep, or goats?"

"Goats, a donkey, and a black dog."

"Then I know who it is," said Pamphile. "It's little Manon's flock. When she saw you she hid herself."

"Why?"

"That's how she is. Sometimes you see her at a distance. But when you get near she's not there anymore. She's quick as lightning!"

"Girls are often like that," said the baker. "But it passes when they grow up."

"How old is she?" asked M. Belloiseau.

"She should be twelve or thirteen years old," said Ugolin.

"What?" cried Pamphile. ". . . I say she's at least fifteen!"

M. Belloiseau cupped his good ear.

"Fifteen years!" repeated Philoxène.

He borrowed a hand from the carpenter to open fifteen fingers, side by side.

"And where does she come from?" cried M. Belloiseau.

"She's the daughter of the poor hunchback," said Pamphile.

In Provence "poor" means the person being spoken of is dead. It is a word used by pagans who believe that a dead man no longer possesses anything.

"Whose daughter?" murmured M. Belloiseau.

Philoxène, abandoning the spoken word, pulled his neck down into his shoulders, which he raised to the level of his ears.

"The hunchback!" he repeated.

"Which hunchback?" asked the teacher.

"A simpleton," said the Papet.

"Not all that simple," replied the carpenter.

"When I say simpleton," continued the old man, "I don't mean imbecile. I mean unreasonable. He thought he could raise thousands of rabbits, and multiplied them on paper."

"And then," said Pamphile, "since he didn't have water, he tried to dig a well . . ."

"And he had to use explosives!" said Ugolin, "although I warned him enough! I said to him: 'Don't play with gunpowder!' But no matter what you said, he had books, and he thought that with books you could do anything. He wouldn't listen to me and his first blast killed him."

"And since then," said Pamphile, "the little one has lived on the hill with her mother, who's a little odd, and Baptistine, Giuseppe's widow, that old woman who looks like a wooden statue . . ."

Ugolin reflected:

"You think she's fifteen?"

"Certainly," said the Papet, ". . . it's the third year of the carnations, and the hunchback's been buried three years . . . She's at least fifteen years old, perhaps sixteen! Have you lost your memory?"

"It's because of the carnations!" said Ugolin. "They take up so much time, the years pass like the birds . . . And since I've no more time to walk on the hill, I've never seen her again!"

"And since she doesn't come to the village," said Philoxène, "nobody knows what she does up there."

"She never comes to the village," said Casimir. "But she sometimes comes to the cemetery . . ."

"Then give us," said M. Belloiseau with the air of a gourmand, "a description of this young person."

"I haven't seen her face," said Casimir.

M. Belloiseau demanded libidinously:

"Then what have you seen?"

"It was last summer, at the cemetery. I had to dig a grave for poor Elzéar, the one from Rastoubles—and I had to hurry because with the heat at that time poor Elzéar couldn't last much longer . . . They told me at four o'clock and by the evening I wasn't even halfway done. The next day I came just before daybreak . . . And when I put the key in the gate I heard a little music, rather sad, but very pretty. It wasn't very light yet, but I could see it was a girl, on her knees in front of a tomb. I listened a little, then suddenly I turned the key. Ah, my friends! In one jump she leaped onto the cross of the Pelissier family, and hop! She flew over the wall! I went to look at the tomb—it was the poor hunchback's and she had brought a big armful from the heath: wild irises, everlasting, fennel flowers. I see flowers like that nearly every month—but I've never seen her close up since her father's burial."

"Well," said Pamphile, "I can tell you she's at least sixteen years old because I've seen her close up."

"Where?" asked Ugolin.

"At the Baume Sourne, up there. I was looking for morels."

Philoxène, pouring his own Pernod, exclaimed.

"Damn it! That's a long way to go to look for morels!"

Pamphile replied mysteriously:

"I know a spot up there that my father showed me . . . Besides, what can I say? It's my vice, I love the hill. As for the trees, I've cut up so many of them, when I see the living ones I daren't look at them too much!

"So, I was up there all alone and suddenly I could feel a storm coming. The pines in the vallon began to sing."

He turned toward the teacher.

"You know, there was absolutely no wind, yet the trees made the noise of the wind . . . And from the top of La Tête Rouge I saw a terrible cloud coming down. It looked like a violet inky smoke. And the front of it curved under itself and it rolled on the Garette garigue and landed right in front of me!"

The baker shuddered loudly.

"That happened to me at the Plan de Précatory under Garlaban. It made my skin crawl!"

"And suddenly," continued Pamphile, "bang badabang bing—the first thunder!"

Claudius the butcher, shivering, murmured:

"Ayayay!"

"I went running to the shelter of that wretched charcoal burner's hut, just on the edge of the Font Breguette escarpment."

"I know it," said the Papet. "I used to kill thrushes up there when I had my good legs . . ."

"Oh! now it's in ruins . . . I fixed the roof a little, lit my pipe, and waited. I could smell burnt powder, and the day was violet. Through the hole for shooting thrushes I saw the bushes all the same, not moving any more than me. And suddenly, on a level with the bushes, I see something passing like a golden bird . . . It flies, it flies, and it arrives in the open, and I see it's this girl running in front of the storm, and the gold is her hair. She stops, she turns round, and she looks at the clouds. The thunder roars and she bursts out laughing and sends it a kiss!"

"That one," said Ange, "she's afraid of nothing!"

"She took the slope, my friends, jumping over the bushes like a wild animal, and may I drop dead this moment if it's not true, the storm didn't catch up with her!"

M. Belloiseau looked at the teacher, and said:

"There's a very interesting young person! My word, since I haven't got a child I feel myself quite disposed to do something for her! Is she pretty?"

"M. Belloiseau," said Pamphile, "her hair is like gold. Her eyes are like the sea; her teeth are like pearls; and what she's got in her ragged bodice, I'm sure it's a very pretty sight!"

At that moment an angry voice, explosively loud, descended from the window above the carpenter's shop. It was Big Amélie, and she cried:

"And you, what do you look like, you satyr? Is that the kind of mushroom you go looking for?"

All the cronies on the terrace burst out laughing, and the Papet cried, "Ay-ayay!"

She continued:

"You never told me about any golden birds!"

In three steps Pamphile was under the window. With his arms open and his chin raised toward his wife, he said in a reasonable voice:

"Amélie, don't take it like that! I didn't mean any harm. It made such an impression on me!"

"Oh, I know what kind of impression it made on you. It's a shame she ran so quickly, hey?"

"You haven't got it right at all, Amélie! I was talking about something artistic!"

Amélie let out a strident burst of laughter, and yelled:

"The artist! Come and look at the artist! Who would think he was the father of four children!"

The unbelievers snickered, and the gossips and the children came running up. Behind Amélie the cries of a baby could be heard.

Then she appealed:

"Listen to his daughter crying of shame. Poor little thing! When she's old enough to understand her father's a satyr, how should I explain it to her? Poor little thing!"

But as the "poor little thing" started bawling, Amélie turned round quickly and yelled herself: "Be quiet, daughter of a satyr!"

Then she addressed the public:

"Monsieur has caught a look at a little shepherdess, and that's knocked him for a loop! And it seems she looks like gold, and she looks like the sea, and her bosom is the most beautiful you ever saw! Tell me, husband, what about me, what's in my bodice, doesn't it look like anything?"

There were great bursts of laughter. Then the exasperated carpenter replied with warmth:

"Oh, those! They look like two melons!"

Amélie uttered a long cry of rage.

"Oh! You insult the mother of your children? This time you've gone too far and you'll pay for it!"

She left the window. Pamphile, already frightened by his own courage, cried:

"Amélie! I wanted to say beautiful melons! BEAUTIFUL, Amélie!"

"Oh, bad luck," said Philoxène, "something tells me this is not going to end well!"

They expected to see her come out the door, broom in hand, but it was at the window that a cooking pot appeared. She held it by the handles over the void. At the same time Amélie said in a caressing voice:

"Who is it that likes mutton stew with fresh green beans? And this one, it's first-rate, with black olives and pickled pork and a little thyme. It's been simmering all night!"

The spectators kept silent, and those on the terrace got up. Pamphile raised his arms pathetically toward the pot and cried:

"Amélie, don't do that! No, Amélie, no! If you ever do that . . ."

She didn't let up:

"But the lovers of golden birds, the artistic satyrs, the scorners of melons, they don't eat ragout of mutton . . . Here's what I'll do with it!"

Pamphile hardly had time to jump backward to avoid the steaming pot, which exploded between his shoes while the onlookers applauded noisily.

He flung himself down to save a few pieces of steaming meat, but two dogs, then three, then four came out from who-knows-where and started a ferocious battle between his legs. He could only extricate himself by cutting such ridiculous capers that the teacher wept great tears and the unbelievers howled with laughter, while Philoxène, with his back to the wall, held his shuddering paunch with both hands and uttered infantile moans.

The Papet and Ugolin returned to the Soubeyran house early. They were expecting M. Trémelat, who was coming to settle the accounts for the first four months of the year. He arrived in a motorcar, rather small, but quite new, and equipped with such a powerful motor that when it idled the car hopped about on the spot. They shut themselves in the dining room—door and shutters closed—and the Papet examined the agent's accounts and compared them with the messenger's. After a fairly long discussion they reached an agreement, and M. Trémelat laid eighty-four golden louis out on the table. Ugolin rang each of them on the fireplace mantel to make sure they were good.

"It's not that I'm suspicious, but you never know, somebody may have deceived you."

The three of them then dined, on a dozen thrushes, some polenta, a big omelette with wild asparagus tips, and a tart weighing a kilo that M. Trémelat had brought from the city, along with a bottle dressed in straw, which appeared to contain champagne.

The conversation was very instructive: M. Trémelat avowed that he had ruined himself at the business of shipping carnations, and that because of competition from the Italians, who had just taken over the foreign markets, he was on the point of selling his motorcar and his country house.

Ugolin and the Papet replied sadly that with the poor price he had allowed them, they had hardly managed to pay for the fertilizer and the insecticide, and they were currently thinking about returning to growing chick-peas. M. Trémelat commended the sagacity of this decision and declared that his only regret would be no longer to meet such charming friends every quarter . . .

After the tart, the shipper popped the cork of the champagne with such a powerful detonation that Ugolin wondered how the bottle had contained it so long. They clinked glasses swarming with a froth of bubbles that entered the mouth only to emerge again through the nose and wished each other long life and prosperity. Then the Papet, feigning indecision, said:

"I wonder what we should do with the fertilizer and the insecticide that are left. They're no use to us with the chick-peas . . ." At which M. Trémelat, after some reflection, replied:

"If you want to try one more season, I would be happy—just to oblige you—to continue to work for you. I wouldn't want to abandon my friends. But then I suggest you pull up the plants at once and put in the new cuttings."

Ugolin protested loudly, because his carnations were still in full flower. The agent replied that it was not a question of getting fine flowers, but of getting the best price. For his part, he considered the season to be over and did not want any more carnations until October. The month of May, which was about to start, was the most detestable of months; five days were ruined by church feasts, which were not saints' days and thus not days for sending greetings; five others were wasted on saints with names like Athanase, Pie, Servais, Urbain, Petronille, so odd that very few people were named after them; moreover, people seldom get married in May; and finally—to the great detriment of florists—people die much less readily in May than in December!

So it was reasonable to sacrifice the poor profit of this month so that the next harvest could start at the beginning of October, which honored Saints Rémy, François, Constant, Brigitte, Denis, Edouard, Thérèse, Leopold, Raphael, Antoinette, Simon, and Arsene: glorious and commercial litany, supplemented on the funereal side by the virulence of the first influenzas, and triumphantly crowned by All Saints' Day and All Souls' Day.

They parted around eleven, quite satisfied with each other, and Ugolin took the path to Les Romarins, hugging the sack of gold pieces that hung from his neck.

Because of the champagne, he stopped every ten meters, shaken by hiccups that sounded like barks; as he passed the clearing in front of Massacan, a cloud broke and hard slanting rain accompanied him all the way to Les Romarins.

He barred the door, counted the louis again, and put the sack under his pillow.

He slept to the sound of sputtering drops on the tiles, while tense echoes shuddered at the claps of thunder and reflected them against the shutters, setting them to quiver until the windows vibrated.

It was doubtless the long, beneficial rain that made him think of poor Monsieur Jean, then of his daughter who hid like a fox and ran faster than the hail . . . Then he saw Pamphile again, jumping in the middle of the dogs, and fell asleep smiling.

When he woke up, the storm was already a good distance away, and the day whitened the slits in the shutters. He immediately slid his hand under his pillow to make sure that his little bag of gold was still there. He lifted it up as high as he could and let it fall on his stomach, to feel the magnificent weight; there was half a kilo of it, and what beautiful music it made! He already possessed four hundred ten louis. He calculated with these eighty-four he should have four ninety-four, and all the expenses of the season were paid. He needed six to make five hundred: he decided to ask the Papet for them—surely he would not refuse. So, idling on his bed, he repeated in an ecstatic whisper: "Five hundred louis! Oh, Ugolin, you have five hundred louis."

He put on his trousers, but opened neither the door nor the shutters, because he had to put the eighty-four new arrivals safely away and add them to his treasure.

Taking a thousand precautions, he loosened the stone on the hearth, lifted up the cover of the cooking pot, and poured the eighty-four pieces on top of the others, then put everything in order as hurriedly as a thief. After he replaced the flat stone he mixed a handful of plaster in a plate and carefully filled in the groove.

Then, while the plaster was still fresh, he took a small twig broom and passed a cloud of soot and cinders over the stone.

"There!" he said. "Even Délie, when she does the house, won't see anything at all . . . And as for thieves, I'm not worried about them . . ."

All the same, to reassure himself, he put on his favorite act—that of a disappointed housebreaker.

He went out, closed the door, then noiselessly opened it again very slowly and carefully, and entered the vast kitchen on tiptoe, with his ear cocked to be sure that the house was empty.

He murmured:

"Nobody. All's well!"

He went up to the bed, picked up the pillow, then spent quite a while feeling the mattress.

"Good," he said. "There's nothing."

He opened the big cupboard, lifted up the sheets, the dusters, the socks, showing the thief's disappointment by a number of grimaces. Then he went to the dresser, opened the two doors, looked at the shelves, took off the cover of the soup tureen, shook an old coffeepot, and murmured in an irritated tone, "But where is it, the hoard? Where has he hidden his money?" He pulled roughly at the drawers of the dresser, muttering insults: then suddenly, raising his head, he was surprised to discover the notice board. He read it in a loud voice, slowly, as if he could hardly make it out.

"'Attention, Burglar!'" appeared to excite his curiosity and he knit his brows. "'Don't waste your time looking for money. It is not here.'"

He smiled ironically, and said:

"Liar!"

He continued:

"'It is in the bank . . .'"

He first pretended to be uneasy, then cried:

"It's true he goes to Aubagne three times a week! He's quite capable of doing that, the pig! And then, he's a modern peasant, since he had the idea of growing carnations. He's not stupid, not him! And which bank?"

He read:

"'In the middle of Aubagne, next door to the gendarmerie.'"

So, terrified by this reminder of gendarmes, the "burglar" took a step backward, mouth open, and leaped toward the door to make a frantic escape. But he stopped on the doorstep, burst out laughing, rubbed his hands joyfully, and cried:

"It's not enough to be a thief: you also have to be smart! And smart is what Ugolin is!"

He went out to look at his beloved carnations, which he had to pull up as quickly as possible. Thanks to the long nocturnal rainfall a large number of buds had opened.

"That's too bad!" he said in a loud voice. "Well, no, I'll wait before I pull them up and if that Trémelat doesn't want any more this year, I'll take them to the florist at Aubagne . . . Even in May I'll sell a few of them . . ."

He walked about for a moment with his hands in his pockets, looking at the toes of his big shoes.

"Frankly, I've nothing to complain about. Five hundred louis soon! Who would have believed that? One mustn't always look on the bad side. If the poor hunchback had earned five hundred louis his daughter wouldn't have to run about the hills like a grasshopper. In the end everyone has his luck, everyone his fate. Other people's business doesn't concern me."

The big sun dispersed the light mists, and the swallows darting about seemed to fly for the pleasure of it. A little belated owl mewed once before going home to sleep, and the cuckoo started singing regularly.

Ugolin raised his head, looked at the sky, then breathed deeply. Finally he took his hands from his pockets and said suddenly:

"And what if I should take a little walk on the hill? Perhaps the first morels have come out . . . And then, the woodcocks are about . . . And then, it'll give me some new ideas . . . When one is rich, one has the right to have fun. Go on then! Today will be Sunday!"

He went back to the house, took a napkin and a big cake of soap, and went to wash himself by the edge of the little pond.

Then, in front of a triangular piece of mirror that was attached by three bent nails to the wall near the window, he shaved himself. His reddish beard was very hard, and the blade of the razor was strangely narrow since the honing stone had eaten up the major part of it. But he was used to it, and in spite of the surprising delicacy of his redhead's skin, his dexterity and patience took him to the end.

He chose a clean shirt, corduroy trousers, and hunting espadrilles with projecting soles. Then he put two thick slices of bread, a handful of broken olives in a tin box, a small goat cheese, a bit of white onion, and a bottle of wine in his game bag. Finally he tightened his belt, took his gun and his game bag, and went out. He closed the shutters, locked the door, hid the key in a hole in the stable wall for Délie, who was coming to clean the house, and left for the high plateaux.

CHAPTER 8

He followed the crests of the hills or the edges of the escarpments. The hunting season was not yet open and he had to be somewhat on the lookout for gendarmes.

It was a very fine morning, still and hot like a summer's day. The bushes carried thousands of little birds that did not merit a cartridge, and knew it, because they sang with open beaks on the highest branches and did not deign to notice the hunter passing by.

In the transparent air the distant chain of Sainte Victoire seemed to have come closer during the night, and the scent of thyme, a little softened by the rain, floated on the garigue of the Plan de l'Aigle.

He slowly followed the edge of the plateau, above the vallon of Le Plantier. At the bottom of the hollow, invisible blackbirds carolled and suddenly burst out laughing.

"Those ones there, at least they don't worry . . . Their biggest job is to make a nest. No clothes, no shoes to pay for . . . They eat for nothing, they sleep when they want to, say what you like, it's a fine life!"

It was rare that his thoughts were elevated to such philosophical heights; he marvelled at them himself and pressed his meditations further.

"Yes, it's a fine life, but it doesn't last long, and always on the condition that you don't receive a shotgun blast in the back . . . or get caught in a trap . . . Everyone has his pleasures and his troubles . . . I wonder why I work . . . With five hundred louis I could live like a blackbird until I inherit from the Papet . . . And never do anything again in my life . . . The truth is, the more you've got, the more you want, and finally, the cemetery. So what good is it?"

He saw that he was above the cave of Le Plantier. He stopped a moment and looked at the landscape like a Sunday hiker.

In front of the wall of the cave, linen was drying on a line. There was nobody in the little vegetable garden, which seemed to be clean and well-tended. He saw some bean stakes, five or six rows of cabbage, some onions, some leeks, a few fine artichoke plants, a fine patch of potatoes already greening, some strawberry plants, and two fine currant bushes. Above these crops a scarecrow spread its stiff arms, from the ends of which hung black gloves. It wore a tattered blue dress and a woman's hat topped by a long feather that seemed extravagant to him.

"A female scarecrow," he said, "I've never seen that . . . Perhaps they didn't dare put the poor hunchback's clothes on it . . . It would be the little one who would not want that . . ."

He noticed that the goats were not there. He continued his walk, made a big detour under Garlaban, then descended toward La Baume Sourne . . . Neither hare, nor rabbit, nor partridge.

"I wonder where they're hiding today . . . But perhaps it's me who's become deaf and blind. I'll have to borrow the baker's basset hound . . ."

He scoured the vallon of Le Jardinier where abandoned crops of sumac had formed an almost impenetrable thicket above the rockrose. A very fine hare suddenly leaped from a patch of brambles, but the branches of the shrubs got in his way and he missed it twice.

"I'm no good at anything anymore!" he said. "At anything! A three-kilo hare, two cartridges at twenty sous apiece, and I lost it all in one go. I'll get that hare . . . First I'll go and have my lunch at the end of Le Taoume. From up there I'll be able to see the whole country. If I'm patient it would be very strange if I didn't see her!"

He climbed up the steep slope, which was interrupted in several places by little ledges that he had to go around.

He arrived at the final plateau; a light breeze cooled his sweaty brow.

At an altitude of seven hundred meters he could look down on the entire district and was surprised by the extent of the countryside.

Like most Bastidians he never climbed to the summits. Neither game nor mushrooms were to be found there, nor dead wood, nor wild asparagus, and these useless climbs were no more than an outdoor exercise for townspeople. His gaze slowly travelled along the horizon, and he said:

"It's big. There's nothing for it, it's big!"

He went to sit on the edge of the perpendicular drop, and lunched with a good appetite, all the while scrutinizing the vallons and ravines plunging around him.

At first he did not recognize these valleys, although he had known their names since infancy, but he could not see Les Bastides, hidden behind La Tête Ronde, and he thought what he was looking at was the normal landscape he was used to but reversed. On his left he distinguished, very small, the cave of Le Plantier, which he had been looking for on his right; then he was able to arrange the landscape properly and name all the vallons. "Good!" he said. "That's Le Plantier down there, that's Le Rascla, that's Le Bec-fin. She can't be there because of the ledge . . . So, either she's stayed on the plateau or she's gone down to Refresquières by the Pas de la Ser . . . It may take me all day, but I'm going to find her!"

He descended toward the plateau that dominated Les Refresquières.

It was a deep valley, mainly hollowed from the blue limestone of Provence by some rugged glacier that had started out during the night of the millenia.

From each side a steep hillside clothed in thick pine woods rose from the bottom of the valley to the foot of the vertical escarpments that sustained the two plateaux. It was a large table of rock furrowed here and there with clefts that the wind and rain had filled with dust, sand, and gravel. The hardy plants of the hills followed the lines of these furrows.

Thyme, rue, lavender, and rockrose had thus formed miniature hedges, and in the larger crevasses cades and junipers, mixed with some twisted pines, had formed little dark green thickets, sometimes burdened with flights of chaffinches.

Right in the middle of the vallon torrential rainfall had carved a bed in the limestone, which was now perfectly bare and polished, like marble, but pierced here and there by circular openings that grew bigger as they deepened, like flattened spheres. They were of all sizes. Many were no bigger than a cooking pot, but others were as much as two meters across.

With every rainfall the vallon received the runoff from the neighboring plateaux. These streams had cut deep ravines down to the bed of rock where the day's torrent rolled and rumbled.

The streams' pounding flight left the holes in the stone filled with bright water, which the birds, the goats, the hunters, and the sun drank dry in a few days.

Because of the storm during the night, all the hollows of the vallon sparkled in the bright rays of the morning sun, and the bigger ones shivered in a breeze that hardly touched the silence.

Ugolin was looking at this calm landscape when he heard the tiny sound of a little bell.

He stopped short and pricked up his ears.

"Hullo!" he said, "that's surely the shepherd from Les Ombrées."

He went forward carefully, as if stalking game, and discovered, in the bed of the torrent, near a grove of spindly pines, a dozen goats and two kids browsing on the meagre grass in the clefts. A black dog was lying on its belly, its muzzle on its outstretched paws.

"Well," he said, as if surprised, "they must be Manon's goats!"

He looked for a long while, but did not see the shepherdess.

"Ho ho!" he continued, "this hussy must be setting her traps and she's surely frightened my hare, who's probably a long way off by now!"

Shaking his head with a worried look, he took two steps backward and looked for a spacious and deep chimney in the ledge. He found one choked with bushes that allowed him to go down to the slope of the hillside without being seen. Hidden by the undergrowth of the pine wood, he resumed his silent walk, with his gun under his arm, his finger on the trigger, and his ear cocked.

Meanwhile he hardly looked in front of him, but more often toward the vallon. At least twenty meters away some partridges flew up with a flurry of noise and suddenly lit up the forest. He raised his gun to his shoulder, but did not fire.

Then, in a whisper, he said:

"Ugolin, you're a fool. A poor fool."

He resumed his walk, crouched behind the gorse, and little by little descended toward the bed of the torrent.

From time to time he stopped and listened. The goat bells were now very near. He noticed that the path did not go down any more but followed a little ledge on the hillside beside a four- or five-meter drop-off, edged by thick bushes of ivy and clematis that hung down to the bed of the torrent.

Hidden behind this thicket, he advanced hesitantly, looking for places to put his cord soles down noiselessly.

He had thus covered about a hundred meters when he stopped suddenly; he had just heard a light sound, a sort of plashing . . . He slowly parted the grey branches of clematis, then the fleshy ivy leaves, and finally saw her whom he had been seeking since dawn and who had drawn him to this place.

Sitting on the edge of a big round hole, trailing the tip of her toe in the water, she was naked.

A collar of sunburn descended from her neck down to her young breast, her forearms were brown up to the elbows and her legs up to the knees; but her torso was white as milk and shone in luminous contrast to the gloves and stockings bronzed by sun.

Immobile as a rock, he stopped breathing . . .

Not far from the shepherdess her dark dress and her blouse were drying in the sun on a burning rock.

Beside her were a square scrap of soap and her little mouth organ.

Pensive, with her head down and her blonde hair hanging down to her breast, she swung her round legs continuously, and the shining drops on the tips of her feet leaped in the sunlight.

He felt the blood mounting to his face and beating in his temples. He swallowed his saliva twice, and was unable to take his eyes from those white and tender thighs, enlarged by their weight on the blue rock. A sombre madness began to mount in him. He raised his head and looked all around—there was nobody. Neither shepherd nor woodsman nor poacher. He listened. Not a sound disturbed the silence that hardly trembled at the sound of a cricket. Then with his eyes he sought the hidden passage that would lead him behind her.

But she suddenly got up, lightly and quickly as a goat, and leaned down to pick up the dress that left its shade on the humid stone. She must have found that the stuff was not yet dry because she draped it over a prickly cedar. Then she bent down again to pick up her mouth organ. She parted the hair from her mouth and blew a few fragile notes that enchanted an echo close by, then she started an old Provençal tune and suddenly, an arm outstretched, she started dancing to the sun.

He heard barking, then a light gallop that sputtered like rain. The goats appeared around a little cap of rock, followed by the black dog that had rallied them to the music.

The dog sat on its hindquarters and looked, while the goats browsed in a semicircle on the green embellishments of the crevasses. But a kid rose on its hind legs, its little beard curled back to its throat and its horns pointed forward . . . It hesitated a few moments, then threw itself toward the dancer. She avoided it with a step to the side, but at the end of its spring it turned about quickly and resumed its game.

So they flung themselves toward each other, yet avoided each other and crossed without the least visible effort, as if carried by the breeze and the joy of their youth; and poor Ugolin of the Soubeyrans, who broke the handles of pickaxes, and never passed through a door without bruising his shoulder on the frame, looked at these arched feet springing back from the elastic rock, this red-haired kid, as light as the music he heard, and did not know anymore if it was she who played this song, or whether the friendly echoes had invented it to sustain their dance. He was wrapped in the mystery of a wonderstruck fear. With his chin in a lavender bush he heard the beating of his heart. He felt obscurely that this dancing girl, still fresh with purifying water from the rain, was the divinity of the hills and the pine woods and the spring.

He didn't notice that he was slowly sliding toward this sorcery, and a little stone rolled down from under his palm.

The dog raised its head, pointed its glossy nose, and growled heavily. The girl stopped her pirouette short, took her breasts in her hands, and ran to hide behind a cedar tree.

He retreated on hands and knees toward the high undergrowth of gorse, but as he penetrated it a handful of gravel ran down the slope. The dog ran to the bottom of the little ledge and barked furiously . . . He got up, but remained bent like the village centenarian and plunged under the fragrant sheet of yellow flowers. He fled without knowing why.

Manon hid in the soft branches of the cedar and followed the course of the sacrilegious intruder by the movement of the gorse, but she could not actually see him and thought it was a youth from the village. Then, furious and naked, she took up her slingshot and hurled buzzing stones at the invisible fugitive swimming under the waves of flowers.

Ugolin stopped from time to time, and as he looked back to assure himself that she could not see him, he received the third projectile in the middle of his forehead.

The pebble was hardly bigger than a nut, but it was not very smooth. It left him stupid for a moment, then he wiped a drop of sweat on the side of his nose with the tip of his forefinger and saw his finger red with blood . . . Instead of anger he felt a sacred terror, and dashed like a boar through the thick branches, chased by the magical stones the hill was hurling at him . . .

He judged he was beyond reach and, out of breath, recovered slowly behind a big hawthorn tree. He saw her from afar through the branches: with arms raised she was pulling on her dress. The golden hair reappeared. Then she tightened her belt and threw herself toward the top of the vallon, uttering the shepherd's cry: "Bilibili . . . Bilibilibili!"

The dog ran about reassembling the goats and they followed her; the flock rose by leaps and bounds on the opposite hillside and disappeared under a black pine wood.

He went to sit under a big rock and give himself up to reflection. He thought of the madness that had taken him, and murmured:

"A little harder! . . ."

Then he wiped the blood from his forehead and felt a soft oval lump under his finger. He said again:

"A little harder and she would have broken my head! . . ."

The partridges sang in the distance and he remembered he had forgotten his gun. He made a big detour to go and look for it, always bent under an inexplicable fear.

The little bells rang in the forest opposite. He glided up to the crest and took to a gallop as soon as he had cleared it. He was in a hurry to see his house, his tools, his table, true things—real, without mystery . . .

He went in; everything was in order, and the chairs were not dancing. The ponderous Adélie had come, the cooking pot whistled on the tripod, the plate, the glass, the bottle, and the bread were soberly placed on the table.

But he locked the door, hung the gun on the wall, and with arms crossed stretched out on his bed.

CHAPTER 9

The Papet woke him up toward five in the evening, on returning from looking for wood on the hill. He tied the faggot-loaded mule to the trellis, then pushed at the door, and its plaints woke the sleeper.

"Well!" said the Papet, "it's five o'clock! You've had quite a nap!"

Ugolin rubbed his eyes, yawned, and mumbled:

"I wonder if I've had a bit of sunstroke . . ."

The Papet opened the shutters and looked at his nephew.

"You're not red," he said. "The fact is, you're behind with your sleep, and now that you haven't got so much to do with the carnations it's a good idea to get some rest."

Ugolin took the water jug, raised it toward the ceiling, and slowly poured the water down his throat.

The Papet declared:

"As for me, I'd rather have some white wine."

He went to the cupboard and took out a glass and a bottle and sat down in front of the table, while Ugolin washed his face and combed his hair.

"Galinette," said the Papet, "I went to collect wood below Le Plantier, but on the way back I detoured over this way because I wanted a private talk with you. The dumb woman doesn't hear anything, but she guesses everything, and what I want to say to you is nobody's business but ours."

The Papet was grave. Ugolin sat down opposite him. The old man drank, wiped his moustaches for a long time, and spoke:

"Galinette," he said, "you will soon be thirty, and you are the last of the Soubeyrans . . ."

Ugolin knew what he was going to say by heart, and knew how this litany usually ended.

"I can see what's coming," he said. "You're going to tell me again . . ."

"Let me speak!" cried the old man. "If I keep telling you the same thing it's your fault, and I'll repeat it again until you understand."

He took his time, and spoke slowly, sometimes with his eyes closed.

"The Soubeyrans—we others—we used to be the biggest family in the village. My father had four mules and two horses . . ."

Ugolin recited what came next:

"You used to have five hundred apricot trees at La Badoque, and an orchard of five hundred trees on the plateau of Le Solitaire."

"Twelve thousand vines on the Plan des Adrets."

"The same on the hillside of Precatori!"

"More than three hundred plum trees on the field below Le Plantier. When we grew chick-peas . . ."

"We produced more than ten cartloads of them."

"Twelve," corrected the old man. "When we grew melons . . ."

"They had to be taken to Marseille because they would kill the price at the market at Aubagne."

"For grandfather's birthday . . ."

"You would have more than thirty at the table."

"All the Soubeyrans, with cooking pots full of gold hidden all over the place in the house. We were known a good long way away, and we were the ones who mended the roof of the church . . ."

"And the cross of the steeple, it was your grandfather who paid for it and put it there. You see I know my lesson very well . . . And I'll answer in the usual way: if all that doesn't last, it's not my fault! It's fate!"

"That's not true!" said the old man forcefully. "Fate doesn't exist. It's the good-for-nothings who talk about fate! You always get what you deserve . . . What happens is the fault of the old people . . . Partly out of pride, and partly not to be separated from their money, they intermarry, cousin to cousin, and even uncles and nieces . . . It's bad for rabbits, and it's not good for people. At the end of four or five generations you get a maniac, like my grand-uncle Elzéar: they say he died in the war of '70, but he was in an asylum for twenty years. Two maniacs, and three suicides. And now there's the two of us, and I don't count anymore. Now the Soubeyran family is you!"

"And you're going to tell me again to get married . . . So this time I'm going to ask you something: you, why didn't you ever take a wife?"

The old man shook his head pensively as he searched for a reply . . . Finally he said:

"It wasn't really in my character . . . Mind you, I thought of it . . . But it never worked out . . . In the end I went off to be a soldier in Africa, like that, stupidly . . . When I came back, naturally I courted girls, as one does at that age . . . If one of them had given me a child, I would have married her at once . . . That never happened. I was like Anglade's fine cherry tree that has lots of flowers but never any fruit . . . And now there's nobody left but you."

"And so you want me to marry instead of you!"

"It must be done, Galinette . . ."

"But why? WHY?"

The old man got up, opened the door, and looked all round to be sure nobody could hear, then came back to Ugolin, and said in a whisper:

"And the treasure? Do you want to let it die out, the treasure of the Soubeyrans? It's not bank notes that the rats can eat. It's gold. A jar of pieces of gold. Yes, it's me who's got the treasure. Because as they died, they told the oldest of the survivors about the hiding place, and so finally everything has come to me! It's you who'll have it, and who do you want to leave it to? To the neighbors? Or to the curé? Or to the earth? And what about our property, which takes up a quarter of the land registry of Les Ombrées? All that—it comes from savings, from privations, from work. Do you want to throw all that away?"

"Certainly not!" said Ugolin. "Me, I love gold."

"Since you love it, you can't leave it without a master. With gold you can have servants until your sons are grown."

"Oh, Papet," said Ugolin. "I think you're dreaming . . . A family, one can't change one's nature like that . . ."

"Galinette, one day the alarm bell will ring and we'll go to a forest fire at Les Bouscarles, and when we get there they'll tell us, 'It's over, it's been put out,' and everybody will go back . . . But at midnight the alarm will ring again in four villages because a single spark has been forgotten in the extinguished cinders.

A red spark, like your hair . . . Come, Galinette, let's go and dine at the Maison Soubeyran, under the roof of our grandfathers; it will give you counsel."

At the table the Papet got down to particulars. He was thinking of Eliacin's sister, as strong as a mare and capable of producing powerful babies . . . Of Anglade's daughter, an industrious brunette who would have the Vala des Alouettes as a dowry, and a share in the concession of the water supply from the fountain, which might mean a new field of carnations. Moreover, she stuttered to the point of being nearly mute.

Finally, there was the daughter of Claudius the butcher: she would have a fairly large dowry of money, because her father adored her, and free meat all her life; her property wasn't very big, but the six little parcels of land she would inherit were the six enclosures (with rights of way) on the Solitaire plateau, pride of the Soubeyrans. Such a marriage would resolve a long peasant grudge . . . But there were also some drawbacks: Clarisse had gone to school in town and was well educated, and it was well known that educated people didn't like real work . . .

So it was necessary to look, to reflect, and to decide once and for all.

Ugolin hardly spoke, but drank big glasses of the black wine with its slight raspberry flavor.

He ended by saying:

"Listen, Papet, I understand what you're saying, but you must still let me wait a little while . . ."

"It's nearly ten years since I spoke to you about it . . ."

"Not as seriously as today . . . Listen, give me one more year. And then let me choose. Those three don't please me."

"So, you've got somebody in mind?"

"Perhaps."

"And you don't want to tell me who it is?"

"Papet, today I had a bit of sunstroke, I've just drunk a lot of wine, and I don't know what's happened to me. I feel a bit stupid. So don't ask me anything. We'll talk about it later."

"Agreed, agreed," said the Papet, smiling. "I'm pleased with you, Galinette. Do what you like, there's only one thing I ask—when you choose a wife, think of the children."

"What d'you mean?"

"I mean don't be taken in by a pretty face. What's needed are wide hips, long legs, and fine big tits. Choose her like a brood mare."

"But if she's got a pretty face as well?"

"If you get that as well, it won't bother me; on the contrary, she'll be La Belle Soubeyrane and I'll have the pleasure of looking at her."

CHAPTER *10*

Ugolin went back to Les Romarins at about half past ten. The moon was full and its light made very black shadows. He went up the steep path to Massacan, stopping from time to time, not for breath, but for reflection.

It was not the Papet's arguments that had struck him, and he gave hardly any thought to his duty to perpetuate the family. He was thinking of the adventure of the morning, of the strange emotion he had experienced over such a small thing.

All the same it was extraordinary that that little girl should so quickly become a person, and it was truly shocking that she should dance quite naked on the hill. Some woodsmen might have passed by, or a poacher from Les Ombrées. A naked girl, that gave you ideas, inevitably . . .

He did not stop at Massacan, which he had abandoned two years ago. The old mulberry tree dreamed in the light of the moon, indifferent and solitary. He suddenly saw the shadow of the little Manon of former times on the path again, following the she-ass carrying the jugs . . . He saw her as if she were real . . . He stopped, rubbed his eyes, and said in a loud voice:

"Oh, Ugolin, isn't that better?"

Then as he approached Les Romarins he heard the little music of the mouth organ; the fragile notes whispered in the leaves of the olive trees . . .

He spoke again:

"This time I'm going mad! . . . Or rather, I'm drunk, that's the truth!"

Without lighting the lamp, he locked the door with the key, took off his shoes, and stretched himself on his bed with his hands crossed under the back of his neck . . .

Toward midnight there was a great reunion of owls, no doubt concerning a subject of common interest because from time to time several of them would ululate in chorus.

Across the long chink in a shutter, a bar of moonlight drew a luminous trace on the blue tiles. His head was heavy, and there was a small droning in his ears.

He said in a whisper:

"He forced the wine on me to make me say yes. But I didn't say yes. Eliacin's sister, to hell with her. The Soubeyrans, to hell with them. They're all finished, the Soubeyrans. And the Papet, he'll die too, and so will I. All that, it's rubbish. In the end you're never satisfied with anything." He yawned loudly, turned on his side, and finally went to sleep.

At once he saw the girl and the little goat dancing; but in his dream it was the girl that had the little golden horns, and who flew with arms outstretched, like a bird . . . Little by little she approached him. He flung himself at her furiously to seize her, and the violent shock woke him up—he had fallen from his bed.

He uttered several oaths in the dark, then got up and groped about for matches. The yellow brilliance of the paraffin lamp chased the shadows up to the ceiling. He stretched, coughed, turned the key in the lock, and went out barefoot onto the terrace.

The chorus of owls had stopped. The moon was enormous, and so brilliant that the stars around it had retreated.

The shadows of the olive trees were black, and in the big patches of moonlight in the middle of the field the red carnations were violet and the white ones were blue.

With his hands in his pockets and his head bent, he walked to the middle of the flowers. Suddenly he stopped, raised his head, and forcefully responded:

"Not at all, no, not at all! The one who's wrong is the one who was wrong in the first place. And who started it? It was you."

He took a few steps, and resumed:

"What was that idea of yours of being a peasant? And what would you have done if I had wanted to be a tax collector? If I had come to you and said: 'Come on! Pay me some taxes, otherwise I'll sell your furniture!' What would you have said?"

He sneered, shrugged his shoulders, and went slowly back to the house.

"The bad thing was what we did to the spring. Yes, but when I did that I didn't know you . . . And then, I've thought about it a lot. But even with the spring it wouldn't have worked. You grew the pumpkins, yes, certainly! But the business with the rabbits wouldn't have worked. I told you that in good friendship; you didn't want to listen to me."

He entered the shadow of the big olive tree and leaned against the trunk.

"Why? Because when there are a hundred rabbits together they die of swollen belly and the shits. And remember that happens fast!"

"And the tip of Saint Esprit, it wasn't my fault! It's been like that since the time of Jesus Christ!"

"I agree, I agree. Yes. Sometimes I think I should have talked to you about it. I should have said to you: 'Well then, let's do the carnations together.' But you wouldn't have wanted to. Always books, statistics. But yes, yes."

"I told you myself to go back to town! I told you frankly. And you, you said to me: 'I know where I'm going' . . . You were going to the cemetery . . . You would have been a hundred times better off with your bottom on a soft chair, collecting other people's money . . . And your little girl, she would have been a fine young lady, instead of dancing quite naked on the hill . . . What does that look like? And what will happen to her? Now you can see everything from up there . . . You must understand that for me, it was the carnations . . . Not wickedness, no . . . I didn't have anything against you, on the contrary . . . You've seen how I never told them to go . . . If they had wanted to stay at the house they would still be there . . . They would be tying bouquets for me, and I would be giving them sous . . . But women alone are like goats without a dog; and that leads to nothing but foolishness . . ."

He sighed deeply and said:

"Finally, all that, it's a time that won't come back, so it's no good talking about it . . . But I can tell you all the same that you've brought me a lot of worry . . ." He went toward the house, where the open door let out the yellow light of the lamp, and murmured with head bowed:

"And perhaps it's not over . . ."

One morning in May Ugolin went down to the railway station at Aubagne to collect some boxes of cuttings that Attilio had sent him. They were Almondos, Aurores, and Gloire de Dijons, especially delicate, selling at the best prices.

He was busy opening the boxes in the shed when the Papet appeared.

"Galinette," he said, "the mayor is complaining that you never come to the municipal council anymore, and this morning they want you, together with Ange and Casimir, to go and clean the pond at La Perdrix, tomorrow morning."

This pond was the one that received the water from the spring, and each night it accumulated a reserve of about a hundred cubic meters. It had to be cleaned every six months because of the reddish sand that deposited in it along with the pine needles and dead leaves that the wind brought.

"Clean the pond!" said Ugolin. "That's not possible. Look at the cuttings I've just got. They're fine, but they mustn't suffer. They must be planted at once, and that's three days' work. I'm sorry about the pond, but I haven't got the time."

"Listen, we'll start working on the cuttings now, and up to midnight if necessary. Tomorrow morning, at four o'clock, we'll continue. At eight o'clock you'll go to the pond while I work with Délie, and you'll come back at midday . . ."

"D'you think it's so important, that pond?"

"Yes, because you've been too successful, and you haven't got the right to refuse. It's a volunteer job, for everybody. A work of friendship. You haven't done it for at least three years. The Soubeyrans have always taken their turn. Go there tomorrow."

That same day Manon left her goats under Bicou's care to go and gather rue on the shoulder of La Tête Ronde, which was just above the gorge of La Perdrix. In the distance, very far off, the sea shone silver.

As she was sitting under a crooked pine tree tying the oily twigs in bundles, she heard voices coming from the bottom of the ravine, then the iron sound of a shovel in gravel. She ran under the junipers to the edge of the escarpment.

In the empty pond three men, stripped to the waist, shovel in hand, were scraping the bottom and throwing a reddish mud over the edge of the pond. She thought she recognized the voice of the seeker for gold.

She went back, took a roundabout route, and installed herself in a narrow chimney from which she could see them all. Indeed it was he. He was kneading a handful of mud and examining it through his magnifying glass.

Pamphile, leaning on the handle of his shovel, said:

"That's got a bit of the color of clay, but it's not clay; it's not sticky."

"It's bauxite powder," said the expert. "It's a fairly soft rock, a mineral containing iron and aluminum—I wonder where this powder could come from . . ."

"The spring brings it after big storms," said Ange, ". . . seven or eight hours later . . . But it doesn't go up to the fountain. It all gets deposited here."

The man with the hat spoke:

"In mine too," he said. ". . . When it rains all night, in the morning about ten my spring begins to run a little red and then afterwards it's like rust on the stones . . ."

The sound of this voice troubled the shepherdess; the man took off his filthy hat and used it to wipe the sweat running down his face. She recognized Ugolin's red curls.

She had not seen him for four years, but this person had played a large part in her past . . . Since her childhood he had inspired in her an irrational aversion, and since he had taken the farm from her, this aversion had turned to hate. Sometimes, however, stretched out under a pine tree, while she relived former times, she wondered whether this hate was clearly justified. Her father had felt friendship for Ugolin, who had often helped him. Without being asked, he had offered the pure water of his well, he gave some tiles the day they arrived, and he had come to help dig the field. And then later, it was he who had found the money they needed so much; on the tragic day, it was he who went for the doctor.

But in the end it was he who lived under those tiles, he who owned the field that had been dug; they had to quit the farm to give back the money he had lent to her father, and it was this money, above all, that had paid for the powder that hurled up the sharp stone that had killed her beloved father . . .

Moreover, he had found the spring!

It was the height of injustice that this imbecile, shaken by tics, had obtained from Providence the gushing water so cruelly denied to the better man . . .

Sometimes, however, she reasoned.

After all, if the rain had not come, if the fatal stone had fallen, if her father had not found the spring, it wasn't the fault of this poor peasant. And if he had found it himself, what could she reproach him for? But the most convincing reasons did not diminish her distrust and rancor, and she was sure that the profitable result of all his good deeds proved their perfidy.

"In fact, it's rust," said the seeker for gold, "it's iron oxide!"

"Then," said Pamphile, "isn't it harmful?"

"Just the opposite!" cried Ugolin. "My grandfather always has nails soaking in the jug of drinking water! Everybody knows that rust fortifies, because it puts iron in the muscles!"

"And where is your spring," asked the gold seeker, "in relation to this pond?"

"What d'you mean, in relation to the pond?"

"Is it higher or lower?"

"It's difficult to say . . ."

"In my opinion," said Ange, "the vallon of Les Romarins is a little higher."

"Then it's quite likely that the village water comes from that vallon, and that Ugolin's spring is a resurgence of it, because it goes through the same layer of bauxite . . . Are there red rocks in the region?"

"Sometimes," said Pamphile. "But no bigger than a nut."

Manon knew them, those stones . . . She looked for them for her sling, because they were heavier than the others and she could fling them further . . . She found them often, at the bottom of the valley of Les Refresquières; but she knew they came from some distance carried by runoff from the rain.

A distant bell sounded. It was the one in Les Bastides.

Ugolin counted the strokes.

"Oh damn!" cried Ange. "I promised to put the water back by midday at the latest!"

"So what's the problem?" said Pamphile. "We'll be done by midday!"

"Exactly," said Ange, "that's what bothers me. Because it will take an hour for the pond to fill up to a good height so that the water covers the pipe. And then it will take another half-hour for the water to get to the village. Let's get going! Let's have a go at it. You, Ugolin, take the broom."

The gold seeker got up and said:

"Gentlemen, your company is most agreeable, but duty calls me to the secretariat at the town hall."

"Don't you have a class on Thursday?" asked Pamphile.

"Certainly not! But don't forget that the *instituteur* is always the secretary of the town hall! The mayor expects me at half past ten for a reading and the commentary of the *Official Journal*!"

Manon was disappointed. He wasn't a seeker after gold . . . He was a teacher, perhaps from Aubagne, perhaps even from the village . . . Yet he was somebody all the same. And he talked about minerals in a pleasant voice . . .

She suddenly thought of the knife, which she had hoped to keep with the excuse of not having found the owner; but now he was right under her nose, and it was the teacher . . . She drew back so as not to be seen and took the lost treasure from her bag. She kissed the polished nickel, threw the knife onto a tuft of grass behind the young man, and flattened herself under the rockrose.

The projectile bent the branches and rang on the gravel. Ugolin raised his head.

"Say," he cried. "Somebody's throwing stones!"

"It's not a stone," declared Pamphile. "It made a little flash."

"Ayayay!" replied Ange. "If you see flashes at nine in the morning, you must have started on the white wine early!"

"On the tomb of my parents," said the carpenter solemnly, "I swear I had nothing but a cup of coffee before coming here."

Meanwhile, the teacher felt the gorse.

He stopped, leaned down, picked up something, and said, astonished:

"It's my knife!"

"Fancy that!" said Pamphile. "You lost it?"

"I lost it in the hills, about four or five days ago."

"Did you come this way?"

"Certainly not, this is the first time I've been in this vallon."

"Then it's extraordinary," said Ugolin.

"Now that I think about it," said the teacher, "I must have lost it when I was having lunch near the old sheepfold, the day I saw the flock without a shepherd . . ."

"Then," said Pamphile, "it's the shepherdess. She saw you having lunch, she found the knife, and she's just returned it to you."

"What, what?" said Ugolin, "do you mean to say Manon?"

"Yes, the hunchback's Manon," said Pamphile. "Who else can it be?"

The teacher raised his head.

"And you think she's hiding up there?"

"Hiding up there! She's scuttled off!" said Pamphile.

"That's a pity," said the teacher, "I would have liked to thank her."

Pamphile winked slyly.

"Oh yes," he said. "That would be quite natural. A polite thanks, perhaps with a little kiss?"

"As for the kiss, she's already gotten it!" said the teacher. "After what you told me the other evening I dreamed about it, and good heavens, I swear I gave her several kisses!"

"And she let you do it?" said Ugolin brusquely.

Pamphile burst out laughing and the teacher replied seriously:

"In my dreams no woman has ever refused me!"

Manon felt she was blushing; she moved back, got up, and took flight.

Hidden under the tumbling branches of the old fig tree, clasping her knees in her arms, she thought about this teacher who wasn't even a seeker for gold, and who spoke about her so lightly.

Since her birth only one man had kissed her brow or her hair, and that was her father. This young stranger, coming from town, was pretty sure of himself!

He had spoken about her with shocking ease and had told his audacious dream to others, which doubled the impropriety. Besides, this story of the dream bothered her a little. Baptistine said that it was very dangerous to venture into other people's dreams. While you slept they called you, they lured you, they made your spirit leave your body, and when you were in their dream you could no longer defend yourself. She cited the example of a girl from her village who had been summoned by a lover to his dreams each night and finally had had a baby without knowing how or why. Manon did not think this was true, but all the same, this young man had made his shadow come into her room, and he had embraced her, holding her in his arms, and perhaps he would do it again this very evening . . . But suddenly she was reassured—he had never seen her. So it was not she, but a creature he imagined according to what he had been told . . .

And they talked about her in the village and said things that made a young teacher dream. That proved that they spoke well of her. But who then? Perhaps this Pamphile, who did not seem to be a brute like the others. However, neither he nor anybody else had met her since the tragedy, when she was no more than a child!

She concluded that some hunter from the village, hidden in a lookout for partridges, had perhaps seen her without her suspecting it, and suddenly she thought of the day she had bathed at Les Refresquières, and of the undulating flight under the gorse of a spy she had not been able to see. So, blushing furiously, she burst out laughing, and hid her face in her hands.

Meanwhile, Ugolin came back down to the village with his shovel on his shoulder, behind Ange and Pamphile. He thought of the insolence of this teacher, who had pronounced words unworthy of his position.

"In dreams everything is easy . . . Me too, I also see her in my dreams sometimes. But I'm polite, I don't even talk to her . . . While he, he imagines himself embracing her, and she doesn't protest! Oh, he's surely got some ideas about her . . . He'd like to amuse himself with her . . . Taking advantage of the fact that she no longer has a father . . . I'll have to keep an eye on that . . . I'm a little to blame that she lives on the hill . . . In memory of poor Monsieur Jean it's up to me to take an interest in her . . ."

Eight hours later, at dinner under the lamp in the old Soubeyran house, the Papet said:

"Galinette, you haven't been looking well for quite a while now, you look as if you might go off the deep end . . ."

"It's true I don't have much appetite," said Ugolin, "and I think it's because of the poison I have to spray on the carnations every evening to protect them from the red spider."

"Why in the evening?"

"Because it's a chemical that can't take daylight. Light decomposes it, kills it, takes all the power out of it. That's why I often don't get to bed until midnight."

The Papet swallowed the chick-peas he had been chewing for some time, drank some white wine, and said:

"Listen, Galinette, it's inconvenient for you to come here for supper since you have to work so late, you lose more than an hour. So this is what we'll do: I'll come to your house around midday and bring food for both of us. I'll work with you in the afternoon and I'll leave you your supper. That way you'll be able to go to bed earlier . . ."

It was true that Ugolin looked after his carnations by lantern light until midnight; but he was lying when he said the chemical did not like the light. In fact he worked at night to make up for the hours lost in the morning, because he left Les Romarins at about six o'clock and did not get back until midday. He explained to Délie that he went to work every morning in an abandoned vineyard belonging to the Papet. He hoped to restore it to fruiting, but it was particularly important not to talk to the old man about it because he wanted to surprise him at the grape harvest.

When he rose from his bed he washed himself carefully, drank his coffee, put a fine onion in his haversack, together with a piece of bread impregnated with oil, and went out into the fresh morning wind.

First he went to visit two dozen traps he had set on the hillside above Les Romarins. Every day he caught some blackbirds, some thrushes, some red-tails, and some chaffinches. For fear of an encounter with the gendarmes he hid the birds under his shirt and in his pockets. Then he climbed up to the Plan de l'Aigle and sat down among the junipers on the edge of the escarpment above the cave of Le Plantier.

Toward seven o'clock Manon came out, opened the goat shed, and went off toward the plateaux or the vallons, according to the weather.

Ugolin followed her at a distance, as carefully as a hunter. He waited until she had gone some distance, then slid along under the bushes of the heath, and in his turn visited the traps she had set. He disarmed them and garnished them with the dead birds he had brought with him, smiling all the while with pleasure, and then applied himself to the artistic restitution of attitudes of agony in the cadavers.

After having carefully eradicated the traces of his passage, he took a roundabout route to avoid being seen on his way to the plateau of the Jas du Baptiste, which overlooked Les Refresquières, where he knew he would find her.

Before reaching his observation post he plunged into the high undergrowth where he could find all the plants of the hill growing around a rock clothed in ivy . . . He emerged with his ginger head hidden under a thick crown of ivy, a garland of clematis rolled around his neck, and the roots of a great tuft of thyme clasped between his teeth.

Thus adorned, he crept up to the edge of the bluff: with his chin poised on the edge, between two stones, he watched her living her life.

She spent some hours on the flat rock, in the shade of the single branch of the hunchbacked mountain ash. She read, she dreamed, she sewed multicolored materials, or slowly combed her hair . . . Suddenly she would get up and hurl stones with her sling, or dance around the mountain ash, dropping curtseys to it. Sometimes she would call the black dog and patiently extract minute thistles from his fur and the sly insects that crept into his ears, and sometimes even into his nostrils . . . When she finished Bicou's toilet she took the shaggy cheeks of the liberated dog between her two hands and talked to him eye to eye. Ugolin was too far away to hear the things she said to him. They certainly were secrets, and perhaps worse, because black dogs, especially those with eyes covered with hair, have never had a good reputation.

Besides that, nearly every day he observed another ceremony, much more surprising. Toward eleven o'clock she would call the big white she-goat and draw a little milk in a tin plate, which she put beside her on the flat rock . . . Then she would put her lips to the mouth organ and play an ancient air, always the same, a long phrase, shrill and fragile, which hardly disturbed the pure silence of the vallon: then the great "limbert" of Les Refresquières, the green lizard, spotted with gold and blue, would leap out from a distant bramble thicket. Like a streak of light it would run toward the music and plunge its horny snout into the bluish milk of the hills.

This limbert had been known in the village for years because of its size, nearly a meter long. It was said to have the eyes of a serpent and to mesmerize little birds, which fell alive into its open jaws. Its forked tongue would lap the milk, but when the mouth organ stopped, it would raise its flat head toward Manon. Then she would smile and speak softly to it. Ugolin, uneasy and charmed, looked at the long glistening beast listening to the luminous girl, and thought: "The old people weren't very wrong when they said she was a witch!"

But one day he murmured, smiling with pleasure:

"When a witch is pretty, well then she's called a fairy!"

The only book he possessed was an anthology of fairy stories, in a children's illustrated edition, a present from Grandmother Soubeyran, who had won this prize at school fifty years earlier. There was nothing left of it but a pile of pages stained with red half-moons and black spots and embroidered on the edges by time and rats.

He laid the pages out on the table and looked at the pictures first—the princesses and the young lords of the fairies surrounded by auras of light . . .

By the yellow light of his lamp he slowly re-read the story of Riqueta la Houppe, then the story of Beauty and the Beast.

The transformation of the beast into a prince seemed absurd, but it worried him a little. This great limbert that ran to the sound of the mouth organ, and looked at her, immobile, for such a long time was perhaps a punished prince whom she would one day free with a kiss, and then he would marry her to the sound of bells . . . He shook off this vision with a sneer and said loudly:

"This is childish . . . And even at the time of King Herod it never existed! . . . It's like Father Christmas and no more."

He went to sleep fairly late and had an atrocious dream. Manon was smiling and talking to the limbert, fondling its head . . . Suddenly there was a golden explosion, but without any sound, and in place of the limbert there was a dark young man, in a blue costume trimmed with gold braid, graciously greeting the shepherdess. This prince was the teacher, and Manon threw herself into his arms . . . Ugolin leaped from his bed crying with rage, and in the dark looking for the matches he knocked over the lamp and the glass burst gaily between his legs. Finally he succeeded in lighting a candle and bathed his face and his temples with cold water. He went back to sit on his bed and expelled a long sigh.

"If it goes on like this, I wonder how it'll end . . . There've already been three lunatics in the family. I don't want to be the fourth."

He soon got into the habit of talking loudly to himself . . . During the day he addressed the shepherdess. He apologized for not being handsome, but boasted about his qualities as a worker, his tenacity, his astuteness, and his fidelity to his only love. He made her visit his fields, talked in whispers about the golden louis hidden under the hearth stone, the second to the left of the first row from the bottom . . . During the night, while pulverizing the chemical to the sound of the owls, he talked to the hunchback and told him about the little girl's morning.

"Firstly, that pig of a teacher didn't come; however I saw him on the hill, but going up the side of La Tête Rouge gathering stones. Anyhow, I believe he was joking the other day and doesn't think that anymore. But all the same, I've got my eye on him. Especially Thursday morning. Not Sunday, because he stays in the village. Count on me. The little one's fine. She's got beautiful calves and a pretty bodice. She often laughs by herself. I don't tell you this just to please you; it's the truth. This morning she went under the old mountain ash as usual. She read books, she played a little music, and she talked to the limbert again, which is not a beast to keep company with. If they knew that in the village it wouldn't do her any good. But after all, she's like that. Afterwards she danced on the rock of La Tête Ronde. Completely dressed. She was waving a piece of golden material. It was very pretty: the hawk from the Plan de la Chèvre came to see what it was . . . Afterwards . . ."

He gave a thousand insignificant details in order to relive his morning by talking.

These soliloquies were embellished by shakings of the head, shrugging of the shoulders, and winks and various grimaces, aggravated by the tics of his eyelids. Yet he did not neglect his carnations. Quite the opposite, he worked like a convict. But not for the love of gold; if he wanted to amass mountains of it, it was for the love of Manon.

On Saturday she did not emerge from the cave until about nine o'clock, in a sombre dress, under a straw hat ornamented with a ribbon, and made a little taller by shoes . . . On the pack on the she-ass there were two or three bags apparently filled to bursting. They were swollen with bunches of aromatic herbs hiding two or three dozen dead birds. Ugolin knew she was going to Aubagne, but he was always disappointed by this departure . . . He watched her leaving and descending toward the crowd of houses. So he wandered in the hills, on the paths favored by his beloved, looking for traces of her passage—little bruised branches, footprints of a rope sole in the sand, recognizable among thousands because the heel was hardly marked . . . Then he approached the flat blue stone that he venerated like an altar—he smelled it, caressed it, and kissed it devotedly . . . He had gathered a number of relics around the sacred place . . . a crust of bread, a bit of frayed ribbon, and especially a little ball of golden hair that she had pulled from her comb. But as he pressed it to his lips he suddenly saw the great lizard—raised on its short feet, the earless beast looked at him fixedly. Frightened by the idea of some evil spell he took flight, but from afar he called:

"You, one of these days I'll blow you to bits with a good crack of my gun!"

CHAPTER 13

For the first two weeks the Papet believed the story of the nocturnal chemical. He came to lunch every day with Galinette, but did not always find him at the farm. Ugolin explained that around midday he felt the need to take a little walk to breathe the pure air and cleanse his lungs, which had been irritated by the chemical.

The old man approved of this prudence, at the same time deploring the indispensable noxiousness of the insecticide. But he soon became intrigued by a change in his nephew's character. He hardly spoke anymore, made only vague responses to the most precise questions, and blinked as rapidly as a star . . .

He thought: "If it's the insecticide, I'll get used to it, but there might be something else there. I think he's worried about something. But what?"

One fine morning about ten the Papet came to the observation post he had abandoned since the death of Monsieur Jean. Up to midday he saw nobody but Délie, who arrived from the village carrying a loaf of bread and a duster knotted at four corners.

He thought, "Galinette's asleep. Good, he needs it. But now I'd better wake him up!"

As he got up to go down to the farm, he saw Ugolin advancing pensively under the pine wood. A haversack, and no gun. And dressed "properly."

"So," he thought, "he went off before ten. And where did he go?"

He waited a moment, then pretended to arrive as usual for lunch.

He did not ask any difficult questions, but watered the carnations until three o'clock, then complained of his rheumatism and said he was going home to rest.

Instead he circled around and returned to his post. For a long time he watched his nephew's deeds and gestures. He saw him talking to invisible interlocutors but was not able to catch a word of what he said. He was frightened by the vivacity and variety of the pantomime that accompanied the soliloquy. Without saying a word he went home, very worried about poor Galinette's mental state. Was the worst of misfortunes going to strike the last of the Soubeyrans?

For four days he came back to his hideout at dawn; four times he saw Ugolin, "properly" dressed, leave at six in the morning, make a tour of his traps, and continue at a rapid pace down the path that joined the road from Aubagne a little farther on . . . The four afternoons were the same as the first—Ugolin did not stop talking . . .

However, about seven o'clock, when Délie had gone, the old man at last had a pleasant surprise. He saw the "loony" drop his pickax, fling himself to his knees, and throw kisses toward Aubagne. The Papet smiled and shook his head; when Ugolin went to sit on a big rock under an olive tree, with his fists on his temples, he went straight down to him without bothering to hide. The thinker was lost in his dream and did not even hear him come. He became aware of the old man's presence only by the arrival of his shadow, lengthened by the setting sun.

He wakened with a start and raised his head. The Papet looked at him gravely and said simply:

"Who is it?"

Ugolin, bewildered, got up and replied stupidly:

"It's me."

"Yes, it's you who's been telling me lies for a month, and it's you who's going nuts. But the woman, who is she?" Ugolin stammered:

"Woman? What woman?"

"The one you go and see every morning at Aubagne!"

"I don't go to Aubagne," said Ugolin.

"And so, where do you go?"

But the other did not reply. He looked at the ground and cracked his knuckles.

"I've been watching you for days. Yes, I've a right to, because you're my responsibility. You leave in the morning at about six. You collect the birds in your traps, and you take them to somebody, because I never see them in the house. I can't follow you because of my aches, but you go toward Aubagne or Roquevaire . . . And in the afternoon, when you're alone, you talk, you wave your arms around, you pray, you send kisses. Who is it?"

Ugolin kept silent.

"I'm not reproaching you for being in love," continued the old man, "although I think you exaggerate, and you take it badly. But it does happen, and when it happens late it sometimes happens too strongly. But after all it's natural. What I reproach you with is keeping it secret from me . . ."

Ugolin raised his shoulders and shook his head, but kept quiet.

"If you don't want to tell me, it must be something not quite proper. Or is it a married woman?"

At these words Ugolin burst out with a demented laugh, pranced about, and cried:

"Yes! Yes! She's married to a limbert! Hahaha!"

He fled toward the house, and the Papet heard the lock click three times. He was astonished and murmured anxiously:

"That's not good, no, it's not good."

He rushed to the locked door and beat it with his stick.

"Open, imbecile!"

"No, I won't open it, but if you want we can talk through the door."

"Why?"

"Because maybe if I don't see you, I'll be able to tell you something."

The Papet reflected for a moment and declared:

"You're as big an idiot as your poor father. Wait while I get a chair to sit down, because my leg's hurting."

"There aren't any chairs, but you could get an empty box from the stable."

The Papet sat down on a box, facing the door, with his hands crossed on his cane.

"What is it you want to tell me?"

"I don't want to tell you anything, it's you that's forcing me. So ask me questions."

"Good. First, tell me why you talked about this limbert. That's what worries me most."

"That was sort of a joke . . . It's because there's a big limbert that comes when she calls it and drinks milk at her feet."

"You saw that at the fair?"

"No, on the hill."

"So, because she knows how to make a limbert come, that's made you dotty?"

"No, no," said Ugolin. "But it intrigues me."

"Me, too, it intrigues me. It proves that you're just as stupid as a limbert. And afterwards?"

"After what?"

"Well then, tell me who it is."

After a short silence Ugolin replied firmly:

"No, I'm not going to tell you."

"Tell me at least whether it's a girl from town."

"Oh no! quite the contrary."

"So much the better. D'you know her?"

"So to speak . . . no."

"Why, so to speak?"

"Listen, Papet, don't ask me questions like that, because you're too smart, and after four questions you could understand without my knowing."

"Therefore I know her?"

"You see? You see? You know I don't want to tell you who it is, and you ask me questions like a gendarme. No, I don't want to tell you!"

"Why not?"

"Because it's my secret. My first love secret. So I'll keep it to myself."

"Good, good," said the Papet. "Keep it to yourself for the moment. Is it with her you have those rendezvous in the morning?"

"Yes, but she doesn't know it."

"If you answer me in riddles it's hardly worth going on. Good-bye."

The Papet got up.

"No, Papet, don't go. I like to talk to you about her."

"It doesn't interest me, since I don't know who she is!"

"Yes, but I know. So it pleases me."

The Papet shrugged his shoulders, sat down on the box again, and asked:

"How does she come to your rendezvous since you say she doesn't know about them?"

"Listen: every morning I know where she is, and I go there. I look at her from a distance. That's the truth!"

The Papet reflected for a moment and said:

"What good's that?"

"It gives me pleasure. Every morning when I see her it's the most beautiful day in my life!"

"Ayayay!" said the Papet. "You'll get over that pretty quickly."

"Oh no! I'll never get over that! Never! On the contrary! It will only get stronger!"

The Papet thought this over while filling his pipe.

Ugolin asked stupidly:

"Have you gone?"

"No. I'm filling my pipe. So, you want to marry this woman?"

"Oh yes, I would like to very much. But I don't think she wants to."

"Why?"

"Because she's beautiful, and me, I'm ugly."

"That's nothing. There are some who're married to Madonnas who're as ugly as you are. But let's talk a little seriously. Has she got any property?"

"Oh no," said Ugolin. "She's got a little, but it's not much."

"So, she won't find a husband very easily. Is she in good health?"

"That, yes," said Ugolin. "She's got fine little muscles. You understand, she's not just a mare! No! But for a woman, she's very strong and fresh!"

"Could she help you with your work?"

"Oh yes, certainly. I've seen her pickaxing. Of course I'm not saying she could dig down to fifty centimeters. But for hoeing my carnations, which is a delicate job—she'd do that better than me. And besides, above all, she's had some education."

"How d'you know that?"

"She reads books all the time. Sometimes for an hour without stopping!"

"That's not too good, Galinette. A poor girl who reads books—I can't say I care for that . . . But after all, you know how I've been wanting you to marry for some time . . . It's not the kind of woman I was hoping for, but after all, I don't want to force you. As for money, while it can never be useless, we've got enough for two. If she is too beautiful it could be a nuisance for us, and besides, a woman who's too beautiful is not well regarded and not always very serious . . . It wouldn't do if she were a tart. Do you think she's honest?"

"Oh, Papet, I'm quite sure of that! She's a wild Holy Virgin. It's difficult to explain, but that's what she's like. If she said yes, she would be an extraordinary wife for me, and I would be happier than you can imagine. But she doesn't want me."

The Papet replied violently:

"A poor girl has never refused a Soubeyran. She must be a hopeless lunatic."

"You, Papet, if she said yes, would you agree?"

"If what you tell me is true, I'll agree, but I can't say yes without knowing who she is. Come on, you big imbecile, open the door and tell me!"

"No, no!" cried Ugolin. "I won't open the door. I must think a bit."

"Take your time," said the Papet, and he lit his pipe.

The setting sun had just plunged into its red clouds, and a timid cricket tried its frail high-pitched music. The Papet raised his head, and across the trellis he saw two Asiatic pumpkins hanging, already as big as oranges, of a fine green, spotted with white.

He was thinking of the hunchback carrying his jar, and of all his useless efforts, when Ugolin spoke:

"Papet, I think I'll tell you. But first you must swear on all the Soubeyrans that you won't say a single word after you hear her name, and that you'll leave— at once."

"Why?"

"Because I don't want you to talk about it this evening. I want you to get used to the idea first . . . Tomorrow, if you like, we'll talk about it. We'll talk about it all the time. But tonight, I'm ashamed."

"Oh, misery!" said the Papet. "What a fool! All right, it will be as you wish!"

"Swear! Swear on all the Soubeyrans!"

The Papet took the pipe out of his mouth, stood up and took off his hat, and swore solemnly.

"Good," said Ugolin. "It's sworn. Now, wait a moment so I can decide."

The Papet raised his eyes to the sky, shrugged his shoulders, and sat down again on the box.

He waited at least two minutes; then he rattled on the door.

"I'm not opening it," said Ugolin. "I'll take out the key. Put your ear to the keyhole!"

The Papet bent down, his ear pressed to the door. Finally Ugolin whispered:

"It's Manon, the hunchback's daughter."

In perfect silence the old man stood up, turned his back to the mute door, and departed to the setting sun.

The next day at lunch, the Papet talked first about the drought that was menacing the vines and fruit trees in the vallon; the village was concerned because it had not rained for five weeks. Ugolin had not even noticed.

"I can't stand water from the sky," said Ugolin. "You can't control it; it's always too much or not enough. Whereas I can control the spring—and since it's snow water it runs faster in the summer than the winter . . . If we're lucky enough to get a lot of heat, like this year, I'll make a fortune because with well-watered carnations, the hotter it is, the more beautiful they are!"

"You can tell when it's going to be very hot," said the Papet. "The crickets are out at least two weeks in advance, and that means the sun's going to drink half the wine!"

Ugolin shrugged his shoulders.

"There'll be enough wine left for us, and it will be all the better!"

They clinked glasses joyously and attacked the dessert—a little basket of fresh figs . . . Then the Papet began:

"Can we talk about it?"

"Oh yes!" said Ugolin.

"Good," said the Papet.

He took a long time stuffing his pipe, without saying a word. Ugolin waited, trembling with impatience, squinting and blinking horribly. After this period of reflection, the Papet smiled and said:

"Yesterday evening you did well to stop me from saying a single word, because I would have said a lot, and it would have been painful for you."

"You don't like it?" said Ugolin all pale.

"Let me talk; I said 'yesterday evening' . . . Well, yesterday evening my first thought was: 'He's mad, this little girl is fifteen, maybe sixteen.' Sixteen years, that's very young for you."

"So, you say no?"

"But let me talk, for God's sake! That's very young. And perhaps in twenty years she'll find you very old, and she'll find a lover."

"You don't know her!" cried Ugolin. ". . . A girl like her, if by chance she wanted me . . ."

"A girl like her is just like other girls. But what does that amount to? In twenty years the little Soubeyrans will be made, and well made, because she's beautiful. She's a creature of the hills, and I agree."

Tears rose to Ugolin's eyes, and the beating of his eyelids sent them flying onto the table.

"And besides," said the Papet, "she looks more than her age. She looks nearly eighteen."

"So," said Ugolin, surprised, "you've seen her?"

"Certainly."

"When?"

The Papet smiled and said:

"This morning."

"That's not possible, because this morning . . ."

"This morning at five," said the old man, "I was hidden at the edge of Saint Esprit, because I knew that was the way you'd go, and it put me a little ahead of you, since I was afraid I might not be able to follow you. And finally I saw everything. While you were hidden above the ledge, I was under the big fig tree by the ruined shepherd's hut."

"She might have seen you!" said Ugolin.

"So what? A good old man surely has the right to look for herbs or mushrooms. In any case, I was nearer than you, and I could see her well. Do you know who she looks like?"

"Nobody," said Ugolin forcefully.

"Be quiet, silly. She looks like somebody you never knew."

He went on pensively:

"She's the exact picture of her grandmother, Florette of Les Romarins, who was born on this farm . . ."

He seemed to dream for a moment, then said shortly:

"When will you speak to her?"

"I don't know . . . For the moment it's enough for me to see her."

"You've got time," said the Papet, "but be sure that nobody more handsome than you comes near her, someone not afraid of talking to her—these things happen . . ."

He dreamed again for a moment.

"Come on, Galinette, to the carnations!"

CHAPTER *14*

One morning, visiting his traps at dawn, Ugolin found the rarest of captures—a little hare, half suffocated. He felled it with a blow behind the ears.

"This time," he said, "she'll be happy . . . It's more than three pounds, and it's easily worth five francs!"

He followed her as usual. She went straight to the little ledge where the mountain ash stood, and he found that this day the traps were set at the bottom of the vallon and on the hillside, quite close to her encampment. He was thus unable to visit them to set the usual scene and deliver the precious game to her without being seen.

She made her rounds, but the east wind had been blowing all night and had hardly fallen. She found no more than a handful of birds and went up again to her flat rock. There she filled her haversack with dried grass, placed it on the stone as a pillow, and went to sleep.

He looked at her for a long time, overwhelmed by the sight. He was reminded of an old lullaby that spoke of the "sleep of innocence" and wept a little. Then he suddenly thought of the hare. He made an immense circle (because of the dog) and arrived at the traps at least a hundred meters from the sleeper. He penetrated the thicket, slid the long-eared head into the first snare he could find, and tightened the running knot. He pulled up several tufts of grass around the body and scratched the earth with his nails. Then he scrambled up a dangerous chimney with difficulty and got up close to her viewpoint. Manon slept all the time.

He thought:

"Today, too bad for the Papet, too bad for the carnations, I'm going to stay here until she goes to her traps. I want to see what she does when she finds the hare. I'm sure she'll dance!"

He resumed his adoring contemplation.

But at the end of a quarter of an hour the black dog, stretched out by his mistress with his muzzle between his legs, got up suddenly. He turned his head toward the bottom of the vallon and growled softly. Manon raised herself on an elbow, then on her palm, and looked in the same direction.

Then the teacher appeared. He was climbing up the gorge of the Pas du Loup with his head bent, studying the least pebble.

On seeing the young man approach, Ugolin was seized by a kind of anguish, and he looked in turn at the girl and at the intruder.

"If she'd seen him, she'd already have gone . . ."

Then he murmured:

"Run, run, look who's coming!"

Meanwhile Manon, as if unconscious of the danger, gathered her hair and tied it with a ribbon; then she tightened the belt of her dress, opened a book, and stretched out on the rock and started to read, with a fennel flower between her teeth.

The teacher picked up a pebble, examined it through his lens, then threw it away. He looked around him and saw the goats, then Manon.

He took a step to the side as if to hide behind the brushwood bordering the path, and advanced on tiptoe without the slightest noise. This stratagem greatly worried Ugolin. He whispered:

"Oh dear! Go quickly. He's a swine. He said he kissed you!"

Meanwhile the villain continued to approach her stealthily, and evidently intended to surprise her . . .

He trembled with pain and rage, and whispered:

"Oh really! She can't let that happen! And if he tries to embrace her by force, I'll go down!"

Manon had heard the young man approaching since his first steps fell in the gorge and the ringing of his hammer had alerted her—the person walking on the pebbles of the Pas du Loup was the insolent young man who had called her during his dreams. She felt her cheeks burning, but she pretended to read, immobile, as if lost in her book.

When he suddenly emerged from the junipers, she raised her head and looked at him without showing the least surprise . . . The teacher advanced, smiling, carrying face-high a shining knife of polished horn and steel.

"Mademoiselle," he said, "I am happy to meet you, to thank you for returning this instrument to me."

Ugolin could not make out the words, but when he saw the knife he understood.

"Good. He's saying thank you to her."

Manon got up, but made no response.

"The truth is," said the teacher, coming toward her, "it fell on me from the sky, but the peasants who were with me divined your presence and told me."

"Monsieur," said Manon, "I found it on the hill, down there, under the big pine tree, near the shepherd's hut."

"But how did you know it belonged to me?"

"I saw you having lunch under the tree one day, at midday."

"And I saw your goats, your dog, and especially your donkey, who was determined to eat my sausage . . ."

"It's a she-donkey," said Manon. "She has her caprices . . ."

"But you, where were you?"

"In the tree. High up."

"Why?"

She shrugged her shoulders, but did not reply.

Ugolin was staring with all his might at this conversation, which he could not hear. He felt his heart beating against his sides, because he saw the teacher smiling as he talked, while Manon listened to him without raising her eyes, smoothing the twig of fennel between her fingers.

The seducer continued:

"They've spoken to me about you, and what they told me is extremely interesting . . ."

"I know," she replied. "I heard the conversation by the side of the pond, before throwing you the knife."

The teacher became embarrassed, because he suddenly remembered "the kiss," and said very quickly:

"I was especially interested by the red powder that forms a deposit at the bottom of the pond after the storms . . . I have a mania, I should say almost a passion, for mineralogy. Since I am the teacher in the village, I want to assemble a little collection of the minerals of these hills in order to teach my pupils the composition of the land where they were born."

"That's why you've got a little hammer and a lens? I thought you were look-ing for gold."

"I would look for that," said he, "if we were on land containing veins of quartz or schist—but that's not the case here."

"Here," said Manon, "we have the Jurassic Cretaceous of the second epoch of the Quaternary."

The teacher's eyes opened so wide they met his eyebrows.

"You're very learned for a shepherdess."

She smiled.

"Oh no . . . I'm doing no more than repeat my father's words . . . And I often read the books he left me. I don't understand them very well, but they remind me of him. He knew everything, absolutely everything!"

She was smiling all the time, but suddenly the tears glistened in her eyes.

The teacher was moved by the dignity of this grief and did not know what to say. That was why he felt in his bag and drew out a second knife, exactly like the first, and made them both flash in the sun.

"There's its brother," he said.

"You bought another?"

"No! . . . The day I bought the first one, when I went home for lunch I found this one under my napkin—it was a present from my mother for Saint Bernard, whom I'd forgotten . . . Naturally I uttered cries of surprise and didn't say a word to her about my purchase. But I've always been afraid she might discover the first knife, and so, if you will accept it, you'll free me of this little worry."

Ugolin was a little reassured by the attitudes of the two young people, who stayed three paces from each other; but he thought their conversation was last-ing rather a long time, and when he saw the two knives, he thought:

"There it is! He bought one for her! A knife worth at least seven francs. That proves he's got ideas about her, and not just in his dreams! Of kisses! Me, I don't care a damn about kisses!"

Meanwhile, Manon was looking at the fine present the young man smilingly held out to her.

She stammered:

"Oh no! Thank you . . . I've got one . . . I've got my own, after all . . . And besides, it's too fine for me!"

"Not at all! A shepherd's knife is not too fine for a shepherdess . . . You know it's got four blades, a corkscrew, an awl, and a nail file . . ."

"And even a little pair of scissors," said Manon, lowering her eyes. "I looked after yours for several days, and I made use of it."

"There then, you can't do without it now. Take it."

"Oh no, thank you," she said, ". . . I can manage . . . Thank you."

The teacher had approached her, and she had not retreated; he kept holding the shining knife, and she kept smoothing the fennel twig without raising her head.

Above, on the brink of the ledge, Ugolin stretched forward like a gargoyle under his crown of ivy. He ground his teeth on a root of thyme and gazed at them in a fearful silence.

But the black dog, seized by a sudden fury, plunged down the path leading to the traps, barking enough to choke himself. Manon bent down, seized her stick, and bounded after him.

The teacher, surprised, followed her and saw a large red buzzard suspended on trembling wings at least ten meters above a thicket. The dog disappeared under the junipers. Manon followed with her stick raised, shouting Piedmontese insults.

The noise of the running, the barking of the dog, and the cries of the shepherdess intimidated the bird of prey, and it flew off in a mounting spiral . . .

"It's a thief," said Manon. "It watches my traps better than I do, and it has already taken a fine partridge from under my nose, and a pigeon as well!"

Talking all the while, she entered the thicket. After a moment her hand rose above the dark foliage, holding a large red hare by the ears.

"There, that's what it wanted, the dirty beast! A hare!"

She came back toward the teacher, flushed with emotion and joy, with her arms raised to show the beauty of the animal she was holding by the ears . . .

"It's the first one I've caught with the snare! It's because it's young. . . . When they're bigger, they take everything with them!"

Ugolin was happy to see her content. He laughed noiselessly, then said:

"It's me that offers it to you, that hare! . . . Yes, it's me, Ugolin!"

He saw them coming up toward the mountain ash again. The teacher was talking all the time, holding out the two knives . . .

"But no," murmured Ugolin, exasperated, "she doesn't want your knife: that's twice she's said no!"

Indeed, Manon was still refusing to take what he was tendering.

Then the teacher looked at his watch and said:

"Quarter to one! My class begins in an hour and a half, and I've hardly got time for lunch . . . Oh well, mademoiselle, I thank you once more, but since you don't want to relieve me of this superfluous instrument, I am leaving it on this stone. It will certainly bring pleasure to someone!"

Ugolin saw the gesture and murmured:

"No, she won't take it! No, no, no . . ."

The teacher went down the path at a rapid pace. The shepherdess, with the hare in her hand, watched him leaving. Ugolin breathed. She had refused the present from the seducer, and she was happy and proud about the hare. In all, it was a victory. But when the teacher reached a bend in the path that plunged between high briars, he turned round and raised his hand in a little gesture of farewell . . .

Then Manon cried:

"I'll look after the knife if you will accept the hare!"

Ugolin blinked three times on hearing these dreadful words.

The seducer responded:

"I agree."

She whirled the red animal and hurled it with such force that the teacher would have received it on his chest if he had not caught it in flight.

He cried, "Bravo, and thank you," then disappeared.

Ugolin groaned:

"My hare!"

The girl was already opening the blades of the shepherd's knife, one after the other.

He went back down toward Les Romarins, heartbroken and trembling with anxiety. Every ten steps he stopped to talk loudly and try to figure out the importance and meaning of the adventure.

"Firstly, she returned his knife. That was something that is not usually done. If you find a knife, you keep it . . . But you could say it was because she was honest . . . That's her father's fault for moralizing too much . . . Besides, how did she know that the teacher was at the pond that day? That's always puzzled me. But after all that could have been chance . . . I was at the pond too . . . and I can't say why . . . Today it was much stranger . . . Yes, he was looking for her. The proof was that he had bought that knife to give to her . . . Yes, quite so, he looked for her, and he found her . . . But the kiss, he didn't do that! Ah, no! He knew quite well that would not succeed."

"Only, only, they talked a good long time. Yes, but it was him talking most of the time . . . It's the custom for townspeople to talk all the time, to run on . . . And the knife, she said 'no' at least twice. That proves she's proud . . . The bad thing, the bad thing was the business of the hare. That's a disaster. She likes his knife better than my hare!"

He took a few steps, quite overwhelmed, then stopped suddenly, and with finger raised, said very quickly:

"Pardon, Monsieur Ugolin, pardon! She did not know that it was my hare. She thought she caught it in her trap!"

"And besides, she did that because she did not want to accept the present! And besides, it was good business—the knife cost at least ten francs, and the hare's worth no more than five! Consequently she did well!"

Nevertheless, although these considerations quieted his anxiety, they did not suppress it, because the fact was that they talked such a long time, and they would probably talk again. That teacher was not going to stop there. He would certainly return, under the pretext of looking for stones (which were useless) and perhaps, because of the present, he would end by winning her. So he resolved to lose no more time, to make his "declaration" as soon as possible.

During the night on his pallet, he had a long conversation with Monsieur Jean. Monsieur Jean unfortunately seemed to favor the teacher and, furthermore, overwhelmed him with reproaches for the regrettable affair of the spring . . . This inimical attitude of the phantom confirmed him in his resolution to "get in the running" immediately, after talking it over with the Papet. The old rascal knew a lot about women . . . But for fear of appearing ridiculous, he decided to say nothing about the schemes of the teacher.

CHAPTER 15

The next day, after Délie had gone, the two of them lunched in the kitchen.

"Papet, what should one do to talk to girls?"

The old man salted some tender green beans and crunched them like sweets. He smiled, winked, and said:

"So, you've decided, at last?"

"Yes, yes, I must start as soon as possible, because she goes to Aubagne from time to time, and she's so beautiful, somebody might take her from me . . . So it would be better to talk to her at once. But you know I'm not used to talking. So tell me a little how to do it . . ."

"Good. Pay attention. First, where will it take place?"

"On the hill, naturally. I will approach her by pretending to look for mushrooms or snails . . . As if I don't see her . . . And suddenly I'll see her and I'll talk to her. But what do I say to her?"

"Not so quickly!" said the Papet. "In the first place, it's not a good idea to be looking for mushrooms or snails. That makes you look poor. When you're rich, you must show it. Better to pretend you're hunting, in a fine hunter's costume. Yes. It's no good showing up with ten francs worth of clothes on your back. A new outfit, and one that makes an impression! . . . A proper hunting suit, with leather gaiters, and a hat of the same material as the suit. And above all, braces!"

"They mustn't show, the braces!"

"You poor simpleton!" cried the Papet. "Just look at the rich—they always have their trousers well supported, whereas peasants, with their woollen belts, the backsides of their trousers hang down to their knees . . . Look at Philoxène, when he does a wedding, or goes to town, he puts on his braces . . . And the teacher, he wears them all the time!"

That was a decisive argument.

"And after that?"

"After that, a hunter's cravat. Like a kind of scarf, to hide the throat . . . Like that, you look like somebody! And we'll go and find all that at Aubagne, at the Happy Worker—not too dear . . ."

Ugolin got up to get the pot of daube simmering on the cinders and refilled their plates. For a moment they did not talk. Ugolin reflected smilingly.

"I've thought of one thing," he said. "I wondered—mind you, I've not yet decided—I wondered whether I should shave my moustache."

"Perhaps," said the Papet, ". . . it depends on what sort of face you've got . . . But sometimes a moustache pleases women . . . There are two you know (and they go to mass at seven every morning) who close their eyes when they stroke mine . . ." ("That," thought Ugolin, "that would be very fine . . . She will never do it to me. It's not her style; and besides, her father never had a moustache and that teacher is clean-shaven.")

"In any case," he said, "it's worth a try . . ."

They ate in silence, without hurrying, and exchanging smiles from time to time. Then Ugolin said timidly:

"A little perfume in the hair—what d'you think of that?"

The Papet—who smelled like a fox—replied:

"I think that would please her, if you can bear it. I never could. It gives me a headache . . ."

The next day they went to Aubagne.

First they paid a visit to the hairdresser—a real hairdresser—and eventually emerged unrecognizable. The Papet regretted having his head washed because this operation revealed that his hair was much whiter than he thought; but he was very pleased with his moustache, the points of which the artist had elegantly turned up with a little curling iron. Ugolin's moustache was sacrificed, but at a profit for his nose, which now seemed twice as long. Since he saw nothing but his full face he did not notice this aggravation of his profile. The Papet was a little uneasy, but said nothing.

They left the Happy Worker an hour later. They had committed follies. The old man had been unable to resist a dark blue velvet suit, the beauty of which obliged him to replace his ancient hat with a wide-brimmed black felt hat. As for Ugolin, a little stiff in his brand new clothing, he looked at himself as he passed shop windows, smiling and blushing with pride.

"Galinette," said the Papet, "with an outfit like that you could marry the Pope's daughter."

"I think it suits me well," said Ugolin. ". . . If I were to meet me I wouldn't dare talk to me."

CHAPTER 16

Manon was climbing the steep path in the ravine that led to the mountain ash, as was her habit, when the big white kid that marched at the head of the flock stopped dead and looked curiously at the thicket of myrtle overlooked by a green oak with several trunks . . . The dog sprang forward, growling.

She had laid her traps under this cover, so she immediately concluded that some animal that preyed on wild birds, perhaps a ferret or a weasel, was devouring her prizes. She threw herself forward with stick raised when there was a noise of breaking branches and a hunter rose up in front of her; it was a stranger from town wearing a partridge feather stuck in the ribbon of his hat.

She drew back ready to fly, while the dog barked furiously and ran around the stranger, who seemed confused, and said in an uncertain voice:

"Pardon, excuse me if I trouble you . . . I am after a hare that I shot up on the plateau that is certain to be wounded . . ."

Manon was surprised by the voice, but while she was still searching for a name to put to the face, the grimace of a tic contracted it suddenly; she recognized Ugolin. He advanced toward the dog, who retreated barking, and with a twitching smile, said in a tone that he thought citified:

"But is it by chance—you wouldn't be little Manon, the daughter of poor Monsieur Jean?"

He had prepared this phrase, and this smile, for a long time, and had hoped for the happiest outcome from them. But Manon did not reply and stared with surprise at the hunting costume and the fawn-colored leggings.

He forced himself to stand very straight.

"I see," he said, "that you do not recognize me, and that's quite natural since I have changed a lot. I am Ugolin, your poor father's friend."

He found her even more beautiful close up, but when she raised her eyes toward him he could not meet them, and he felt his heart beating. He had to speak at any price.

"And you too, you have changed . . . You've become a real young lady. One has to look hard to recognize you . . ."

He spoke very kindly, but she was ill at ease, as in the past.

"You must be surprised that in such a long time on the hill we have not met. But up to now I haven't had the time to hunt . . . It's because of the carnations . . . Did you know that I've been growing carnations?"

"No, I didn't know that."

"Didn't they talk about it in Aubagne?"

"No."

"All the same, everybody talks about it, because I'm the only one in the country who's had the idea of growing carnations. And besides, it's not only the idea—you must know how . . . it takes good land and a lot of work."

She answered sharply:

"And a spring."

"Oh yes," he said. "That's probably the most important."

"I know that."

"And so, you can see I've succeeded very well. I've made a lot of money . . . Hum. A lot of money . . ."

Manon looked at this triumphant idiot and did not doubt his success, which aggravated her father's defeat; the new suit reminded her of his tattered jacket, the fawn shoes insulted the painful memory of his bare feet.

He approached her and said in a low voice:

"And all this money, it's in pieces of gold, well hidden . . . I've never told that to anybody, but I'm telling you, because it shows your father was right . . . In two years I've saved up at least fifty thousand francs! What do you think of that?"

"That's none of my business," said Manon. "If you are rich, so much the worse for us."

She leaped lightly from the path to rejoin her goats on the other side of the undergrowth.

He followed her, talking all the time.

"Listen, don't go. I want to say something important to you. Yes, a message for your mother."

She stopped, surprised.

"Is it true you live at Le Plantier with Baptistine?"

"Yes. It's all that's left, but it's home for us."

"Well, it worries me to think that you're three women alone up there—it even makes me ashamed. But it's not my fault. I said you could stay at Les Romarins, and then you left without a word. But all the same, sometimes I'm ashamed."

"Why? It's none of your business!"

"I agree, but I often think about it. Would you like to come back to Les Romarins?"

She replied brusquely.

"With you?"

He answered very quickly, and almost humbly:

"But no, no! I've always got my little house at Massacan, where I was perfectly content, and I don't feel at home in Les Romarins, because it's always been Monsieur Jean's house, but I was forced to stay there because of the carnations . . . They're very delicate, a lot of things can go wrong, and they need to be looked after . . . If the house were empty, the rabbits would do a lot of damage . . . And besides, the carnations are expensive and someone could come and steal them some night . . . But if you were there, with your mother and Baptistine, I would go back to Massacan . . . You could use the spring, and you could live in the midst of the flowers that your mother likes so much . . ."

Again a good deed, again a generous offer? What did he want from it? Despite her suspicion and her repulsion, she hesitated to answer him too sharply. She caressed her dog's head and he pressed against her dress and licked her hands between barks directed at the intruder.

Finally she replied:

"I thank you, but I've already told you, we are very well at Le Plantier; and Les Romarins, for us, would be too sad. No thank you."

She started off again.

"Manon, listen. I know very well why you say no. It's because you're proud. You don't ever want to accept presents . . . Even when you were small you would run off if I brought you a handful of almonds . . . Listen, as for your pride, don't worry about that. Let me explain."

Out of sheer curiosity, she stopped.

"I've told you: my work is carnations. But it's not enough to plough and to plant. They must be watered and plucked, and then made into bouquets . . . And that's what women can do. So you, your mother, and Baptistine could help me a lot, and the pay would not be too bad . . ."

Manon was relieved.

"Ah, good!" she said, smiling bitterly. "I understand! You need domestics?"

He blushed and replied forcefully:

"But no! No! Don't take it like that! In memory of your father I'm offering you your house and a little work. Like that you won't think it's a charity . . . But above all, it will enable you to leave the savage conditions you now live in, and you will help a friend!"

She replied brutally:

"You're very keen on giving help, but it always ends with your profiting from it! You helped my father, now you're living in his house. You found the spring, and now it's you who're rich! Perhaps you haven't deliberately done us harm, but it seems to me your help has brought us misfortune. So don't worry about us—we don't need anybody, and especially not you!"

She turned her back to him, went up toward her goats, and moved away under the escarpment, along the stony hillside.

He called:

"Manon! Listen, Manon . . ."

She did not even turn.

Poor Ugolin stood frozen. He had thought that time would soften this aversion, which he considered unjustified since Manon had never known the true history of the spring . . . Certainly he had not dared to hope she would fall into his arms, but he thought the proposition he had made was marvellously advantageous for a poor shepherdess . . . Nevertheless, she had refused him scornfully and told him that he had brought them misfortune . . . What a disaster . . . He felt a pain in his side and tears in his eyes.

When she was far enough away, she turned round to make sure he had not followed her. She did not see anybody and stopped to gather some peppermint from a long row growing under the escarpment.

The encounter with Ugolin had revived the past—not that she had forgotten it, but her keen, youthful joy of living, which so quickly caused foreign bodies to be expelled, softened the contours of the bad memories and obscured the cruel colors, and ended by giving them the unreality of a story read in a book.

The presence of this man, his tics and the sound of his voice, had wiped out the beneficial effect of the last four years; and it evoked her father's personality very clearly: with his bulk and his weight; and the sound of his very steps on the rolling stones of the scree, walking under the weight of the jar. She started to run.

Suddenly a heartrending voice cried her name twice.

She stopped, looked behind her, then raised her head. She saw him up against the sky, leaning over the perpendicular drop.

He cried:

"Manon! Don't run! Listen to me a minute! Manon, it's not true! To make you work! It's because I love you! Manon, I love you! I'm in love with you!"

These cries he tore from his chest echoed and re-echoed, and from the other side of the vallon the sheets of rock moaned three times, "Love!"

The astonished girl stared at the gesticulating puppet. Her mouth hung open with surprise and disgust.

He continued to cry:

"Manon! I didn't dare tell you when I was near you, but I am sick with love. It chokes me. It's a long time since it happened. It was at Refresquières after the big storm! I was hiding for partridges . . . I saw you when you were bathing in the rain pool . . . I looked at you for a long time, you were so beautiful. I was afraid of committing a crime! I went off under the broom, and you threw stones at me!"

Manon blushed indignantly and cupped her hands to shout insults in Piedmontese because she didn't know any others. She terminated this short litany by shouting loudly, "Old pig!," and took to the path again behind her goats. Ugolin ran along the escarpment, shouting:

"It's not true, I'm not old! I'll be thirty years old and I'll have fifty thousand francs next year! And it's not for my amusement! I want to marry you! It will be a fine household! And besides, I've got no family! Nobody to feed! My grandfather is dead! My grandmother is dead! My father hanged himself when I was little, my mother died of flu. There's only the Papet! He's my godfather! He's rich and he'll leave me everything because I am the last of the Soubeyrans! He's old and he'll die soon, the Papet! We will have the big house in the village! And all those carnations, I grew them for you! Yes, for you, in God's name! Because I love you! I love you!"

The whole valley echoed to these moanings, and the dog replied with furious barks. Manon, nauseated, continued her course, but the unfortunate man followed her, galloping on the edge of the escarpment and stopping from time to time to continue his declarations.

"Manon! You'll be like a queen! I'll pay for two housemaids for you! I'll get you everything you want! I'll bring you coffee in bed every morning, yes, in God's name, because I love you!"

But as he stretched his arms toward her, moaning, "My love, my love . . . ," his voice stopped suddenly in a hiccup and he doubled up with his hands on his stomach. He had just received, full in the belly, a stone hurled from the shepherdess's sling. She fled lightly, followed by the tinkling goats and the bounding dog . . .

Poor Ugolin fought to find his breath. Bent in two he swung his torso about and ended by falling on his knees in the thyme.

Finally the pain allowed him a moment's respite, and he said in a strangled voice:

"It's unbelievable how adroit she is!"

The spasm contracted his muscles again, and he was down on all fours on the gravel of the garigue, when he spotted a flint that was nearly round, a little honey-colored egg. It was the stone that had hit him. He picked it up and kissed it, then put it in his pocket and got up. Manon had disappeared behind a spur of the escarpment, and he could not even hear the goat bells . . . He went to pick up his gun and slowly descended toward Les Romarins.

CHAPTER *17*

He found the Papet among the cuttings, busy with planting stakes.

"So? Did you speak to her?"

"I didn't see her today," he replied. "She must have taken some game to Aubagne, or perhaps to Pichauris."

"If not today, then tomorrow."

"Or even later," said Ugolin. "I ought to get used to this outfit . . ."

"You are superb! You look like a hunter from Marseille! Hurry up and change!"

They worked at the carnations until the evening. While Ugolin kept an eye on the irrigation streams, he reflected. Despite the harshness of Manon's response he regained some courage little by little; he found consoling explanations and gave himself reasons for hope.

"In the first place, she's a wild one, she's not used to talking to people . . . Secondly, she's quite new, like goats the first time they see the billy goat, they're afraid of it. It's quite natural. And then perhaps my costume is too fancy. It surprises her, and so it doesn't seem serious . . . And besides, I shouldn't have told her I saw her bathing—that's what made her cross. That annoyed her . . . It was all my fault, everything."

Nevertheless, after his solitary dinner eaten in a few bites, he remained seated for a long time with his elbows on the table and his head in his hands. He saw again the big sea-blue eyes, the golden mane of hair, the full soft lips, and he murmured:

"It's terrible, it's terrible . . . She's too beautiful, it's terrible . . . If she were less beautiful I would still love her, and it would be easier . . . And besides, there's that teacher, he worries me . . . What can I do? What can I do?"

During the days that followed he noticed that she had become suspicious. All along the path she made her dog search the undergrowth; then, before sitting down under the mountain ash, she carefully examined the landscape. Because he was high up on the escarpment, flattened under his garlands and behind his tuft of thyme, she could not see him; but she certainly felt his presence, because at the slightest movement of the bushes around her she whirled her sling and flung cruel stones that broke the heart of the poor enamored one.

"If only she would let me talk to her! I'm sure I could change her mind . . . That's what is needed, to change her mind. But how?"

CHAPTER 18

One night, wakened by an extraordinary concert of owls under a moon red as a bloodshot eye, he judged the moment favorable for a magical ceremony.

Having written Manon's name on a piece of paper, he placed it in the middle of the table and surrounded it with his relics—the little scrap of green ribbon, the ball of hair, a mother-of-pearl button, three olive pips. Then he dug up his precious cooking pot and surrounded this collection in turn with a big circle of gold louis, as if to imprison Manon with his riches. Then, in order to reinforce this charm, he joined his hands and invoked the Holy Virgin, who was no doubt surprised by these incongruous appeals.

When the owls quieted down he put his gold back in the pot; then he buried the precious ball of gold hair among the glittering coins, tied the lid with a double wire, and replaced the pot under the hearthstone. He hoped the gold, with its well-known magical powers, would exert a powerful influence on the captive hairs, which would send the message to the hair on his darling. Then he would be able to put ideas in her head (especially while she slept), and finally, one fine morning when he opened the door, he would find her sitting on the doorstep . . .

He took the ribbon, looked at it, caressed it, kissed it, then suddenly got up to open the drawer of the little cupboard. There he found some thread and a needle, which he did not find easy to thread. He took off his shirt, sat with his chest bare on a chair near the lamp, and started to sew the green ribbon onto his left breast. The needle was thick and the blood spurted out in drops. He clenched his teeth and pulled on the rough double thread, tearing his flesh. Four times he pushed the needle in and drew the thread tight. The fifth time he pierced only the ribbon and tied a dressmaker's knot. Finally, his face pale and drenched with sweat and tears, he took the piece of mirror from the wall and gazed at the blood-spattered green ribbon hanging from the soft red hair on his chest.

"That way," he said, "it will always be over my heart."

Then he drank a large glass of wine and stretched himself out on the bed, with a hand clasped to his burning heart.

That is to say, poor Ugolin of the Soubeyrans was going mad, and visibly wasting away.

CHAPTER 19

One afternoon at the bottom of the vallon of Les Refresquières, Manon was sitting in the dry grass, looking at the yellow carapace of a little prehistoric monster that had planted its claws on a branch of Queen Anne's lace. The big insect stayed perfectly immobile but something was happening inside because suddenly its back split along almost its whole length and a tender green animal struggled for a long time to free itself from this prison. It was enveloped in damp, crushed wings and climbed slowly and awkwardly to the end of the branch, where it rested motionless under the burning July sun. It was a cicada. Its body browned visibly, and its wings unfolded and became transparent and rigid, like mica veined with gold.

Manon was waiting for the little insect's first flight when she saw in the distance two hunters descending into the vallon. With their guns slung on their shoulders, they followed a nearly imperceptible path on the flank of the hillside; but they suddenly left the path and disappeared behind a wide thicket stretching along the foot of the escarpment . . . She waited for the sound of firing, but nothing disturbed the silence, not even the light clatter of stones under their espadrilles. She became a little uneasy because she had set four precious rabbit traps in the thicket, and perhaps these hunters came from Les Ombrées—with people like that you never knew. She abandoned the cicada, made the dog sit down, and made a wide circle on the plateau to arrive above them without being seen.

She slid under the junipers up to the edge of the slope; through the branches of a turpentine tree that flung itself horizontally into space, she saw the two men sitting under a holm oak, eating a snack with great appetite.

She recognized Pamphile, the carpenter who had made her father's coffin.

She did not know the other one, who was very small with a big head—it was Cabridan.

As he removed the skin from a slice of sausage, the carpenter said:

"Me, I never touch other people's traps. For me traps are sacred. Especially all those."

She was astonished by this particular respect.

"Why those?" asked the other.

"Because they belong to the daughter of the hunchback . . . Yesterday evening I was hidden up there waiting for the thrushes to go to sleep, and I saw her setting them . . ."

Cabridan chewed slowly. The carpenter poured himself a glass of wine. He drank, wiped his lips with the back of his hand, and said:

"She's got no more than that to live on—it would be criminal to take her traps from her after what we did to her . . ."

"What, what, what?" said the other with his mouth full. "I never did anything to her . . . And as for the incident of the *boule*, you know perfectly well it wasn't my fault!"

"I agree!" said Pamphile. "But that's not what I'm talking about."

"Then what is it?"

"The spring. You don't know it, do you, the spring at Les Romarins? You don't know that it's been there for fifty years?"

"Don't forget I'm younger than you others."

"You never saw it running?"

Cabridan hesitated before replying.

"Perhaps once, when I was small. Hunting with my father . . . We drank in a little stream. I think it was there."

"Why d'you think? There have never been any others in the whole countryside. And you must know that Ugolin plugged it, before the hunchback arrived."

"I know it and I don't know it," said Cabridan. "In any case, it's not my business. And besides, the Papet told me it was lost a long time ago."

"Lost!" sneered the carpenter. "Not lost for the Soubeyrans! They made it run quickly enough when they were able to put their hands on the farm . . ."

Manon froze—she heard these words, and her mind registered them, but they had not yet touched her heart, and she doubted their meaning. Still she felt shivers down her back and she breathed faster.

The conversation continued through the chewing of bread and sausage.

The carpenter continued:

"Didn't it mean anything to you to see that poor man die for nothing?"

"At least," said Cabridan, "it never made me laugh like the others . . . When they talked about it, I went away because I preferred not to think about it . . . You know I'm good, and honest, but courage, I don't have any. Besides, I must tell you that for five years I owed the Papet two hundred francs. When my little ones had measles . . . I paid him back ten francs at a time. And when I couldn't, he said to me: 'Don't worry about it, you give it back to me when you can.' So, you can understand that I wasn't about to meddle in the affairs of the Soubeyrans, on account of a story I wasn't quite sure about, and that didn't even concern me . . ."

"The Soubeyrans," said Pamphile, "are bastards. And the old man lent you that money so you wouldn't talk about the spring. And he figured correctly!"

Cabridan drank his glass of wine and timidly took up the attack:

"And you, why didn't you say anything?"

The carpenter cut several rounds of sausage, and said:

"Me, because of Amélie. One day I saw the hunchback in the distance, looking for water with a divining rod . . . I thought he was going to find it and I was very pleased. But dammit! He was completely unaware of it and passed it several times only twenty meters away, and the next day I saw him digging in the wrong spot . . . It bothered me all night that the man should have to walk barefoot, with his jar on his hump, while all the time he had the most beautiful spring in the country under his feet . . . So, in the morning I said to Amélie, 'We're all criminals, and it can't go on like this. I'm going to tell him.' Oh, misery! She made a terrible scene! I was going to take my children's bread from their mouths! It was shameful to meddle in other people's business! Hunchbacks brought bad luck! He was from Crespin etcetera etcetera, and finally she followed me right up to my workshop, and she kept up her litany. In the end I promised I would say nothing. She said: 'A promise is not enough. Swear on your workbench.' Well, it doesn't bother me to swear—me, I don't think much of those things. I stretched my hand over the workbench and swore. Then she fixed me with a glacial eye and said to me: 'Take a little peek at what you've sworn on!' She lifted up my T-square and showed me a photograph she had slipped under it—it was my daughter, taking her first communion, with her prayer book in her hand!"

"Ayayay!" said Cabridan, "she had you there!"

"Oh yes! Oh, she's clever! Suddenly there was nothing I could say, but it bothered me all the same. So one morning, out hunting, I took a little pot of black paint with me and painted two arrows on white rocks, twenty-five meters apart, on the side of the road overlooking the hunchback's house."

"Why?"

"The two arrows pointed to the spring! That way I hadn't talked about it, but if the poor hunchback had got the idea of aiming with the two arrows, he would have dug in the right place and after four blows with his pickax the water would have hit him in the face!"

"That wasn't easy to figure out," said Cabridan. ". . . I would have thought . . ."

The carpenter quickly put his finger to his lips, opened his eyes wide, and cupped his ear. A partridge could be heard cackling for his family . . . They got up very quietly, took their guns under their elbows, and quickly disappeared on tiptoe into the gorse.

Manon, frozen with horror, looked at four slices of sausage, red and white on a scrap of yellow paper, and a bottle leaning up against a stone. Two gunshots woke her up. She walked aimlessly through the pine woods.

She walked a long time. The flock, gathered and directed by Bicou, followed her at a distance . . . Slowly the pain gathered strength and pressed her breast.

Thus, the long suffering of her father, his three years of heroic effort, had become almost ridiculous . . .

The little hunter had said that people had laughed at him. It was not the blind forces of nature, or the cruelty of fate, that he had fought for such a long time, but the tricks and hypocrisy of stupid peasants, sustained by the silence of a coalition of miserable wretches, whose spirit was as low as their feet. He was no longer a vanquished hero, but the pitiable victim of a monstrous farce, a weakling who had employed all his efforts for the amusement of an entire village . . .

She walked in the lavender, her breath short, her teeth clenched, her cheeks on fire, and her spirit as empty as the garigue . . . Without any conscious decision, and as if led by her legs, she found herself suddenly in front of the mountain ash. Then she ran toward it, and crying like a wounded animal, she clasped it in her arms, rubbed her scratched cheek against the hard bark, and wept at last.

The sun was sinking behind the Tête Rouge, the evening breeze rose toward the summits; a partridge called on the escarpment . . . Her goats browsed around her, her dog stood on its hind legs and licked her hands.

She saw again the happy days of their hard times, the black forelock on his pale face, the fine eyes that always laughed, the big hands, the prickly cheeks . . . No, he was not vanquished! It was his glory not to have comprehended the brutality of these insects. This black soul of Ugolin—he had illuminated it with his own light and had not been able to divine a hypocrisy that he could not even conceive. But as for herself, her instinct had warned her—she had always known this man was the enemy . . . She saw again with horror his friendly gestures, the too-numerous little presents, the useless help he offered without cease . . . And while he talked, and while he deplored the drought, the spring was there in his head, the water ran under his red curls, and this brute seated in front of a glass of white wine had only to say three words to work a miracle. Now, enriched by his crime, he had had the audacity to cry his love for her, to propose to serve her! Her grief gave way to a heavy and profound rage that clenched her fists. No, this wretch would not profit from his ignoble success. She ran toward Les Romarins.

She did not know what she was going to do. In any case, she would see the scene of the crime again and prepare her revenge. She went down on La Garette, crossed the vallon of Le Plantier, climbed the slopes of Saint Esprit, and reached the crest of the hillside that plunged toward the house of her childhood. She entered the thick pine woods that trembled in the evening breeze, but was surprised to see that the big pines no longer went down to the field.

Without the ravenous trees the woodcutters had removed, the junipers, gorse, and hawthorns had taken on a new vigor. Sole masters of the richness of the soil, they formed a nearly impenetrable thicket, tall yellow plants dried by the summer. Ugolin's sickle had not intervened because their plunging roots could not reach the carnation beds.

She slid under the brushwood and did not recognize the field, which seemed immense because of the massacre of the olive trees; but the view of the beloved house, with the three big pine trees of the owls stretching their branches over the roof, made her tears rise.

Ugolin emerged from the outbuilding harnessed to a sulfate sprayer, and started a slow walk along the rows of green cuttings, emitting little bluish clouds from the end of a copper tube.

He seemed dejected, crushed, and stopped from time to time for no reason, with his head bowed. She remembered that there were still a dozen cartridges in an old biscuit tin and that her father's gun lay resting on two wooden pins on the wall in the cave. She had only to come one morning before dawn. She would hide in the thicket, quite near the house, and as soon as he came out she would shoot him like a skunk. She had never handled a gun, but she would soon learn . . .

When Ugolin got to the end of the field, she crept into the undergrowth again and climbed to the crest without the least noise.

Evening fell. She followed her goats with slow steps on the path to the sheepfold, but she stopped at the fountain at La Ser to bathe her tear-reddened eyes with cold water, because she had decided not to reveal the terrible truth to her mother, or to Baptistine; she was afraid it would diminish her father's memory, and besides, she wanted to act alone. So she forced herself to contain her pain and anger and went to bed pleading a headache.

There, with eyes closed, she thought for a long time, then suddenly said to herself:

"The gun is dangerous. I might miss. And besides, the gendarmes will come because they'll know he's been killed. There's something better—a fire."

She saw again the high shrubs on the hillside, the dry bushy grass, the closed circle of pine woods, the four big olive trees in front of the house, the large resinous branches stretched over the roof, which they caressed during the mistral.

She saw herself hiding down there one evening; he returned from the village, and she waited until he had put out the lamp. She prepared little stacks of grass in four corners, and toward one in the morning, when sleep was deepest, she started the fire . . . The red dance ran through the undergrowth. Then the broom and the junipers blazed, then the big pine trees twisted their arms in the smoke and burst into flames in an instant, like torches.

When the people came from the village, it was too late, and it was not until the next day that the firemen from Les Ombrées found, in the remains of the ruined house, or perhaps stretched near the spring, a blackened corpse twisted like the stump of an old olive tree . . .

A little appeased by this vision, she slept until daybreak.

In the morning she took her sheep to the escarpments of Saint Esprit and went down toward Les Romarins.

Ugolin had gone to Massacan with the mule . . . She was able to complete a survey of the pine woods, to make sure that the fire would not leave any trace of the criminal. She noticed that on the side near the village the bottom of the vallon was less wooded because of the road, but the dried grass was very high; and in the brushwood she saw the varnished leaves of a good number of turpentine trees shining—they would be set alight by a single spark and burn for a long time . . . She thought they would suffice to stop the flight of a man crazed by the flames and lost in the smoke.

That same evening, while her mother slept, she stole out of Le Plantier, and under a horned moon she again took, after such a long time, the horrible path on the flank of the hillside, the path where they had carried the water. She followed her father's staggering steps as he hung onto the tail of the she-ass. She came to the resting place, under the helpful branch from which the iron S still hung . . . She saw him again, wiping his brow, eyes closed . . . She kneeled for a minute, and went off again, pale and resolute, holding a little box of matches in her fist.

Among the big pine trees behind the house the owls were answering each other as they had formerly. The windows were black . . . Had Ugolin come back? She waited a few minutes. Then she heard the approach of hobnailed boots on the stones, a dragging step that stopped from time to time, and a shadow crossed the fields slowly, head bowed, hands in pockets. She heard the key grate in the lock, then the beloved plaint of the hinges . . . A yellow gleam feebly illuminated the dirty windowpanes. After a minute a window opened; then the wooden shutters clattered and the French window groaned as it had in the evenings of the happy times. The quickened light shone through the slits in the shutters. She waited a moment. The frail croaking of an insolent frog cruelly proclaimed the presence of the spring . . . Then she got up and prepared the little stacks of dry grass from which the first flames would leap. But as she was putting the second one in place the moon veiled itself, then disappeared.

She raised her head—a thick storm cloud mounting from the sea extinguished the stars one by one. Five minutes later distant thunder rumbled slowly, and a large drop of water struck her face. Tears of rage rose to her eyes . . .

The rain, which had eluded her father for so long, came to the rescue of the murderer. She scattered the piles of grass and ran in the night, under the storm.

In her bed she regained her courage. Perhaps this sudden rain had been great luck for her. She was in too much of a hurry—it had not occurred to her that it would be better to wait for a day when the mistral was blowing . . . At the time of the great fire at Pichauris, when two firemen had been killed, her father had said: "When there's no wind, the pine trees burn more or less where they are, and the fire doesn't progress, except by going up the hillside. But when the mistral blows, the fire runs in all directions, as quick as a galloping horse!" It would be wiser to wait for the great red horses of the wind and the long horizontal flames that threw the resinous pinecones like showers of comets.

It rained for two long days, a beneficent rain that penetrated deeply into the soil, a rain that could have saved her father . . . Manon was nervous and hardly ate and hardly slept and woke up surrounded by flames. She estimated it would take three days of sun, or two days of wind, to dry the pine woods. It was the beginning of August, and nothing was lost. All that was needed was a little patience.

After the rainy days, devoted to the gathering of snails, the sun reappeared and the steaming hills turned green. She went with her animals the length of Les Refresquières, where the cavities of the rocks shone like mirrors. At the foot of the slope, under the turpentine trees, she was setting her traps under the watchful eye of her dog, when he pricked his ears and shot off like an arrow. A very young goat, a little foolhardy male, had got away from the flock and was bounding from rock to rock in the scree high up on the hillside, under the escarpment. She hardly worried about it, sure that Bicou would fetch it with his usual turning maneuvers and his warning barks with their simulated ferocity; but the tiny billy goat suddenly disappeared in a hollow at the foot of the escarpment. Bicou followed it. Then Manon heard the barking grow faint, followed by a moaning that expressed real alarm. She sprang forward immediately, ran across the hollow in her turn, and found herself in front of the narrow opening of a crevasse from which the desolate cries of her dog were emerging.

She slid into it on all fours.

At the bottom of a short passage Bicou was scratching the floor with rage, trying to enlarge a hole too small for him to pass through. When he had torn up the earth and the moss, his claws grated on the rock. Manon seized his tail with both hands and pulled him backward, then thrust her head into an opening that was too small to admit her shoulders. She heard desperate bleating, amplified and prolonged by the echoing of a vault. She thought: "a cave!"

So she called the little animal lost in the dark . . . "Bilibili" . . . Long echoes responded, then some bleats that sounded farther away . . . She drew back to let the light in, and examined the sides of the opening. It was not living rock, but a whitish smooth stone, almost opaline, which she could scratch with the point of a knife.

She left her flock under Bicou's care and ran to Le Plantier. Her mother and Baptistine were at Les Ombrées, but she found some potatoes under the cinders and a rabbit stew simmering on the corner of the fire and a basket of figs . . . She lunched very quickly, all excited by her discovery—a cave she did not know, perhaps never entered before!

Without doubt there would be galleries that went up to Les Bastides, and chambers glistening with rock crystals, as she had seen in the geology book . . . There certainly would not be any large animals because the entry had been too narrow . . . but snakes perhaps? In any case, there couldn't be anything but common snakes, which took flight at first sight; besides, Bicou knew how to kill them with a single bite, so quickly it was impossible to see how.

She departed, eating some figs. But instead of her stick, she carried a little, pointed, iron mining bar, and in her haversack she had a mason's hammer, three candles, some matches, and a ball of string, which she intended to attach to the entry, in order to find her way back through the galleries . . .

She saw at once that the vagabond goat had rejoined the flock, but that the faithful Bicou was not at his post . . . She went up to the opening and called; a pack of dogs responded. In her absence Bicou had succeeded in getting through the entry, but was unable to get out . . .

She started work. It was not an easy task because she did not have enough room for a clear swing of the hammer. Fortunately the lime deposit did not adhere very strongly to the rock, and she was able to detach several layers by forcing the point of the mining bar into cracks that were barely visible.

At the end of an hour she managed to knock away a thick white plaque, and the opening was now big enough for her to crawl through. But before starting on the mysterious adventure, she withdrew from the crevasse to examine the surroundings. Nobody. The goats grazed peacefully in the distance, around the she-ass. She listened for a long time, inspected the horizon, then slid into the hole. Kneeling, she first lit a candle, then advanced resolutely toward the voice of her dog.

The narrow tunnel gradually grew bigger, and suddenly opened into a big space; but her candle lit a mossy rock at the base of a step. She attached her candle to a projection on the rock. The dog continuously barked his appeals, and she heard him running . . . She pressed both hands on the moss and climbed carefully to disengage her body from the narrow tunnel. Finally she was able to stand up and take the little candle again.

No, it was not a subterranean cathedral, but a sort of mine gallery, decorated with candles of reddish stone: some hung from the ceiling, others rose from the floor. She slid between the stalagmites. Her dog preceded her, and came back from time to time to tell her something she did not understand.

When she had gone about ten meters, she heard a noise, a sort of continuous murmur, which came from the bottom of the gallery, and she felt the floor descending under her feet at a slight angle.

Finally the gallery emerged into a fairly low chamber, under a portcullis of stalactites.

The murmur was stronger; it was a ringing crystalline song . . . She stopped, raised the little flame over her head, and saw, on the floor, a star dancing; as she leaned down, a face came toward her—it was hers.

She was on the edge of a sheet of water, an oval sheet, a good six paces long. It was not deep—the dog went through it without losing its footing.

On the right, at the foot of the wall of rock, a little stream tumbled from a mossy slit and plunged under the trembling sheet. At the other end of the ellipse, a little whirlpool sucked the water through an invisible hole.

Tears rose to her eyes. It was the water of the hills, which could have saved her father, and instead wasted its richness in the sterile rocks and the subterranean night . . .

Level with the surface, on the wall opposite, the gallery plunged into the night. It could serve as an overflow when the level rose. That was why the water never came out of the cave, and the fine spring had remained unknown . . .

Step by step she entered the icy mirror of shadows where the inverse reflections of the stalactites trembled. Under her feet little dark clouds rose up. She plunged her hand down to the bottom and brought up a fistful of sand that seemed nearly black . . . She climbed up the tunnel into the light of day, and in her wide-open palm the sun, at last generous, illuminated the red sand of the pond of La Perdrix.

CHAPTER 20

She came back the next morning with a small saw hanging from her belt and a little rake without a handle in her hand . . . In the vallon she spent quite a while finding a long, nearly straight branch—there were very few of these in the hills, where the trees pushed out their knotted and humped branches with great difficulty. In the end she chose a young pine that had risen directly to meet the light through the high undergrowth; she cut off the branches, smoothed the knots with her knife, and managed to attach the little rake to this handle and fix it with a nail. Then, after studying the four horizons for a long time, she slid into the secret cave and set four candles on bumps on the walls.

The water flowed continuously, limpid and musical. She plunged the rake into it and scratched the bottom of the pool. A red cloud rose to the surface at once and spread rapidly. Patiently she continued this action for more than two hours . . . When the iron teeth ground against the rock, she scratched the sides and pushed the red powder into the water.

About midday she finally came out into the sun and went to bury the rake under the gravel of the scree. Then she lunched under a pine tree, surrounded by her flock.

She was idly mulling over her experience. The man had said that the water in the pond reddened slightly after big storms. But how long after? She tried to remember his words exactly . . . It seemed to her he had said several hours. Seven or eight hours? She could not remember the exact figure, but it could not be more than eight . . . After lunch she went with her goats, toward the pond.

The water in it was perfectly clear; in front of the entry pipe, which emerged from the wall a foot from the bottom, she could see a transparent tremor . . . There were still some red particles on the grey cement; these were old particles that had escaped the shovels and brooms of the cleaners.

She explored the area around the pond, sat down under the tree where the teacher had sat, and opened a book.

Every ten minutes she went to lean over the mirror of water, but during the afternoon the spring remained pitilessly pure. Toward six in the evening she began to despair.

"No," she thought, "this water does not come from up there . . . But then, perhaps I didn't stir the bottom enough . . ."

Since she did not know what to do, she leaned toward the icy water, drank in long drafts like a goat, and washed her face. Then, while she was looking at herself in the water, trying to do her hair, she saw, gushing into the bottom of the pond, a reddish thread that opened out in a spiral, mounted slowly to the surface, then redescended in a circular motion . . . Within two minutes the cloud enlarged to touch both sides. So she knew that Providence had provided her with the ruination of Ugolin and punishment for the village . . . The miraculous carnations would die like the corn and the pumpkins; the rich vegetable gardens of Les Bastides would be dead on their feet in a few days. She ran to announce the news to the mountain ash, trembling with an emotion so wild that she burst into laughter as she wept . . .

She started her preparations immediately. First of all, she went up on the slopes to explore the countryside; she feared the unforeseen passage of a hunter, or the surveillance of Ugolin. Then with the she-ass she descended a little ravine of Les Refresquières where the rainwater had left a long trail of blue clay, nearly pure. With the precious knife she cut some loaves of it. She loaded them into the esparto grass pouches and made two trips to the cave. Finally, she went back to Le Plantier and made a little square sack of jute folded and sewn in the fashion of cobblers, with a nail and a double thread. She filled it with some crumbly cement, old but probably still capable of hardening in water.

"What are you going to do?" asked Baptistine.

"Perhaps I'll tell you tomorrow evening."

After dinner she went off in the moonlight with her dog, the little bag of cement on her shoulder. She walked in the shade of the hills, and stopped frequently to listen, while Bicou, nose pointed, sniffed the breeze . . . She made him sit sentinel in front of the entrance, gave him several instructions in a whisper, and entered the tunnel.

With four candles lit, and her clothes knotted above her belt, she entered the icy water, which came up to her knees. She pushed the bag of cement into the drain hole, and rammed it with the handle of her rake. Finally she kneaded the loaves of clay in the water and molded them against the bag of cement and the rock surrounding it.

The water rose slowly, and when she had finished her work, her hands were like gourds and she could not feel her legs anymore. She painfully returned to the bank of the flooded pool and had to clamber over rocky projections in order to sit on the step of the tunnel . . . As she rubbed her icy thighs she saw the glistening water reach the threshold of the gallery opposite, suddenly go over it, and plunge down the slope . . . She heard the murmur of the little cascade that would take away Ugolin's gold and the harvests of his accomplices during the night. She said in a low voice:

"There are some who laughed at him!"

She listened for a long time to the delicious sound, then she gathered up her tools, blew out the flames of the dying candles, and slid outside the cave . . . The dog was waiting for her; conscious of his mission he pricked his ears at the least noise. Then she slowly pushed some stones into the crevasse, for fear that a fleeing rabbit might look for refuge in the cave, soon to be followed by a dog, then by a hunter. Finally, by the gleam of the stars, she went and pulled a turpentine tree and a big spiny juniper up by the roots and planted them in front of the blocked-up entrance. Then, heavily loaded with her tools and preceded by her guardian, she climbed to Le Plantier.

Her mother was asleep with a book in her hands and the lamp still alight. The alarm clock on the commode marked midnight. She blew out the yellow flame and lay down and went through her calculations again.

The water would probably stop reaching the pond about seven in the morning. But the spring at Les Romarins, which was a little nearer the cave, would certainly dry up sooner, while the fountain in the village, fed by the pond, would go on running until midday, and perhaps later . . .

In any case, it was going to be a great and beautiful day.

At first she had intended to hide in the pine woods of Les Romarins to witness Ugolin's surprise and despair, then to go through the village, on the pretext of a visit to the cemetery, to make sure of the death of the fountain. But she thought it would not be wise to approach the scene of the disaster too soon, because those who knew about the crime that had killed her father might perhaps put two and two together and their suspicions would lead to her . . . It would be better to send old Baptistine to the village to find out the results.

Exhausted, she slept deeply until the great day.

Baptistine was milking the goats in front of the shelter.

"My beauty," said Manon, "I need you. Soon we are going to gather some flowers on the hills and then you are going to take them to the cemetery."

"Good," said the old woman. "That's just what I'd like to do. I'll ask the blacksmith for the key, and I'll go and talk with my Giuseppe and our master."

"Then you can do some shopping. Two big loaves, salt, pepper, three cutlets . . ."

"Write it on a piece of paper for me," said the old woman. "I'll show it to the shopkeeper and he'll understand. Shall I go at once?"

"No, at eleven o'clock. I'll go with you to the slope of Saint Esprit, with the goats, and I'll wait for you."

CHAPTER *21*

On the terrace of Philoxène's café on the town square the unbelievers were drinking their midday aperitif. The teacher was giving them a little lecture on a very old Provençal proverb that went, in French: "Vent de nuit dure un pain cuit," that is, "the night wind lasts the time it takes to cook a loaf."

"In my opinion," he said, "it's a typical misinterpretation. I think the real proverb said: 'Ven de nuei duro pas ancuei' and by contraction 'pancuei.' This would mean 'the wind that comes up in the night will not last today.'"

"That's just speculation!" said the baker, who saw himself being eliminated from a proverb.

"Even so," said M. Belloiseau, "I think you're perfectly right, because 'lasts the time it takes to cook a loaf' gives the night wind a fixed duration, limited to less than an hour, whereas it often rises before midnight and falls at sunrise! I would say even more, because . . ."

No, M. Belloiseau did not manage to say any more, because a powerful voice cut his words short. Old Baptistine, who had passed by an hour before to ask Casimir for the key to the cemetery, had just appeared at the end of the plaza; she was roaring insults and curses. Some laughing children were following her, and women appeared at their doors. The Piedmontese came up to the terrace. She shouted continuously, with a man's voice, and suddenly threw the cemetery key at Casimir's head. He escaped it by a miracle, and a glass from the bar went flying and broke into splinters.

"Hey!" cried Philoxène. "You're mad, my poor old friend! What does this mean, breaking people's glasses? Especially when you haven't got a franc to pay the damage?"

But she continued shouting, her face contorted with rage and wet with tears, shaking her fist at Casimir. He quickly explained the drama.

The day before, he had been forced to transfer Giuseppe's body to the communal grave because the miserly "entraprenoure" had paid a fee for only two years, and he had had to make space for old Jeannette de Bouscarles, who had just received her last sacraments.

"I explained it to her when I gave her the key," said Casimir, "but she didn't understand, until now . . . Listen to me, Baptistine . . ."

But she howled like an animal, with such insane gestures that three dogs surrounded her, barking furiously, while Philoxène's fox terrier treacherously stole up behind and tore off a big piece of her dress . . . She drove it away with a kick, climbed two of M. Belloiseau's stairs, and with arms raised proclaimed a solemn curse:

"Let the pigs die! Let the goats die! Let the olive trees fall! Dry up the beans! The women sterile! The men blind in one eye! The pip in the henhouse! Rats in the cellar! Fire in the barn! Thunder on the church!"

This terrible litany, dimly understood, brought tears of laughter to the unbelievers, and the children shouted with joy . . . But two old ladies fled terrified, crossing themselves. Big Amélie appeared at her window and cried desperately:

"Listen! Keep her quiet! She's casting a spell on us!"

Pamphile and the baker closed their fists with the forefinger and little finger sticking out and pointed them seven times running at the witch, shouting the exorcism:

"Hi . . . Hi . . . hiii . . ."

But she was still shouting, terrifyingly, when M. the curé's housekeeper, expert in exorcism, appeared with a basin in her hand—it was holy water, and she threw it courageously in the face of the excited woman. The Piedmontese recovered, crossed herself, came down the steps, and cried:

"That's the curse! You are all lost!"

She turned her back on them and departed to the sound of their jeers.

Manon had spent an hour lying impatiently in the grass, waiting in the midst of her browsing goats for the return of her friend, not taking her eyes off the village.

Since she could not see the town square, surrounded by houses, she hoped the people would run down the streets shouting, with their arms raised to the sky, with all the agitation of an overturned anthill. But everything remained calm under the burning midday sun . . . An idea suddenly worried her—the gallery toward which she had diverted the streamlet might perhaps rejoin the same canal underground, and all she had done would serve no purpose . . . It was not only possible, it was probable—because the water followed the slopes and the slopes led to the pond . . .

She was in the midst of these discouraging reflections when she saw Baptistine leave the village, followed by shouting and jeering children . . . The Piedmontese suddenly turned toward them brandishing her stick and let out such terrible shouts that they took flight. Then she came down the steep path that plunged into the vallon and came up toward Manon, who ran to meet her.

"What have you got, Baptistine, my beauty? What did they do?"

The Piedmontese tried to speak, but her lips trembled and she dissolved into tears . . . Manon put her arms around her and made her sit against a rock under a cluster of pines. Then Baptistine gave an account of her misfortunes, accompanied by lamentations.

"They took out the beautiful box, because they said it took up too much room . . . And they mixed him all up with the others, with people he didn't know, and perhaps they had dirty diseases . . . And in the same hole with Pepito the butcher, a Spaniard as nasty as scabies, whom Giuseppe had knocked out twice because he had stolen his wine from his basket, and made faces to mock him and then run off . . . And now that was going to start all over again, for eternity . . . And at the Last Judgment, how was he going to find his bones, because they look like everybody else's, and besides nobody can recognize his own bones because he's never seen them and it would be easy to make a mistake . . . And now that he's all scattered, even I don't know how to put him together again. And besides, what's the use of saying prayers for him, on this grave? You can be sure the others will steal half of him! But these people from the village are a bunch of pigs, and I have cast the worst possible curse on them, and that's going to bring them misfortune."

Manon consoled her as best she could, and told her that for the Last Judgment the Madonna would fix everything, and that she would certainly see her Giuseppe again, all together. Then she suddenly asked:

"And my father? They haven't touched his grave, have they?"

"I don't know," said Baptistine. "I was so unhappy, I didn't look properly. They've made holes all over . . ."

Manon got up and ran toward the village.

Meanwhile the group on the bar terrace had gained some reinforcements— Big Amélie with her fists on her hips, the teacher's mother carrying a basket full of vegetables, Anglade coming back from the fields with his pickax on his shoulder, Cabridan standing on crutches, and old Sidonie.

The Papet said with a sneer:

"All that, it's just talk."

"You'll see, you'll see," replied Sidonie. ". . . I knew a witch at Les Ombrées who could kill a mule or a goat with four words!"

Amélie cried:

"And the Piedmontese said more than four! Me, I think things will go badly for us!"

"In any case," said Cabridan, "my wife was coming back from the garden when the old woman cast the spell and when she got home the ragout was all burnt, and my grandmother had fallen down the stairs and has a lump on her forehead the size of a plum!"

"And according to you," said the teacher, "these two misfortunes are the first results of the curse?"

"I'm not positive, but I'm inclined to think so!"

"If your grandmother drank fresh water. . . ," said the Papet.

"Hey, hey, hey," said Pamphile suddenly, "what's that I see?"

The teacher followed his look. Manon, disheveled, arrived running. She saw the teacher and stopped in front of him. She was pale and pearls of sweat glistened on her forehead.

She said quickly:

"What have they done at the cemetery?"

Philoxène replied at once:

"We have changed the place of the poor woodsman, because he hadn't been paid up in perpetuity!"

"And . . . my father?"

"He hasn't been touched, and he'll never be touched!" She closed her eyes and breathed deeply.

"Make her sit down!" cried Magali. "Can't you see she's about to fall?"

The teacher had already taken her by the shoulders, but she had recovered. She blushed and pushed him away gently.

"Thank you," she said, ". . . I thank you . . . Can I have the key to the cemetery?"

"Certainly," said Casimir.

"On condition," said Philoxène, "that you don't come back and break another of my glasses, like your friend!"

"But make her drink something!" said Magali. ". . . At least a little coffee!"

"No, thank you, madame," said Manon. "Don't bother . . . thank you . . ."

M. Belloiseau looked at her with a very lively interest and said—he thought he was whispering—"Amazing and adorable creature!"

Amélie turned to Pamphile:

"All the same, it must be a pleasure to see her so near, your golden bird!"

Pamphile replied with sudden ferocity:

"You, go home at once! Go home, or be quiet, because you'll get a couple of clouts in front of everybody."

Amélie, hands on hips, shouted:

"Me, a couple of clouts? Me?"

"This is getting interesting," said M. Belloiseau.

But this pleasant scene was abruptly interrupted by a desperate voice calling: "Papet! Papet!"

Ugolin arrived at a gallop, covered with mud, face drawn, and out of breath . . . At ten paces he called:

"Papet! The spring! The spring! . . . It's stopped!"

"What are you saying?" said the old man.

"Since this morning, it hasn't run anymore! . . ."

"Not at all?"

"Not a drop!"

A sombre joy warmed Manon's heart. This face convulsed by tics, these haggard eyes, these trousers streaked with mud, it was a very fine sight . . . He continued, panting:

"Since nine this morning . . . I dug a little trench, I pushed sticks in the hole . . . Nothing, nothing . . . Holy Mother of God, what can I do?"

"They're capricious, these springs!" said Pamphile. "Especially yours! Formerly it flowed . . . Then when the monseiur from town came it stopped . . .

Then when you came, it flowed for you. Then suddenly it stopped. That's its character . . . But don't worry—three months from now it'll come back!"

"But unfortunately all my carnations are in bud! The deluxe carnations, the specialties!"

"There are fifteen thousand!" said the Papet.

"All my fortune, everything I've made, I've put into this crop! And with this sun, eight hours without water, and everything's finished!"

Then Manon's clear voice rang out:

"You've still got the cistern!"

"It will give me two days, but no more!"

In his confusion he had not recognized the voice, but he saw her suddenly and was bewildered for a moment.

"It's you? Well you, you know that you can't do anything with the cistern!"

"Yes," said Pamphile, ". . . she's in a good position to know that."

"You can figure I need eight meters a day. If I don't get them I'll be ruined in five or six days! And this sun! Look at the sun! It's the same as the one that killed the pumpkins, and now it's going to burn my carnations!"

He fell on his knees, raised his eyes to the sky, and moaned:

"Holy Mother! Holy Mother!"

"That'll do!" said the Papet brutally. "Get up, imbecile! First, perhaps the water's already come back while we've been talking . . . And if we have to wait for it, there's the fountain. With two mules, and even four mules if necessary, and four men, we can hold out . . . First let's go and look up there!"

He turned to Ange:

"Are you coming with us, fountaineer?"

"I'll go and eat first," said Ange. "It's half past twelve! I'll come up afterwards."

"Me too," said Cabridan.

"Come by my house first," said Anglade. "I'll lend you my little pump . . ."

A female voice suddenly called:

"Say, you others, come and have a look!"

It was Bérarde, Anglade's wife, who was holding her jar under the spout of the fountain.

"What's happened?" said Anglade.

"It seems to me the fountain isn't running well—it's no more than my little finger!"

"Not possible!" said Anglade.

He ran to Bérarde, and nearly everybody followed him. For years the copper pipe had run full, but now its flow had been cut in half.

In a profound silence the men exchanged uneasy looks.

"It can't be the same thing that struck Ugolin!" said Anglade.

"That's not possible!" said Philoxène. "It has never stopped, not for fifty years!"

But under their eyes the trickle of water got smaller minute by minute. Manon looked at these people she did not know, these people who had kept the secret of her father's spring and were now looking at their own spring dying. She did not dare think of it anymore. Her legs trembled; Magali made her sit on a terrace chair, while everybody approached the fountain. In the silence she heard the sound of water falling into the jar, and suddenly a strange gurgling, and then the pipe sighed lengthily, and was quiet.

Ugolin, haggard, cried:

"This one too! Papet, we are lost!"

Ange was stunned. He felt the pipe, and the loud voice of Amélie said:

"I told you she cursed us! You had a good laugh, didn't you? And now see what's happened. There's only one thing to do—put the woodsman back in his box. Without that, the fountain will never flow again!"

"And if she won't lift the curse out of friendship," cried Sidonie, "we'll make her drink a liter of holy water, and we'll heat her feet over a good fire!"

Manon became afraid for her friend. These savages were quite capable of avenging themselves on her. But M. Belloiseau intervened.

"Mesdames, you're lacking in logic!" he said.

"What logic? After what she's done to us?"

"I mean to say," continued the notary, "that if she has supernatural powers, it would be very imprudent to torture her—and if she hasn't any, as I think, then it would be better to look elsewhere for the cause of this accident."

"Oh, fountaineer," said Philoxène, "you're the one who looks after it! What has happened?"

"I don't know any more than you," said Ange. ". . . Perhaps there's a frog blocking the pipe, or a grass snake . . . In any case, I'm going to look at the pond . . ."

He left at a gallop.

"In my opinion," said the teacher, "it's not an accident with the pipeline, because Ugolin's spring, which is higher than the pond, stopped first . . . This stoppage, which is certainly temporary, is no doubt due to the drought . . ."

"I don't think so," said Anglade. "It's true it hasn't rained for ten days, and we've had a fiery sun . . . But ten days, that's often happened, and the water's never stopped before!"

The baker was dismayed.

"If it lasts eight hours, what am I going to make bread with?"

"And what can we put in the pastis?" said Philoxène.

The Papet led away Ugolin, who was in a daze, while the plaza was invaded by children and gossips, and M. the curé came loping up, followed by his servant.

The children, who were not very interested in the fountain, came to look at Manon, a little frightened by the arrival of all these people. She took the key of the cemetery from the table and got up. She was so pale that Magali said to her:

"I think I'd better go with you."

"I thank you, madame, but I'm used to living alone on the hill . . ."

"I know!" said Magali. "You are the one who found my son's knife and gave it back to him . . . I'll go with you to the gate . . ."

They set off. Manon kept quiet.

"I adore the hills," said Magali. "Sometimes I go with my son, on Thursdays. We go and lunch on the Tête Rouge, or under the escarpments of Saint Esprit . . . One day, from far away, he showed me your . . . habitation . . . It must be marvellous to live in an old sheepfold—but perhaps not very convenient?"

"We're quite used to it. We have a spring in the kitchen. An absolutely pure spring, and icy . . ."

"My God," said Magali, frightened, "it hasn't stopped too, has it?"

"This morning it was flowing as usual . . ."

Two out-of-breath peasants hurrying up the hillside approached them.

"What's happened, Madame Magali? The water hasn't come to our pond! Has Ange cut it off?"

"Good heavens," said Magali, "I know there's something wrong at the fountain, and people are looking worried . . ."

"This is terrible!" said Polyte, "this is not the time for us to have no water! I've got a thousand tomato plants, just bedded out at the end of June . . . It will be a great disaster . . ."

They flung themselves up the rising slope . . . The women arrived at the cemetery gate.

"So, I'll leave you here?"

"Yes, madame. Thank you. Thank you."

She opened the heavy gate, while Magali went back on the road to the village; but she was curious, so she stopped and retraced her steps, not daring to go right up to the gate. Then through the sonorous haze of the cicadas, she heard music, music from a mouth organ; but the tune it played was a dance.

She went closer and risked a look through the bars of the gate. Manon was kneeling with her back to the gate, and her joyful little music astonished the calm of the cemetery. Magali took a step back, started to go, stopped again, and said:

"She's strange, this little one . . . Yes, very strange . . . But how pretty she is!"

CHAPTER 22

As Manon was climbing up to the hills again, she met the Piedmontese, who was waiting for her on the Baou. Baptistine danced with joy when she heard the spring had gone dry . . . She wanted to return to the village to snap her fingers in the faces of those "chick-pea eaters," and make a few additions to her curse. Manon talked her out of it, telling her she better not show herself for some time, since they were capable of roasting her feet.

Manon stayed in the hills for several days, looking after her goats and her traps as usual. She was proud of having accomplished her duty, and sure of her just cause, since it must have been Providence that had revealed the secret of the spring to her; but she wondered whether the water would dissolve the clay-and-cement plug so hastily put in place; or, on the other hand, whether the new course of the underground spring would find some indirect route to join the old course . . . Every morning and evening she slipped under the undergrowth to the edge of the escarpment above the pond to make sure that the water had not come back; but no, she saw the rectangle of cement whitened by the sun, and two or three urchins charged with the duty of announcing the resurrection of the spring. While they waited they hunted for limberts, cracked pine nuts between stones, or scratched the bellies of cicadas to make them sing.

In the village it was disaster.

Every morning Philoxène telephoned the prefect, who had promised to send a specialist in agricultural engineering, but the technician was slow in coming, and the situation got worse every day. The fine vegetables in the vegetable gardens dried on the plants, and the wells were empty, except for the

Papet's, which had a padlock on its cover. He was thus able to provide two liters of water a day for the aperitifs of the unbelievers.

In the town square the women sneered as they looked at poor Ange. Stunned with shame, he foolishly polished the copper pipe of the fountain, as if he thought this proof of solicitude would encourage it to resume its song. The delighted baker had resolved his problem with an abominable blackmail; he had cynically declared:

"If you want bread, bring me water!"

That was why a peasant went off every morning with a little caravan of three donkeys attached one behind the other, to go and get "bread water" at the fountain of Les Ombrées.

Anglade's twins, who were desperately trying to keep some fine beds of cabbages alive, took two mules to Ruissatel every day. As for the unhappy Ugolin, he travelled to and fro between Les Romarins and Les Quatre-Saisons with three carts laden with barrels, because the Papet had hired two Italian carters with their equipment.

He left at dawn every morning; all day long he walked under the devouring sun at the head of the convoy, and in the evening when the Piedmontese wanted a rest for their animals, he made another two journeys, pulling the Papet's phantomlike mule at the end of his arm. Its painful progress was really no more than a series of forward falls miraculously retarded at each step . . . At night he talked to "poor Monsieur Jean."

"Go on, go on, I know very well you've cut off the spring . . . It's been well done, I'll grant you that. But you know perfectly well that I'm not working for myself! You know that all these flowers, they're for her, to get sous for her! Listen, I know you, you're a good man, you're in Paradise. You can see my feet are blown up so huge I can't pull my shoes on, you can see the mule's going to die, and that if this goes on for eight days the carnations will be lost anyway . . . Come on, in the name of the Father, the Son, and the Holy Ghost, give us the spring of your daughter, as it was in the beginning, is now, and ever shall be, amen, in the name of God!"

One morning about seven Manon saw Casimir the blacksmith coming up toward Le Plantier, accompanied by Big Amélie and Nathalie. It was a delegation come to ask Baptistine to withdraw the curse since the fountain remained mute and the villagers were overcome with anguish.

Casimir assured her that the bones of Giuseppe had been solemnly recovered, his coffin had been restored to newness, and M. the curé was going to say a mass to appease his spirit, no doubt irritated by two removals. While the women were pleading with the Piedmontese, Casimir winked at Manon, and came over to tell her in a whisper that he did not have the tiniest belief in these sorceries, but that Baptistine would do well to go down to the village and regale them with some pretence of retraction to calm the old women who were inciting the males against her. He added that the village was painful to see, and complacently described the reeling Ugolin's calvary: he was probably going to die at the same time as his carnations.

In the hope of witnessing such a pleasant spectacle Manon accompanied her friend to Les Bastides.

Giuseppe had the honors of a new ceremony at the cemetery. The unbelievers were doubtful about its power to console, since Casimir had confided to them that he was not at all sure the recovered bones were those of the woodsman; but in any case they added up correctly. After an expiatory mass, Baptistine performed the "counter-charm" in front of the fountain.

First she warned the audience: the water would not flow today because it had to come back from a long way. Then she burnt a tuft of dry verbena and began a litany of benedictions that wiped out the previous maledictions one by one. This magical operation had a great effect on the women and children, but none on the fountain, which confirmed the infallibility of the witch.

Manon was in a hurry to go up to the path from which she would be able to see Ugolin passing with his mules; but the teacher stopped her on the way with a beautiful friendly smile and said:

"I've been looking for you—they're waiting for you in the mayor's office."

She was surprised and already worried. What did they want?

The teacher continued:

"The mayor has got the prefecture to send us an agricultural engineer to solve the mystery of the spring. Ugolin has already taken him to Les Romarins, because that's where the disaster started. But he wants somebody to show him the water sources that aren't shown on his charts, and we thought of you. Come."

He led her toward the town hall.

"Why me?"

"Because one day an old man looking for asparagus on the hill called you 'the girl of the springs.'"

Manon's fears grew. This engineer was going to ask her questions and she had to reply without the least hesitation, looking him straight in the eye. He was certainly a savant; perhaps, with calculations and reasoning, he was going to discover the secret of the cave; perhaps it was even marked on his maps . . . And then they would find the remains of the candles, and her footprints.

The mayor and the agricultural engineer were examining a colored map spread out on the big table.

The engineer was a young man with very dark hair, gold-rimmed spectacles, wearing a hunting jacket.

"Little one," said Philoxène, "look at this map. The springs we know are marked with blue circles. Are there any others?"

The engineer pushed the map under Manon's eyes, then with the end of a pencil he pointed to La Perdrix, Le Plantier, and La Font du Berger. She saw with great relief that the cave was not marked, and immediately mentioned four unknown springs: Le Laurier, La Font de la Ser, La Niche, and le Pétèlier, but was not sure how to locate them on the paper.

"In any case," said the teacher, "you can lead us there?"

"Yes, certainly."

The engineer got up.

"Good, we'll follow you."

On the way he explained, in a very fine Narbonne accent, that the position of the different water sources might reveal the underground path of the dried-up spring, and that these researches were an excellent opportunity to complete the orography of the region. He'd take a long look at the landscape and then unfold his map to make mysterious signs on it. During this time Bernard asked Manon a thousand questions.

"Since you were eight years old you never had any little friends?"

"No, my companions were my she-ass, my dog, my goats, and Enzo and Giacomo. They are woodsmen from Piedmont, like Baptistine."

"And you didn't find it boring, this solitude?"

"One is never alone on the hill. There are so many animals you don't see, looking at you . . . And often there are people you see, and they don't see you . . ."

"Like me, the first day."

"Yes, like you."

"Do you think you're going to stay on the heath for the rest of your life?"

"I would like to very much. But I say that now, and then perhaps I'll change my mind later . . ."

"You're seventeen?"

"No, not yet. Almost sixteen."

"I should have thought more . . ."

"No doubt it's the open-air life . . . the natural life . . . Stop, here's the Laurier spring."

She showed them a little dry-stone construction covered with a big slab of rock under a very old twisted laurel; a very thin streamlet issued from it and was immediately lost under the surrounding stones.

The engineer approached and wet his hands in the water.

"Is this its normal yield?"

"Yes. It takes a big storm to make it run a little stronger."

He examined the surroundings and took more notes.

The teacher was picking up stones, and Manon was gathering bunches of savory herbs, when Bicou suddenly arrived, running faster than a hare. He made extravagant demonstrations of joy at finding his beloved mistress, whom he thought lost forever when she left him for an hour. Then he started burrowing in the bushes, looking for a grass snake or a field mouse.

Going to the Font de la Ser, a meagre spring in Les Refresquières, they passed not far from the secret cave. Manon averted her eyes and forced herself to call everybody's attention to the other side of the vallon, saying that she most often kept her goats there because it had a certain amount of humidity and the grass stayed green for a long time. But Bicou, who had a good memory, went off like an arrow toward the cave, calling his mistress with enthusiastic barks. Manon was worried and called him back immediately.

"Here! Here at once!"

The dog returned at a gallop, ran around her with a number of joyful bounds, and tried to drag her to the fatal spot, pulling at the bottom of her dress. The teacher seemed surprised.

"The dog wants to show you something," he said.

"Certainly," said Manon. "A green lizard, or a gerbil . . ."

But Bicou went off again and scratched the ground at the foot of the false screen in front of the entrance to the gallery. Manon was panic-stricken. She took her sling from her haversack and hurled a round stone as big as a crab apple in his direction. She intended, as usual, to miss him slightly to frighten him, but she was so frightened herself that he received the stone on the head. He uttered a piercing howl and fled toward Le Plantier, his mournful protests multiplied by echoes. Manon was horrified to see that he did not run straight, but with his body askew.

The teacher looked at her with surprise.

"You are adroit, but cruel. I heard his skull ringing . . ."

"Too bad for him," replied the savant. "He only had to obey."

"You're right," said the teacher.

"Stop," said Manon, "here's the Font de la Ser."

They finished their tour of the hills around noon. When they separated, on the shoulder of the Tête Rouge, Manon gave the young man a big bouquet of savory herbs tied with a shoot of broom.

"It's for your mother," she said. "The best savory herb in the country . . . Especially with jugged rabbit."

"Thank you on her behalf—and on mine! . . . Tomorrow morning our savant will give his report on the situation at the public meeting of the municipal council. Won't you come?"

"Perhaps."

"My dear mayor," said the engineer, "unfortunately I have nothing very pleasant to say to all these good people."

"That's why," said Philoxène, "you should be the one who says it."

They were in the mayor's office, with the teacher.

"You see," Philoxène went on, "I need their votes to be elected, so I don't like announcing bad news. But it doesn't make any difference to you. You only have to read them your report."

"I've written it for my superiors. It's in technical language—they won't understand it at all."

"So much the better. That way they'll think it's serious, and they'll have a little hope."

"They've been waiting for half an hour," said the teacher.

Philoxène got up.

"Let's go!"

The big hall was filled with a silent crowd, standing on three sides of the table behind a white barrier.

The councillors (the Papet, Anglade, Ugolin, Pamphile, the baker, Ange, and the butcher) sat motionless with arms crossed and elbows resting on the green cloth.

With a certain solemnity Philoxène invited the agricultural engineer to sit at his side, while the teacher, secretary to the council, went to sit at the end of the table behind a pile of registers and dossiers. He ran his eye over the fifty faces lined up behind the barrier—practically all the peasants were there, and there was also a good number of women: Big Amélie, Bérarde, Miette, and even Marinette, M. the curé's housekeeper, whom Philoxène considered to be a "Jesuit spy." Bernard found Manon at the front of the hall. Her hair was tied in a blue scarf that outlined her oval face. She was in the first row, her brown hands resting on the white barrier. Behind her rose the tall silhouette of M. Belloiseau, under his fine pearl grey hat. He seemed to be charmed with this proximity, and his nostrils quivered.

Manon was grave and tense. She was afraid of the savant's report. Ugolin stared at her with all his strength, and the Papet never let her out of his sight.

At last, in a gloomy silence, the mayor's bell sounded, and he said:

"The meeting is open."

Although he spoke freely on the terrace of his café, he was nevertheless incapable of making a speech on a subject fixed in advance. The sight of several people silently looking at him paralyzed him. He said, "It muddles my ideas, it makes me stutter in the brain."

Finally he declared:

"You see, I have called a meeting of the council to discuss the question of the water."

Ugolin stood up quickly and said forcibly:

"It's not a question, it's a catastrophe!"

The crowd received this vigorous clarification with murmurs of approval . . . Ugolin looked at Manon with a proud smile and sat down.

"Exactly," said Philoxène, "it's a catastrophe. But thanks to my personal efforts, and thanks to my telephone, I have been able to call the agricultural engineer to our rescue. And here is the agricultural engineer."

The engineer nodded his head in greeting and took the floor.

"Gentlemen, I have studied your problem, and I can't do better than read you the report I have drawn up tonight for M. the engineer in chief . . ."

A murmur of hope went through the assembly.

"First of all, I want to thank the charming shepherdess whose collaboration was most valuable. By informing us of a number of unknown water sources she has enabled us to draw up a more precise local map."

Ugolin stood up at once and clapped his hands, crying, "Bravo!" but only the teacher and M. Belloiseau discreetly followed his lead, while Manon blushed to her ears.

"Here is my report."

He drew a little file of papers from his briefcase and started the lecture.

"The spring of La Perdrix, which feeds the village fountain, is the most important and the most constant in the region. It emerges from a fissure between two layers of calcareous rock belonging to the superior Cretaceous. Therefore it is not a spring issuing from a diaclase but from a resurgence of the Vauclusian type."

Philoxène assumed a grave look, looked at the audience, raised his finger, and said:

"Let us not confuse them."

The engineer continued, pronouncing all his syllables carefully:

"It is not from phreatic water, nor from a capillary fold, as is shown by an examination of the surface of the upper stratum, or of the walls."

The baker leaned toward the teacher and whispered, "He's a savant, a true savant . . ."

The crowd listened in uneasy silence while the true savant continued:

"Therefore, it is clear that the permeable layer outcropped and was contained between two impermeable layers. The water flowed on the roof of the impermeable inferior layer, but was contained by the ceiling of the impermeable superior layer and so came under pressure, and thus formed a captive sheet that fed the pond by means of a resurgence, and the pond itself fed the fountain by means of a pipe that brought the water to the village by gravity."

Ugolin lugubriously murmured:

"Oh yes! There's no mistake about that! What gravity!"

"Then, on the last twenty-sixth of August, the fountain suddenly dried up, and the village found itself totally deprived of water. Summoned by M. the mayor, and mandated by the administration, we have looked for the cause or causes of this deplorable occurrence. First of all, what was the origin of this water? Fortunately we have a very precious document."

A thrill of hope ran through the crowd while he unfolded a big colored map on the table. Manon stretched up on the tips of her toes but saw nothing more than blobs of green, red, and blue.

Philoxène, after examining the "very precious document," nodded his head twice and smiled, which gave the assembly confidence. Pamphile leaned over his shoulder and said loudly:

"This is getting interesting!"

The teacher looked at Manon, who seemed worried to him. The agricultural engineer continued:

"This is a study by M. the chief engineer that summarizes and explains in the clearest and most useful terms the experience that has been gained in the last five years in this region."

Nobody realized that these eulogies had no other purpose than to flatter the vanity of the powerful chief to whom this report was addressed. There was an attentive silence, and Ugolin looked like a hunter waiting for a rabbit to emerge from its hole.

"In fact," continued the young savant, "our services have taken the trouble to color all the springs in the chain of La Sainte Baume green with tetraoxylphtalophenone anhydride, better known by the name of fluorescein. These experiments have enabled us to definitely trace the isochronochromatic curve, which, combined with the isogradhydrotimetric curve, gives us a perfect representation of the orography of the hydrogeological basin."

These words, aggravated by the rumbling r's of his Narbonne accent, were overpoweringly scientific, and they made a big impression. But the Papet sneered and said very loudly:

"Up yours!"

All looks turned to him, but the engineer continued:

"Now, an inquiry on the spot has proved that the spring of Les Bastides Blanches was not colored by the fluorescein."

"Ah!" cried Philoxène suddenly, "I remember one day a well-dressed, bearded man came and spent all day on my café terrace. He drank pastis. He had a dozen. And then from time to time he got up and filled his glass at the fountain, but instead of drinking it, he looked at the sun through the water, and then threw it away. He told me he was verifying the color of the water, and if by chance it should run green, I should telephone the prefecture, extension 102."

"That's my office," said the engineer.

"Well," avowed Philoxène, "I took him for a loony who hoped that by drinking enough pastis he would see it flowing in the fountain!"

The engineer smiled and replied:

"It's thanks to this 'loony' that this spring does not appear on the precious diagram of M. the chief engineer, and that we know that it's not possible to integrate it in the orography of the Huveaune, or one of its tributaries."

"And how does that help us?" asked the Papet.

"It's a big step, in fact!" said the engineer. "Since we know with absolute certainty that the water does not come from this neighborhood, we can therefore conclude that it comes from a distance."

"That doesn't get us very far," riposted the old man.

"Clearly it doesn't resolve our problem, but it enables us to place it correctly, and to tell you that it is not going to be easy to find the solution!"

The Papet sneered so vigorously that he had a fit of coughing. The engineer gave him a severe look and continued:

"Now, the length of the subterranean course also makes it more difficult to locate the occurrence, which can perhaps be explained by four different hypotheses."

At this point Ugolin raised his hand.

"I want to speak!"

"It's not the right time," said Philoxène.

"What I want to say won't take long: I think that instead of talking so much you should give us back the water and then explain it to us AFTERWARDS."

"My dear sir," replied the engineer, "it seems you are mistaking me for the fountaineer, who only has to open the hydrants with his key."

He continued:

"First hypothesis: the drought. There is no doubt that our region has not been favored with rain. To tell the truth, it's not a matter of a true drought, and in the last fifty years your spring has supported far worse ones. But it is possible that a slight fall in the subterranean levels could be the cause of your troubles. Indeed, since the resurgence is surrounded by parallel chains of dolomites in the Jurassic series it must certainly get through them by a system of siphons— Do you know what a siphon is?"

"Yes," said Ugolin. "It's when you draw wine with a rubber tube."

"Exactly. Very well, it is probable that at the first rain the siphon, or siphons, will get primed again after the level of the subterranean lake that supplies you has returned to normal."

The affirmation of the existence of this lake was greeted by optimistic murmurs, and Philoxène, with raised finger, said forcibly:

"A subterranean lake!"

Then he looked severely at the Papet and added:

"Those who argue with progress are not always right!"

Ugolin stood up, radiant, and stretched his arms toward the engineer.

"If progress brings back the water, me, I'll embrace it! In any case, as soon as my spring flows there's a hundred francs for progress! There!"

And he placed a bill folded in four on the table.

The Papet's voice was raised again.

"Wait for the end! The end of this baloney!"

There was some laughing, while the agricultural engineer continued:

"We can now offer three other explanations for the occurrence."

"Here we go," cried Philoxène. "Listen!"

"Second hypothesis: the water, by a natural phenomenon, has finally worn away the inferior impermeable layer at some point in its journey and has plunged God-knows-where to emerge somewhere else, perhaps even in the sea."

There was a stunned silence, then some murmurs, and the Papet cried:

"There's a fine hypothesis! It's a joke, your hypothesis!"

Philoxène rang his bell and cried:

"But wait! He said three other explanations! Continue, M. the engineer . . ."

"Third hypothesis: the underground stream, having cut through its bed, then fell into an impermeable cavern, or into a system of such caverns. When the caverns are full, the water will reach its former level, and the spring will flow again."

"There, that's better already!" said Philoxène. "It's acceptable!"

"And in how many days?" asked Ugolin.

"It's impossible to say exactly," said the engineer. "Perhaps two days, perhaps two years."

"Perhaps a hundred years!" cried the Papet.

"That's not out of the question," replied the savant coldly.

Ugolin promptly made his hundred-franc note do a vanishing trick, while a murmur of indignation swept through the audience; but without deigning to explain, the savant continued his lecture.

"Fourth hypothesis: a subterranean subsidence. Such an occurrence is the more probable since we have a number of lignite wells in this region that cause mines to explode when they go through a seam of rock. The vibrations caused by these explosions can be transmitted great distances, and could have caused a piling up of soft or unstable layers that have blocked the canal."

A murmur of anxiety from the crowd was dominated by a number of desolate exclamations.

"Ayayay!" said Pamphile, while Anglade shook his head, saying, "That's done us."

"Well, no!" replied the engineer. "Don't alarm yourselves, because in this case we have a hope."

"Listen! Pay attention!" cried Philoxène.

"Indeed, it is possible that the plug would be composed of sand and gravel, or perhaps of clay. In that case the water, acting under pressure, is capable of going through it, or breaking it up, or dissolving it away. It is possible that such an operation would be accomplished in the relatively short time . . ."

Faces cleared, but the engineer added very quietly:

". . . of six days to a month, because experience shows that after a month it becomes unreasonable to hope."

"But then," cried Ugolin, "what will become of us?"

"And the bread?" cried the baker.

The murmuring of the crowd grew.

"But after all," said the engineer, "you've got wells."

"There are no more than three in the village," replied the baker, "and now they're dry! Every day we've got to go kilometers for water for the bread and the soup!"

"And rainwater cisterns?" asked the engineer. "Usually every house has its cistern!"

"Certainly," said Casimir, "but they haven't been used for a long time. They've been turned into cellars. Naturally they could be put back into service, but what's the use if it doesn't rain? And besides, for watering, one cistern only lasts a week!"

"And so," said Ugolin, "what can you do for us?"

"I can send you water for your domestic needs."

"And for my carnations?"

"Let's not worry our guts over your carnations," cried the baker brutally. "Your carnations, they're nothing but money, and that's exactly what you don't need."

"And your bread, don't you make that for money?" cried the Papet. But Philoxène rang his bell and decreed:

"Bread first. Flowers are for the cemetery; they can wait. Continue, M. the engineer."

"I will. What is the population of your village?"

The teacher opened his registers.

"One hundred and forty-three people," he said.

"Plus the animals!" said Anglade. "At least a dozen mules and about twenty donkeys!"

"And the pigs!" said the butcher, "every family has at least one pig!"

As Nathalie burst out laughing he added:

"I mean on four legs with long ears!"

"That makes how many pigs?"

"About fifty," said the teacher.

The engineer made a little calculation with his pencil, and announced:

"I can send five thousand liters a day."

Ugolin got up nervously.

"And my carnations? How much will you send for my carnations?"

Pamphile and Casimir, inspired by a single thought, cupped their hands and shouted:

"SHIT!"

The savant judged this response to be sufficient, and continued:

"The daily lorry will be enough to cover your most urgent needs, but it will be a very big effort for my administration, and it is doubtful whether it can be continued for more than a month."

"And then, if the water does not return in a month," said the Papet, "what can you do for us?"

The engineer replied amiably:

"I can offer you my condolences, and advise you to cultivate the ground somewhere else. There're plenty of depopulated villages with plenty of water that would be happy to receive you."

Violent protests were raised, and Philoxène declared with sovereign authority:

"No, sir, no! The municipal council cannot accept that."

"I think I can affirm," said the savant gravely, "that the authority of municipal councils over subterranean phenomena can be measured with a number close to zero."

While Philoxène's eyes opened wide, the Papet's voice resounded:

"Fifth hypothesis!" he cried. "And it's a good one!"

"You will give us a great pleasure if you will explain it to us!" replied the engineer.

The Papet, leaning on the table with both hands, had already got up.

"M. the engineer told us recently that he had put a green powder in the springs. Well, I say this powder has all gone into a paste, like mortar, and that's what's plugged the fountain!"

These absurd words seemed to have a great effect on the old peasants, and they shook their heads, while the teacher shrugged, and M. Belloiseau burst out laughing.

But the Papet turned to Bernard and responded forcefully:

"Don't forget it's a CHEMICAL powder, and those chemicals, we know what they are!"

The engineer replied with a derisive smile:

"Quite precisely NO, you don't know them, and you don't know that it takes only a handful of this powder to color a river for many kilometers!"

"Nonsense!" cried the old man, "when you consider how much Pernod it takes to turn a glass of water green, I tell you it would take fifty tons to change the color of a river."

The engineer gathered up his papers and laughed as he looked at Bernard. He said:

"In spite of the interest of this scientific discussion, I think it is time I went and got busy with your water lorry."

While he was closing his briefcase, the Papet pounded on the table and cried:

"I'm sure of it! I knew it would end like this! Him, he's a liar, the mayor is a fool, and me, I'm laughing. That's the administration! Look at the administration!"

The engineer replied with perfect serenity:

"Monsieur, I have the honor to inform you that the administration is bored stiff with you. The lorry will come on Sunday, the day after tomorrow. Ladies and gentlemen, I thank you."

In the meantime a little boy had been standing with his ear to the window and had heard the discussion. He cried:

"It's the man from town who blocked the spring with a lorry full of green powder!"

That was why two dozen children accompanied his departure with cries and shouts and followed him up to the boulevard, where the withering intervention of M. the curé dispersed them.

CHAPTER 24

The crowd left in silence—some with heads bowed, others running to visit their fields. Ugolin and the Papet were the first to go, followed by Casimir and Pamphile. There was nobody left around the table but Philoxène, the teacher, the baker, and the butcher. They were trying to draw reassuring conclusions from the terrible report they had just heard.

Manon was slowly crossing the courtyard of the town hall when M. Belloiseau joined her and said in the most gallant tone:

"So, mademoiselle, I have the impression that that learned young man, in spite of your help, did not know any more than we did and was in no position to rescue us from this business! Fortunately we've still got the curé!"

And since she looked at him with surprise, he continued:

"Yes. His faithful servant has just told her friends that he knows the secret of the spring and is going to reveal it in his sermon on Sunday morning."

"And how does he know it?"

"Bless me," said M. Belloiseau, "the servant maintains that while he was preparing his sermon in his room she heard him say forcefully: 'Who has blocked the spring? Well, I know, and I am going to tell you!' Between you and me, I suppose . . ."

But M. Belloiseau did not suppose any further and said in a worried tone: "What's that?"

Eliacin, the big brute who worked a little farm in the hills, was running toward the town hall. He had just knocked old Phrasie over on the way, without deigning to turn round and respond to her well-deserved insults.

With a big stick in his hand and his black felt hat pulled down to his eyes, he passed near them without looking and strode toward the council chamber. He stormed in and brutally banged the door so that the glass trembled. Soon his powerful, rough voice could be heard. Manon, followed by M. Belloiseau, ran to the closed window to try to hear and see him.

Eliacin, hands on hips, was shouting in Philoxène's face:

"Who is the president of the water syndicate? It's not me, it's you!"

Bernard, the baker, and the butcher got up quickly and they too put their hands on their hips.

With great calmness, and with perfect dignity, Philoxène replied:

"I am president of the water because I am the mayor, and I am mayor because I've got the telephone."

Then Eliacin drew a sheet of paper from his pocket and brandished it under the eyes of the teacher.

"And this? What does this say?"

The teacher replied coldly:

"I see that it is the receipt for your subscription for the water."

"Exactly!" cried the giant. "Fifty-two francs, and the stamp! You really have taken them, haven't you, my sous? So, where is it, this water I've paid for?"

"Eliacin," said the teacher, "be reasonable! Our spring isn't flowing, for the moment . . ."

Claudius the butcher declared in a peremptory tone: "If you had come this morning the engineer would have explained the orography to you."

Philoxène raised his forefinger and affirmed:

"You should take orography into account."

But Eliacin replied sharply:

"I don't take anything into account, especially that! Ah! If you had said to me: 'We're making a water syndicate, but it's only to take your sous,' then I would have looked after my sous and I would not have looked after my little meadow. But now it's superb and there are two cows on it . . . So, I've paid for the water, now I want my water."

"Listen," said Philoxène, "a water lorry is going to come every day until the fountain flows. You've only got to come with your mule and two barrels and I will see that you get a hundred and fifty liters a day . . ."

"In the first place, I haven't got a mule. In the second place, a hundred and fifty liters is fine for a bistro but not for a meadow. In the third place, I've paid for spring water and not lorry water!"

"As far as I know," said the teacher, "the lorry water comes from a spring."

"Not from mine!" cried Eliacin. "I've paid for my water, I want my water!"

"Don't shout so loud," said Philoxène. "You'll wear yourself out, you'll wear us out, and it'll do no good."

"O Holy Mother," groaned Eliacin.

He closed his eyes. Visions passed through his thick skull. He raised his arms to the sky and bellowed desperately.

"And my eggplants! Two hundred eggplants, they were coming on so well and now they're already droopy . . . And six hundred potato plants, already as big as your fist—they're green now, and green they'll stay? Ah no! No! It's not possible!"

Tears ran down his face. The teacher stood up.

"Eliacin," he said, "you have to realize that we are as miserable as you . . . But it's a general misfortune, it's a case of force majeure . . ."

The other cried furiously:

"Me too, I'm major! That's why I want my water."

The carpenter shouted in his turn.

"But since the fountain isn't flowing anymore, where do you want us to get it?"

"Get it where you like, but make it come out of my pipe! And besides, it doesn't matter to you. You have become a fine municipal councillor, I didn't vote for you. So don't you get mixed up in this affair, or you'll get a stick to the mouth!"

"Who from? Who from?" cried Pamphile.

He was good and angry and suddenly seized a croquet mallet, while Philoxène advanced bellowing.

"So in the end you come and take it out on us! Where do you think you are, you gorilla from the hills!"

"Among the water stealers!" shouted the "gorilla."

Then seized by a sudden rage, he splintered the plaster bust of the Republic with a single blow of his cudgel, and raised his arm toward the carpenter, who had just climbed onto the table. Philoxène held back the cudgel from behind, and this allowed Pamphile to land a good blow with the mallet on Eliacin's hat. He was stunned for no more than two seconds since he carried a Neanderthal cranium on his shoulders, but Philoxène had the time to cross his arms under the maniac's chin; despite the weight of the mayor hanging on his back, the brute threw himself on the table and gripped Pamphile's legs. He fell down, but savagely gripped the thick crop of hair. While the three men battled with pants and grunts of rage, the baker leaped onto the table in his turn. Hanging by one hand from the ceiling lamp, he swung onto the barbarian's neck and tramped on it like a wine harvester in the fermenting vat . . . In an attempt to separate the combatants, the teacher took three steps on the green tablecloth and plunged into the melee, but the table could bear no more; it cracked and then collapsed with a horrendous noise.

Outside, Manon and M. Belloiseau could not distinguish the protagonists in this epic battle because the glass was dirty, but they could hear the fracas very well.

"What carnage!" said the notary, "we should call for help."

Manon cried:

"Come quickly! They're fighting!"

Ange the fountaineer, who was passing by on the road, came into the courtyard, moving as if he were taking a walk, and said:

"You think it's serious?"

Anglade's twins came in their turn . . .

An uproar of breaking chairs and raucous cries still sounded, and suddenly an inkwell came flying through the tinkling glass. Then M. Belloiseau marched toward the door in a determined fashion. But it opened suddenly and Eliacin appeared, his hair on end, his chin inflamed, his nose red, and foam on his lips, carrying a sleeve of his jacket in his hand.

"Look, my friend," said M. Belloiseau, "is that reasonable?"

What followed was still less reasonable, for the monster seized the brim of the pearl grey hat and pulled it violently down over the face of the benevolent moralist.

Just then the four croquet players appeared at the door, mallets in hand.

Eliacin turned to them and shouted:

"If I haven't got my water tomorrow, I'll come back and set fire to the place!"

"I advise you," replied the mayor, "to carry a match that's longer than the handle of this mallet!"

Eliacin shrugged his shoulders furiously; then he knocked down the twins, gave the amazed fountaineer a clout in passing, and, pushing his way through the curious onlookers—who retreated a good distance—went rapidly up toward the hill, carrying his sleeve in his hand.

That Sunday morning the esplanade was crowded with mules and donkeys loaded with barrels and drums, and at the foot of the wall there was a display of jars, watering cans, and buckets. They were awaiting the arrival of the water lorry.

Their owners were gathered together in the plaza, all in their Sunday best because of the mass. The first stroke of the bell had just sounded.

They were assembled in little groups, and they talked together about the disaster, almost in whispers.

It was the sixth day of the drought; the little ponds were empty and the sky had refused to refill the repaired cisterns.

Around the mute fountain there was a big watchful circle. The young people were blowing into the pipe, and Ange the fountaineer was leaning with his back against the ancient mulberry tree and turning his key in his fingers without looking at anybody, overcome with shame.

Meanwhile on the café terrace Philoxène was serving his acolytes: Pamphile, the baker, Claudius the butcher, and Casimir. They looked worried, like everybody else, but they were already drinking their aperitifs.

"Teacher" soon arrived, accompanied by the agricultural engineer, who had come to supervise the distribution of the water. His passage through the crowd had provoked an almost inaudible murmur, because he had predicted that the fountain might never flow again, and this prediction seemed to be nearly equivalent to Baptistine's curse. Then M. Belloiseau could be seen descending the outside stairs of his terrace, under his panama hat, in a light grey suit, already smoking a cigar. He went through the crowd, nodding his head in passing, to sit with the unbelievers, who shook his hand vigorously and made room for him.

When the second bell for mass rang the women started going into the church. Then Ugolin could be seen arriving in his fine hunter's suit, and the Papet, squeezed into his Sunday clothes. They stopped in front of the terrace on their way.

"Oh, you others," said the Papet, "aren't you going to mass? The curé's going to talk about the fountain."

"And so?" said Philoxène, "we're going to talk about it too."

The agricultural engineer's eyes widened.

"I don't think much," he said, "of the efficacy of a sermon in repriming a siphon."

It was then that Manon appeared on the little street that led to the plaza. In her pretty Provençal dress, with her yellow leather shoes and her mane of golden hair under a mantilla of blue lace, she looked like a young lady from town. In fact that is what the teacher thought, but Ugolin recognized her.

She approached with eyes lowered, with a natural grace, almost dancing. Ugolin coughed and blinked three times in a row. Forgetting the carnations and the spring, he gazed at her, and the beating of his heart shot fiery arrows into the swollen abscess under the green ribbon.

As she passed the terrace she quickly raised her eyes and the ghost of a fugitive smile crossed her lips.

"Hey, hey," said Pamphile. "What's she smiling at?"

And he winked at the teacher.

"It's at me," cried Philoxène. "Isn't that so, M. the schoolmaster?"

She went into the church.

"So," asked Bernard suddenly, "are we going in?"

"Yes, we're going in," replied Philoxène. "Because I think it's going to be interesting today. Let's go!"

"If we go in," said Pamphile, "we'd better wait for the sermon, otherwise we'll have to put up with the whole mass."

"A mass never hurt anybody," said the Papet. "Besides, if we wait any longer everybody else will have gone in and there won't be a single seat left."

"Let's go," said the baker.

He got up.

"Wait," said Philoxène. "They mustn't think we're going to church, because they'll all run like hares, and that'll cause a scrimmage. Leave your hats on the table, and follow me."

As usual the faithful were waiting in little groups, having a last cigarette while the women went in, when they saw the unbelievers get up and cross the plaza in a hurry, as if they were on urgent business. A few wanted to follow to see what was happening. But as Philoxène passed in front of the portico he made a quick right turn, and the whole band went into the church.

The women's seats were fully occupied, and Manon had gone to sit in the only empty seat, just under the pulpit.

Ugolin saw her and went up to the first row on the men's side, in front of the organ, to be near her. The Papet followed him, grumbling, while Philoxène led the others toward the steps that went up to the balcony. They sat down, and five of them could be seen leaning over the rail as if they were at the theatre.

But when the mass started, M. Belloiseau made them adopt a more respectful attitude, and they followed the divine service with a fair show of correctness, even if they were a little slow in getting up and sitting down.

At last, M. the curé turned toward the audience, before mounting to the pulpit. He seemed surprised and delighted at the sight of so many parishioners, and he smiled when he saw the row of unbelievers.

When he got to his place he attacked his sermon with a clear voice and a familiar tone.

"My brothers, I am very happy. Yes, very happy to see you all gathered together in our dear little church. All the parish is here, and I can even see a group of very intelligent people—perhaps too intelligent—who are in the habit of passing the time of the holy mass on the terrace of a café. I will not say which café, especially since there is only one, and I will not name these people since everybody can see them. This might embarrass them—if the hardness of their hearts does not make them laugh."

All heads were turned to look at the unbelievers, who indeed laughed, but in a rather self-conscious way.

After a short silence the curé continued in a more serious tone.

"At last they have come to the church. Fine, they are welcome! Indeed I want to show them that I have prepared today's sermon with them in mind.

"So, I am very happy to see everybody. But on the other hand I am sad, ashamed, furious; and I am going to tell you why.

"When I was young (my father was a peasant like you in a little hamlet near

Sisteron) we had a cousin named Adolphin. He lived in another village not far from ours, but nevertheless, he never came to see us, neither for fêtes, nor for births, nor even for deaths. But from time to time (about once a year) I would hear my father say, 'Well, look, Adolphin's turned up. He must want something!'

"Adolphin would come up the path, in his Sunday best. He would make friendly remarks, pay compliments, and talk about the family until he brought tears to our eyes. And then, when he had embraced everybody, as he was leaving, he would say, 'By the way, Felicien, you haven't got a plough you could spare? I broke mine on the stump of an olive tree.' Another time it was a bundle of vine shoots for his grafts—because my father made a famous wine—or then his horse had the colic and he wanted to borrow the mule. My father never refused, but I often heard him say: 'Adolphin, he's not a good character!'"

He leaned over the edge of the pulpit, swept the audience with his eyes, and said forcefully:

"Well, my friends, what you are doing today to the Good Lord is Adolphin's kind of trick! He hardly ever sees you, then suddenly you all arrive, with your hands joined, full of emotion, all bursting with faith and repentance. Go! Go, you band of Adolphins! Don't imagine the Good Lord is more naive than my poor father, that he doesn't understand you right down to the very bottom of your petty spitefulnesses! The Good Lord knows very well that there are quite a few here who have not come to offer Him sincere repentance, or to take a step on the way to their eternal salvation! . . . He knows very well that you are here because the spring is not flowing anymore!"

Many of the parishioners bowed their heads, much as they might when the consecrated host was elevated. Some because they were ashamed, others to hide a smile.

M. the curé looked at them for a moment as he pulled a snow-white handkerchief from his sleeve to wipe his face. Then he continued in a rather sarcastic tone, turning his gaze on all sides:

"There are some who are worried about the garden, others about the meadow, others about the pigs, and others because they don't know what to put in their pastis! These prayers you have had the audacity to offer Him, they are prayers for beans, orations for tomatoes, hallelujahs for artichokes, hosannas for pumpkins! Go on! They are all Adolphin's prayers—they can't rise to heaven because they have no more wings than a plucked turkey!"

In the silence that followed, the voice of M. Belloiseau could be heard by everybody but himself: "Familiar eloquence—they don't give a damn about it."

M. the curé no doubt understood only the first part of this interruption, for he gave a slightly confused little smile and continued in a more conversational tone:

"Now the spring, I must talk to you seriously about it. I admit that since yesterday I have thought about nothing else, and I have ceaselessly asked myself the same question: this water, so pure, so abundant, and so constant until now, why has it stopped, and at the moment of our need? At the request of M. the mayor, whose telephone has more than once done wonders"—he looked at Philoxène, who smiled in turn and seemed flattered—"the state sent us a young engineer, who is certainly a savant"—the agricultural engineer made a little "hum" of demurral. "The municipal council was convened, and I can tell you how it went. This technician started by baffling everybody with kilometer-long words. Then, with a lot of science, he said perhaps the water will come back, and perhaps it will not. And he advised us to load our furniture on carts and go and live somewhere else . . . Nothing more!"

Shaking his head with a reproachful air, he stared fixedly at the agricultural engineer, who spread his open palms in a gesture of helplessness and resignation. Then with true emotion, but deliberately controlled and directed, the curé launched into a moving declamatory speech:

"Abandon these houses where you were born, desert the fields where your fathers and your grandfathers have deposited so much courage and patience, leave this church where you came for the first time in the arms of your godparent, and to which you will all return one day for your last mass—yes, all of you, there, there in front of the altar, on two trestles—all! And our little cemetery, where you have more friends than in the village, and where you will go and sleep one day in the peace of Our Lord, to the song of cicadas who suck the clear gum on the apricot trees that lean over the wall . . . Yes, all that will have to be abandoned because his miserable science has not found any way of saving us. Well, I don't know this savant, because I don't trust engineers. They are people who dig all the time and don't plant anything but pylons. This one did not talk about anything except layers of clay, of siphons that got unprimed, of lorries that cost a lot. In short, he talked of nothing but material things, and he couldn't do otherwise because he doesn't know anything but material things!"

Once more the agricultural engineer made his gesture of impotence, while the teacher sneered silently.

"But I," continued the orator, "I regard our misfortune from a much loftier point of view. And it seems to me that to explain it, and to make the water return, we must go further than the things we can see. Because in the world created by the All Powerful, everything has a reason, everything is directed, and not one cicada sings without God's permission. So, what we must try to understand, what we must find, is not the material accident that stopped our spring, but the reason why God allowed it, and perhaps wished it."

After these solemn words he drew out his handkerchief again and wiped his face.

All the parish listened in a truly religious silence, except Eliacin, who was sitting in the first row. Turning round to look at the crowd, he finally spotted the carpenter high up in the balcony and cast threatening looks at him, to which the other responded with shrugs interspersed with insulting thrusts of his chin.

M. the curé continued his harangue:

"I once read in a profane book—a Greek tragedy—the history of the unhappy city of Thebes, which was struck by a consuming plague because its king had committed crimes. And I asked myself: is there a criminal amongst us? It's not at all impossible—the worst crimes are not those you see in the newspapers . . . Many remain unknown to the justice of men, but the Good Lord knows them all."

It was at this moment that Manon turned her head toward Ugolin, whose eyes had not left her. Now she looked at him, unmoving and icy, as if she were waiting for something. He lowered his head and pushed his arm against the Papet's . . . The old man, who was listening to the sermon with eyes closed, opened them at once, and met the eyes of the girl. He tried to smile. But she looked at him unseeingly and suddenly raised her head toward the voice of M. the curé. He said movingly:

"It is to this unknown criminal, if he exists, that I want to address myself first, and I want to say to him: 'My brother, there is no fault that cannot be pardoned, no crime that cannot be atoned. Sincere repentance effaces everything, and our Lord Jesus Christ has himself said these surprising words: "There will be more room in Paradise for a repentant sinner than for a hundred just men!" Whatever your fault may be, however great your offence, try to mend it, and repent. You will be saved, and our spring will flow more beautifully than ever before!'"

Ugolin nudged his elbow twice in the Papet's side, but he did not respond. Then he raised his head to see if the preacher was looking at him. No. The curé wiped his forehead and his cheeks once more, and continued:

"Now (I am telling you things as they come to me) it seems to me, after reflection, that the True God of Christians—our God—will not punish everybody because of the crime of a single one. So, if we have not got one big criminal, perhaps we are satisfied with several guilty ones. I'm not talking of murderers; I mean sinners who have, collectively or singly, done some bad things."

Ugolin was reassured, and breathed a sigh of relief, but the parishioners looked at one another, since each once had some peccadillos to reproach his neighbors with. Eliacin profited from the general agitation and once more turned toward the carpenter, carrying his hand to his throat and promising to strangle him.

"That is why," continued the curé, "I ask you all to examine your consciences. But not just a hasty examination, sitting on the edge of the bed pulling on your shoes; no, on your knees! That's better for reflecting. And then ask yourself the question: 'Have I done anything bad? Where? When? How? Why?' And you will look closely, very closely, with your spectacles well cleaned, like grandmother looked for fleas on the baby. And when you have completely finished the review, you will offer your repentance to God; and to prove your sincerity you will come and confess. If you are ashamed—quite often it is shame that paralyzes good intentions—you only have to pass by the sacristy, or even the garden, with a packet under your arm, as if you were bringing me a dozen eggs (and in parentheses, if you do bring them to me, I'll take them since I really need them). Or else with tools, as if you were coming to do a job for me (actually the drain is blocked, and Marinette pushed a three-meter stick in it and I haven't got it out yet).

"I will take your confession without solemnity, because a good confession can quite easily begin with a glass of white wine. What counts, my brothers, is sincerity, is repentance. You must look your faults in the face and ask God's forgiveness—He likes nothing so much as to forgive.

"And now—as I talk ideas come to me, so I'm going to change once again—perhaps there aren't any truly guilty among us; I mean people who have done a really bad deed. But are there many who have done good deeds?"

At these words Philoxène murmured sarcastically: "That depends on what you call a good deed." As for Ugolin, he turned to the Papet and whispered: "You lent him four thousand francs." Ange, who was standing at the back of the nave, briefly pantomimed Eliacin and answered the curé with a terrible grimace; he pulled back his lip and stuck his tongue out between his teeth, squinting as hard as he could.

"That," said M. the curé, "that may be the big point. My very dear brothers, you are not brothers. I have seen you working, laughing, and joking; but I have never seen one of you go and dig, for pleasure, the abandoned vineyard of a widow or an orphan . . . On the other hand, my predecessor, the good Abbé Signole, told me about the dreadful affair of La Bastide Fendue, which I want to recall for you today."

He assumed the tone of a narrator, and it was easy to see that he was addressing himself particularly to M. the schoolmaster, to M. Belloiseau, and to the agricultural engineer, who probably did not know the story.

"One fine day there came from the town (naturally) a house agent (even worse than an engineer). He had bought a ruin at the foot of the slope. It was called La Bastide Fendue because it had gaps in the walls big enough to pass an arm through. He put a roof on it, he filled the holes, and he covered it with a handsome roughcast plaster. A pensioner from town bought it for a stiff price, and called it Villa Monplaisir. When the Abbé Signole arrived here—he was not au courant, you see—he asked why everybody laughed when they spoke of the Villa Monplaisir, especially the builders.

"One fine day the pensioner, who had delusions of grandeur, had the idea of putting in a bath. He bought a pump for the cistern, some pipes, a bath, and wanted to have a big water-tank installed in the attic. The builders came, laughing harder than ever. They installed the water-tank, a cement box holding more than a thousand liters, and they told the pensioner that he should let it dry out first, and that they did not advise filling the box before the day after next, at four in the afternoon.

"That day the whole village came down the road, and they watched the Villa Monplaisir as if they were at the circus. The pensioner had already started the pump and was smoking his pipe at an upstairs window, looking as if he were wondering what all these people were expecting. He never knew, because at half past four Monplaisir fell down on his head, and he was buried the next day."

Many parishioners were unable to restrain themselves from laughing at this reminder of such a pleasant farce, because the squashed pensioner was nothing but a "foreigner from town"; and on top of that a pensioner generally is an orphan, and often a widower, who looks at other people working and lives on the taxes they pay.

The unbelievers could not restrain a scandalized hilarity, and M. the curé, with his arms raised to the sky, cried:

"And that makes them laugh. Lord, forgive them, for they know not what they do!"

He leaned over the side of the pulpit and cried:

"You are ALL responsible for the death of that good man! The first guilty ones were the agent and the builders. But all those who *knew* and did not warn that man are perhaps more guilty than they. The builders wanted two days' work, the house agent wanted a little more money . . . It's not an excuse, but at least it is a motive. While you, what was the reason you kept your mouths shut? I can't see anything but a natural brutality—you don't need a curé, you need a missionary!"

There was a great silence, and nearly everybody looked at their shoes. The voice of the preacher rang against the vaulted roof, and the old women became so small that the backs of their chairs hid everything but their meagre chignons.

A great flourish of the handkerchief, and the voice was raised anew:

"You will find him again, that pensioner! Not here, but in the sky. And it won't be his poor spirit you'll find, because I hope it is in Paradise, smoking the clouds in a diamond pipe . . . What you will find will be his body, in St. Peter's balance, and on the wrong side of the balance. And you know it weighs heavy, the dead body of a poor old man, all torn with bursts of laughter, as if the chickens had started eating him . . . Think of that, and repent, because you've still got time . . ."

There were a number of whispered protests.

"I know very well that my words astonish you and you are saying to yourselves: 'But it's not me who made that water-tank! It's not me who touched the money! Me, I don't concern myself with other people's business,' so 'there is nothing I can be reproached with!' Well, don't deceive yourselves! You have to be concerned with other people's business in order to help them, and that's called Christian charity. Because, you see, to be loved by God it is not enough not to do harm; virtue is not keeping quiet and closing your eyes and not moving. Virtue is acting, it's doing good. We haven't got many opportunities. That's why, when the opportunity for a good deed is presented, all ready, in marching order, right in front of your nose, it's because the Good Lord is offering it to you. He who doesn't jump onto the running board, but goes off with his hands in his pockets, is a poor idiot who's missed the train. There are many of you like this, and I regret to tell you that it is perhaps this lack of generosity, this lack of fraternity, this lack of charity, that is costing you so dear today.

"You know what the fountaineer does when somebody doesn't pay for the water? He comes along with his big key and he turns it off. That's why you pay regularly at the town hall. But what is it that you pay for at the town hall? You pay for the piping, for the soldering, for the fountaineer; but the water, it's not the town hall that makes the water; it's God whom you must pay, with acts of grace, with prayers, with good deeds. You must have a pretty big account in arrears, and that's why the celestial administration has shut off your stopcock.

"But it is not enough to lament this state of affairs; something must be done. I propose a procession for Sunday to ask for the intervention of our great Saint Dominique, whose goodwill the faithful can hardly be said to cultivate; he does not see even three candles a month! Nevertheless, I have confidence in his goodness. During his earthly life he performed several miracles—just think what he could do today from up there in the sky!

"Starting tomorrow we will decorate him with banners and show him our afflictions, that is, our thirsty and powdery fields . . . I hope the sight of our languishing crops, so painful for us, won't be any less for him, and that he will intercede in our favor, as he has always done, like Our Lord. I therefore ask the Sunday School children, as well as the Penitents Gris, to prepare the banners for Saint Dominique, the candles, the costumes, and the bouquets.

"Thus we will all walk under the parish banners through our fields that are dying of thirst. And while we are in the procession, nothing must be heard but the distant bell, the song of the cicadas, and the sound of our feet. Then, humbly and sincerely, we will lift our spirits toward God. Because it is not the banners that guarantee the success of a procession, it is the pure hearts . . . And if only some of you (it would be too beautiful if I could count on everybody), if only some of you will take with you a solemn vow to do at least one good deed, or to repair the harm you have done, then I am sure that the Great Fountaineer who cut off your water and who is only waiting for your repentance, will give it back to you."

For the last time M. the curé sponged the sweat from his forehead, and then he came down from the pulpit. Under the fingers of Madame Clarisse the organ began a psalm, and the tart voices of the skinny Sunday school children were raised, enlivened by much sly innocence. The suppliant voices of the old women soon joined them with involuntary tremolos whose crystalline purity resulted from the absence of hormones and the inexplicable fear of beneficent death. Then the baritone of the curé, a little thick, but clear, restored order to the wandering melody, powerfully sustained by the liturgical bellowings of Eliacin.

A great peace descended on the parish, and the surprised unbelievers were listening motionless when there was a cry at the door and an unknown voice shouted:

"The water lorry has arrived!"

A hundred chairs grated on the tiles, and the faithful dashed out in a panic such as is seen only at a fire.

For all that, there was no scuffling at the distribution of the water; they were all too worried, suddenly drawn together by the common misfortune . . . The only murmur was when two great barrels were seen approaching on a cart . . . That seemed pretentious, but since they were for the baker the murmur soon died down.

Meanwhile Ugolin and the Papet stayed out of the way—two jugs of water would not save two carnation plants, and, not only that, everyone knew they had wells. If they seemed to be generously leaving their share of the lorry water to others, then they must not be asked to do more.

The sermon had moved Ugolin profoundly.

He whispered:

"Papet, he didn't talk about anything else, and he looked at me three times."

The old man too was worried and tormented, but refused to admit it.

"Nonsense," he said. "It's because you're stupid enough to think about it all the time that you think people are talking about it! Me, I've forgotten all that! And besides, what do you think he knows? It hasn't been a year since he got here."

"Yes, but perhaps somebody talked to him in confession . . ."

The Papet was silent for a moment, then he admitted:

"I wouldn't put it past Anglade . . . That one, he's so sanctimonious that he's quite capable of confessing the sins of others. But after all, how can that affect us?"

They went up toward Philoxène's café.

"What worries me," said the Papet, "is the little girl . . ."

"Me too," said Ugolin.

"She looked at you in a peculiar way."

"That's true. She looked at me twice, and in a way that upset me . . . She looked as if she was saying, 'You're the criminal . . .'"

"That's your imagination again," replied the Papet. "She knows no more than the others . . . Perhaps she is jealous of the spring, but nothing more."

"Then why did you tell me she worries you?"

The old man hesitated for a moment, then he admitted:

"Because I've got the idea she doesn't want you."

"Why?"

"I don't know. It's just an impression . . ."

Ugolin made no reply. He was looking at Manon, who was coming out of the church with slow steps. She saw him and turned her eyes away to smile at the teacher's mother, who was coming from the lorry carrying a watering can and a jug, spurting little jets of water at each step. As she passed, Manon took the watering can despite Magali's protests, and they went off together.

Ugolin's heart contracted under the damp ribbon sewn to his burning skin.

"That too is not a good sign," he said.

"Why?"

"I saw the teacher talking to her on the hill."

"When?"

"Last month."

"You didn't tell me."

"I was ashamed."

"It doesn't surprise me that he should want to amuse himself with her . . . You had better ask her as soon as possible . . ."

They arrived at the terrace, where the unbelievers, after an orderly retreat, were already seated, talking about the sermon as they looked at the passing donkeys loaded with cans, and women with arms lengthened by the weight of buckets and jars . . . Some men near the fountain surrounded Ange and the fountaineer from Les Ombrées, who had come to offer his technical assistance. His capacities were limited to repeating, "It's all because of the drought, if it doesn't rain in a week it will be the same thing with us." The others listened to him, dejected or nervous, old Médéric looking stupid with his mouth open. Jonas and Josias were biting their nails while poor Ange, with his hands in his pockets and eyes downcast, was scratching the earth with the toe of his shoe.

It was then that the unbelievers saw Eliacin arriving. Wearing a black felt hat, he was following a donkey loaded with two cans, and he himself was carrying two jars. He came straight toward the terrace, and while the donkey followed the familiar return road, its master stopped three paces from the drinkers, put the jars on the ground, planted his big fists on his hips, and looked defiantly at the group. Anglade, who was passing, stopped to see what would happen next. Then two gossips, an old lady, and some children ran up. Eliacin looked fixedly at the group, whose faces were turned to him.

Then Philoxène, immobile, closed his left eye, opened the other wide, made a lump of his right cheek with the tip of his tongue. Casimir, with his elbows on the table, bent his hand at a right angle to his forearm, like the head of a duck; then, folding index and ring fingers down on either side of the middle finger, he pointed this rigid finger in Eliacin's face. Eliacin did not know that this insulting gesture had already been described by Juvenal, but he knew the significance of it, and it demanded a response. He spat with force at the legs of the table.

Then the baker seized the soda siphon and directed a jet toward the enemy's shoes, while Pamphile blew a contemptuous raspberry with his tongue between his teeth. The curious onlookers, already more numerous, burst out laughing. Eliacin immediately struck a great blow. He turned his back, lifted his leg, and directed a veritable battery of farts in their direction. It would have done honor to an elephant. Then he faced them again, grasped the edge of his felt hat, waved grandly, took up his jars, and departed gaily at a little trot in the tracks of his donkey . . . The unbelievers followed him with a variety of insults, such as "cochon," "porcas," and "cago ei braio," but he did not bother to return them.

The water carriers were still filing by lugubriously, stumbling on their damp shoes. Philoxène could stand this spectacle no longer.

"Messieurs," he said, "to escape from all these emotions I suggest we have a big drink, but since all these people are pulling such terrible long faces, let's go sit down, one by one, with a sad look, in my dining room."

"Such delicacy of feeling enchants me!" said M. Belloiseau.

"It's not delicacy," replied the mayor. "It's so I don't shock the electorate!"

"Well," said Bernard, "I've got something better to suggest! In spite of the catastrophe, it's my birthday today and (let me whisper) a festive drink awaits you in the courtyard of the school. Follow me."

"Us too?" asked Pamphile.

"You too," said Bernard. "And there's the Papet and Ugolin, just in time to go with us . . ."

"To your place?" asked Ugolin.

He trembled with emotion, and thought:

"Perhaps she's still there. And what do they want to say in front of everybody?"

"Yes," said Bernard, "at the school. Let's go."

Philoxène murmured:

"A little sadness, if you please. Don't forget we haven't got any more water."

On the way they picked up Claudius the butcher and then Cabridan, who hardly ever came to the daily reunion because they couldn't afford the drinks. The teacher took them by the arm and drew them along. The old ladies, seeing their little group passing by, concluded they were going to have a meeting to discuss the sermon and the fountain.

As Bernard opened the garden gate he found himself face to face with Manon, who was leaving.

"Ah no!" he said, "no! Today you're going to have a drink with us!"

Ugolin was delighted. He leaned toward the Papet and winked joyfully, whispering: "He said 'vous' to her."

But Manon was frightened by the arrival of all these men and wanted to flee. Bernard barred her passage and laughingly seized her wrist, and poor Ugolin saw him conduct his beloved to a long table loaded with glasses and bottles in the cool shade of the acacias. Meanwhile Magali was giving a big welcome to everybody. Then the guests sat down on the chairs or on the wall bordering the yard.

"So, that sermon, what did you think of it, you people?" asked Magali.

"What d'you want us to think?" replied the Papet. ". . . The whole thing was nothing but words . . ."

"They were words, but they had a mysterious meaning," said Bernard. "Mind you, I don't think the fountain was stopped by divine intervention . . ."

"As for that," said his mother, "we know you're an unbeliever, so much the worse for you."

"I'm none the worse for it," replied Bernard.

"Still, the preacher seemed to be alluding to a crime that he knew about, but couldn't describe clearly, probably because he'd heard it in a confession."

"And what crime?" said the Papet. "If anyone committed a crime in the village it would be known."

Pamphile, seated on the wall between Casimir and the butcher with his legs hanging down, was kicking the wall with his heel and looking at the ground. Without lifting his eyes, he said:

"It's not always done with a knife or a revolver!"

"It seemed to me," said Bernard, "the speech was addressed to somebody . . ."

The Papet looked him in the eye and asked unpleasantly:

"Who?"

"Yes, who?" insisted Ugolin.

"It seemed to me," said the baker, "he looked at Ugolin several times . . ."

Pamphile pretended to laugh, and continued:

"Especially when he spoke of the king who had the plague and didn't give a damn about anybody!"

"What, what, what?" cried Ugolin, "you're not going to tell me I've got the plague?"

"These are not things to repeat!" said the Papet severely. "Not even joking. And in the first place he was talking to all of us. Yes, certainly, I could see that very well. He said, 'The Good Lord will not punish everybody for the crime of one man.' That's what he said. And then he told about La Bastide Fendue, and he said everybody was responsible—because they could have spoken about it, and *they said nothing*."

He looked around at them, one after the other, and Bernard was surprised to see them avoid his eye, while Pamphile, crushed, bowed his head, opened his arms, and let them fall again.

Philoxène himself seemed ill at ease for a few moments. He suddenly seized a bottle, drew the cork, and said laughing:

"All that struck me in that sermon was that he used the catastrophe to ask for a dozen eggs and someone to come and unblock his drain!"

Then he filled all the glasses in a great silence, raised his own, and said gaily:

"Your health, Monsieur Bernard."

At this moment the farther gate opened and Anglade appeared, hat in hand.

He came forward, humble and smiling.

"Ho ho!" cried Philoxène, "you smelled pastis?"

"Oh no!" said Anglade, "Madame Magali, excuse me, and please don't think I've invited myself!"

"But you are invited!" said Bernard. "Come on in and sit down!"

"I thank you, M. the schoolmaster, but don't bother . . . What with the things that have been happening, I don't want a drink . . . It's not pastis I've come for, it's water. The children told me the little shepherdess was here, and it's her I want to talk to because I've got something important to say to her."

Manon, surprised, went pale.

"To me?"

"Yes, to you, because you, if you want to, can bring us the water."

She was suddenly frightened. This old man knew the truth, and he was going to tell it in front of everybody. She stammered:

"Me? But how?"

"By coming to the procession on Sunday! Are you coming?"

She blushed, and suddenly, in spite of herself, said abruptly:

"No."

The tone of her response surprised everyone and Anglade seemed overwhelmed . . .

"Then," he said, "the fountain will never flow again."

"And why?" asked Philoxène. "D'you think she's a saint already?"

Bernard turned to Anglade.

"Aren't you attaching too much importance to her presence?"

The old peasant looked embarrassed. He hesitated, shook his head several times, and finally said:

"You understand, she lost her father . . . She has no one else to protect her . . . In cases like that the Good Lord often takes charge . . . The prayer of an orphan girl goes straight up to the sky like a lark, and Our Lord Jesus Christ gladly listens to its song . . . As for the rest of us, it's clear that he has punished us, the curé spelled that out . . . But she, she is innocent, and even more . . . If she came to pray for us, we would be saved."

He spoke with profound conviction, and he waited, slowly turning his hat in front of his flat chest. Ugolin stood up, and said very quickly:

"Yes, yes, Manon, you must come . . . You must save our carnations . . ."

A sudden anger made the girl clench her fists. Without thinking what she was doing, she got up, took three steps, stopped, went back to her place, then passed behind her chair, and with two hands grasping the back of it, she looked Ugolin in the eye. She was pale. They thought she was going to talk, but she changed her mind and remained silent.

"Little one," said Philoxène, "I know perfectly well that this procession's going to be a load of baloney, it would be better to have a giant corkscrew to resuscitate the spring . . . But Anglade thinks it will work, and I can tell you he's not the only one in the village—make them happy! If you don't come, they'll think it's your fault if the procession flops!"

Magali approached Manon and put her pretty hand on the shepherdess's shoulder.

"Do you have a reason for not going?"

For the first time since the death of her father, the young girl felt protected, by the presence of Bernard, by the maternal hand on her shoulder, and by the warm looks given her by Pamphile, secret friend of the black arrows. She recovered her composure and said clearly:

"I don't want to pray for water for the criminals who stole my father's water."

Pamphile could not contain himself and cried, "Bravo!"

All heads were bent, but Bernard and M. Belloiseau opened startled eyes, and the Papet reddened. Ugolin, who was looking at her as hard as he could, smiled to see her so beautiful, and did not understand her words.

"What do you mean?" cried Magali.

"I don't understand!" said Bernard.

Manon pointed her finger.

"Them, they understand! Look at them! They know what I'm talking about, and why God has punished them."

"Perhaps," said Bernard. "But I, I don't know what you are saying!"

Magali, bewildered, asked:

"So, the unknown criminal, you know who it is?"

"There are two of them," said Manon. "There they are."

She pointed her finger at them.

Ugolin was frightened and turned a storm of tics toward the Papet, whose eyes glistened with fury and whose face was white. But he shrugged his shoulders, sneered, and quickly spoke up:

"I think I can guess what this is about! I must tell you, madame, that my nephew, who thought of growing carnations here, has made a lot of money these last three years . . . Naturally that has caused a lot of talk in the village, and naturally they didn't have anything good to say about it . . . There were lies and stories . . . I don't know what spiteful tales may have been told to the little girl, but she accepted them readily because Ugolin has become rich and her father was ruined. That's the real truth!"

"Ayayay!" said Pamphile in a low voice.

But the old hypocrite did not waver and added with an aggrieved air:

"Mind you, it was not right that her father did not succeed, and it's quite true he had no luck, but it wasn't our fault. That's all I have to say. And anyway, if we've been invited here to talk about criminals, thanks for the invitation, but I would rather go home!"

He turned toward the gate.

"Papet," M. Belloiseau said suddenly, "this hasty retreat does not plead in your favor. One would think . . ."

"I don't give a damn what one would think," said the Papet. "Me, I keep my conscience to myself. So, are you coming, Galinette?"

"No. Not right away. I want her to say what she's accusing me of, because I can explain everything!"

Bernard was surprised by the dialogue and by the embarrassed expressions of the onlookers. M. Belloiseau leaned toward him and spoke in what he thought was a whisper:

"I smell," he said in a loud voice, "some sordid peasant story . . ."

"And you're right!" replied Pamphile.

"What I would really like to know," said Bernard, "is how they stole your father's water?"

The Papet immediately responded violently:

"It's pure imagination! It's true her father lacked water all his life, and that's probably what ruined him. Since he was a very intelligent man he knew there must be a spring on his land. He looked for it a long time, and he would certainly have found it if he had not been killed in an accident . . . So, my nephew and I, when we saw the women alone, we bought this little property . . . partly because we liked it, to tell the truth, and partly to help them, and then we looked for this spring and we were lucky—we found it. That's what she calls stealing her father's water!"

He added with great bitterness:

"Do a dog a good turn, and he'll turn around and bite you! Come on, Galinette . . ."

M. Belloiseau stood up and said with the authority of a president of a tribunal:

"Wait a bit. We are all ready to render you justice. Young shepherdess, is that what happened?"

Manon, with a voice vibrating with indignation, cried:

"It's not true! He's lying! The truth is that the spring has always existed! When the owner died they thought the farm would be sold at auction, and they plugged the spring, and that's the truth!"

Magali, surprised, asked:

"And why should they do that?"

"Yes, why?" cried the Papet hypocritically. "Come, Galinette."

But M. Belloiseau glared at him and replied to Magali:

"Because without water, that farm was worth nothing, and they could have it for a piece of bread!"

"And so," said Manon, "my father never knew that we had a spring at our front door. For three years he went to get water at Le Plantier, and he died of overwork because of these murderers."

Ugolin took a step forward and was going to speak, but the Papet pushed him back brutally and cried:

"That's what they call calumny. Yes, calumny. You saw me looking for it with a watch! Tell the truth! You were with your mother, and you had a pumpkin in your arms . . . With the watch!"

He pulled out his watch, which hung on a silver chain, and swung it like a water diviner; then running his eyes over the onlookers he proclaimed:

"I found it with the watch!"

"In less than an hour!" said Manon.

M. Belloiseau, with a scornful expression, raised his forefinger to make the devastating remark:

"I think, I think the spring must have said to you what God himself said to Pascal: 'You will not look for me if you have not already found me!'"

This magnificent quotation, so well placed, won him a joyful smile from the teacher, but it plunged the Bastidians into an abyss of perplexity, because Pascal, he was the fountaineer at Les Quatre-Saisons.

"I don't give a damn about Pascal," replied the Papet furiously. "I met him only once and he was so rude that I gave him two clouts! Oh, you can laugh, it's the truth! And so, see what we've come to: what she saw, she doubts, and what she didn't see, she believes! Who saw us plugging the spring?"

This was met with a great silence, so he repeated triumphantly:

"Who saw us plugging the spring?"

But this time a raucous and powerful voice was raised.

"Me, I saw you!"

It was Eliacin. He had just arrived and had not dared to come in, but he was standing on a stone, leaning his elbows on the top of the courtyard wall. He repeated:

"Me! I saw both of you."

"Liar," cried the Papet.

"This is getting interesting," said M. Belloiseau.

"And what could you have seen, poor idiot?"

The old man turned to Bernard.

"He has never been able to tell his right hand from his left hand! In the army he wrote them on his hands, but since he can't read, that didn't help much, and they finally sent him back!"

Eliacin started laughing and leaped into the courtyard.

"And I was very pleased!" he said. "It wasn't easy, but I succeeded. The major was suspicious, then one day he said to me . . ."

"That doesn't interest us today," said M. Belloiseau. "We want to know what you saw!"

"Yes," said the Papet, "what did you see in your dream?"

"I NEVER dream," replied Eliacin. "It happened five or six years ago."

"You see!" cried the Papet. "He doesn't even know the date."

"It was about a fortnight after the death of Pique-Bouffigue. I had gone up to Les Romarins for the partridges . . . The spring was not flowing anymore . . ."

"So it was already blocked!" said the Papet.

"Not completely . . . there was a little pool of water in the undergrowth, on the side of the field, and the partridges came to drink there, since the farm was empty . . . Then, one morning, early in the day, I went up to the shed . . ."

"And how did you get inside?" asked Ugolin sharply. "The door was locked with a key!"

A little embarrassed, Eliacin explained:

"I lifted the hook of the shutter by poking a hacksaw blade through a slit."

"That's a fine thing, breaking into a dead man's house!" cried the Papet. "What you've just told us would be interesting to the gendarmes!"

"That's not the question," said Bernard. "And then?"

"And then there were two tiny windows, just under the gutter. Pique-Bouffigue put them there for shooting thrushes . . . So I sat down on an old chair, and what do you think I saw? It was these two, with their tools!"

The Papet looked contemptuous.

"He fell asleep in the chair, and voilà, he started dreaming."

But Eliacin continued:

"I thought they were passing by, but not at all! They stopped on the hillside opposite, twenty-five meters from the house. They had a good look all round, the Papet got up on a little ledge to hide, and Ugolin started digging with a hoe. I said to myself, 'They're putting down rabbit traps, and they're afraid of gendarmes.' "

"Fine," said the Papet, "at last you've said something reasonable . . . Yes, we often put down rabbit traps. And you, don't you ever set them?"

He addressed M. Belloiseau:

"You have to dig a hole, you see, to place a rabbit trap! That's what he saw, this idiot . . . Let's go, Galinette, we're leaving."

He went toward the gate, but Ugolin did not follow him. He got up, his face purple, and cried:

"No, no, I've got something to say, too!"

"Later, later," said M. Belloiseau. "Eliacin, you haven't told us about the spring yet."

"I'm getting to it! So, since they were doing so much digging, I thought they had probably bought the little property and were looking for the spring . . . I was furious, because my morning was shot . . . I didn't dare go out, because I was in the wrong, having opened that window. . . To kill some time I ate the bread and cheese I had brought . . . And the other one kept on digging and the Papet kept on the lookout . . . And suddenly the leg of my chair broke . . ."

"And that's when you woke up," said the Papet, "and saw there was nobody there . . ."

"I saw that you were frightened, and I heard Ugolin say to you: 'It's not a ghost, it's the rats! They're as big as rabbits!' And he dug some more, and suddenly the water shot out of the hole . . . Then you mixed up some mortar, and you plugged the hole with a round piece of wood. Then you put the earth back and left, and the partridges never came . . . That's what I saw and I tell you . . ."

"You could have told that to my father."

"What could I do," said the colossus, "it wasn't my business . . . But now I can see that they're the criminals M. the curé spoke about . . . The Good Lord wants to punish them; only, to cut off their water he had to cut off ours as well . . . Suddenly my meadow's like raffia, my eggplants are starting to die, and so now this is my business . . ."

"There's a very categorical witness," said M. Belloiseau. ". . . What do the accused think of him?"

"I think he's been dreaming," said the Papet. "Besides, a single witness doesn't count."

"That's right! You need at least two!"

"There is another one," said Manon.

The Papet, incredulous, demanded:

"And who is the other?"

"The spring."

The old man seemed surprised by this unexpected reply, but M. Belloiseau was charmed with it.

"That's certainly reasonable! In any case it's an argument that impresses the tribunal!"

The Papet's eyes blazed.

"What tribunal? Who's talking about a tribunal?"

"Me!" said M. Belloiseau. "One could argue that you knowingly depreciated the property, that you forced the owner into efforts that exhausted him, that he died of it, that you then bought the property at a low price despite the existence of a minor who could claim restitution, not to say a big indemnity!"

Ugolin had not taken his eyes from his beloved, but she did not once look at him and seemed to hear nothing. But he suddenly got up, and after a mad burst of laughter, he cried:

"An indemnity! Holy Virgin, an indemnity! Don't you realize that I want to give her everything, the spring, the carnations, the house, and all the Soubeyran inheritance, the lands, the house, the treasure, my name, and my life?"

He advanced toward her.

"You know that—I told you that on the hill! Listen, and listen all of you! Suppose it were true, everything she said against me . . . It's not true, but just suppose it were . . . Picture, Manon, all of you, that I wanted this farm for years for growing carnations, and as luck would have it, I succeeded. So I was happy, I thought about nothing but my flowers and my money . . . And then suddenly I saw you, and I fell in love with you, in a way that's impossible to describe . . . I saw you all the time, I talked to you all the time . . . Sleep was finished for me, when I ate everything had lost its flavor. If you don't want me, I'll die, or I'll go mad . . ."

"Shut up, imbecile," said the Papet, "shut up, come on."

He tried to take him by the shoulders, but Ugolin brushed him off and returned, panting, to Manon.

"Think about it a little, think . . . Don't think it will be a terrible mixture: try and forget the harm I've done you. Don't you see how I will work for you? I know that I'm ugly, but I'm good, and you are beautiful enough for two . . . And among the little ones you'll make for us, if by chance there is one who is . . . like your father, he'll be my favorite, my friend, my prettiest, and I'll ask his pardon every day, on my knees in front of his cradle . . ."

He kneeled in front of her and stretched his arms to her with great tears running down his cheeks, and he moaned:

"Manon . . . my love . . . my love . . ."

Frightened and disgusted, she got up and stood behind the teacher's chair. As Ugolin advanced on his knees toward her, Bernard held him back by the shoulders, while Manon murmured:

"It's horrible . . . Make him go . . ."

Pamphile too stood up.

"Come on, stop being a fool! Get up, go!"

Ugolin jumped to his feet and pushed him away without looking at him.

"Manon," he said, "think about it . . ."

"Let's go," said Bernard curtly, "after the crime you have just admitted, these declarations are indecent."

"He hasn't admitted anything at all," cried the Papet.

"He confessed in front of witnesses!" cried Bernard.

"It's not true! It's not true!" cried Ugolin. "I said just supposing . . . Haven't you ever made suppositions? And besides, who's this teacher, who arrived the day before yesterday and goes and talks with her on the hill? Of course he wants to amuse himself with her! If she didn't have pretty tits he wouldn't have spoken against me! And the other fool, the big idiot who saw everything and weeps for his eggplants! And the others who don't say anything! Manon, your father is dead, he's got no more cares. Now I've got them. He saw his pumpkins wither, and that made everybody weep. But me, in the same place, I'm going to see my carnations die, and I'm going to die of love for you, and that won't bother anybody."

The Papet shouted from the gate:

"Come on, Galinette! Come home!"

Ugolin turned to him roughly, his face grimacing and drenched with tears.

"No, no. It's all your fault! It's you who made me lose everything! If I had known! If I had known . . ."

He hid his face in his hands. The Papet went toward him.

"Listen, Galinette . . ."

But Ugolin drew back quickly, jumped over the wall, landed on his feet in the broom five meters down, and fled. They saw him run like a madman through the kermes oaks on the slope and disappear in the pine wood.

The Papet returned to the middle of the group:

"Well, I'll stay. Since everybody's against him, I'll stay and defend him."

"That's difficult," said Bernard, "and first you'll have to defend yourself!"

"But, M. the schoolmaster, let me explain! You've seen how this little girl has driven him mad! I'm not saying she did it on purpose, but that's how it is! He doesn't know what he's saying anymore, and he doesn't know what he's doing anymore! The day before yesterday the deaf-and-dumb woman grilled us some mushrooms, they were delicious. In the evening he didn't want to eat and he said to me: 'I've got a bit of a stomachache. I ate too many snails at lunch, and now they're coming back on me!' So, everything he says is nonsense! That story of the spring, it won't stand up!"

He turned to the Bastidians one by one with a look that demanded their complicity, and cried:

"There never was a spring at Les Romarins. A little pool perhaps—but the real source, I found it! Come on, you people, you're from Les Bastides, like me. Tell him there never was a spring!"

They all remained silent, but they exchanged uncertain looks. Only Eliacin, with his hands in his pockets, shrugged his shoulders and started to speak before the Papet cried solemnly:

"Be careful! If you knew there was a spring, *you never told the hunchback*, so it's you who are responsible for his death!"

"Bastard!" murmured Pamphile. "Old bastard!"

Manon, teeth clenched, looked at each of the men, not one of whom dared to speak. Bernard broke the silence.

"Let's see, M. the mayor, is he saying that you knew about that spring?"

Philoxène, hesitant and embarrassed, replied:

"You know, me, I don't go to the hills too much . . . I don't go hunting, except occasionally with a friend. Les Romarins is a long way . . ."

"You didn't hear talk about the spring?"

"Hear talk? That, yes, certainly . . . I heard that Pique-Bouffigue had a spring, and that he hadn't used it for a long time. I understood it was dead."

"And the rest of you," continued Bernard, "you knew nothing?"

They exchanged worried looks under the glistening eyes of the Papet. It was Pamphile again who decided.

"Certainly we knew . . . Everybody knew it!"

"Me," said Casimir, "when I was small my father often sent me there to fetch a jar of water to wet the hatchets or the blades of the plane . . . It wasn't a big stream . . . no bigger than my wrist, but it ran fast; and there were big white rosemary roots floating on the edges . . ."

"And you, Anglade, did you know about it?"

"Unfortunately, yes . . . Pique-Bouffigue's father, Big Camoins, grew vegetables with that water . . . He took full cartloads to the market . . ."

"And you also know that a man killed himself carrying water with his wife and his child?"

"Everybody knew that," said Pamphile. "From the top of the hill you could see them coming and going with cans and jars . . ."

"In the end he ran," said Cabridan. ". . . I thought he was going to fall . . . but I was too poor to concern myself with other people's business."

Bernard was indignant.

"So you all knew, and not a single one of you had the courage to go and say two words to this man to reveal his riches to him, and certainly to save his life!"

"I don't want to annoy anybody," said M. Belloiseau, "but you all have been accomplices in a crime you could have prevented with two words, or even a simple gesture . . ."

They bowed their heads, and the Papet was going to speak, when Manon, without raising her eyes, said quietly:

"There was one who tried to save us. He was the one who painted black arrows on two white stones . . . We didn't understand them. That one, he's a man, and I thank him. But the others, all the others . . ."

The tears gushed suddenly, and she cried:

"It must take a rotten heart to refuse to work a miracle when the Good Lord makes it possible!"

She sobbed so hard that Magali took her in her arms.

"You are right," said Anglade, "but a miracle, you can work one on Sunday . . . Your misfortune is our sin . . . If you come to the procession, your prayer will be our pardon . . ."

M. Belloiseau said dryly:

"It is a bit much to ask the victim to pray for her hangman!"

"Nevertheless, that is what Our Lord did," said Anglade quietly, "and perhaps that was His chance to gain His Paradise. She would be wrong to miss such a chance, because it doesn't happen often. Sometimes I am sorry that I don't have any enemies since that deprives me of the opportunity to pray for them . . ."

"With such fine sentiments, how could you let her father die?"

Anglade raised his eyes to heaven, stretched out his arms and let them fall humbly, and dropped his head.

"The truth," said Philoxène, "the truth is that nobody dared stand up to the Soubeyrans, to defend a man who wasn't from here, and especially, especially, someone from Crespin . . . You understand, the people of Crespin . . ."

"Oh yes," said Bernard sarcastically, "they can die, the people from Crespin . . ."

"And not only that," murmured Manon, "they detested my grandmother, and they took their revenge on her son."

Anglade, surprised, demanded:

"Your grandmother? Which grandmother?"

"The one who left Les Bastides to get married in Crespin."

"What did she say?" said Casimir.

"Foolishness," said the Papet. "Tsk, I've had enough, I'm going . . ."

He took two steps toward the gate, while Anglade asked quietly:

"What was her name, your grandmother?"

He asked the question even though he had already divined the answer.

"You know perfectly well," said Manon.

Anglade put his hands together and moved toward her.

"You're not going to tell us it was . . . Florette?"

"Yes, it was Florette Camoins, who was born on the farm where her son died!"

"Ayayay!" said Pamphile, dismayed. "Nobody here ever knew that!"

"That old thief over there always knew it, and Ugolin knew it too . . ."

The Papet had reached the gate.

"Oh, Papet," cried Casimir, "did you know it was Florette's son?"

He replied coldly:

"What difference does that make?"

For them it made all the difference. An amateur peasant from Crespin was fair game on the whole; but to have abandoned the son of Florette of Les Bastides to his sad fate, not a tenant or a foreign buyer, but the legitimate owner of a family property, acquired by maternal inheritance.

"That's different," said Anglade, "he's my cousin's son! O Holy Virgin, what have we done! . . . He came back to us, and his own people killed him!"

"He was related to me too," said Casimir.

"In any case," cried Pamphile, "he was from here!"

"It's not true!" cried the Papet furiously. "It's the father that makes a son! And the proof is that the son bears his name and is looked after by him all his life. He was called Cadoret, like his father, the blacksmith at Crespin, and he was born at Crespin! And Florette, she was a tart! If she had stayed with us she would have had straight children like the rest of us, and none of this would have happened! It's all her fault, everything, and I wash my hands of it!"

He opened the gate with an abrupt gesture and left.

"I always knew," said Pamphile, "that the Soubeyrans were bastards, but I never would have guessed just how far they'd go!"

"Now," said Anglade, "I understand. I understand everything."

"What's that?" asked Bernard.

Anglade shook his head several times. Finally he said in a low voice:

"It's because of Florette that he never married."

The Papet, furious, and muttering insults addressed at his nephew, entered the Soubeyran house, where he expected to find his Sunday lunch. A fine chicken was turning in front of the fire of vine shoots, but Ugolin was not there, to the dismay of the deaf-mute, who was worried about her bird.

The Papet thought:

"He's ashamed of what he said, that imbecile . . . And that girl, she's just like her grandmother . . . She never wanted him . . ."

The anger that he had felt was still making his old legs shake . . . He sat at the table, stuffed his pipe, and poured a big glass of white wine. At half past one the deaf-mute laid half the chicken before him, already a little overdone. He ate mechanically, with melancholy.

He had no remorse, but was greatly disappointed by the feebleness and na-ïveté of the last of the Soubeyrans.

"He should weep on his bed, like the idiot he is . . ."

And besides, the Bastidians had refused him false witness, contrary to their tradition. He said loudly:

"They've got a phony morality! A band of pigs who'd betray their fathers and their mothers . . ."

He ate some figs, then said:

"I know where he is! He's gone with the mule to get some water. Well done. That's the most important. The tribunal! And the mortgage, so, means nothing?—Tsk, I'd better have a little nap to cool off my anger—and then I'll go and find him."

Meanwhile, the news had gone round the village. Reactions were in full flow, and in every family the relationships were being explained.

During the delayed meal Anglade talked for a long time with his wife, Bér-arde, in front of the ravenous but attentive twins.

"Think a little: my grandfather Clarius married the sister of Camoins Bar-bette, who was the father of Big Camoins. And Big Camoins was the father of Florette. That makes Clarius the uncle of Big Camoins. Good. Then he was the grand-uncle of Florette. I am the grandson of the grand-uncle through my grandmother, Elisa Camoins. Consequently, Florette was my cousin, and her son, the poor hunchback, was my grand-cousin . . . No, wait, I think I'm a bit mixed up, so I have to start over. So . . ."

Jonas intervened:

"So, teuf . . . teuf."

"Don't wear yourself out," said Josias. "Because they nic . . . nic . . ."

"I don't understand that at all," said Jonas.

"In any case," said Bérarde, "we're related on my side too. I can't say how, but the property of Canteperdrix, which my father gave us for our wedding, that came to him by an inheritance from a Camoins daughter. Don't you remember the notary read that to us on a paper?"

"Well, my children," said Anglade, "you're related twice over to that little girl . . ."

"Me," said Jonas, "if she wants we can be . . ."

"Related once more," said Josias. "And it would please me if you married her because t . . ."

"Twins," said Jonas, "they sh . . ."

"They share everything," said Josias.

CHAPTER 27

It was a gloomy Sunday afternoon. To relieve the general feeling of uneasiness, Philoxène announced a *boules* competition, with a first prize of twenty francs and a second prize of ten francs . . . He managed to assemble more than a dozen players—two of whom were visitors from Les Ombrées, the postman and a young layabout passing through. These two people, who had water at home, cheerfully took both prizes, with the Bastidians frequently leaving the game to run to the plaza where a ring of demoralized men surrounded the fountain, while the women prayed devotedly at vespers.

They were talking about the hunchback, about the greed of the Soubeyrans, about the drought that got worse every day, and about Cabridan, who was preparing to move to a different house; and old Médéric announced his intention, if the water did not come back, of retiring to town, that is to say, Roquevaire, where he could be watchman at a solitary villa. Above the village, in the open area, there was a lookout watching the vallon of La Perdrix from afar. In fact Ange was spending the day near the pond and was going to announce the return of the water with a firecracker . . . Toward six o'clock the unbelievers came to sit as usual, but the Papet did not appear. Philoxène was right in the middle of explaining the Soubeyran character and the slight chance there was of obtaining restitution for the property stolen by these two rogues, when a boy of twelve, Tonin de Rosette, came up to the teacher, a little out of breath.

"M'sieu," he said, "the Papet told me to tell you he would like to see you, and also M. the mayor, and also M. Loiseau. He said it would give you great pleasure."

"What for?" said Philoxène.

"I don't know," said the boy. "He said you should come quickly, and that it would give you great pleasure."

"Where is he?" asked Bernard.

"He's at Les Romarins," said the boy. "He is sitting on the doorstep. He's smoking a pipe.

"It will give you great pleasure."

"There!" said M. Belloiseau. "Let's go—he's thought better of it!"

"I'd be amazed!" said Philoxène. "But let's go all the same."

They found him sitting on the doorstep of the farmhouse smoking his pipe, as the little boy said. He let them approach without saying a word, then he raised a white face to them, a wild look on it, and pointed his finger at something behind them . . .

From the plunging branches of the big olive tree, above a ladder fallen in the grass, Ugolin was slowly rotating at the end of a rope. It was attached to the ring from which the swing had formerly hung.

Pamphile leaped to him, clasped his legs to his chest, and lifted the body while the teacher climbed the ladder and cut the rope with his knife.

"Is there any hope?" asked M. Belloiseau.

Pamphile replied:

"He's as stiff as a stockfish."

The four of them carried him to his bed in the kitchen. Bernard placed a napkin on the long purple tongue.

"There," said the Papet, "look what you've done."

"Come, come," said Philoxène. "You know quite well that he had gone mad! You said so this morning!"

Pamphile covered the dead man.

"It won't be possible to dress him," said Casimir. ". . . It's too late."

"Tomorrow evening perhaps," said Bernard.

"Do you think," asked Casimir, "it would be possible to push back his tongue?"

"I'm not sure, but it's not very important."

"I ask," replied Casimir, "because if he shows up looking like that at the pearly gate, St. Peter will think he's being rude."

Then he realized he had just recognized the existence of St. Peter, and added, as a good unbeliever:

"Of course, I don't think so. But he might think so. It would worry him."

M. Belloiseau, who had just gone over to the little sideboard, stretched out his hand and took an envelope.

"What's this?" he said. "A letter for me! And there's another for the Papet."

The old man's eyes glistened suddenly.

"Give them to me, give them to me!" he said.

"There's yours," replied M. Belloiseau. "The other is addressed to M. Belloiseau, notary. I can't relinquish a document that might be a will . . ."

He tore open the envelope, while the Papet slid his into his pocket unopened, and read the hanged man's message silently to himself.

To M. the notary Beloisot
I am writing to you becaus it is a matter for a notary; it is my will, which I want you to carry out exaxtly. They must not think I am afraid. Firstly, none of that is true, and moreover there were not two witnesses. And it is not for the carnations, so what if they die, they are nothing but flouers. It is because of my Love, and I now see that she never wants me. Never. I douted it, because my ribbon of love made an absess that burned me. And then when I told her in front of everybody that I wanted to marry her, and give her everything, etcetera, she spat on my words, and furthermore she took refuge with the teacher. First I saw them talking on the hill. She did not shoot him in the stomach with a stone, and she listened to him while she looked at the ground, and when he finished she wanted him to start again! And he wasn't surprised, he thought it was natural. I wanted to kill him, Oh yes, but that would be sad for her, so, so much the worse, I did not want to deprive her. That man doesnt know his good fortune, but I know my misfortune, and I can't stand it anymore. Now my testament begins:

I leave the farm of Les Romarins to Madmoiselle Manon Cadoré, the daughter of the hunchback Jean Cadoré of Crespin. I leave her the farm and everything on it. Everything. M. the curé said that if the criminal wanted to make emends for his wrongdoing, the water would come back. I make emends, the spring will flow, the carnations will be beuatiful, they will sell well. The address of M. Trémela is quai du Canal, number 6. The Papé knows it.
So; farewell, good day to everybody.
This is my testament. Last wish is sacred.
Official signature, Ugolin Soubeyran. The date
is 6 September, today.

When he finished his silent reading M. Belloiseau seemed to reflect, then he said:

"A will is clearly meant to be publicized, otherwise it can't be executed. Therefore I think I can read this to you."

They listened, immobile. Bernard seemed surprised and embarrassed by the passage concerning him, which M. Belloiseau underlined with a look, but Bernard shrugged and tapped his forehead with the tip of his finger. The Papet remained impassive, but when the reading was finished he demanded:

"What is it, this 'ribbon of love'?"

Pamphile, who was trying to do the dead man's toilet, replied:

"Come and look; it must be this . . ."

He half-opened the shirt, and they looked with amazement at the green ribbon stained black with blood, on a red-and-yellow lump almost as big as a girl's breast.

"It's that little tart's ribbon!" said the Papet. ". . . Get it off! Throw it in the fire!"

"I'm not going to touch it," said Pamphile. ". . . The wishes of a dead man are sacred."

"The wishes of a dead madman," replied the old man, "they don't count."

Bernard examined the abscess and suggested:

"Perhaps it was this infection that troubled his spirit."

"You know better than I what made him mad," replied the old man.

Pamphile suddenly asked:

"But to you, Papet, what did he say to you in his letter?"

"I'll read it when I'm alone."

His face was hard and impassive, his eyes dry.

"Now, all of you, go to the village. Tell the deaf-mute to take some wax candles to the church. At least six, the biggest. Then, an old linen sheet, which his grandmother spun and wove. You, go and make the box. You've got oak planks in the loft. Old oak that I thought of for me . . ."

"I know," said Pamphile. "You're the one who ordered them."

"Take them for him. And then above all, all of you, say that he fell from a tree. Keep the secret for at least three days, just after the cemetery, because otherwise the curé won't want to give him a proper burial. Now go . . ."

"I'll stay with you," said Philoxène.

"No, don't bother. Come back, if you want, for the vigil."

They left one after the other, after a last look at poor Ugolin. They had not gone five steps when the Papet came to the door and shouted:

"Tell her to bring me something to eat."

Evening fell. They walked down toward the village. Pamphile and Casimir went ahead to start work on the coffin and the Soubeyran tomb.

Philoxène, Bernard, and M. Belloiseau were strolling and talking about what had happened.

"Me," said Philoxène, "I've never understood love stories."

"You're not the only one," replied M. Belloiseau.

"And this little girl, who lives in a hole, in the middle of a desert, who refused the last of the Soubeyrans, sole heir to the biggest fortune in the village, that's beyond me."

"He was really ugly," said Bernard.

"All men are ugly," replied Philoxène. "And he, he was decent. Yes, perfectly. And besides, I didn't say she had to love him. I said she should have married him. That would have been a better revenge. She could have walked on his head . . ."

"In that position," said M. Belloiseau, "I don't see what pleasure she could get out of it; but what I couldn't help thinking was that poor Ugolin, stupid as he was, understood the situation very well . . ."

"And what was that?" asked Philoxène.

"They say love is blind, but painful jealousy sometimes gives it second sight that sees through all secrets."

He turned to Bernard.

"It's quite true the pretty shepherdess turned to you and not to me."

"My God," replied the young man, "that's because she was nearer to me."

"No doubt; but she was near you because she went there, after pushing the Papet, Eliacin, and Philoxène aside."

"I don't think she did that on purpose."

"I don't think so either. That's why I've got the feeling that if you care to undertake a little pastoral, autumnal, and mineralogical idyll . . ."

"Don't even think about it," said Bernard. ". . . She's a proud creature, rather like an untamed animal, and she behaves quite naively and without ulterior motives . . . And besides, even if I had the opportunity to abuse her youth, I would certainly do nothing of the sort; that would be a very wicked thing."

"Good heavens," said M. Belloiseau, "if I were your age I wouldn't be looking at it from that angle . . . If you really want, we'll go first thing tomorrow to bring her the good news and tell her about the will that gives her all his property."

Meanwhile the Papet had lit a bundle of vine cuttings in the hearth; then he went through the drawers in the sideboard and found a pair of scissors.

Then with a grimace of horror and pity, he cut the sticky threads that held the green ribbon, seized it with the fire tongs, and burned it in the purifying flame.

This duly done, he stuck two wax candles—in lieu of church candles—at the head of the bed and then lit them. He moved his chair near the body and drew the letter from his pocket.

Papé, I'm going because I cant go on anymore. I dont want to see what happens next, you understand everything I want has gone wrong. I gave her the farm, also everything that's hidden you understand under the stone to the left of the fire that you know. There are 494 add six to make 500. I told her I had 500 I dont want to be a liar especially now you understand and then dont blame her its not her fault, its not my fault, its not your fault its fate watch out that Trémela doesn't fiddle the price. And then have a Mass said for me because up there I'll have to axplain myself because of the spring. I never did anything else bad my shoes hurt the hunchback surely talked to them about it so whats going to happen to me. Get them to say a Mass at once.

Farewell my Papé it grieves me to leave you but I cant stay. You must tell everybody shes now got 500 and the farm and the carnations she'll be a good match, not to amuse oneself with, she can marry who she wants, even somebody very well educated. I embrace you.

When he had reread the letter twice, he murmured, "Poor idiot! Poor Galinette!"

He took a long time stuffing his pipe.

"You're quite wrong if you think I'm going to let her have that pot . . . And the carnations, they'll die because the water will never come back, and the village too, it will die; they deserve that . . . They all spoke against you . . ."

He leaned his pipe toward the flame of a candle, puffed a few times, and continued the conversation.

"Ah yes, it's the Soubeyrans . . . Three mad, three hanged, and me all alone with a no-good leg . . . And nobody after me . . . Nobody, nobody, nobody . . ."

Manon was sitting in front of the cave under the stars, with her dog. Baptistine and her mother were sleeping.

She was thinking back on all the events, of such great importance to her. She did not know of the most important one.

She had seen all: the Soubeyrans had lost the fruit of their crime, the village had no more water, her father was avenged, and the burning drought that was going to complete the disaster proved the complicity of Providence. As she thought of Ugolin's carnations she laughed very softly and decided to go the next day and witness the agony of the criminal flowers.

While she was undressing a worry came to her; she had been very imprudent to reveal to these people that she knew all—some of them might see that there was an exact correspondence between their crime and their punishment, and they might conclude it was a matter of vengeance.

Then they would come and look for her with forks and sticks and force her to return the water . . . She knew she could not lie without blushing up to her eyebrows, but she certainly had the strength to keep silent. And besides, the teacher and his mother would protect her, and perhaps also M. Belloiseau, and perhaps the mayor . . .

At seven in the morning M. Belloiseau, Philoxène, and Bernard left Les Bastides to bring Manon the news of Ugolin's death and to inform her that she had regained possession of her father's property.

M. Belloiseau took his role of testamentary executor very seriously and had put on a dark jacket and a hard collar. The mayor, excited by his example, wore town clothes, while Bernard kept to his old hunting jacket, and the geological box hanging from his shoulder rattled at every step.

It was a sultry day. Summer lingered into September, there was not a breath of wind, and thousands of cicadas chirped in the pine trees.

When they arrived at the Jas de Baptiste, M. Belloiseau was hobbling. He stopped and said:

"Excuse me, I've got a scruple!"

He went and sat on a big stone and started unbuttoning his boot.

"A scruple?" asked Philoxène. "Is it about the will?"

"Not at all," said the learned notary. "A scruple, in Latin, is a little stone in a shoe that impedes walking and wounds the foot. It is a charming metaphor that has caused us to give the word its moral sense."

He shook his boot and a minute grain of gravel fell out.

The teacher started laughing.

"My word, although I don't know Latin, I've also got a scruple, but it's not in my shoe. First tell me if you're going to read this will to the shepherdess."

"Obviously," said M. Belloiseau. "I must inform her of her good fortune. It's my duty."

"In that case," said Bernard, "I would rather not be present at the reading, because certain phrases are rather embarrassing. Not so much for me, but for her . . . I won't go and see those women until later . . . Right now I'm going to take a walk around Les Refresquières, where I have found a layer of admirably preserved fossil oysters."

As he spoke he went off at an angle down a ravine . . .

"That's a delicacy that does you honor!" called M. Belloiseau. "See you soon."

They went off along the stony hillside.

Manon was busy milking her goats, and Aimée had gone to Les Ombrées to post her letters that were never answered. Baptistine was digging in the garden; she stood up suddenly and cupped her ear.

"'Quiet, listen."

A distant bell sounded. The Piedmontese said:

"Somebody has died in the village."

Manon crossed herself and replied:

"That must be the old lady who wanted to take Giuseppe's place . . ."

"The thief! Let the devil . . ."

She stopped in the middle of a curse.

"No. One mustn't speak ill of the dead."

She crossed herself too and was saying a little prayer when Manon said:

"There are two townspeople who look like they're on their way here!"

"They're wearing Sunday clothes . . . Perhaps they're going to the funeral and have taken a wrong turn."

"No," said Manon. "It's the mayor and M. Belloiseau. What have they come here for?"

After Philoxène greeted her pleasantly and M. Belloiseau greeted her ceremoniously, the notary took the floor.

"Mme. your mother, might we see her?"

"She's gone to Les Ombrées," said Manon. "I don't know what time she'll come back."

"That's unfortunate," said M. Belloiseau, "but you can tell her the news I bring. It concerns you personally. Allow me to be seated because the road here was long and remarkably stony."

He sat down on a big stone; Baptistine went to look for a chair for M. the mayor, but he preferred to remain standing. Manon wondered what news these unexpected visitors were bringing.

"That bell you hear ringing in the distance," said M. Belloiseau, "is telling you of the death of Ugolin, who has charged me with the proper execution of his last wishes. I am bringing you his will because he left you the farm of Les Romarins."

Manon was astonished and wondered if she weren't dreaming.

"But . . . what did he die of?" she asked.

"He hanged himself!" Philoxène said bluntly, "hanged from the olive tree where your swing used to be!"

"Why?"

"Let his will tell you."

M. Belloiseau had drawn an envelope from his pocket.

"I will read it to you because the spelling of the deceased would pose some problems for you."

As he unfolded the will, Manon translated the news to Baptistine; for the first time since the death of her Giuseppe she burst out laughing, and ran to hide in the house.

M. Belloiseau slowly, and with perfect articulation, read the last message of the hopeless florist. He interrupted himself to explain the "ribbon of love" sewn to his chest. She made a little grimace of disgust at the idea of her ribbon simmering so long in the bloody sweat of this madman. But when M. Belloiseau read the phrase that reproached her for fleeing to the teacher, she blushed a little, and seemed surprised, as if she had no memory of such an incident.

The notary concluded by giving her another envelope.

"Here," he said, "is a copy of the document in which I have respected the spelling, which demanded careful reading. I will keep the original, and I will go this very morning and deposit it with the notary in Aubagne. And now allow me to congratulate you on recovering your farm."

"Too late," said Manon, "too late . . ."

"I know," said Philoxène, ". . . but perhaps one day the spring will come back and you can sell it for a good price and use it for a dowry . . . Good, so that's settled. But I want to say something else to you. Look at what's happened—the water hasn't come back and things are going badly in the village. The vegetable gardens are about to die, and the lorry water, it hasn't got a natural taste. We'll go and look for drinking water at Les Quatre-Saisons. So there's a lot of talk. The women think we're being punished because of you . . . Others say—in passing—that you know the springs in the hills very well, perhaps you know what's happening . . . So, in short, I suggest you come to their procession. Of course, that won't get us the water, but I think it will make people shut up; and now that they know that your poor father was the son of Florette you will be at home in the village. That is what I want to tell you— but you do what you want. Now I have to go down and wait for the doctor to sign the death certificate, because before signing it he's going to ask a lot of questions, and there may even be gendarmes to make sure he really hanged himself. So farewell, and don't worry."

"And I," said M. Belloiseau, "I'm going to Aubagne to look after your affairs. Good-bye, and all my heart will be with you."

They left.

Manon gathered the goats and went down to the beloved mountain ash, to think. The already high sun exalted the frenzy of the cicadas, and the sea breeze had not yet come up. Worn out by a sleepless night, she didn't have the energy to take a tour of her traps. Sitting under the mountain ash, she thought about Ugolin's suicide with more astonishment than pity, and without the least gratitude . . . She re-read his last message, whose strange spelling had been interpreted in an admirable calligraphy by the notary clerk.

The unhappy man's declaration of love inspired nothing but a shuddering revulsion. She thought that God had sent him this extravagant passion to punish him for his crime, and that the legacy of the farm was no more than the delayed restitution of a theft. But she re-read the part concerning the teacher several times. Yes, he had spoken to her on the hill, but he had never said anything that merited "a stone on the stomach." On the contrary, he had always been polite and discreet. It was true that on the day of the pond he had told the others about his dream of "the kiss," but he did not know that she was listening, and that hanged imbecile did not know it either.

On the other hand, she hardly knew him. She had seen him no more than six times. Twice without being seen herself—the day he lunched under the pine tree, and the day of the pond. Then he had spoken to her on the day of the hare, exchanged for the knife. Then the morning the fountain stopped, then the day of the walk with the engineer, finally the previous day, after the sermon, when she told everything. As to whether in fact she had "fled to him" on retreating from the mad Ugolin, she had not done it on purpose. There was nothing extraordinary in that, he was a young man from town, like her father, in the midst of all those villagers who had so cruelly kept the secret of the spring—it was quite natural that she should go to him. The hanged man, in his folly, had drawn the conclusion that she was in love with him; it was absurd.

Certainly this handsome young man inspired a true interest, and it was true she often thought about him; but it was because of the marvellous knife. Every morning she sharpened its edge by honing it on a sandstone moistened with spit, and she could cut the hardest wood almost without effort. The little saw blade, which could be considered no more than a superfluous flourish, easily sawed big branches, and it had won the admiration of Enzo, a connoisseur, who said, "It's Swedish steel, the same as what they use for razors." The awl pierced leather straps or soles of shoes, and as for the little scissors they were a miracle of elegance and precision; finally, with the nail file, she could now look after her hands, which she otherwise hid under her cloak when she went to Aubagne . . . Yes, this knife was a treasure; she kissed it every time she put it in her haversack, and since she used it ten times a day, it was quite natural that she should think of the one who gave it to her. It was gratitude, but not love . . .

First, there must be two to love; you could not go and love somebody who did not love you. The teacher was at least twenty-five years old, and he was probably engaged to some young girl in town and could not be interested—except for natural generosity—in a poor shepherdess like her. Nevertheless, he had dreamed of "the kiss," which made one think. But then a kiss like that was not a real kiss, it was like a kiss for a child, or a father, or a friend. The huge Enzo always kissed her like that when he came to Le Plantier on Sundays. And besides, the teacher had certainly said it as a joke, without attaching the least importance to it . . . Moreover, this very morning, he had not accompanied the mayor and M. Belloiseau to tell her the good news. Although he was on holiday, it was a fact that he had not come . . .

Meanwhile the vengeance had been more complete and more terrible than she had hoped . . . She stretched out on the stone in the shade of the mountain ash; her eyelids were heavy, as in the wonderful days of the "sandman."

She shut her eyes and went to sleep.

The mayor's words about the people in the village soon troubled her sleep and provoked a frightening dream. She saw several groups of peasants coming up toward the cave brandishing cudgels and forks. They advanced slowly, step by step, in perfect silence—then suddenly the women appeared, a crowd of the old ones, uttering cries of hatred.

She wanted to flee; she realized with terror that she was unable to move . . . But suddenly the teacher rose up, stood in front of her, and shouted in a powerful voice:

"Yes, she blocked the spring, and you thoroughly deserved it! It was her duty, and so it was her right. I warn you, if anyone tries to touch her, they'll have to deal with me!"

The old women fled crying with fear; the men stopped and nearly all raised their hats to salute the valiant champion. She kept herself hidden behind him, and suddenly made an extraordinary discovery—he was hunchbacked! Not just stooping, but ornamented with a great and beautiful hump, which could carry a heavy jar full of water! She was woken by a powerful and sweet emotion, with her eyes full of happy tears; and she knew she was in love with him.

She was sitting on the polished rock, leaning back on her arms and looking at the distant bluish escarpments of Les Refresquières. She was moved by a happy restlessness, and a kind of pride, when a soft little bark called her. She turned her head—the black dog was stretched out at Bernard's feet. He was sitting in the lavender on the slope and smiling. She got up quickly and smiled back, blushing.

"So," he said, "you know?"

"Yes."

"And now, what are you going to do?"

"I don't know . . . I don't think we'll go back down there. It has many bad memories for me, and for my mother . . . And besides, I'll always see that man hanging in the place of my swing . . . And above all, he must have left his smell in the house . . ."

"I understand you," said Bernard, "but what have you decided about the other things?"

"The mayor has advised me to go to that procession."

The teacher stood up and said, stressing every word:

"If the water doesn't come back, if you are sure it can't come back, I also advise you to go there. They say one must howl with the wolves; I believe it's also necessary to bleat with the sheep, when one belongs to the flock."

The blue eyes became sombre.

"I don't belong to that flock!"

"One doesn't choose one's flock. That village, it's your grandmother's village. And there are many others you're related to."

"My grandmother detested them. She said they were brutes and they certainly proved it. I know that my father wanted to be . . . their friend. He never said it, it's true, but I felt it . . . We went to the village once and they threw a ball at him. At his back."

"I know," said Bernard, "I know. It was a stupid accident, a piece of bad luck . . . It was that nice man Cabridan who threw it, and he regrets it to this day. The true culprits were the Soubeyrans. They deceived the village about you; they deceived you when they talked about the village. It was their second crime, engendered by the first. But if your father had come one morning to see the mayor, with corduroy trousers and big boots, and if he had said, "I am Florette's son," the village would have accepted him. In their way, obviously.

No doubt they would have poked fun at him (under their breath), and his pumpkins and his rabbits; they probably would not have denounced the Soubeyrans . . . But in the days of the drought the Anglade twins, or perhaps Pamphile or Casimir, would have gone up to Les Romarins with their picks on their shoulders, and under the pretext of digging for winged ants—for their traps— they would have opened up the spring and flooded the field."

Manon listened to the man's fine voice and looked at his dark brown eyes, like her father's, shining in his brown face . . . She suddenly seemed very moved, and murmured:

"Are you saying my father was wrong?"

"No," he said, "no . . . But victims are rarely completely innocent. And, in any case, he has been revenged. The main culprit is dead, and the surviving one is no more than a beaten old man, half mad with rage and disappointment. The others, whose only fault was to keep silent, have lost half their harvest; they have wives and children."

"My father also had a wife and a child."

He was silent for a moment, then replied:

"Who was it who painted the black arrows?"

She raised her eyes and said:

"The carpenter."

"I suspected that. What's more, he told you your father's coffin was given by the community. It wasn't true. He gave it."

She was silent for a moment, then she said:

"He's not a peasant. He doesn't need water."

"But he needs a village. If the young people left, he'd be forced to go and settle somewhere else . . ."

She made no reply, her eyes were lowered. He continued:

"I have a Protestant grandmother who sometimes reads the Bible to me. I remember a phrase spoken by the God of Israel, although he was severe and cruel: 'If there is a single just man left in this town, it will not be destroyed.'"

She still did not reply and nervously twisted a sprig of fennel.

He said softly:

"If your father were still living, and he had the power to give them back the spring, what would he do?"

She suddenly raised her eyes glistening with tears.

"Oh, him," she said, "he . . ."

"Well then, in his memory you must do what he would have done."

Then, as she wept, she turned to the dog, and said:

"All right, Bicou, do you want us to go and look for that gerbil that got away from you the other day, when you were so surprised to get a stone on your head?"

So in the first hours of the night they found themselves in front of the artificial debris that blocked the entrance to the little cave. The full moon rose like a balloon behind the pine woods on the crest of the hill, the wind was warm, two crickets were calling to each other. Bernard wore espadrilles and made no more noise than a shadow. Manon, her hair tied under a black mantilla, helped him move the debris aside. He was surprised at the strength and dexterity of the shepherdess, who noiselessly manipulated fifty-pound stones.

It was difficult to get through the entrance of the tunnel; they did not dare enlarge it because of the danger that hammer blows might arouse nocturnal echoes. Manon went in first and lit the candles; then Bernard, having changed into a bathing suit in order to take up less room, entered the crevasse in his turn. But even after painful contortions his shoulders could not clear the narrow tunnel and he was stuck. The girl seized both his hands and pulled with all her strength. She tugged several times, pulling hard on the palms of the prisoner. At last his shoulders passed through and he suddenly slid in easily. Manon thought confusedly of the birth of a kid goat.

She put four candles down at the edge of the water and they descended into the pool, the level of which had risen. They could hear the waterfall in the other gallery. With great effort he lifted the sheets of rock she had detached from the sides and leaned them against the bank; she helped him without a word, and saw the play of male muscles indifferent to the streaks of blood on his back. From time to time she went out for a moment to scan the night and to caress Bicou who silently kept watch . . . The cement plug resisted the mining bar for quite a while, but little by little it was crumbling and they suddenly heard the profound fall of liberated water.

He plunged his arms in and gathered up some handfuls of clay.

"There it is," he said.

His face was shining with sweat, and a damp slick of black hair hung down his forehead.

"Does your back hurt?"

"Of course," he said smiling. "It's burning."

"It's the sharp points of rock that've wounded you. I'll go and break them off with the hammer."

She crawled slowly up the tunnel on her elbows, holding the tool in one hand and a candle in the other. One by one she broke the cruel points and the jagged ridges. For fear of noise she only made little taps, and her work lasted long minutes. He followed her, also crawling. He felt the mossy vault of the narrow tunnel on the nape of his neck. The tunnel was almost blocked by their bodies, and her bare feet strained at the prehistoric clay under his eyes. Leaning on his palms in the dancing shadows he smelled the tender, wild odor of the girl of the springs, and he could feel his heart beating through the soft music of the underground water.

Suddenly the gleam of the candle was extinguished and the night air refreshed his face.

She whispered:

"I think you can get through."

He reached out again to seize the girl's hands. She pushed her foot against the vertical side and threw her body back, and by the light of the stars he got out, without letting Manon's hands go. He looked at her with eyes so shining that she lowered hers and said very quickly:

"We haven't finished. We must put the stones back." She took a step back and freed her hands to tie the ribbon in her hair.

Side by side together they rolled two great blocks up to the opening. In their efforts their shoulders touched from time to time and drops of sweat fell on their hands.

Manon felt her cheeks warm and her legs trembling. When the entry was perfectly hidden she sat on a block of stone, breathed deeply, and said:

"I couldn't have done it alone. It's easier to let stones fall than to lift them up!"

She wiped the sweat that wet her face with her scarf.

"All we have to do is replant two or three junipers," said Bernard. "I'll do that . . ."

"I think it would be better to wait for daylight to put them in good places . . . I'll come back tomorrow morning . . ."

"You're right," he said. ". . . Besides, the water's already moving toward the pond. When it's filled nobody's going to look where it came from!"

He went behind the gorse to get dressed.

"You don't regret anything?" he asked.

"What's done's done. If you hadn't talked to me about my father . . . But finally, I think you were right."

"By your calculation the water should be at the pond tomorrow morning about seven or eight o'clock and half an hour later the fountain will flow."

He heard a metallic clanking.

"What are you doing?"

"I'm hiding the tools. They're very heavy. I'll come back tomorrow with the she-donkey and fetch them."

"I can carry them to your place now," he said. "It's such a beautiful night I'd like to walk in the moonlight!"

She did not reply.

As he adjusted his socks he continued:

"There'll be rejoicing in the village, but the curé will be disappointed to give up his procession the day after tomorrow . . . Bah! . . . He'll have it anyway, only to give thanks to the Lord for his bounty! . . . It's also possible that the water will return a lot quicker than we think."

As he laced his espadrilles he explained his theory.

"According to Ange the water in the pond reddens about eight hours after a storm . . . But how long before it gets to the little cave? Perhaps three or four hours, and the delay in getting from the cave to the pond will be decreased by that amount!"

Again she did not reply.

He buttoned his shirt, buckled his belt, and wiped his face.

"What annoys me is that I haven't got the time to make some bets with the mayor, who thinks the spring will never flow again. I could have won some good bottles . . ."

While he was talking, a brief barking sounded some distance away.

He lowered his voice:

"Listen. Somebody . . ."

He listened, then said:

"Perhaps it's a fox?"

As she still did not reply, he asked:

"What d'you think, is it a dog or a fox?"

He was met with silence.

He came out of the undergrowth noiselessly: Manon was no longer on the rock. He called softly:

"Manon!—Where are you?"

He suddenly heard stones rolling and raised his head: on the opposite side, along the length of a little ledge of white rock, she was running with her dog in the moonlight.

CHAPTER 29

At about seven in the morning, after a meticulous toilet—in which the scissors and the nail file of the precious knife played their part—she left Le Plantier behind her flock. She was happy and pensive, and reviewed all the scenes of the previous night, as she had before going to sleep. She asked herself once again if she had been right to flee without a word . . . Certainly in romances moonlight is always dangerous for young girls; but romances are not life. After all, he had probably never walked in the hills at night before; he had been seduced by the beauty of the stars, the nocturnal perfume of the plants, and that blue silence of the moon, enhanced by the singing of the crickets. It was unjust to ascribe intentions to him that he never had, since he had not said a single audacious word, he had not made a single disturbing gesture, and that ridiculous flight must have made him smile with pity . . . She decided that if it happened again, she would not sneak away, if only to know where she stood.

She danced down to the doomed cave and saw that from afar the false debris seemed quite natural, except for three stones that had been placed upside down—the sides that could be seen were encrusted with earth and little roots . . . She repaired this and then planted tufts of thyme between the stones, and a fine juniper that she pulled up on the ledge above. Then she walked away and came back several times to make sure her work looked natural—it blended perfectly with the background, with nothing to attract attention.

Then she left for the pond, walking and trotting so quickly that Bicou could not force the flock to follow her—this delayed her finding out whether the water had already returned as her accomplice had predicted, and was she also thinking he might be there?

In fact he was there, sitting on the edge of the reservoir with his legs hanging down, and he was looking at the bottom of the big cement tank, already criss-crossed with cracks. He looked at her approaching and said:

"It hasn't come yet, and I wonder why . . . It'll be nine o'clock soon . . ."

Manon jumped into the reservoir, kneeled down, and pressed her ear to the entry pipe.

He admired the grace and precision of her movements, and found her unique—not just like a young lady, but like a squirrel or an ermine.

She listened for a long time.

"I can't hear anything," she said.

She heaved herself up onto the side of the pond and came over to him to say in a low voice:

"D'you think it will come back?"

"I think so, at least if the little canal isn't blocked by debris from the plug that I broke up . . . Or there's a siphon on the way, or several little siphons, that are unprimed but will function again when the water reaches its normal level . . ."

"An idea torments me," she said. "What if the water doesn't come back until after the procession?"

"Well?"

"Well then, they'll think the saint has performed a miracle."

"One that'll be worth three dozen wax candles, and one M. the curé won't fail to hold up for the edification of the unbelievers!"

"Yes, but me, when I go to confession . . ."

"One confesses only one's faults, and you have wiped out yours since you have restored the water to the village . . . And besides, we're short of miracles at present; it wouldn't be very charitable to renounce that one—if it happens . . ."

He looked at his wristwatch.

"This morning," he said, "I can't stay with you—I must go to Ugolin's funeral. It's at ten o'clock . . ."

"He's having a service at the church?"

"No. The curé was told that he had fallen from a tree, and he seemed to believe it. But the gendarmes came and so he learned the whole story . . . In spite of that, he'll give him absolution at the cemetery."

"Good for him!" she said.

"It won't bring him back to life."

"Not to this life; but to the next?"

"Let's hope so!" said the teacher, and he got up.

"And if the water never returns?"

Manon shrugged her shoulders.

"That will be a sign that the Good Lord admits I was right . . ."

She returned to the pond in the afternoon. But when she got to the cliff that overlooked the valley, she saw a little caravan following the bottom some distance away—four or five mules loaded with drums, accompanied by five or six men. She hid among the junipers. What were these people doing? It suddenly occurred to her that the spring had begun to flow again, but that the water had not yet reached the village, so they had come to fill their drums at the pond, which she could not see. As they approached she first recognized M. Belloiseau's panama hat, then Philoxène, then Ange the fountaineer, and little Cabridan. Behind the mules, the teacher was talking with Pamphile, who was carrying a glazed jug.

She crawled under the junipers to the edge of the escarpment to look at the pond—it was as empty as the day before, and she thought the arrivals would be greatly disappointed. But they showed no surprise, and started emptying their drums onto the burning cement, which the heat of the sun had divided into slabs . . .

"We've come too late!" said the mayor simply. "We must repair the coating . . ."

He was carrying a bottle under his arm, which he uncorked, while Cabridan distributed the glasses he had brought in an esparto grass hamper. Then they sat in a circle under the fig tree. Pamphile, who had not emptied his jug into the pond, poured a thin stream of water from it into the absinthe, clouding it purposefully.

Then they talked, as was their custom. A desolate Cabridan announced his decision to leave the next day and take his wife to live with cousins at La Bouilladisse, since she was on the point of having a baby. He justified this desertion by saying:

"A child is not like a chick-pea—you can't dry it out . . . What's more, if the water doesn't come, I'll go down there too. My cousins have big crops of young vegetables and they've often suggested I come and work with them . . . Besides, they haven't got children."

Claudius declared that he was considering moving to La Valentine and going into business with Pampette the butcher, who could no longer serve all his customers because of his rheumatism.

Ange was dismayed, and cried:

"So, you think there won't be anybody left in the village?"

"The old people will stay," said Claudius, "and old people, they're miserly and they've got no teeth—they don't eat meat . . ."

Philoxène was pessimistic. In his opinion it was no good having illusions. The spring was dead and the village would have to be abandoned.

"As far as money goes, it's all the same to me. With my pension and my savings and some packets of tobacco, I can always get by . . ."

He turned to Bernard, who didn't show any emotion.

"And you, Monsieur Bernard? If the young people go, they'll take the children away . . . It was a lot of trouble to get that school . . . If there aren't enough left, they're capable of closing it!"

"I'm a civil servant," said Bernard, "and you know that last year I refused to go to Saint Loup . . . If I'm not here, I'll be sent somewhere else, and it's even likely I'll get a promotion!"

He spoke cheerfully. She drew back noiselessly and returned to Le Plantier. She walked quickly, with her head down, pulling up sprigs of fennel as she went.

CHAPTER *30*

The news of the catastrophe made a big impression at Les Ombrées and at Ruissatel; it was a threat to the springs that nourished these two big villages, and the danger had aroused peasant compassion. That is why the neighbors, without particularly liking "them from Les Bastides," had delegated some of their own people to take part in the procession to ask the heavens to restore the fountain and renounce this kind of punishment, which was too cruelly appropriate to the aridity of the country.

While the "officiants" were getting ready in the too-small church, the crowd surrounding the dead fountain overflowed the plaza up to the esplanade at the bottom of the steps. Yet not a sound could be heard, because while some talked in whispers, practically everybody was quiet, except, of course, the unbelievers. They were sitting in the café terrace, making rather unorthodox remarks.

"In the old days," said M. Belloiseau, "the priests would try and appease the anger of the gods by slaughtering the most beautiful girl in the country on the altar, while our kind curés suppose that the Christian God will be satisfied with a march-past, and some songs accompanied by the cornet, which Saint Dominique up in heaven has requested . . . You have to admit that's tremendous progress!"

"And do you think," said the baker, "that it will do anything?"

The teacher shook his head and assumed a mysterious air. He said:

"You never know!"

"What?" cried Philoxène. "You're not going to tell me . . ."

"No," replied Bernard, "I'm not going to tell you, but I wonder what I would think if, at the first prayer, the fountain started to flow!"

"Well," said the baker, "that would have a terrible effect on me, because it would change my ideas! I wouldn't know anymore what to say to my wife, and I would have to go to confession at once!"

"There!" said Philoxène sarcastically. "That's the danger, because unfortunately if the water should return today, I know many idiots who would think like him! That would make us all a village of churchgoers, and I would certainly lose the mayorship!"

"That's for sure," said Casimir, ". . . a miracle, that doesn't pardon!"

"I'm not thinking of a miracle!" said Philoxène. "I'm thinking more of some trick by the master of the Jesuits!"

"Ho ho!" said the teacher seriously, "that wouldn't surprise me!"

"Come on, come on," said M. Belloiseau incredulously, "how would they do it?"

"I never know how they do it!" replied Philoxène. "They're scholars, and mysterious, but fortunately I don't think they're going to bother about the town hall of Les Bastides. It's too small to interest them!"

A peal of bells suddenly rang out. The saint emerged from his church, on a litter carried by the Anglade twins, old Médéric, and Barnabé de Baptistine. The curé followed them, surrounded by his choirboys; behind him Anglade proudly carried the saint's banner, at the side of the sacristan of Les Ombrées, who was the prior of the Penitents of Saint Leonard. There were four of them, under their grey cowls, which hid everything but their eyes. Behind them Ange had pushed the staff of an embroidered standard in his belt, to the great merriment of the unbelievers, who did not spare him their sneers and shrugs. But Philoxène excused him, saying: "Because of the fountain he doesn't know what to do anymore. Just think, he hasn't had a single drink for a whole week!"

The people of Ruissatel were represented by a choral society of old people and a dozen bonny Sunday school children, led by the verger.

The group was organized at once; under the direction of M. the curé, Eliacin had formed the ranks with the dedication of a sheepdog.

Meanwhile Anglade seemed to be worried and looked around him ceaselessly, as if he were waiting for somebody. Suddenly he smiled—Manon had just appeared, with the teacher's mother. With her hair tied under a hood of grey foulard, she followed Magali, who was smiling under a large straw hat.

Manon walked with her eyes lowered, but she felt the presence of all the motionless people; and when she saw the crowd dominated by the banners and the gilded saint she was frightened by the fullness and the gravity of the ceremony. She thought: "If these people knew what I have done they would tear me to pieces." But first of all nobody knew anything, except Bernard; and not only that, he was there, on the terrace, capable of defending her against all . . . And as it happened, he was looking at her with a grave air, frowning; she divined that he was having great difficulty restraining a violent desire to laugh, and she lowered her eyes. Then, the sight of the duped priest, who had turned to her with visible benevolence, troubled her . . . His faith, without bigotry, deep and sincere, reproached her for having organized a false miracle, one that would doubtless be talked about for a long time. Bernard could laugh at it, but Saint Dominique, from the height of the sky, could see her sacrilege, and she did not dare look at the statue.

As she passed, Anglade put his hand on her shoulder. He smiled, with tears in his eyes.

"Little cousin," he said, "come with me! We'll pray together . . ."

Then M. the curé intoned a psalm, joined by the entire choral society, whose musical architecture reposed in Eliacin's bellowings. The procession started its march. When it reached the terrace, M. Belloiseau showed the largeness of his spirit by getting up, and, with his panama at the end of his arm, bowing deeply at the passage of the saint.

The singing procession left the plaza and made a long tour of the village. It stopped at the sides of the fields, to show their misery to the Protector, and the curé blessed the earth, already powdery under the pitiless sun. Every so often Manon sneaked a glance at the village; she was waiting to see someone—perhaps the teacher—rush out with hands cupped to mouth, shouting, "The water has come!"

Meanwhile, facing the empty plaza, the unbelievers continued their conversation.

"In my opinion," said Bernard, "the spring isn't permanently dead. I'm not saying this procession is going to bring it back, I'm saying the water will come back one of these days, and perhaps very soon."

"I don't think so," said Philoxène. "And I bet you three bottles of Pernod, and I hope I lose them."

"It's a bet!" said the teacher. "I'll even go to four bottles if you agree."

"I agree to four!"

"I approve of this bet," said M. Belloiseau, "because whatever happens we're the ones who'll drink to the health of the loser."

Meanwhile Bernard never took his eyes off the fountain; he was amazed by its silence, and wondered whether the stoppage of the spring for more than a week had not drained it forever . . .

From afar the procession was chanting its singsong supplications, a solitary cicada chirped in the old mulberry tree, and the unbelievers fell silent, worried . . . Suddenly Philoxène cried:

"Come on, come on, let's not let it get us down. We can still have a drink and play a game of manille."

They were playing their fifth round when the singing approached, then the procession appeared and went to surround the fountain. Everybody seemed discouraged, and Manon gave Bernard a worried look, but Anglade smiled all the time.

M. the curé started a litany in his fine, clear voice, and the crowd gave their responses with pathetic fervor.

Just then a strange figure was seen approaching.

Between an extremely large black felt hat, and the double bow of an artist's cravat, he displayed a round florid face around a large nose, and two fine eyes shining like anthracite. He wore a huge suit of midnight blue velvet and in his hand he carried a stick with a silver knob.

With a rather theatrical authority, he made his way through the crowd and went to stand in the first row, beside M. the curé. He uncovered his head before the saint with a solemn gesture; then, with eyes raised to the sky, he responded feelingly to the litany in a strong, clear voice.

Philoxène, suspicious, asked:

"Who's that character, there?"

"The general of the Jesuits," said Bernard gravely.

At this moment Ange was seen to turn quickly; he put the staff of his banner in the hands of a Penitent Gris and went up to the fountain. He pressed his ear to the copper pipe, and cried:

"Something's happening!"

The soft litany stopped abruptly and in a truly religious silence Ange listened again, and said:

"It's breathing!"

The men advanced. There was a sigh, which slowly grew louder. The unbelievers stood up as one man, and M. Belloiseau asked in a ringing voice:

"What's going on?"

"The pipe is blowing!" said the baker, and he ran up to Ange.

Philoxène was pale, the teacher looked at Manon, who stubbornly kept her eyes to the ground, while Anglade, openmouthed, clenched his wrinkled hands on the staff of his banner. As M. Belloiseau crossed the crowd to try to hear, the fountain sneezed three times, a thin stream of water appeared, wavering and deformed by the air current; then the copper pipe coughed, the jet rounded up suddenly and struck the stone of the shell, which started to sing. Anglade cried, "Miracle!" while the sacristan of Les Ombrées, remarkably excited, shouted, "To your knees! Everybody, to your knees!"

The crowd fell down, while the priest, arms raised, threw his solemn thanks to the heavens with his generous voice:

"Thank you, Lord, for the humble vegetable garden, thank you for the orchard, the vine, and the meadow . . . Thank you for the frailest of our blades of grass that will grow green again tonight!"

But while he was pronouncing these noble words, the men suddenly flew off in all directions, as if a bomb had just exploded in the plaza. They were running to their ponds. Only the bearers of the saint and old Anglade remained heroically at their posts.

Then a strong resonant voice began the "Hallelujah." It was the stranger singing the Latin words. M. le curé, surprised and charmed, followed at once and was joined by the chorus. The stranger, turning his back to the fountain and clasping his hat between his knees, started to wave both arms to the music, with the authority of a conductor, and the hymn of thanks and joy swelled to fill the plaza . . .

"I told you!" repeated Philoxène. "There's the man from the Jesuits! Look at the organization of the miracle! He sings Latin better than the curé!"

"Let's go then!" said M. Belloiseau. "It's neither a true nor a false miracle . . . It's a coincidence, that's all!"

"Lucky coincidence!" said the teacher, "because there's our water come back, and just in time to water the four bottles of Pernod that M. the mayor has lost!"

"Those bottles," said Philoxène, "that's right, I'll go and find the first one. But the town hall, we haven't got them there!"

After the "Hallelujah," in a silence animated by the antique song of the fountain, M. the curé blessed the fountain. Then he turned toward the disconcerted Manon and blessed her, before a radiant Anglade . . .

She bowed her head, as if ashamed, but the priest said solemnly:

"The true miracles are those that God makes in the soul."

Then he turned to the crowd, and although he saw only women, he said:

"My brothers! Let us take our great Saint Dominique, who has just saved our village, back into his house, and let us give thanks in front of the altar!"

Preceded by the banners, he went toward the church, followed by the crowd of women. Manon, thoughtful, stayed in the middle of the plaza, and looked at the fountain flowing, while the unknown singer went toward the café terrace, where Philoxène was serving the drinks.

"Ho ho!" said Philoxène, "he hasn't gone into the church because he's trying to cover up his trick! You can say what you like, but that's just what the Jesuits do! And now he's coming to spy on us!"

Philoxène attacked at once.

"You sing very well, sir, especially religious songs. One can see that you're used to it."

"It's not my specialty," said the stranger smiling, "but quite often I am called upon to accompany important religious ceremonies in church . . . I am Victor Perissol."

He looked at the audience as if to judge the effect of this revelation. There was none.

Only M. Belloiseau responded:

"Enchanted, sir."

Philoxène, with his fists on his hips and his chin raised, looked fixedly at the stranger.

"Me," he said, "I am the LAY mayor of this community, and miracles don't frighten me."

And as the other seemed perplexed, he added in a defiant tone:

"On the contrary!"

"The one we've just seen was rather pleasant, however," said Victor Perissol, "and I can't see why it should frighten anyone. But what I can see clearly is that in this charming village my name is quite unknown, as no doubt is Caruso's. I observe that without bitterness."

"You are a singer then?" asked Bernard.

"Yes, sir, yes, and I have enjoyed my hour of fame. But that is not what we're concerned with—and in the absence of the ovation that I haven't merited today, you can perhaps tell me something . . . I'm looking for a place called Le Plantier. Do you know Le Plantier?"

"Certainly," said Bernard, "and there's a young girl who lives right there."

"Ho ho!" said the stranger, "she wouldn't be little Manon?"

"Herself! D'you know her?"

"That is perfect!" cried the singer.

He went up to Manon. She was surprised, but reassured when she saw Bernard following him.

"Young lady, let me introduce myself: I am Victor Perissol. Yes, himself."

Manon had never heard the name and did not know what to say, but the tenor continued:

"And you, you're the daughter of little Aimée Barral?"

"Yes, that's my mother's name," said Manon.

"Well then, you've no doubt heard her talk about me!"

Suddenly she said:

"Victor! It's you, Monsieur Victor!"

"But of course!" cried he.

"She wrote you a lot of letters."

"More than fifty!" cried Victor. "She didn't know I was in Marseille, and she wrote to me at the Comic Opera in Paris, to invite me to dinner in the most charming fashion, but without giving me any address except 'Château du Plantier,' Bouche-du-Rhone . . . This Plantier, I searched for it on all the maps, in all the travel agencies, I asked postmen . . . Nothing . . . And since these letters were rather poetic—and finally rather incoherent—I wondered whether Château du Plantier wasn't a kind of . . . nursing home . . . Finally, I got a letter yesterday—as usual forwarded from Paris—but it was stamped by the post office of the village of Les Ombrées. I found it immediately in the telephone directory, and I went there this morning. The lady at the post office advised me to try Les Bastides, and that's why I'm here. Let's go to Le Plantier!"

Manon was very embarrassed and said very quickly:

"I can't go right now . . . I've got to do some shopping for my mother . . ."

"Good," he said. "I'll go and wait on the terrace of that café and have a drink!"

At a look from Manon, Bernard followed her. When they had gone around the corner of the little street she whispered:

"I don't know what my mother told him, but that man thinks he's going to dine in a château. What can I do?"

"Laugh!" said Bernard . . .

And he started laughing heartily.

"But I'm ashamed," she said. "He'll see that she's been telling him lies!"

"He's an artiste. He'll have no trouble understanding that. I'll warn him on the way."

"Oh yes. But he'll want to eat . . . He's big . . . We haven't got much. Some eggs . . . Some tomatoes . . . We don't eat much . . . There's no wine . . . I must buy some food. I've got a gold coin. Do you think they'll take it?"

Bernard smiled.

"First," he said, "let's go and see my mother!"

The good Magali listened to her son's explanations and declared:

"It's all quite simple. Go and get four or five bottles of wine from the cellar. Then, on the second shelf, three tins of sardines, the little jar of gherkins, etc. . . . . And as you go through the village get some bread. I've got a fine rabbit stew on the fire—I'll bring it about eight o'clock."

"Oh!" said Manon. "You can't go all that way! And besides, you don't know where it is."

"My poor little one, Bernard has shown me your pretty sheepfold so I know perfectly well where it is. And as far as walking in the hills, I'm not afraid of anyone. Don't worry about me, and make a tomato omelette—I'll arrive at eight. Me, I'm curious. In the first place I want to meet your mother. And then I want to see the sheepfold. And then I would enjoy talking to that tenor . . . I adore tenors, but I've always seen them from a distance. And moreover, a tenor in a sheepfold, that's rather unusual, and if we ask him, perhaps he'll sing us a tune from an opera! Go! And don't forget the bread."

They found the guest singing the ballad "If I Were King" to Philoxène, Pamphile, Casimir, and a charmed M. Belloiseau. He held the last note for a long time, and bowed while the audience applauded.

"Is it far?" asked Victor.

"Two kilometers," said Bernard.

"Then we'll take my car. I left it on the esplanade . . ."

"Let it stay there," said Bernard, "because when we get out of the village there's nothing but a path!"

"I'm delighted!" cried Victor, "but I want to carry that rack of bottles!"

He took it from Bernard, who was already loaded down with his Tyrolean rucksack.

They went up on the road along the crests of the hills. The tenor never stopped talking the whole way.

"I knew her during a tour of *Werther* . . . Very young, a little debutante. A strong pretty voice, a dramatic soprano, not yet well placed, but most agreeable . . . She was the first soprano in the chorus, and she doubled for the prima donna in case of mishap . . . And there! at Castelnaudary, our Charlotte—an enormous ogress—but with an admirable voice—a nightingale in a baobab tree—got terrible indigestion from a cassoulet, and when we arrived at Toulouse they told me that the long beans had blocked her high notes, and little Aimée would have to perform that night! At Toulouse! Would you believe it!"

He drew a handkerchief from his pocket to wipe his streaming brow, repeating, "At Toulouse!"

He let out a sigh of anguish and continued:

"They told me that at nine in the morning, while I was shaving. I thought to myself: they're going to hiss at the little one, and they're going to hiss at me, Victor Perissol. I'll take her to the theatre at once, with a pianist, and I'll make her repeat her part all day. We'll lunch on a sandwich . . . I worried like mad. Well, my dear, that evening, do you know what happened that evening?" He stopped, planted his cane in the ground, and waited.

"Obviously we don't know," replied Bernard smiling, "but you're going to tell us!"

"Well, that evening at Toulouse I had a triumph! I had to encore the cavatina of the first, the ballad of the second, and at the end of 'Clair de Lune,' a hurricane of bravos! They called me back three times! I must say that night I was in a state of grace . . . It was perhaps my most beautiful soirée."

"And Maman?" asked Manon.

"She didn't bother me at all! And besides, she was so pretty! And then, don't you know, she was carried by the enthusiasm of the public—and in spite of a rather dubious B-flat they applauded her at the end of the third. At the final curtain for the bows during the ovation I went and took her by the hand"—he took Manon's hand—"and pushed her toward the public . . . then the audience went wild! Ever since that night I've been interested in her."

He winked a mysterious wink that contracted the side of his face on the teacher's side.

"I moved her voice, which was a little too low in her throat, and we made many tours together, *Manon*, *Werther*, *Lakmé*, *If I Were King* . . . And then America called me." He stopped, shook his head, and continued:

"When I say America, I mean that an impresario invited me to be the partner of the illustrious Massiarova. This lady, who had the dimensions of a locomotive, also had its whistle. I was given a lot of money to sing beside her. The Americans took a lively interest in her whistle. My voice pleased them. It was thus that I married a charming girl from Texas who gave me all sorts of trouble before dying from an excess of corn whisky, leaving me mixed memories and a rather large inheritance. I came back to France. The war was on—I did my service in the army theatre—and I didn't see little Aimée again. They told me she had had a pleasant career on theatrical tour, then she had found her Great Love and had married a financier. That's why I wasn't surprised when she wrote and told me she lived in a château!"

Manon cast a desperate look at Bernard, who intervened at once.

"What Manon is trying to say is that she has an imagination that makes her very happy on the whole, because she embellishes everything . . . She transforms, she transmutes . . ."

"She was always a little like that," affirmed Victor, "but her letters suggest the tendency has increased . . ."

"It's since the death of my father," said Manon. "She dreams wide-awake . . ."

Victor stopped again, knit his brows:

"So, you're telling me it's not a château. So, it's a simple villa?"

"Not even that."

"Well, so much the better!" cried Victor. "Nothing is more beautiful than an old farmhouse!"

Manon gathered all her courage and said:

"It's not even a farmhouse. It's an old sheepfold."

Victor Perissol stopped dead, and repeated in a low voice, in a dramatic tone:

"A sheepfold?"

"Yes. In a cave . . . But it's arranged quite nicely . . . It's got furniture, it looks like a house . . ."

But the portly Victor was not listening. He took off his big hat, looked at the sky, and said:

"God in heaven, the cycle is completed."

Then he looked at the two young people one after the other and continued in a confidential tone:

"You're too young to know, as everybody knows, that from the age of ten to seventeen years I was a shepherd. Yes, I looked after sheep in the mountains of the Basses-Alpes and I didn't even know how to read. Then one day the celebrated Altchewsky heard me singing in the village church. And so . . ."

He stopped short and changed his tone:

"I'll tell you everything at the table. It's too important—and too grand—to resume this account in a conversation in the open air. So, it's a sheepfold, and you see me bowled over by it, because one day a gypsy said to me, 'You came from a sheepfold, and you'll go back—for one evening—to a sheepfold.' Don't you find it extraordinary?"

"It's amazing!" said Bernard.

"And that's not all, everything that happens to me is extraordinary," continued Victor. "I'll tell you other things that'll leave you flabbergasted!"

"Do you still sing in operas?" asked Manon.

"Sometimes, yes—but I'm not too proud to admit that I have been betrayed by my physique, which has been devastated by my appetite . . . It would be ridiculous to play Werther or Des Brieux looking like a gurgling barrel . . . Oh yes. And besides I'm rather old. I'm fifty years old, oh yes . . ."

He shook his head mournfully, then suddenly and violently he said:

"And why bother to tell lies? I'm on the wrong side of fifty-four. In other words, fifty-five. As to my voice, I haven't lost it. But I've . . ."

He hesitated some moments, as before a painful confession, then continued humbly . . .

"I've become a baritone . . . Oh yes. It's the fate of a tenor . . . The pure clear pitch that he once had gets obscured by age and descends into the throat, then to the chest, then the navel, then the boots, and winds up the deep note of the old Hebrew in *The Jewess* . . . I'm not yet there, no . . . and I still have a very pretty falsetto. But I admit I can't sing an entire opera anymore without weakening . . . And it's a great pity, because after making a few allowances, I sing much better than before . . . I mean to say . . . Now I know how to sing . . ."

During this speech Manon was thinking about the relations this man could have had with her mother. Like nearly all children, she knew next to nothing of the early life of her parents. He had said that her mother was very young, a little debutante, and that he had helped and protected her . . . She herself had said during her soliloquies that she was surprised to get no response from Victor, because he was a good and generous man . . . Manon looked at him talking and gesticulating. He seemed a little ridiculous because he talked about nothing but himself—but he had the great black eyes of a child, and she gave him her friendship.

They approached Le Plantier, walking along the hillside under the high blue ledge whose summit was reddened by the setting sun, on the side of the narrow rocky vallon. In the distance they could already see the wall of the sheepfold. Victor stopped and looked at the landscape.

"It's beautiful," he said. "This vallon would be sensational for Walpurgis Night in *Faust*. These rocks look as if they're made of cardboard, like the Opera. It's marvellous!"

At this moment, and although nobody was in sight, a woman's voice sang a long phrase from the last act of *Manon*. Victor opened his eyes wide and stopped; he listened for some moments and said:

"It's her!"

He suddenly set the basket of bottles on the path and threw his cane and his hat on the kermes oaks, while Aimée emerged from the turpentine trees holding a sheaf of hill irises to her breast. She sang: "Ah! Oh, that I could die!"

Then, rising toward her while she descended toward him, he replied, "No, live! And henceforth that I could safely follow. Two by two, the path where all will blossom once more . . ." Then he took her in his arms. Cheek to cheek, and alone in the world, they sang the final duet, and the echoes in the valley sent cries into infinity. The young people listened, without moving, surprised at the strength and the delicacy of these voices, and by the tenderness of this fat man, who had not been celebrated for nothing.

When the young people finally drew near, Manon did not recognize her mother's face. Her eyes shone with a new light, and Manon realized obscurely that this woman had sacrificed herself to her husband. Victor wiped his tears with a lace handkerchief and said with utmost simplicity:

"You have come down a little toward the mezzo, but you still easily sing the contra-fa, and the timbre is beautiful . . ."

He raised a finger for a qualification:

"A little faint in the high notes. But we'll easily put that right . . ."

Magali arrived while Manon was preparing the tomato omelette and Bernard was opening the cans and Baptistine was basting a dozen blackbirds and thrushes. In the sheepfold Victor was helping Aimée lay the table while he hummed the *Tales of Hoffmann*.

At the table the marvellous appetite of the tenor did not stop him from talking . . . He told them about his tours of America where ferocious Indian chiefs melted in tears on hearing the death of Werther; his triumphs in Mexico; his apotheosis in Philadelphia, where he was nearly suffocated by the dozens of bouquets of flowers in his dressing room, lavished on him by women of dazzling beauty.

Magali listened with her mouth open, and Aimée laughed with pleasure and applauded with joy.

Manon regarded Victor with admiration throughout the meal and laughed at his flashes of wit, but Bernard saw a shadow passing over her face from time to time; he thought that the singer's familiarity with her mother embarrassed her because of the memory of her father. He was soon to see that she had something else to worry about.

Indeed, while he was breaking almonds with his fist and making the plates jump on the table, Victor declared:

"Now, let's talk about serious matters. This sheepfold, it's picturesque, it's charming, it's touching. I want to sleep in front of the door tonight, rolled up in a blanket under the stars, as a souvenir of my childhood. But I don't want to leave you here. With women alone in this deserted place, you never know what's going to happen!"

"But no," said Manon, "no. Enzo and Giacomo are always nearby, and people come by here sometimes, hunters or poor old people gathering herbs, and there are no ferocious animals. We're very happy here!"

"You think you're happy because you don't know anything else. And besides, you, you run like a goat, you live like a goat, and you're not yet seventeen years old. For your mother it's quite a different matter."

"Monsieur is quite right," said Magali. "For a woman who's still young and beautiful, and with a pretty voice, it's a sin to stay in a cave, to talk to herself!"

"Listen to what I propose. I'm now a professor at the conservatory in Marseille, and head of the chorus at the Opera. It's not a very desirable situation from the pecuniary point of view—but that doesn't matter to me, thanks to the blessed memory of Mildred. I've got a very large apartment with several rooms on the Old Port, close to the Opera. I live there with my sister, who is an absolutely charming old lady. Tomorrow I'm going to take both of you down there. You will sing in the chorus of the Opera, as first soprano, and in the summer we will give a number of performances in the casinos. And this little one, we're going to civilize her a bit. We'll turn her over to an instructor. She'll be taught how to do her hair, how to dress; to dance, and perhaps to sing."

Manon lowered her eyes and said in a soft voice:

"Me, in town, I'll fall sick and I'll die."

"Don't say such stupid things!" replied Victor. ". . . When you see the shops, the streets lit up, the Opera . . ."

"And my dog? And my goats? And the she-ass? And the hills?"

She succeeded in restraining her tears, but her chin trembled.

"Victor is right," said Aimée. "You can't judge what you don't know . . ."

"We must get things right," said Bernard. "Manon's got a primitive mentality, the spirit of a bird that you can't put in a cage, but on the other hand, I agree with Monsieur Victor. Her mother should—if she can—return to civilized life, because it's obvious this solitude hasn't done her any good . . ."

"So," said Victor, "the problem's insoluble! . . ."

"Listen," said Magali suddenly, "I've got an idea. It's true this little one mustn't change her life too abruptly. To see all the hustle and bustle of a city, it would drive her mad, she wouldn't be able to breathe, she'd weep in the night, she'd wither away . . . I suggest she stay in the village for a while, it would be like a stop on the way. She'd get used to seeing people, and talking to them . . . Sometimes she'd go to town with me, we'd say good day as we pass, and little by little she'd be tamed."

"I would rather live at Les Romarins," said Manon.

"Why Romarins?" said Magali. "You could take your animals there, and you could walk there as much as you like, but a girl your age can't sleep quite alone in a farmhouse in the hills. We've got room at the house, and you could live with us for some time. You could help me in the house and I'd teach you how to cook, and to sew, and everything else. What do you say to that?"

Manon did not reply. She pressed her clasped hands between her knees and looked at the tablecloth under the drooping candlewicks.

"And you, Bernard, what do you think?" asked Victor. The young man raised his eyes and smiled:

"If she wants to come and live in our house, I think that she mustn't ever leave it again."

He stretched his arms across the table and placed his open hands before the girl of the springs.

She made a droll little face, got up suddenly, and fled into the night.

Dressed in his fine black frock coat (the same one he wore to visit M. the prefect), girdled with his tricolor sash, and crowned with his top hat, M. the mayor took three jumps and made a "square," a feat applauded by the onlookers, to the great consternation of Casimir, who thought himself already the winner . . . M. Belloiseau, who was arbitrating this duel, announced, "Fourteen to fourteen."

The gallery in their Sunday best admired his marine blue jacket, his large cravat—with its shining fat pearl—and especially his silk hat, which was so tall that nobody would have been surprised if he had pulled live rabbits from it.

However, it was not a parish feast, nor even a Sunday; it was a fine April morning, and the very day of the wedding of M. the schoolmaster. But while awaiting the arrival of the soon-to-be married couple the mayor and Casimir could not resist the sight of a basket of *boules*; and Philoxène had immediately taken off his white gloves and offered "to teach the blacksmith a lesson"—a proposition the other accepted with a smile of pity.

So they were fourteen-to-fourteen, and the next "lead" was critical—it had to be the last—and its agonizing difficulty tightened the throats of the mute spectators. Just then the nuptial party appeared.

At its head was the bride, little Manon, so tall on her lady's heels that she would not have been recognized from any distance had it not been for the traditional dress of white tulle and the crown of real orange flowers on her golden hair. This was a precious gift from Pamphile and Casimir. They had gone in the night to steal it from the notary at Les Ombrées, an eccentric who had a Seville orange tree growing in a little greenhouse at the bottom of his garden. In addition, as a souvenir of her dear hills, she had inserted among the soft white clusters four large flat flowers, of a violet red—what the English call "rockrose," and the Provençals "messugue."

As she came down the slope that led to the town hall, she leaned on the arm of Victor, a grandiose Victor, draped in the black cape in which he had played Werther. It floated on the varnished boots of the Postilion of Longjumeau, the reflections from which had dazzled more than one prompter in his box.

Behind them slowly walked Bernard and his mother. She was dressed from head to foot in beige lace, and smiled through a light veil that floated around her large straw hat, while Bernard stood very tall in what was obviously a brand new suit—which certainly came from La Belle Jardinière. In addition, under his turned-down hard collar, he wore a cravat of azure silk, pierced by a sapphire pin. That is to say both of them were even more beautiful than usual; they quite obviously knew it and were not at all modest.

Next came Anglade, who had bought a beautiful grey felt hat for the wedding of his "cousinette."

With a dignified air, he lent the support of his arm to Aimée, whose makeup (which had seemed insufficient for a scene in an opera) was perhaps a little too brilliant for the town hall of a village, but her broad-brimmed tulle hat shaded her beautiful eyes advantageously . . .

Finally, behind her, marched four gentlemen all dressed the same in black frock coats and bowler hats. They were Victor's guests, whose role we will soon understand.

As they entered the esplanade, Philoxène raised his hand to stop them and cried:

"One second, for the final attack!"

He confided his top hat to Pamphile, leaned backward, and held the ball at eye level for a moment; then, as all talk ceased, he leaped forward: the "square" could be heard clattering, then the crackling of applause.

Philoxène bowed modestly, and everybody was entering the town hall when the bride suddenly left Victor's arm, lifted up her beautiful dress, and ran toward a group half-hidden behind the trunk of a plane tree: Enzo, Giacomo, and Baptistine. The woodsmen were marvellously clean, but in their gala costumes they looked like gigantic parrots—olive green hats, pink cravats, blue jackets, light yellow shoes with green heels. Manon took their arms, but Baptistine, dressed entirely in grey, took flight—it was Bernard who caught her and put her in the hands of Pamphile, half-strangled in his starched collar.

The cortege entered the town hall, which was decorated with rosemary and young flowering gorse.

All the schoolchildren, whom Eliacin stopped from entering the holy of holies, cried with disappointment—but they were compensated by a most remarkable episode.

M. Belloiseau, having greeted the bride most gallantly, put his marvellous silk hat under his arm, and with a quick gesture flattened it like a pancake . . . The children, charmed by this sudden attack of madness, went to press their noses against the windows, in the hope of seeing other manifestations, but M. Belloiseau sat down with perfect dignity, and put an end to his extravagance by exposing a face that was dull without the headgear, while M. the mayor began his speech.

During this time, behind the house at Massacan, besieged by rockrose and fennel since Ugolin had left it, the Papet, all alone, was prodding the wild vegetation with the end of his stick. He was wearing a new suit of black velvet, a black hat, and a black tie. From time to time he plunged his hand into the undergrowth and pulled out a handful of red-and-white carnations. They were the survivors of Ugolin's first cuttings, planted when he came back from military service. The plants had reproduced at random, and their flowers were numerous but small, and M. Trémelat would certainly have refused them. The old man suddenly raised his head—the church bells were ringing for the wedding. He tied the sheaf with a few turns of raffia and went down toward the village.

The mayor's speech was applauded a long time, and especially by M. Belloiseau, who had been the author of it. Manon was profoundly moved by a short passage that evoked the memory of the "child of the village betrayed by her own people," and "the bitter regret of all the Bastidians at the thought of this precious friendship lost."

As the party left the town hall, the children witnessed a new exploit by M. Belloiseau. They were waiting for him, hoping to enjoy his surprise when he tried to put the hat he had so comically and unwittingly flattened back on his head; but the surprise was theirs, for M. Belloiseau, talking to Anglade all the while, took the black pancake he was carrying under his arm, and with a simple flick of the finger, which produced a small explosion, he made a completely new hat, which he placed on his head without a pause in the conversation.

The ceremony in the church was a complete success. Manon did not show any emotion, except for some blushes and some pallor, which were suitable for a bride, and Bernard was superb with assurance and authority. Naturally Magali wept. Aimée and Victor were not seated near the married couple, but up in the balcony near the organ, with their mysterious guests.

One of these, a little old man, was an organist. He revealed the true beauty of their antique instrument to the Bastidians. The three others were the best singers in the chorus of the Marseille Opera. Their trained voices were harmoniously superimposed on the bass of the organ and formed a background for the touching voice of Victor and the angelic soprano of Aimée. The vault of the little church was hearing their voices for the first time, and it reflected them onto the congregation so well that this celestial music seemed truly to descend from heaven. Moreover, M. Belloiseau himself affirmed later that this sung mass would have done honor to a cathedral on the day of a princely wedding.

It was as they were leaving, and the teacher was throwing handfuls of ten-sou pieces to the children in front of the church, that the Papet came into view at the bottom of the plaza. His left arm clutched a thick bouquet of carnations to his chest, and he came down toward the church. He did not have a stick, and it was obvious that he was making an effort to walk with a confident step. This arrival seemed to surprise the whole company. Because of the beauty of his suit, and his solemn air, they thought he had come to offer these flowers to the bride as a sign of reconciliation, and that perhaps she had invited him to the wedding. The children stopped running and shouting, and everybody was still and quiet. Manon, worried and embarrassed, clutched her husband's arm. She whispered, "I won't know what to say to him . . ."

But the old man passed in front of the group without seeing them. His eyes were fixed on the horizon, and a heavy key shone in his right hand. It was the cemetery key.

The silent wedding guests watched him go down to the esplanade. Then he moved on without turning back, solitary, unique, trailing his leg and his grief, but stiff in his pride and carrying high the hard head of the last of the Soubeyrans.

A year later the village was still the same, and the spirit of Les Bastides had not changed. But the teacher, and especially his wife, had won the friendship of everybody, so much so that the mayor had gone, with the assent of the interested party, to the prefecture in Marseille—silk hat on his head, gloves in his hand—to ask M. the director of the academy to annul the nomination of M. Bernard Olivier to Pomme, and instead to grant him his promotion there and then.

Manon's mother, married to the generous Victor, lived in Marseille in a very large apartment on the Old Port, two steps from the Opera. Both of them were at the height of happiness, and Manon received triumphant letters from Victor, of this type:

> *My dear child,*
> *I'm sending you some news of your mother: she is getting on very well, and I will take advantage of that to tell you that I have doubled—at a moment's notice—for Ricardo Goldoni in the role of Albert (Werther). I sang baritone with the greatest ease and I tell you without vanity that I had a very beautiful success. We had eight encores! Your mother's voice dominated the chorus. It's quite simple—they listened to nobody but her.*
> *Love and kisses*
> *P.S.—Did you see my photograph in* Le Petit Provençal? *It is superb. I am seventh on the right in the second row. We are going to dine Tuesday off a leg of lamb, truffles, a Saint-Honoré, and some champagne. Eight encores in Marseille are worth sixteen in Paris.*

The meetings of the unbelievers continued to take place on the café terrace, but their group was augmented by an important new member—M. the curé, who had started by remaining standing as he talked, in passing, but ended by sitting at their table. He was a gay companion, but his presence imposed a certain restraint on the conversation, at least until the hour of the evening prayer.

Now, at last, Pamphile and Casimir went to mass on Sunday, to "show politeness."

M. Belloiseau had changed his maid, or rather, his maid had changed her master, because she left for Marseille, saying she had had enough of putting up with the fantasies of an old skinflint in a village of dodderers.

She also changed her occupation.

The new servant, who was eighteen years old, was a charming slattern, who now and then called her master "tu," and addressed him rather familiarly as Jean. About which M. Belloiseau said indulgently, "She's a child . . ."

The Papet had become really old. He hardly worked anymore, and it was Pamphile who tended his vineyard in the vallon, but he went up every morning to Massacan where he cultivated three beds of carnations that he put on Ugolin's grave every Sunday. He still gladly played manille on the terrace every day, and never complained, except one evening, when Manon passed by and smiled at her husband. As they watched her going, Philoxène declared:

"It's extraordinary how beautiful she's become . . ."

The teacher looked very pleased with himself, and the Papet murmured:

"She has always been. To my misfortune."

A tear slid down to his moustache. He sniffed twice, and said:

"So what's the trump card?"

Baptistine was living at Les Romarins, with the goats, the she-ass, the dog, and Giuseppe's great axes. She continued her errant life, her herbs, and her cheeses, while the Anglade twins cultivated the field. They had abandoned the carnations because it involved too much thinking and besides it was very delicate work. But thanks to the spring they had taken up Old Camoins' crops again, and in the summer they went down to the market at Aubagne with cartloads of vegetables.

On Thursdays or Sundays Manon, Bernard, and Magali often came to lunch with Baptistine, always seated in front of the fireplace: sometimes the two lovers left at dawn for the hills. He looked for stones for his "school museum," which won him the congratulations of the school inspector, and she set her traps ("like the old days," she said). Then they would lunch under the old mountain ash.

Manon always took a little flask of milk in her haversack, intended for the limbert, but the great lizard, no doubt because of a Freudian repulsion, refused to emerge from its hole while the beautiful Bernard was present. The husband went off, feigning a smiling indulgence but profoundly vexed. Sometimes Pamphile accompanied them, with his gun under his arm. Manon preserved a true tenderness for him, because of the black arrows. He grilled cutlets or sausages on a thick thyme ember and seasoned them with savory herbs, while Manon climbed the pine trees and threw pine nuts down to her husband's feet.

But in September they had to give up these excursions: she walked leaning backwards and, for the first time, on her heels. Pamphile went secretly to put a wax candle in the church at Ruissatel, so that the little one should not be a hunchback.

CHAPTER 33

It was that year that old Delphine, the aunt of Ange the fountaineer, returned to the village. She had been married to Médéric's son, the customs officer at Marseille. He had put a fair amount of money on the side, and had fully realized his goal of qualifying for a pension. They had lived very happily to an advanced age, but unfortunately poor Delphine had gradually lost her sight, and her husband, whose tenderness had helped her to bear her infirmity, had died on the very day of their golden wedding anniversary . . . So she had come, with her little hoard and half of the pension, to seek refuge with her nephew, who was triply content.

Delphine was very tall, very broad, and very thin. Pamphile said that she would have made a magnificent scarecrow. The children were afraid of her, because the wrinkles on her face were as big as a man's and were permanently fixed in a hard white mask like marble when her husband died.

Every afternoon, pretty Clairette, her niece, led the blind old woman to the esplanade and sat her on a bench in the sun. She always wore a black lace mantilla over her white hair, held under her chin by a clasp that might have been gold, and a black velvet cape, a little worn, on her shoulders. With her two hands clasped on the knob of her stick, she dreamed in silence and listened to the noises of the village, which had not changed since her childhood . . . Nearly all the passersby stopped for a little chat, and the Papet, who had known her formerly, often came to sit with her. They talked about the old days when corn-fed chickens cost a dozen sous a pair, when the seasons were in order, and they had black hair . . .

One autumn evening they were gossiping as usual with their backs to the setting sun to warm their shoulders with its last rays.

The Papet was talking about Africa, about entire sheep being roasted in holes, and little Arab dancing girls doing belly dances to the sound of flutes and tambourines. The old woman listened without a word, then turned her dead eyes to him and said:

"It's very pretty, the belly dance, but you did a stupid thing when you were down there . . ."

"Me?"

"Yes, you. I say a stupid thing, but it was practically a crime!"

"What stupid thing?"

"I'm very surprised you've forgotten it."

"Well, I don't know what you're talking about. All the officers were satisfied with me, since they gave me a medal! When I was wounded they made me a corporal."

"That's another matter. I'm thinking of a letter you got."

"What letter?"

"One that certainly deserved a reply. And you, you never answered."

He looked at her, knitting his thick grey eyebrows.

"A letter from whom?"

"Fine!" she said. "I see you don't want to talk because you think I don't know who it was."

"Delphine, I swear to you . . ."

"Don't swear, you great unbeliever! Pardon me for making you think of something that upsets you. Listen, I hear Clairette coming . . . Come, my girl! The wind is beginning to freshen and I would much rather be in the corner by the fire. Good-bye, César. Until tomorrow. And don't worry—I've never told anybody, and I'll never mention it again!"

The Papet thought for a long time. Who could have written to him in Africa? He had not received more than three or four letters from his father, who gave him news of the harvest, the mule, the dog, and the family. His mother had added a friendly word and that was all . . . Anglade had sent him one or two postcards. And besides them, who? Nobody. Absolutely nobody. Delphine must have been mistaken. Or perhaps she had invented it to tease him? Or perhaps she had started to lose her mind? . . . At her age it was not impossible. But he soon gave up this facile explanation. Delphine never spoke to say nothing, and her memory had remained infallible. There was certainly something, but what?

He was in his bed when he suddenly remembered it. He had indeed received a letter from Castagne, a celebrated drunkard; the Papet's father had lent him some money and then threatened to foreclose on him.

This Castagne had begged him to intervene with the old man and had announced that if his property were foreclosed he would commit suicide. The Papet had not believed a word of it and had not even deigned to reply. Two months later among the trivial news in his father's letter was the information that Castagne had hanged himself.

"If that's what she's talking about, really it's not important!"

Nevertheless he thought about it again in the morning while shaving.

"And besides," he said loudly, "when one lends money to somebody, it's up to him to return it. Even if I had replied to Castagne, and if I had written to my father, it wouldn't have changed anything. The old man was more obstinate than me, and moreover he was right!"

He found her again on the esplanade, at five o'clock.

"I recognized your step," she said.

"Your ear is as sharp as an eye!"

"It doesn't take its place, César. No, it doesn't take its place . . ."

"Tell me, Delphine, that letter you told me about yesterday, I've thought of what it is."

"Yes," she said, "you didn't have to look too hard. But since it bothers you, let's talk about something else."

"And why should it bother me? He was no friend of mine, Castagne. And besides, it wasn't my fault he hanged himself. He was always an old soak, and so . . ."

"And so, I see you continue to pretend it's nothing, but you're wasting your time and your hypocrisy. This Castagne, I don't even remember him and that's not what I was talking about."

"So, who was it who wrote to me?"

"You know very well, you can't have forgotten."

"Delphine, we're in front of the church and I see the cross up there on the bell tower. Well, before that cross I swear I'm not joking. I swear I never got any letters except from my father, Anglade, and Castagne."

The old woman turned her dead eyes to him.

"Then," she said, "it was a disaster."

"Why?"

"Swear to me again that you're not pretending."

"Once more, I swear it. Who was it who wrote to me?"

She hesitated a moment, then leaned toward him and said in a low voice:

"Florette."

The Papet started.

"Florette Camoins?"

"You know quite well there weren't two of them."

"Are you sure she wrote to me?"

"I was the one who gave the letter to the postman, because she didn't want anybody to know."

"Delphine, I swear before God I never received that letter . . . Because I could not have forgotten a letter from her. If you want to know the truth, something I've never told anybody, I've still got a two-word note from her, half rubbed out, and a black hairpin. Oh yes. But when I got back she wasn't in the village anymore. She had married the blacksmith at Crespin, and they had even had a baby already!"

Delphine clasped her hands.

"How could the letter have gotten lost?"

"You know, down there, we were always moving about, up country or in the mountains . . . Sometimes we didn't get food, or even cartridges . . . It was quite possible for letters to get lost . . . If I had got that letter I would still have it next to my heart . . ."

The old woman let her chin fall to her breast. She murmured:

"So if that's true, it's terrible."

The Papet whispered:

"Do you think she loved me?"

"Imbecile!"

"She never wanted to tell me that. Even afterwards . . . what happened one evening when we came back from a dance, I thought she was teasing me."

"That's how she was. But she told me everything, and I know she loved you; and the letter, I read it."

She remained silent for a while, pensive and drowned in the past. The Papet dared not speak, but pulled his neck down into his shoulders and bowed his head, as if expecting a blow from the sky. Finally she murmured:

"She told you that she loved you, and that she never loved anybody but you."

The Papet cleared his throat three times.

"And then?"

"She also said she was pregnant."

"What?"

"Oh yes. You had been gone for about three weeks . . . And so she told you that if you would write to her father and promise him you would marry her, she would wait for you . . . Then she'd be able to show the letter to everybody in the village and nobody would jeer at her."

He tried to get up, but fell back on the bench. He murmured:

"Delphine, Delphine, you're sure? . . ."

"I tell you I read her letter, and I even helped her to write it . . . She couldn't sleep anymore, poor thing . . . so she tried to get rid of the baby, with devil's tisanes . . . In the hills she jumped from the tops of rocks . . . But it was well embedded. So she detested you. She went to a dance in Aubagne and there she found a fine big man, that blacksmith at Crespin. She took him so she could quit the village, and nobody knew when the child was born . . ."

"Was it born . . . alive?"

"Yes, alive. But hunchbacked."

The Papet felt a great coldness rising from his belly and his heart swelled suddenly between his paralyzed sides. He did not suffer, but he could no longer breathe.

The blind woman continued:

"She wrote to me many times, at the beginning. She told me her husband was a marvel, and that the little boy was very intelligent . . . She hoped that as he grew he would become like the others. And then I got married and I lived in Marseille . . . When you're far away, you forget quickly . . . She didn't write to me anymore, and I never saw her again . . . They told me she died, and her husband also . . . But the little one, I never knew what became of him. He must still be at Crespin. You should go and see him, César. You're alone in the world, you're rich, perhaps he needs you . . ."

She was silent for a long time, as if absent, beside the immobile Papet.

The bell slowly rang the evening prayer, and two little old ladies hurried along the esplanade.

"Oh, Delphine, it's not very nice to flirt with this old devil while the Good Lord is calling you!"

Delphine got up.

"It's not my fault. Clairette is late! Come and give me a hand, my pretty . . . Until tomorrow, César. I'll go and pray for you."

Two hours later, M. the schoolmaster left the club, where he had gone to explain some obscure lines in the *Official Journal* to Philoxène, something about the "common rights on communal land."

Night had fallen. A fine rain was falling in the darkness, hardly yellowed by the street lamps, and the evening wind blew the dead leaves around in little whirls.

The teacher, holding his hat to his head, ran along the esplanade in a hurry to see his dear wife again. But he suddenly slowed down, then stopped, because he had just seen a black shade on a bench. He approached.

The Papet was there, quite alone in the rain . . . Immobile, chin on his hands crossed on the end of his stick, he was gathered in on himself.

"Good evening, Papet . . . Something wrong?"

The old man raised his waxen face, drenched with rain under his black hat, his mouth open under the white hair.

"Don't stay here," said Bernard. "Come, I'll go with you to your house."

He helped him get up.

"Lean against me."

The Papet took his arms, like those of an old friend. His head was bowed and he wept softly, with stifled sighs.

"Are you suffering?"

He could not answer.

They passed a ladder with Ange at the top lighting the streetlights.

He said:

"Hello! Something wrong?"

The Papet appeared not to hear, but the teacher replied:

"Yes, he's not very strong, and I'm taking him home."

"A good tisane with a little brandy, that'll put him right . . . Papet, be careful.

At your age a little current of air can blow out the lamp! Don't do anything silly, and go to bed at once!"

In the open space by the house the old man stopped. He was trembling from head to foot . . .

"I think," said Bernard, "that you'd better call a doctor . . . If you like I'll go and telephone Les Ombrées."

He replied in a small husky voice:

"No. Thank you. I know what I've got. I know . . . I know . . ."

The deaf-mute, who was watching for his return, appeared at the door and came down to meet him, uttering desolated little cries. She took his arms and drew him into the house.

The next day Philoxène saw him come down, dressed in his Sunday clothes, but he uttered a surprised cry when he saw him three paces away.

"Oh, Papet, what have you got?"

His face was shrunken and his grey hair was as white as snow.

"I'm going to Les Ombrées," he said. "I've got things to do down there."

He stumped off.

"What's happened?" wondered Philoxène. "Something must have happened."

Pamphile, who was smoking a cigarette on the doorstep of his workshop, called out:

"Have you seen the Papet? His face looked like death."

After that day he was seen at seven o'clock mass every morning.

"It's not a good sign," said Pamphile. ". . . I think I'd better start on his box!"

Next, the baker, whose back window looked onto the vallon, saw him go up to Massacan almost every day. He did not come down until the evening.

"It worries me," said the baker's wife. "He goes there to think about his nephew. He's quite alone now, the poor man . . . and he can hardly drag himself along . . ."

Some days later he seemed to have recovered his strength; he was seen on the esplanade with Delphine. Every evening he made her retell the story of the letter, and confidences about Florette, but he never admitted anything himself.

In the morning he sat near the bakery. The baker's wife, who had an infallible eye, noticed that he was always waiting for Manon when she came to get her bread. He never let her out of his sight, and when she went he followed her, as if he were hypnotized.

"Hey, hey!" said the baker's wife to her husband one day. "The old gallant still likes the girls!"

The baker shrugged his shoulders.

"You mean he's gaga!"

It was on Christmas Eve that he summoned M. the curé to receive the last sacraments.

He was lying down, very pale, his cheeks hollow, but he talked as usual and his gaze was clear.

"My dear friend," said the curé, "I don't see that you are on the point of death!"

"But I know I'm there," he said, "and I know I'm going tonight."

"What makes you think that?"

"I'm going to die because I don't want to live anymore. Come on, take my confession. You know I've got good reason to need it."

"You know," said the preacher, "that suicide is a mortal sin?"

"I don't need to commit suicide," said the Papet. "All I have to do is let myself go. Take my full confession, and anoint me with oil the proper way."

M. the curé stayed in the Soubeyran house for a long time. He left deep in thought. On the doorstep, in the grey day and the icy wind, were Philoxène, Ange, and Pamphile, their hands in their pockets and their shoulders raised. They had come for news. They acknowledged the passage of the holy oil, then Pamphile knocked on the door.

It did not open, but the mute's face appeared behind the glass. Laying her cheek on two joined hands she showed them he was sleeping, and they went down to the club again for a game of manille.

At the sound of the bells for midnight mass the Papet got up noiselessly. He wrote a long letter. Then he shaved carefully and brushed his snowy hair. Next he put on his best suit, the black velvet suit, the woollen embroidered waistcoat, and the cravat with silk tufts. His gold ring on his little finger, and a rosary wound around his joined hands, he stretched himself out on the bed.

The next morning the baker's wife let it be known that Manon's child had been born. They knew it was a boy, but nothing else. But toward ten o'clock M. the schoolmaster came in—he came to choose the bread himself, instead of his mother, but this was quite obviously only a pretext, and he had really come to receive congratulations. He was as proud as if he had produced the baby all by himself. The ladies were shocked.

He declared that his son was born at 5:35 in the morning, on Christmas day, as if this were an event without precedent. Then he revealed that the midwife from Les Ombrées estimated the weight of the boy at more than eight pounds. He had blue eyes, like his mother, blond hair like his mother, but apart from these details, he was the exact picture of his grandfather, the teacher's father, who had been a swarthy man from Montpellier, and whom his son had never seen, except in a photograph. Finally he added—as an amusing detail—that the back of the baby was marvellously straight, and that he had slipped out like a letter in a postbox, but in the opposite direction, of course. At which the baker's wife recounted the perilous birth of her own son—at his arrival he had a body so small and a head so big that she thought she was giving birth to a cup-and-ball toy, which even had the cord. But at twelve years he was already a handsome boy.

M. the schoolmaster did not appreciate this recital because if one admitted that babies born ugly became beautiful, it must be concluded that those born beautiful would become ugly. He therefore stated with authority that his little boy was physically perfect, and his perfection could only be embellished as he grew. He added modestly that he was not claiming responsibility, it was only a matter of luck; but his smile belied his words and it was easy to see that he was congratulating himself on having produced a child such as had never been seen before.

Just then Pamphile entered the shop. With his meter-stick in his hand, he announced the death of the Papet. This sad news surprised no one.

"I've just been measuring him," he said. "I had expected 1.75, but he was no more than 1.68. So much the better. If I had been wrong in the other direction we would have had to raise his knees and he wouldn't have been comfortable."

"Did he die last night?" asked the teacher.

"Oh yes," said Pamphile. "He must have gone between five and half past five, because at eight o'clock, when the mute brought him his coffee, he was as stiff as justice is for a poor man . . . But he was beautiful to see—all shaved, all fresh, all clean and tidy, with a sort of smile. It's funny all the same how death can change your character!"

The obsequies were solemn. Nearly everyone in the village accompanied the last of the Soubeyrans to the cemetery. A cantor came from Saint Menet, and M. the curé delivered a beautiful sermon. He revealed that during the last days of his life the Good Lord had sent grace to the poor sinner, which made Philoxène, Pamphile, and M. Belloiseau sneer.

After the cemetery, the moment he had taken the sacrament back to the church, M. the curé went to knock at the teacher's door. Magali received him, all smiles. On the table there was a great pile of napkins, bibs, and vests, around a little pink porcelain chamber pot.

"Good day, M. the curé. I bet you've come to settle the date for the christening?"

"We'll talk about that too," said the priest mysteriously.

Bernard was sitting on his wife's bed, as if on holiday, and she had her hand on the cradle. Her pretty face lay in the middle of a sunburst of golden hair, which stretched in an aureole on the pillow. He was talking, and she was laughing. It was known in the village, from the gossip of Céline, who did the housework, that these two never stopped talking, laughing, and embracing, as if they were alone in the world.

When Magali announced M. the curé's visit, the teacher was puzzled, but Manon was very proud that this holy man should come and congratulate her at home.

The priest first paid his compliments to the happy parents, then he said:

"Obviously I know that the papa isn't a good Christian, but I think that with him it's political rather than religious, and I'm sure he won't stop the mother from baptizing her child."

"Certainly not!" said Bernard. "My mother-in-law would die—she wants to be his godmother."

"Good. I would therefore advise you to christen him tomorrow. It's a little soon for the first excursion of a newborn, but I've got a very good reason for it. It is that this child having been born on the same day as Our Lord, it would be a good thing to baptize him on the feast of Saint John the Evangelist, who was his favorite disciple."

"And not only that," said Manon, "he's called Jean!"

"There, that's perfect!" said M. the curé. "Have you got a godfather?"

"Yes. It's M. Belloiseau."

M. the curé knitted his brows.

"Another unbeliever," he said, "and one of doubtful morals."

"I know," said Manon, "but he's named Jean, and he's been baptized, and we don't know another Jean."

"Done. I'll be pleased to take his confession! So, tomorrow. Now I've got another mission to fulfil."

He drew a sealed letter from the pocket of his soutane.

"César Soubeyran, who has just died, and who had—I am happy to tell you—a Christian end after a very dangerous life, asked me to bring you this letter. I must put it in madame's own hands."

"To my wife?" said Bernard. "That's rather strange. Their relations were never very cordial."

"He was a criminal," said Manon.

"He has received absolution," said the priest gravely, "and is now before his Judge."

He presented the letter to her.

"So, until tomorrow morning, about eleven o'clock."

He blessed the child and withdrew.

Magali saw him out and came running back.

"What's this all about?"

Bernard's eyes widened so much that there were lines on his forehead, while Manon tore open the envelope.

"I've never talked to you about it," she said, "but for some time he was quite gaga."

"How?"

"He waited for me every morning at the baker's, and he followed me everywhere."

"He passed in front of the house ten times a day," said Magali. "He used to stop and look up at the windows!"

"And his eyes were strange," said Manon.

"Did he talk to you?"

"No, but I had the impression he wanted to talk to me. In the end I was afraid! Imagine, one evening I was alone at the fountain. He looked at me from a distance for a long time, and when I left he blew me a kiss!"

"Hey, hey!" said Bernard. ". . . Quite often the senility of old men is tainted with lubricity. You'll see, this letter is a declaration of love!"

"That's all you need," cried Magali. "After what he did to your father!"

Bernard sat on the bed and they started reading, cheek to cheek.

Dear little Manon,
The notary at Les Ombrées will tell you Ive left you all my property.

"Ho ho!" cried her husband. "It's very kind of the old fool to be so familiar with you!"

I know you will be amazed, but it is the truth befor God. There is much land, and three houses. The notary will give you the papers and all the dedes. Look carefully at the little house at Massacan. Tell your husband to dig in the kitchen, under the bed. Rigt in the middle, under the paving brick in the middle. He must take out the brick and break the plaster under it. Then he must take out some gravle and he will find a big jar buried. Full to the top with golden Louis. There are six thousand.

"Six thousand louis!" cried Magali. "It's not possible! He's dreaming, or he's making fun of us!"

"Wait, Maman," said Manon, and she went on reading.

It is the Soubeyran treasure, which was started during the Revolution, to stay in the family. But it is not for you—it goes over your head, and it is for the child who is going to be born, who is my great-granson.

"What does that mean?" she asked.

"It means," said Magali, "that your child is his great-grandson."

"That's absurd!" said Bernard. "Or does he imagine it's Ugolin's child?"

"Wait!" said Manon. "Listen."

Becaus your father was my son, my Soubeyran that I missed all my life, and whom I let die little by little, because I did not now who he was. I had only to tell him about the spring, and he would still be playing his mouth organ, and all of you would have come to live in our family hous. Instead of that, a lingering death. Nobody knows it, but all the same I am ashamed before every-

body, even the trees. In the vilage there is somone who nows all about it, and if you tell her about my letter, she will explain—it is Delphine, the old blind woman. She will tell you it is all the fault of Africa. Ask her. It is Africa. Ask her for the love of God! I do not deserve to tell you that I embrace you and that I never dared to talk to you but perhaps now you can forgive me, and sometimes offer a little prayer for poor Ugolin and for poor me. I even feel pity for myself.

I always kept away from him. I did not know his voice, nor his face. I never saw his eyes close by, which were perhaps like my mothers. I only saw his hump and his distres, all the harm I did him. Now you understand why I long to die, because compared with the thougts that torment me Hell is a pleasure. And then up there I will see him. I have no fear of him on the contrary. Now he knows he is a Soubeyran he is not a hunchback anymore becaus of my falt, he has understood that it is all because of a stupidity, and I am sure that instead of attacking me he will defend me.

> Adessias, ma pitchounette
> Your grandfather
> César Soubeyran